THE BLACK EARTH

By Philip Kazan

The Black Earth
The Phoenix of Florence

THE BLACK EARTH

Philip Kazan

Allison & Busby Limited
11 Wardour Mews
London W1F 8AN
allisonandbusby.com

First published in Great Britain by Allison & Busby in 2018.
This paperback edition published by Allison & Busby in 2019.

Copyright © 2018 by PHILIP KAZAN

Permission to reproduce extracts from The Waste Land by T. S. Eliot
granted by Faber and Faber Ltd

A CIP catalogue record for this book is available from
the British Library.

10 9 8 7 6 5 4 3 2 1

ISBN 978-0-7490-2208-2

Typeset in 10.5/15.5 pt Adobe Garamond Pro by
Allison & Busby Ltd

The paper used for this Allison & Busby publication
has been produced from trees that have been legally sourced
from well-managed and credibly certified forests.

Printed and bound by
CPI Group (UK) Ltd, Croydon, CR0 4YY

For Helen

BOOK I

CHAPTER ONE

Smyrna, Asia Minor, 18th September 1922

All night long she lies in the bow of the *Thetis* and listens to the water beneath her. Curled into the sharp angle between the low gunwales and the varnished pole of the bowsprit, chin propped on the shiny wood, the jib sail creaking just above her head, she stares out into the darkness of the great bay. There is hardly any wind and the yacht is gliding smoothly across low, even waves. She is wearing her favourite white sailor suit, freshly laundered and smelling comfortingly of sunshine and soap. Perhaps she'll see a flying fish. She hopes she will – or are they sleeping? Is she passing over shoals of dreaming fish, suspended on outspread silver wings? She strains her eyes into the night but there is nothing. The fish won't fly tonight, she realises. The air is too thick. Why would they throw themselves up out of their cool world into this dense, stinking air?

She stares into the west, where the sun went down huge and deep magenta red, the colour of wild gladiolus flowers. West towards . . . she doesn't know. There is nothing to the east. Nothing to the north and south. *Thetis* can't fly up. So they are sliding out beyond the bay, out to the edge of the world. Ever since she can remember, which seems like an eternity, although she is only six, she has stared out of her bedroom window towards that line, which swallows up the sun every night, where ships appear and disappear. But she has never been further than Uzunada, the long island, sailing out for parties with their friends, while the flying fish skip like mercury across the blue water. Beyond that, the open sea.

If she could just ask her father . . . She can hear him behind her, whispering to Mama as he holds the wheel steady. But she doesn't dare turn round. Mama and Papa have forbidden it: as they had settled her down in the prow of the *Thetis* – Papa's yacht, his pride and joy – they had told her that, whatever happened, she mustn't look back. She had asked why, and they had just shaken their heads – so calm and sensible in spite of all the commotion on the dock, those two heads. There's nothing behind us, *kopella mou*. Everything is ahead. Just keep looking ahead, little darling, little bird. And when the sun comes up, it will all be fine.

Why couldn't she bring Rosie, her pony? Why isn't Cook with them, or Miss Butland? Why had they had to bundle all their things into Papa's motor car and drive to Cordelio through crowds of people, Mama sitting beside her in the back, murmuring, 'Don't worry, don't worry,' like a prayer while Papa's hands gripped the steering wheel so hard that she could see the shape of his finger bones? Papa, who never drove, but always sat behind Murat the chauffeur. When they had gone aboard the *Thetis*, Papa had kissed her and said, 'It's just like the holidays, isn't it, my little angel?' But it hadn't been. No one had said why they'd had to leave home so quickly. *Papa is always right, but this doesn't seem like a holiday.* She curls up more tightly on the bed she has claimed for herself, the big rug from the drawing room, folded into the angle of the prow, and closes her eyes. Home is there, pretty as an iced cake: her own house, safe inside its railings. Pink plaster, fretwork gables, chimneys. Lots of chimneys – she loves them. She counts them now inside her head, and it makes her feel better. What else does she love? The front gate. The tree with blossoms like stars. Their wide, clean street. From the front gate you can see the church; if you wait, you'll hear the shrill, jolly whistle of the train. Mountains behind; in front, quite far off, the blue sea.

Something in the air is making her feel sick. She presses her face into the scratchy, salty rug and tries to go home again. The street swims back into her head, the iron railings, the trees, whitewashed stones lining the swept gravel of the roadway, the whistle of the train . . . A voice, calling through the carved marble frame of a doorway. Clipped, high-pitched.

'Zoë!'

'Yes, Miss Butland!'

A short figure in pleats and lace, a shadow over by the old fig tree, the buzz of wasps in the figs, the green, resinous scent of fig . . . The shadow ripples, shifts to reveal a face, not young but not old either: tight skin; sharp, upturned nose; round chin; mouth that looks as if it doesn't know how to smile, but when it does . . . She'll do anything to tease out that smile.

'*Érchomai*, Miss Butland!'

'In *English*, Zoë!'

'I'm coming, Miss Butland . . .'

Tea and cakes inside, English tea, English chocolate biscuits from Xenopoulo on Rue des Franques. Running up the path, taking care not to land on the gaps between the paving stones, because she doesn't want to invite the evil eye. Skipping up the front steps, brushing past Miss Butland, breathing in the smell of

11

sunlight on freshly ironed linen, clean heat and rosewater. Looking up to catch the smile as they both pass into the cool house. Inside, the ticking of many clocks, the soft voice of Mama and her friends coming from an inner room. A ribbon of sweet tobacco smoke. The train whistle again, telling her that Papa is on his way back from the city, from Smyrna, bringing her a little present as he always does: a box of loukoumi from Orisdiback, tied up with a pretty ribbon; a wooden dancing bear from the Turkish man on the corner of Trassa Street.

Until this summer, the biscuits were always from Xenopoulo and the cakes from Portier, but now those things are gone, and when she thinks of them they are slipping past her, slipping past like a carriage of the little train that always whistles as it pulls into Bournabat Station. It has been days since the train last whistled. She went every day to listen for it, and then one day . . . She hugs herself tightly, but the memory still comes.

'Zoë! Come here at once!'

Outside the painted black iron of the garden gate, a man lying on his face, half on, half off the line of whitewashed stones. There is a smear of dark red on the whitewash, and flies are buzzing. A Greek man. She can tell by his clothes. There is a hole in his back.

Miss Butland ran down the path and swept her up in her arms, carried her back to Cook, and there was a submarine to make her feel better: ice-cold water in a misted glass, and submerged in it, a spoon of thick grape jam to lick. It was going to be all right, everyone was saying. They told her that, and then Mama told Cook. But the train never whistled again, and then Cook went off into Smyrna and never came back. The next day she found out, from Aleko the groom, that the Greek soldiers had eaten Rosie. And then Papa took Miss Butland to the British Consulate when the Greek soldiers had left and the Turkish soldiers arrived. 'She will be quite safe. They've put her on a battleship,' he told them when he returned, looking ruffled, more out of sorts than she had ever seen him. But Cook won't be safe, and nor will the other servants. No safer than Rosie. But she can't think about Rosie. She has decided she will never think of her, ever again.

She can hear something else behind her, above her parents' soft voices. A low growl, like thunder rolling behind Nymph Dagh, but so low and powerful that she can feel it in her insides. And now it is louder. The wind has shifted slightly: she feels the boat jump forward. The sail above her snaps and ropes creak against wood. Her eyes begin to sting. There is a terrifying smell: burning, but not the friendly smell of a bonfire or a kitchen fire.

The girl sits up. She wants Mama to send the smoke and the noise away, so she turns around and, though she knows she shouldn't, she looks behind her. She sees her father, arms spread across the spokes of the wheel, the faint glimmer of his smart white captain's cap. And there is Mama, beside him, wearing her shooting clothes, a scarf tied around her head. But behind her parents, something else. Where the lights of the city should be is dense blackness slashed open to reveal a pulsing wound, dirty orange-red, almost too bright to look at. It throbs. It roars. She opens her mouth to scream. Perhaps she does scream. As the light pulses she sees other boats all around them, each one filled with shadows, and from them comes a sound, a thin wail that rises and falls, made up of whispers and sobbing.

She calls out again, and this time Mama hears her. For a moment the girl is frightened, because she has been disobedient. She has looked back. But Mama leans and whispers something to Papa, and then she makes her way along the rail to where the girl is

13

sitting, hugging her knees, on the damp rug. 'My poor little bird,' she says, gathering up her skirts and sitting down. She takes her daughter in her arms and pulls her close. The girl smells salty tweed and perfume, Coty powder. One of Mama's fair ringlets has come loose and the girl winds it around her fingers and holds it against her face. 'Are you frightened?'

'Mmm hmm.' The girl nods, letting the rough cloth scratch her forehead. It feels so ordinary; it feels like home. A little spark of bravery ignites inside her. 'A little bit.'

'Everything is going to be absolutely fine, my dearest one.' Mama is speaking English, which is their special language; Papa talks to her in Greek, though his English is as perfect as Mama's. So many languages at home: English, French and Turkish; Greek, of course. 'Do you know where we're going?' The girl shakes her head. 'To Athens. Isn't that exciting? Papa is moving his shop there.'

'Can you move a shop?' The girl rubs her eyes, thinking. 'What about the windows?'

Mama laughs and ruffles the girl's hair. 'He's left the windows. But all the precious things, all the lovely things are on board with us. He'll find another shop in Athens, and we'll find another house.'

'But what's wrong with our house?'

'Nothing. Nothing at all. But sometimes one has to do something . . . something new. And exciting! An adventure!'

'An adventure?' The girl sniffs. She takes her mother's hand and, out of long habit, takes the big gold ring Mama always wears, the ring with the old ruby from India, and puts it gently between her teeth. *This does feel like an adventure, all of a sudden*, she thinks, catching the faint, lemony taste of the gold. She lifts her head and looks over the rail. They are sailing past big ships, all lit up in the night like ghostly ballrooms. There are lights high up in the distance, the little villages on the mountains that surround the bay. Suddenly there is a whirring of wings and a flock of cormorants shoots past the end of the bowsprit, black necks outstretched, wings beating frenziedly. Their eyes reflect the fire behind them, glowing like the gems in a garnet necklace she had watched Papa lay out for a customer the last time he had taken her to the shop, his business: G. Haggitiris et Cie, Goldsmiths. The most beautiful shop on Frank Street, where all the shops are beautiful. But now there will be a new shop, in Athens. 'Do they have Xenopoulo in Athens?' she asks Mama. Whenever Papa takes her to work with him, they always go to the department store, the most wonderful place she has ever been, and ride up and down on the escalators. Then they go to the Cafe Trieste, where she eats ice cream and listens to the singers. The singers, with their kohl-ringed eyes and languid movements and their sad, lovely songs. 'Why are the songs so unhappy?' she once asked Papa, and he laughed. 'Well, my little empress, they are so very, very sad that they've gone all the way around again and become happy. Can't you feel it, here?' And he put his finger, very gently, over her heart.

'I'm sure they have somewhere like Xenopoulo. It's a very lovely city,' Mama is saying. She takes a deep breath and the girl senses that she is not quite sure. 'We shall buy a house in . . . I don't know, perhaps Kolonaki. And then I am going to take you to Paris, and London. My goodness! What fun we're going to have!' Mama's voice sounds as if she is making a face, though she is still smiling in the dirty red light, staring back towards Papa at the wheel. The girl wonders if the garnet necklace – the woman hadn't bought it – is somewhere on *Thetis*, in one of the big, heavy boxes the men on the dock at Cordelio had carried on board. They had been angry, and Papa had given them a lot of money before they had done what

15

he asked. There are so many boxes – from the shop and from the house – that the cabin is full. But it makes her feel safer to know that all those precious things are here with her. She looks back at Papa and waves. He grins and sweeps off his neat white cap and waves it at her. She laughs, delighted, but then the line of glowing red in the distance pulses and she snuggles closer to Mama.

'It looks like a monster,' she says. 'Maybe a giant . . . a giant's mouth.'

'Then don't look, dearest. Go to sleep. And when you wake up, there won't be any giant.'

'Papa? When will we get there?' the girl calls out, her voice muffled by the thick air. But he grins and pats the varnished wheel.

'We'll be in Piraeus in time for tea, little Zoë. I promise.'

The yacht slides on. Long before dawn, she is still awake, shivering under a blanket, when she hears a voice: a woman, crying. Then the soft plash of oars, far away through the drifting smoke. The voice comes a little closer and the girl hears that it isn't sobbing but singing. She stares out towards the sound but there is nothing to be seen. Just the voice, and its song.

A person must give some thought to the hour of his death;
when he will go down into the black earth
and his name will be erased.

The girl opens her eyes to a faintly glowing whiteness: milky, suffused with pink and orange, like the opal brooch Papa had once let her wear to the Cafe Trieste. When she breathes in, the air is clean, damp and salty. The thick, dirty stench from last night has all gone. Above her, the sails are hanging almost empty. Mama is sitting next to her on the rug, winding a bright silk scarf, yellow roses on a field of black and red, around the crown of her broad-brimmed hat. 'What do you think?' she asks as she puts on the hat, pins it into place and ties the ends of the scarf under her chin with a flouncy bow.

'I like that one,' says the girl, nodding. 'Mama, where has the sea gone?'

'It's just mist, darling. It will blow away soon. And the sun is rising. Isn't it beautiful?'

'Where are we?'

'I don't quite know,' Mama says. She stands up and brushes down her tweed skirt. 'Somewhere near Andros, I think. I shall go and ask Papa.'

'And ask him about Athens,' the girl says. She reaches out for Mama but her fingers only catch a tiny fold of cloth and it twitches out of her grasp. 'Do they have singers there? Do they have ice cream?'

'Of course they have ice cream, *koukla*!' Mama makes her way around the cabin to where Papa stands behind the wheel. *He hasn't moved at all while I've been asleep*, she thinks. Morning seems to have sent away the horrors of last night. The soft mist that surrounds them muffles their voices and makes *Thetis* seem like a funny sort of long, whitewashed room. Dew shines on polished brass and varnished wood. The girl yawns loudly and stretches. She sees Mama lean against Papa and put her arm around his waist. Beyond the rail, there is a narrow strip of water, as slick and shimmery as blue glass, across which *Thetis* is moving so slowly that she is barely leaving a wake, and then white mist, a soft, undulating wall. She hears the clink of china, the sound deadened by the mist. Mama is coming back towards her, edging along the narrow walkway between the cabin and the rail. She

17

is carrying a pink plate. On the plate is a white napkin, folded crisply into a square, and on the cloth rests a piece of sweet milk pudding. The girl sees it all with perfect clarity: the knife-sharp corners of the napkin, the pale yellow custard held between two layers of brown, crisp pastry.

'Breakfast!' Mama calls.

'Mary?' There is something sharp in Papa's voice. He is looking over his left shoulder, staring intently into the mist. 'Can you hear something?'

'What, darling?'

'There.' Papa pushes his cap back on his head and frowns. 'There! Engines!'

'I don't . . . Yes, yes, there is something!'

As Mama says the words, the girl hears it: a low thrum, a deep pulse inside the glowing mist. 'Too near,' Papa says. He stoops behind the binnacle, and when he stands up again he is holding something that the girl has never seen before: a large black pistol. The pulse has suddenly become much louder. The girl thinks of the sound she heard last night: the roar of the monster.

'George . . .' Mama says. Papa thrusts his arm into the air and there is a deafening bang. The girl sees smoke, and another flash, and then the bang comes again. Mama is still holding the plate and as Papa fires again and shouts at the top of his voice, the girl is staring at the square of milk pudding so she only sees, out of the corner of her eye, a shape, an angle with no top and no bottom, black and sharp, slicing through the opal glow of the mist. She opens her mouth and then she is looking at a black wall that hisses as it moves effortlessly through the wood and brass and canvas of *Thetis*. She has just enough time to realise that Mama and Papa are on the other side of the wall when the yacht seems to tumble. Green water, no longer glassy but roiling and lacy with foam, is above her, all around her. There is water in her eyes, in her mouth, freezing, stifling. A deafening throb beats at her ears. *It's the monster*, she thinks. *It found us after all.*

She is rolling, weightless one moment, heavy as a stone the next. Through the sizzle of panic she can see her arms stretched out in front of her, hands clawing at nothing. They look colourless, dead. She can't feel them, though her head is bursting. She needs to breathe: the pain in her chest is worse than anything she has ever known. If she opens her mouth, the pain will go away. If she opens her mouth . . . She is sinking, through strings of bubbles and bright things whirling past her. A porthole from the cabin glides by, going down. She reaches, reaches. And then something touches her hand. A yellow rose. She clutches at it in a frenzy, sinking her hand into red silk and undulating flowers, and as she does so something takes hold of her. She is no longer falling, but rising up, towards gauzy light. She sees a hand clutching the front of her sailor suit, and on one finger, surely, a gold ring with a blood-red stone. Everything has become still and calm. The girl reaches for the hand, because the only thing she wants to do, the only thing left to do, is to put the ring between her teeth, taste the sour gold and the sweetness of her mother's skin, sweet as love itself.

What her fingers find is something hard and slippery, and though she doesn't want to, she grabs on with all her might and lets herself be carried, faster and faster, up towards the light, to where she doesn't want to go. She doesn't want to leave, now. She wants to stay down there, to take the hand and let it take her home. But instead she is thrown into the air. She gasps, retches, breathes. The thing she is clutching is a long piece of smooth, varnished wood:

part of a mast. She watches her hands scrabble like small, white creatures. They can't be hers. Then she sees, just beyond her fingers, a piece of filmy cloth. A ripple catches it, and the girl sees a yellow rose and a swirl of red, but it is already blackening in the water, fluttering out of sight like a drowning butterfly.

She screams. One word: Mama. The mist takes her little voice and smothers it like a wet pillow pressed across her face. But she fights it. Panic makes her fight. She screams because of the hand that had pushed her up towards the shifting roof of the sea. She screams at her own hands, alien as crabs, that grip the slippery wood with a strength she doesn't understand. She screams again, and again, at the empty sea.

Time must pass, because the mist melts into the sea and the sun rises to show the girl that she is a speck on a vast mirror. The light flashes off the water and blinds her. The sun burns a line into her scalp while the water turns her legs numb. She screams until she can taste blood in her mouth. When she closes her eyes she sees the plate, the napkin and the square of pie, Mama's hand with its ring curved around the white china. She can't really think but if she has a thought, it is that the world can't end as long as she keeps calling for Mama, that she can't be lost as long as Mama can hear her voice. Because Mama can hear her. Mama and Papa are somewhere behind the flash and shear of sunlight, waiting for her.

When the ship rises up out of the orange morning light, the girl has long since screamed herself into silence. It appears behind her, a low cliff of white paint streaked with rust. She looks up to see faces, more than she can count, an endless line of noses and eyes and mouths, blinking and wailing like seagulls. A white circle floats towards her, hitting the water and splashing her so that she almost lets go of the wood. 'Lifebelt!' someone shouts, and she flails herself into it. A couple of sailors haul her up and pull her out of the lifebelt as casually as if they are shucking an oyster. No one speaks to her and she is shaking too hard, and her throat is too raw, to say anything herself. After the sailors dry her off they ask her some half-hearted questions. She can't answer. *Are my mama and papa here?* she wants to ask, but something tells her that if she asks, the world will end. So they just push her into the packed mass of people which fill every inch of space on the boat, and she ends up trapped against the railing, a fat woman's legs pressing her hard into the sharp edges of the blistered paint. She is grateful, at first, for the warmth of the woman's doughy body. She can't think of anything except how cold she is: when she tries, her thoughts have no reality. Her mind drifts, febrile and raw, through an endless series of pictures flicking like a picture book in a breeze. Mama, smiling. Papa's hat. The pistol. A rose, sinking into darkness. Above her, the woman keeps up a whining litany of prayers for hours, muttering at the Holy Virgin as if she hopes that the Theotokos will give in out of sheer boredom. The endless wheedling voice, the throb of the engines, the groans, screams and prayers of the crowd fill air already thick with bad smells: smoke, oil, sweat, stale perfume, an overflowing lavatory. And all the time, the girl is forced to stare out at the sea, blue-green and calm. 'I'm going to see Mama and Papa,' she starts to whisper, in time to the fat woman's prayers. 'They're waiting for me.' And she tries to believe it, though she is too frightened to make that part of her do what she wants it to do: to make her feel like she does when she prays in church, or to the icon at home: that warm certainty that invisible things will help her. 'My every hope I place in you, Mother of God; keep me under your protection,' the woman mutters, but the girl can feel her flesh trembling through her damp skirt, and she knows that the words aren't helping the woman either.

The boat stops, once, at a tiny port, just a stone jetty flung out into the sea from a featureless brown island. The jetty is seething with people. The woman shifts, and more people crowd in on either side of the girl, trapping her arms at her sides. She has almost no strength after gripping the bowsprit in the freezing cold, and though she struggles as hard as she can, she can't free them. She starts to cry, but no one notices. Her sobs are lost in the ceaseless babble of voices speaking Greek, Armenian, Turkish, Ladino. Desperate for the lavatory, as Mama had always insisted she call it, she stands in agony until her body takes over and a warm gush runs down her legs. Still, no one notices. Then they are among other ships, and she finds herself looking for *Thetis* among the masts, which makes her cry again. Islands pass by, and more ships, all of them as crowded as hers. Then they pass beneath some sort of cliff, a looming shadow, and the girl, who can only lift her head, looks up to see the prow of a gigantic ship, stark black, striped with white and painted with letters bigger than her: NARKUNDA. And high up, a little white figure . . . He catches her eye, even though the huge ship's rail is lined with nice-looking people, well dressed, well fed. Why? What has she seen? The bright white of his sailor suit? The flash of something shiny in his hands? She can just about tell that he is a boy, a little boy. Then he looks down, and sees their boat. Light flashes on glass around his face. And then he raises his hand. Is he waving at her? She wants so badly to wave back. It is her world, up there: clean clothes, light glinting off varnished wood and polished brass. Perhaps Mama and Papa . . . The big ship could have picked them up, couldn't it? That was where they belong. It had just been a mistake that this rusty old boat had found her before they had. These thoughts, vague and desperate, make her whimper. She tries to raise her arm, but it only moves enough for the sharp edges of the paint to cut into her. So she has to watch the great ship glide past as the tears stream down her face, the woman behind her still muttering fretfully at the Virgin. When she can't turn her head far enough to keep the boy in sight, she turns it the other way, and sees the harbour.

CHAPTER TWO

Every evening, Tommy Collyer walks, hand clasped tightly in his mother's, along the varnished walkways of the ocean liner until they are facing the dense, vivid striations of the tropical sunset. They have left the monsoon behind them in Bombay but every night the clouds stack themselves above the horizon like slatted blinds. His mother has a box of paints in her cabin, a heavy wooden case with a red NEEDED ON VOYAGE label pasted onto it. Every day he begs her to open it, and every day, after a ritual set of objections from her, which he finds intensely pleasing, she clicks open the catches and shows him the contents. The brushes, the porcelain palette, the water flask. But what he wants to see are the paints. The little lozenges of colour, silky-shiny like sweets, each with a dip worn into it, some more worn than others. He runs his fingers gently across the rows of pigment; secretly he wants to eat them, because they are so unbearably pretty, or squeeze them like rubber tree sap between his fingers. They intoxicate him, like the rich headache fumes of petrol, or the leafy perfume of his father's cigars.

'My Indian colours,' his mother calls them, and sometimes

mutters about having to change them when they get home, which makes no sense to him. Why change these lovely colours? And isn't *home* the place they are leaving behind? Gamboge, cadmium yellow deep, cadmium orange, scarlet lake, rose doreé, permanent carmine, cerulean blue, viridian, Hooker's green, yellow ochre, burnt sienna, Indian red. These are the colours of the vast monsoon sunsets. His mother, on their first evening at sea, had brought out her paints and her easel and set to work while he watched over her shoulder, Daddy being somewhere else – Daddy is always somewhere else. She had made thick stripes of blue, purple, violet, red and orange, and blurred each into the other with a watery brush, which he had thought quite splendid but which Mummy herself did not seem to care for.

'And now it's gone,' she had said, with a touch of irritation, as if sunsets were just one more thing that could not be trusted. It was the voice she usually reserves for remarks about Daddy, in fact. Tom had recognised it immediately.

They are heading for England, the place Mummy and Daddy call home. It doesn't seem possible to Tom, as he plays on the decks and walkways of SS *Narkunda*, that a little more than a week ago he had been playing on the verandah of the bungalow in Koovappally, watching bird-wing butterflies drift past like living kites in the muggy, spicy monsoon air. Looking down the hill at the dark lines of rubber trees, at the pepper vines swarming over the telephone poles. At his ayah, Malini, drifting past the ferns by the well, trailing her white sari like a ghost. Waking in the morning to church bells and the call of the muezzin rising up from the valley. That was home. Daddy, and the other white people in Koovappally and Kanjirappally and Ernakulam, spent a lot of time talking about England, as if India was nothing more than a big, dirty house they were visiting. *But I was born here*, Tom would think, listening to them.

'What's England like?' he asks Mummy, when they are back in their cabin, getting ready for supper. He is standing on Mummy's bed, doing up the buttons on the back of her ballgown. It must be the hundredth time he's asked, but Mummy leans her head patiently and smiles at him in the cheval glass.

'It rains quite a lot,' she says.

'It rains a lot in Kerala,' Tom points out.

'True. Let me see . . . It's very green.'

'Koovappally is green.'

'Different green. All different sorts.'

'Viridian?' asks Tom, tapping the paint box.

'Not . . . not very often,' Mummy concedes.

'Well then. What colours would you use to paint England?'

Mummy furrows her brow. 'Let me think,' she says. 'Hmm. All the colours I took out of my set when I came to India . . .' She clicks open the box and looks at the blocks of pigment. Underneath the white china palette she finds a folded square of printed paper, which she squints at. 'Here we are. Sepia. Vandyke brown. Payne's grey. Caput mortuum. Windsor green. Terre vert. *Olive* green. I told you: lots of greens.'

'And grey. They sound like ugly colours,' Tom says, frowning.

'No, no. They're lovely. They're . . . just different. There's no such thing as an ugly colour, I don't think!'

There is a brisk knock, and the door opens to reveal Daddy, in immaculate white tie.

'Shall we go down, Evelyn?' he asks.

'One minute, Jim.' Mummy wets a comb and runs it through Tom's hair. She adjusts the collar of his sailor suit and pats his head. 'There.'

'Captain Collyer, Mrs Collyer.' The steward greets them at the door to the dining room, ignoring Tom, who expects to be ignored. They are seated next to Mr and Mrs Forde, Major Rowland, the Reverend and Mrs Woodleigh, as usual. There have been four of these suppers so far, and Tom, who is neither spoken to nor expected to speak, has become minutely acquainted with the details of his fellow diners' faces, their clothing and hands. Reverend Woodleigh has long, pale, smooth hands on which the heavy dark yellow staining – yellow ochre, Tom decides – from his cigarettes stands out like a wound. His wife's ears have unusually long lobes. Major Rowland's moustache partly hides a white scar. Mr Forde has a tic in one eye and a sharp, bobbing Adam's apple. Tom goes to work on his plate of fish – bony and trapped in a claggy, cheesy sauce – and listens to the grown-ups talk. Reverend Woodleigh has just finished describing, for the third time, his work at a mission for unmarried ladies at Sangor. Mummy and Mrs Forde are discussing bridge. His father is telling Major Rowland about his time in the War. Tom knows about the War from five years of tea parties, of drinks on the verandah, of polo games. He also knows about polo, duck shooting in the Punjab, and pigsticking. He picks a bone out of his fish, and half listens to his father's clipped voice.

'Came out to India straight after Sandhurst, in '10, Major. Stationed in Secunderabad – yes, that's the one: N Battery. We were in France by the end of '14. Caught some shrapnel at Loos. That was a business . . . You were there, of course. I got a Blighty one at La Boisselle. Wanted to go back to the front, but my lords and masters sent me to W Battery instead – India again. We were supposed to be sent to the Middle East but nothing came of it in the end. Meanwhile, I met my dear wife while on leave in Mussoorie; I rather think that I owe my good fortune to the shortage of eligible men in the hill stations that year, rather than my charms . . .'

'Nonsense, darling,' Tom's mother puts in, automatically, and the major chuckles obligingly.

'And then to Kerala,' the major says, blotting claret out of his moustache with his napkin.

'Yes. Evelyn's uncle plants rubber down there. After the Armistice I went on the Reserve List, you know . . . at loose ends. Thought I'd try my hand.'

'Now, you see, I'm curious,' says the major, leaning forward. Tom sees more scars on his neck, white lines radiating from the shadows under his collar. The two men fall into a heavy discussion of the economics of the rubber trade. Tom doesn't understand the word *economics* but he knows what rubber is. Daddy seems to be telling Major Rowland a kind of story about why they have left India: Mummy is homesick, it seems, and the climate does not agree with her. Or with Tom, apparently. There is an important job waiting for Daddy, though this is the first Tom has heard of it. *Mummy loves the weather in Kerala*, he wants to say. *And there's nothing wrong with my lungs. My lungs are fine. And the colours. What about the colours?* But of course he doesn't say anything. He just keeps chewing on the gluey white sauce. Daddy's story is funny, he thinks, but it isn't the one he has learnt off by heart over the past year. That story, as it runs through his head, is like a book for very little children, full of big, crude pictures painted by Daddy's yelling. The *trees*. The *markets*. Tom can see him pacing up and down in the sitting room, a big glass of whisky-soda in his hand. *The bloody workers. Your bloody father, Evelyn, and his bloody nagging. I know he lent me money, Evelyn! I bloody know that! Well, he's got enough of the bloody stuff, hasn't he? And why shouldn't I play a few games of polo? Anyway, doesn't your father like a flutter?* A flutter is betting, Tom knows, though he doesn't really understand what betting is. Something Daddy does a lot. Too much, even. And his grandfather, Major General Heywood – Da – doesn't seem like the sort of person who *flutters*. Not at all. Da, tall, thick round the middle, with a bulbous nose and swirling grey moustaches, is the only grown-up, apart from Mummy, who has ever looked Tom straight in the eyes and listened to him. Well, that isn't quite true. Malini had listened. The gardener, the cook . . . All his Indian friends had listened. *Are there Indians*, he wonders, *in England?* He very much hopes that there are. Because if there aren't any kind, patient Indians, who is going to listen to him?

A few days later, they pass through the Suez Canal. Flat desert on either side, pale brown like the fur of a dead deer he had found one day in Mussoorie. Raw Umber. Raw Sienna. The huge liner dwarfs the flocks of little boats with sharp, triangular sails that dart around the *Narkunda* as it inches along the strange, dead-straight waterway, passing other big ships: rusty cargo vessels flying flags he has never seen before; coal ships; an Italian cruiser, which has all the *Narkunda*'s passengers lined up along the rails, ooh-ing and aah-ing and waving at the smart Italian sailors. Another ocean liner glides by, and Tom feels a stab of raw envy: the people on its decks are going to India.

They put in at Port Said. Mummy and Daddy go ashore, but Tom is left on board with the Woodleighs, and has to listen to Mrs Woodleigh muttering darkly to her husband about women – whom she may or may not actually know – doing things she doesn't approve of while the two of them drink tea and forget to offer him so much as a biscuit. He desperately wants to lean over the rail and listen to all the noise of Egypt, smell all the smells, watch the orange sellers and the luggage carriers and the beggars and soldiers. But instead he sits stiffly beside Mrs Woodleigh, trapped in a cloud of lavender water and the starchy tang of moral superiority. Mummy comes back alone, reporting that Daddy has bumped into someone he knows from the War. The sigh and slight shake of her head with which she relates this is familiar to Tom. But at least she has brought him some presents: a funny cut-out figure of a fat man in a fez; and a toy, four wooden camels on a wooden paddle, that nod their heads if you pull on a piece of dangling string. He is entranced, and thinks about nothing else for the rest of the day. When he wakes up the next morning, they are at sea again. Daddy eats his breakfast kedgeree in frowning silence. His face is red and puffy, and Mummy narrows her eyes whenever she has occasion to glance at him.

Major Rowland, who is revealing himself as something of a gossip, comes over to tell them that they have someone important on board. An American consul, apparently. The *Narkunda* is making a slight detour, to Piraeus, on this American's account. 'Hitching a ride,' says the major, twitching his eyebrows, perhaps with disapproval, perhaps with admiration. 'Americans . . .'

The breakfast party murmur and shake their heads. It is something to do with an awful happening in Smyrna, Tom hears, though where Smyrna might be is not explained.

Mrs Woodleigh is very upset at what she calls *outrages*. Mr Forde remembers a visit before the War – 'Motor cars and department stores, just like Oxford Street,' he says. All burnt, now. Nothing left at all.

'Poor bloody Greeks,' says the major, ordering himself another poached egg on toast, with anchovies.

The *Narkunda* sails between low, brown islands. Further off, a golden-brown land spreads mountainous arms wide to receive them. White villages tumble like sugar cubes towards the bluest water Tom has ever seen. In the distance, a bay full of ships, and further off, a hill crowned with a broken cage of white stone. The major lets Tom, who is standing on a chair, peer at Athens through his field glasses. 'Piraeus over here, Athens over there,' the major explains. 'You'll be learning about it in school soon, old chap. Aristotle and all that.' The broken cage is something called the Parthenon. Very, very old, and terribly important. The field glasses are heavy and Tom lets them droop down towards the harbour, Piraeus, which has come much closer. Inside the figure-of-eight of his vision, a screen of masts and funnels, and behind that, a quayside swarming with people. Surely those can't be tents? A big flag, a red cross on white ground. Smoke is rising from cooking fires. It looks a bit like India to Tom, but India had never seemed broken. Chaotic, yes, sometimes scary. But India was always getting on with itself. This harbour, these people . . . Something is wrong here.

A motor launch comes alongside, a tall man in a white suit climbs down into it and is taken away to Piraeus. As Tom is staring after it, another ship chugs across the *Narkunda*'s bows. Wide and low in the water, it is trailing black smoke from its funnel, which drifts into Tom's face, almost choking him with its carbolic reek. As he rubs his eyes, he looks down and sees that the decks of the ship are crammed with people. They are packed together, grown-ups and children, most standing, some sitting among a chaos of suitcases, bags and bundles, some just lying on the deck, crowded by the feet of the others. They are all dirty, all exhausted. Mostly women and children. Some of the women are wearing bright, modern clothes, but all stained and filthy; others are swathed in black like the nuns from the monastery in Kanjirappally, their faces all but hidden by scarves. Tom looks down in amazement. Faces turn up to him, blank, or pleading. Angry, perhaps, some of them. A woman is suckling her baby. When she looks up at the great bow of the *Narkunda*, her face is streaked with soot and tears.

As the ship slips by, Tom sees a little girl in a sailor suit just like his. She is crushed up against the rail by the crowd, so small that she is almost swallowed by the skirts of a large woman who is clinging to a stick-thin man in a dented bowler hat. Her long, wavy blonde hair is plastered across her face, which is disgracefully dirty. *If those people are her parents,* Tom thinks, *they jolly well ought to take care of her. How unfair.* And because fairness is something Tom understands, something he has been taught to believe in, and because the girl is around his age and looks so unhappy, he lifts his arm and waves. She sees him; she lifts her streaked face and her eyes meet his. Then he sees that she can't wave back; her arms are trapped against the painted iron of the ship's railings. She is trapped. He heaves the field glasses up to his eyes and fiddles desperately with the focus wheel. Sweeping the glasses clumsily from side to side, he finds the boat. There are people crammed onto the decks, clinging to funnels, masts, rigging. The boats on the river at Cochin are crowded, but he has never seen anything like this. With a huge effort he keeps the glasses still enough to find the fat woman, and in front of her, pushed so hard against the rail that it seems to be cutting her in two, is the little girl in the sailor suit. Her arms are by her sides, caught between the rail and the people pushing in around her. With a little stab of something he can't identify – fear? Wonder? – he sees she is looking straight at him. He has time to see that her eyes might be green, and that she has been crying, when the ship clears the *Narkunda*'s bow and is gone, swallowed by bristling masts and funnels of the harbour. Tom cranes his neck after her and tries to find the ship again with the wavering field glasses, but it is useless.

Lowering the field glasses carefully, he finds that his heart is beating very fast. The poor girl. He feels a little bit ashamed of himself for not noticing that she was so unhappy. He hopes he hasn't made her feel worse. What had she been doing there? And all those crowded, frightened people? They might have been ghosts. He might have seen a ghost ship, it had slipped by so silently. He'll ask his mother, he tells himself, but then the *Narkunda*'s steam whistle begins to shriek and the houses and hills start to swing around in front of his eyes. He goes to find his parents, but the memory of what he has seen lingers in an uncomfortable way and he decides not to say anything about it. Perhaps they'll think he made it up. Perhaps they'll tell him he shouldn't have waved at all those dirty people.

'The captain has told us we can go ashore!' At tea, Mummy is the happiest that Tom has seen her since they left Bombay. He gathers that the *Narkunda* is stopping here until tomorrow evening – something administrative, says Major Rowland, and the grown-ups all roll their eyes knowingly. 'The Parthenon, Jim! We'll go, of course!'

'Can't say I fancy it much,' says Daddy, cocking his head jovially towards the reverend and his wife, who chuckle in agreement. 'Seems rather a mess. Frightful mob on the waterfront.'

'Quite a picture,' Mrs Woodleigh agrees primly.

'They are refugees,' says Mummy, her voice sounding pained. 'Not a *mob*. One can't imagine what they must have been through.'

'Never had much time for the Classics. Frightfully dull,' Daddy states blandly, ignoring her.

'Well, I shall go.' Mummy sits back, glaring at Daddy. 'And Tommy shall come with me.'

'Tommy?' Daddy laughs, not all that kindly.

'Yes. Why not? It will be good for him.'

'I don't see—'

But the major interrupts, surprisingly deftly. 'I rather like the idea, myself. If you'd care for an old man's company, I'd be happy to tag along with you and this young chap.'

'That would be wonderful, Major.' Mummy beams at him gratefully.

That seems to settle it, though Mummy and Daddy do not talk very much that evening, and the next morning, Daddy chews his breakfast kedgeree angrily, moustache twitching, eyes fixed on Tommy's smart tropical-weight blazer, which is getting a little small.

'You'll never wear *that* again,' he says. 'I'll buy you some proper clothes as soon as we get home. Tweed.'

'What's tweed, Daddy?' It is often dangerous to talk to Daddy when he is in one of these moods, but a new word is always interesting to Tommy. Mummy and Daddy lock eyes and Tommy's stomach clenches but, fortunately, Major Rowland chooses that moment to enter the dining room. He smiles at Tommy and raises a hand in greeting, and Tommy, wilting with relief at a quarrel averted, waves back. Mummy gives Daddy a tight little grin and stands up.

'Come along, Tommy,' she says pointedly. 'We're going to have such fun.' Daddy dismisses them with a wave of his fork. 'Honestly,' Mummy says under her breath.

The *Narkunda* is anchored a little way from the quayside. The first thing Tommy notices when he steps out onto the deck, following his mother and the major to where a smartly dressed ship's officer is waiting by a gate in the rail, is the noise. A shout, an endless shout made up of countless individual shouts: that is what it sounds like, noise so harsh and dense that Tommy almost

34

lets go of his mother's hand, tries to let go and get away, but she is holding on to him tightly, wincing at the noise and at the stench, an equally dense miasma of smoke, cooking, unwashed human beings and their waste. Tommy, though he is used to the smells of India, coughs and pulls on Mummy's arm, but she just shakes her head.

'Oh, those poor people,' she mutters, and bends down to ruffle his hair. 'Don't worry, Tomtom. We shan't be going near them. We're off to see the Acropolis.' Tommy notices that the holiday jollity of her words is not quite sincere, but he steels himself and follows her over to the rail. It is a short ride to the quayside. The boatmen, genially savage-looking men with thick dark hair and bristling moustaches, make for a clear section of the waterfront near a gaudy domed church, but as they begin to guide the launch in, a small tug boat, belching black smoke, nips in ahead of them. There is much guttural cursing as they try to put in further along, only to be waved away by an angry harbour official. When they finally tie the launch up, it is to a bollard only a few yards from the rough planking barricades that are containing the throng of refugees.

Tommy doesn't want to get out of the boat. He looks over the side at the water, glinting with rainbow swirls of oil. Further down, a cloud of tiny silver fish moves back and forth. It must be silent down there. The roar of voices coming from the refugees is frightening. He hangs back, but Mummy still has a firm grip on his hand and before he knows it he is half climbing, half being hauled up onto the quayside. The major is standing, jaw set, pointing to where a line of horse-drawn carriages are waiting in the shade of some palm trees.

'Over there, Mrs Collyer. Those are cabs, I think.'

Mummy follows the major across the wide expanse of pavement and tram rails, Mummy pulling Tommy, who shuffles along unwillingly, as only he seems to have noticed what is streaming towards them along the quay: a straggling column of people, mostly women and children with a few old men, being herded by a few soldiers in dusty uniforms and one single nurse in a blindingly white uniform. Tommy has time to note her starched wimple with its red cross in the centre and her steel-rimmed spectacles before the column reaches them and they are swamped. Instantly, Tommy is caught by the dragging black skirts of two women walking almost shoulder to shoulder. He trips, and feels his fingers being dragged out of his mother's grasp. Squeezed between hips and thighs, he staggers in this new direction, terrified in case he falls and is trampled. He looks up and sees red faces framed by black headscarves, dirty hands gripping a baby, a bundle of rags. He catches his breath, and the air is full of sweat, mustiness, onions and, very faint, cinnamon. And words, incomprehensible, soft and hard at the same time, nothing like Malayalam or Hindi or English, the only languages he has ever heard. He trips, catches hold of rough cloth, rights himself. Someone treads, hard, on one of his sandal-clad feet. The women lurch to one side and come to a sudden, complaining halt. Tommy claws his way out from inside the quivering forest of skirts and legs and looks around, frantically, for his mother, but all he sees are dark, dusty people towering around him. To his horror, he finds he is behind the wooden barricade. There, looming not very far away in the harbour, is the huge bulk of the *Narkunda*. But here . . . He whimpers and thumbs hot tears from his eyes.

He tries to push through the crowd, but no one moves to let him through, no one even seems to notice him. The smells, the strange language, rising and falling in raw cadences of grief, frustration and despair, are overwhelming him. Turning, trying to prise people apart – is he blubbing? He must be – he becomes aware of another sound, not loud, in fact rather weak and thin, but . . . Someone is singing. Here, in this nightmare. It sounds like a child. Something makes him turn away from the wall of people and shove his way through more legs towards the voice. Perhaps it is because the singer sounds as small and lost as he feels at that moment. He elbows between an old man's filthy pinstripe trousers and a woman's once-bright calico skirt and has to catch himself, because he is right at the edge of the quay. A narrow strip of dirty marble is all that separates him from that greasy, rainbow water. But he can still hear the singing, and there, sitting beside an iron bollard with her legs dangling, is a little girl. She has tangled, dark gold hair and the torn and stained clothes she is wearing had once been a sailor suit very much like his own. Face turned towards the open sea, where tawny brown islands are shimmering in the heat haze, she is singing to nobody. Her voice hovers and twists like the murmurations of silver fish that flash deep beneath her dirty bare feet, and pulls him through the crowd until he is looking down at the matted cords of her blonde hair and the blue collar of the creased and grimy sailor suit. With a shock, he recognises her.

'You were on that boat,' he says, standing over her. 'With all those people. I waved at you!'

She turns at his words and raises her face to his. It is sunburnt and dirty: she has cried, and rubbed her cheeks, cried again, until her skin is a hundred shades of dingy brown. She is staring at him so intently that her eyes seem brighter than the dazzling sunshine. They are a clear, mossy green, and Tom's mind immediately runs across the pigments in his mother's paintbox. *Sap Green*, he thinks. 'Hello!' he says again. His heart is thumping.

'Hello,' she says, in perfect English, though her voice is all scratchy. 'I have lost my mama and my papa. Have they sent you to get me?' She is trembling, Tommy notices, but she can't be cold. The seafront is boiling hot. And she is staring at him with those eyes.

'I don't know . . .' he stammers, but what he is thinking is that she is British. How utterly amazing! That means he'll be safe. And it must be – of course – why he had picked her out among all those other people. 'I just heard you singing.' The girl gives him one more desperate glare and bursts into tears. But Tom is too overcome with relief and surprise – she is English, so that means he is safe – that he doesn't notice. He squats down next to her. 'What's your name? What were you singing?'

The girl buries her face in her hands. Her shoulders are heaving. Tom has no brothers and sisters; his playmates have been the children of his parents' Indian servants, who would never dream of crying in front of a little sahib. To his distress, he finds he doesn't know what to do.

'I bet you'll find them in no time,' he says briskly. 'What's your name? Mine's Tommy. Tommy Collyer. I'm from India.'

'My name is Zoë Haggitiris,' the girl mumbles hollowly through her cupped hands. She sniffs. Her shoulders are still quivering. 'I live in . . .' She lifts her head and swallows with a great effort. 'I live at number 32 in the Street of the English Church . . . in Bournabat,' she adds, frowning, as though he is an idiot for not knowing.

'I'm from India,' he repeats. 'Is your house near here, then?'

'India?' She frowns, and the dirt around her eyes cracks into tiny lines. 'Mama has a ring from India. Don't you know where Bournabat is? It's in Smyrna.'

'Oh.' Tom racks his brains. He's sure he has heard the grown-ups mention that word. A faint memory surfaces. 'Do you have lots of figs there, or something?'

The girl frowns. 'Figs?' But Tom, overcome with relief that she isn't crying any more, rambles on.

'Smyrna . . . Do they have giant butterflies in Smyrna? In Koovappally – that's my home – they have butterflies as big as this!' He spreads his hands.

'Ooh.' The girl's eyes narrow, and Tom knows instantly that she is picturing the butterflies, the drifting, lazy beauty of them.

'Transparent yellow.' He is so happy to have cheered her up that he forgets he is speaking. 'Indian yellow. Cadmium scarlet. French ultramarine.'

'What are you saying?' The girl is listening intently.

'Oh!' He has been running his fingers across the paintbox in his mind, chanting the name of each shiny square that he might use to paint a butterfly. 'Colours,' he says, a bit embarrassed. 'Um . . . gold ochre . . .'

'I saw a horrible red,' the girl says, drawing her knees up under her chin. Her feet are bare and filthy. 'The *most* horrible red. Like the mouth of a monster.'

'Crikey.' Tom closes his eyes and thinks, touches a cube of paint, reads its label. 'Like alizarin crimson?'

To his horror the girl starts to cry again. Not just blubbing, though: her body looks like it is being bent and unbent by something he can't see, and the air is going in and out of her mouth in great ragged gasps. 'Oh, gosh, don't,' he says, helplessly.

'It was smoky and dirty,' she gasps. 'The fire. All the people were burning up in it. But Papa was taking us to Athens and we were going to have ice cream . . . And now he's gone! Mama's gone!'

'Maybe they've just gone to see the ice cream man,' Tom decides. In a hot, smelly place like this, there's bound to be someone selling ice cream.

'I fell in the sea,' the girl says, shaking her head. Her face is in her hands again. Her shoulders quiver. *Please don't blub*, Tom pleads, silently. He has been brought up, for the six years of his life, to be a grown-up in miniature, a little sahib, a little Englishman. But Tom has come to the limit of this false adulthood. Squatting in his shorts, socks and sandals, trapped between a forest of legs and the oily sea, he feels very small and scared. He wants his mummy. She would know what to do. What *would* Mummy do?

'It was so cold,' the girl is saying. 'And I was all alone. I don't know what happened to *Thetis*.' She glances at him through her fingers. 'Maybe they swam away? But that man said they had . . . had . . .' She starts to sob harder.

'Crikey,' says Tom. This news seems far too big to be coming from this little girl. 'I think . . . My mummy and daddy will know what to do. My daddy was in the army and Mummy's good at everything.' To his surprise, he finds that he has reached out and taken the girl's hand in his own. It is rather sticky and very hot. 'Don't worry, Zo . . . Zo . . .'

'Zoë.' She sniffs, and grips his hand tightly.

'Zo-ee. I liked your song.'

'Papa . . . Papa says I oughtn't to sing songs like that, from the cafes. But Papa is . . . is . . .' She doubles over and lets out a terrible wail.

Tom doesn't know what to do. It is as if everything his father has ever said about foreigners, and women for that matter, is here before him, wearing a dirty sailor suit. He doesn't understand most of those things but he does understand that, like most things except horses, they trouble Daddy and make him angry. Zoë doesn't make Tom angry, though. She is making him feel sad and upset, but her hand in his . . . Tom isn't alone. He is quite lost in an ocean of strangers, but he has someone else. 'Are you going to sing again?' he asks.

The girl wipes her nose with the back of her hand and shakes her head. 'I can't.'

'Go on! Sing that one again – that you were singing before. What was it about?'

'A black stone sitting on a beach.' She blinks at him. Tom sees that salt has dried in her hair and crusted on her forehead. He is about to ask her again, to coax her into singing, when he feels a hand descend on his shoulder, gripping it so hard that he is sure the fingers are digging right into his flesh. He is wrenched upright, feet kicking for a moment in thin air, and, before he can say anything, the girl's hand is ripped out of his and he is being carried, a strong arm around his chest, his feet kicking helplessly, through the dense crowd of noisy, smelly people.

He opens his mouth to protest, and then the major is barking orders at a Greek policeman, a barricade is drawn back and he is deposited, gently, in front of his mother, who is shouting at him, half in tears, half laughing. She pushes him again and again with the heels of her hands; then she is kneeling in front of him, pulling up his socks. 'Oh, Tommy, Tommy,' she is whispering, like a prayer. He is in a panic. His head is spinning. He looks out desperately over the top of Mummy's wide straw hat, but all he sees is a wall of people. The girl is somewhere in there. She was going to sing . . .

'What about my friend?' he says, almost in tears.

'Your friend?' Mummy stands up and grabs his hand. 'Don't be so silly.' She tugs him in the direction of the cabs, then stops abruptly and gathers him up in a stifling hug. 'I was so frightened, Tomtom! I thought I'd never see you again!'

'There was a girl,' Tom insists. 'She was called Zo-ee! She fell in the sea!'

'Come along, my darling. Let's not stay here.'

'But I talked to her . . .' Tom pulls fretfully against Mummy's firm grip. 'We'd better go back and find her, Mummy. She was English! She's lost her mummy and daddy!'

'The poor little chap's had a bit of a shock,' the major says, and begins to wave briskly at a cab driver.

They are on their way again.

By sunset the *Narkunda* is steaming around Cape Matapan towards Italy, and Tom is at supper, ignored among the grown-ups, sitting silently, chewing a lamb chop and listening to the reverend, who is telling them, for the tenth or twentieth time, about a duchess who had come to visit his mission for unmarried ladies. Tom has already forgotten Piraeus, or at least has put it away where he keeps his bad dreams, though the Acropolis is a bright white arrangement of angles in his memory: white stone, blue sky and, far below, a disordered lake of tawny rooftops, church domes, spiky cypress trees. The next day that too is fading. He doesn't feel well, and Mummy has to find the bottle of castor oil.

CHAPTER THREE

Piraeus, Greece, October 1922

The little girl is walking along a street. Shuffling, really; she is a small, grubby bead in a necklace of shuffling people that stretches for miles in either direction. Since they left the dockside camp in Piraeus that afternoon, she has been staring at the backs of the woman and her two children who are walking in front of her. The woman is heavyset, with thick lead-coloured hair. She is wearing a dress of block-printed cotton, the pattern of which – golden roses on a background of burnt-bread brown – has been mesmerising the girl for hours. The woman's calves are swathed in drooping, laddered stockings that might once have been a fetching pink but now resemble pork rind that has been in the sun for too long. She is clutching a child's hand in each of her own. One of them, a boy of around ten, wearing what might be a school uniform, is marching along like a wind-up toy, complaining in a loud, sharp-edged voice about everything. The other child is a younger girl, who is dragging her feet, keeping up a low, relentless whine. The back of her linen dress is stained brown down to the hem, she smells horrible and she has already fallen over twice, crying for water. The mother – if she is their mother – has just

43

scolded her in a raspy, exhausted voice. From her accent, she is from one of the towns up the coast from Smyrna.

The line slows and comes to a stop. Voices start up all along its length: prayers, curses, wails of relief. The girl stands, swaying. Her legs don't feel as if they are joined to her body. The boy in front turns around and pulls a face at her, but she just stares at him. The woman cuffs him, not gently, on the head. Behind, in the line, an old man starts coughing, a wretched, gluey cough. Suddenly she feels dizzy. How long has it been since she last ate? Some soup last night, ladled out by a beady-eyed foreign woman in an odd black and red uniform. Just one ladleful, and not enough. There hadn't been any breakfast. There is a lamp post next to her, and as she puts out her hand to lean against it she catches sight of someone standing in a shop window. A small, meagre little girl wearing a frightful, sagging sailor suit, once white but now streaked with tea-like stains, the jaunty blue collar soiled and half torn away from her neck. Bare-legged, bare filthy black feet. The apparition raises her hand to scratch her matted hair and of course the girl's nails are raking her own scalp, because despite everything she recognises the girl in the window. Zoë Haggitiris.

'What is your name? Your name?' The woman, tall and middle-aged, wearing a flouncy white dress that looked too heavy for Piraeus in September, leant down and put her hand on Zoë's cheek for a moment as she asked her question in dreadful Greek. That had been two days ago. 'What's your name, sweetheart?' she repeated, more gently. Her voice was rounded in the way Zoë recognised as American.

'My name is Zoë Haggitiris,' Zoë answered obediently. 'Please, do you know my mama and papa?'

The woman blinked in surprise. 'Heavens! You speak such good English! Are you English, sweetheart?'

'My mama and papa speak English. And Greek. And Turkish. And Armenian,' she added proudly.

'My goodness! And who is your father, sweetheart?' the American woman said, brightly.

'His name is—' She screwed her eyes shut and found Papa, striding up the garden path, holding her hand on the chugging escalator in Xenopoulo, grinning as he lets her hold a slippery bracelet of woven gold. 'Kyrios—*Mister* George Haggitiris. He has a jewellery shop on Frank Street. Do you know it?'

'Where?' The woman smiled kindly.

'Smyrna, of course! Don't you know . . .' Then Zoë saw that the American woman didn't know George Haggitiris & Cie, had never been to Frank Street or even to Smyrna. Not ever. She was holding a sort of writing pad, a board with pieces of paper fixed onto it, and a pencil, the end of which she nibbled, now and then, with rather large, very white teeth. The top sheet was full of names scribbled onto lined paper, and beneath it were many, many more sheets.

'Oh. Of course. Go on, darling.' The woman glanced at something on the sheet of paper and frowned. Zoë suddenly felt smaller than the ants she had used to watch, just a few days before, crawling around under the hollyhocks in the garden at home.

'I think they fell in the sea,' she whispered, and started to cry. She stuck her knuckles in her eyes to hide them from the woman, though what she wanted to do was bury her head in her skirts that would smell, she knew, of lavender. Of Mama. But Miss Butland always taught her not to cry in front of strangers.

'I . . . oh, dear.' Kindness fought with impatience in the woman's voice and won. 'Can you tell me a little more, honey?'

'Do I have to?'

'I know it's hard . . .'

'I don't know!' Zoë had been twisting the hem of her tunic so tightly in her hands that her fingers hurt. 'I don't!'

Just then, another man appeared out of the crowd, a nice-looking older man with a funny little beard. He looked a little bit like Mr Venizelos, the prime minister, whose pictures were on every lamp post and wall in Smyrna. He talked to the woman behind his hand, but too loudly, and Zoë heard everything.

'I know about this one, Miss Denham,' he said – another American, not Mr Venizelos after all. 'She was pulled out of the sea near Kea by one of the transports. The captain reported drifting wreckage – this little thing was clinging on to the mast. Likely they were run down by another ship. Three navies operating in those waters that night, and it was dark . . .' He shrugged. 'No other survivors, I'm afraid – the transport reported two bodies in the water.' He tapped his finger on the woman's writing pad. 'Orphan,' he said briskly. 'When you're finished here, we need you over by the medical tent.'

The American woman – Miss Denham, Zoë remembered, because a polite young person always remembers people's names – turned back to her, mouth set in a pout of sympathy, rather like the one that Miss Butland would give her when she wasn't really sorry for telling her off. Lucky Miss Butland, who had gone off on an English battleship after giving her a kiss and whispering, *See you soon, petal*, into her ear. But Zoë had decided that Miss Denham really was sorry for her, a little bit.

'It was dark,' she told her, the words spilling out, English words, because suddenly it struck her that she might never speak English again. 'It was morning, and we were sailing along.' She licked her dry lips, remembering. 'I was looking right at Mama and Papa and then they weren't there. Then it was dark. I was so cold. In the water.'

'Oh, you poor little thing,' the woman said, squatting down in front of her. She really did look sorry. But even then, Zoë saw that she was already looking past her, at the next people who needed to tell their story, at whatever Mr Venizelos wanted her to do.

'I saw her,' Zoë whispered. She desperately wanted to put her arms around the woman, but she was so dirty and the woman's dress was so starchy white. 'Mama. In the water. I was sinking. She caught me.'

'Oh. My.'

'I . . . I want her to come back!'

'Well now, Zoë, I'm just going to give you this.' Zoë saw that what the woman was writing on was a label, the sort she had seen tied onto luggage when the big luxury liners came into Smyrna harbour. The woman, quick as a flash, tied the string of the label onto one of the points of Zoë's sailor scarf, and, as she straightened up, planted a kiss on the top of Zoë's head. 'Good luck, honey,' she whispered. And then she was gone.

Orphan. It is the same word in Greek, more or less. *Orfanós.* She had known. She *had* known, hadn't she? As she had clung to the slippery timber, listening with all her might and hearing only her own frightened little breaths, she must have known.

She had never seen the American woman again. Since then, the official men and women had ignored her. She had been utterly alone in the great crowd that filled the waterfront of Piraeus. She couldn't make sense of the big label that slapped her in the face every time the wind blew off the sea. The American woman who had wished her luck was nowhere to be found. Zoë kept

47

moving through the crowds in an agony of panic, which buzzed through every inch of her, as if there were wasps in her veins instead of blood. The waterfront was an ocean of faces, and every face had been made frightening by grief or rage or despair. She made herself look into every one of them, though, in case . . . but she knew. Why would Mama and Papa be here? They would be somewhere cool and nice, waiting for her. *But I'm looking for them*, she told herself over and over again. *If I keep searching, I'll find them. If I stop . . .*

Every now and again she would stop and look up over the milling heads of the crowd to where brown mountains rose in the distance. They must be in Athens already, she would tell herself, and then she would start to cry. Every now and again a woman, usually a young woman, would start wailing at Zoë, grabbing for her so that she would have to scramble to get away. These women always called out to her by name, but it was never *her* name. So she kept weaving through the forest of legs, shivering with fear, not staying still long enough for anybody's eyes to rest on her, even though all she craved was the comfort of a soft voice, a gentle hand. She followed the desperate, jostling lines of people to where food was doled out. It wasn't really food, just water with cabbage, bits of gristle and bone floating in it, but she slurped it down and wanted more, though there wasn't any more to be had. Eventually she found a place to sleep under some folded tarpaulins near one of the medical tents and curled up, rigid with fear, as the sun set and turned the crowd blood red.

Towards the end of her second day on the docks of Piraeus, Zoë's aimless wanderings took her to the edge of the mass of people. Not the edge: rather, she came to a place where the throng had pulled back from something, like the tide. And, like the tide, it had left things stranded. Zoë saw a wall and, beyond it, an ugly, new-looking church. There was a big plane tree beside the church and she was just thinking that she would like to go and sit down in its shade when she saw a row of people laid out in a neat row, heads almost touching the wall, feet towards the sea. A small child, when faced with neat rows of things, is often tempted to count them. Zoë had counted to four when she realised, with a surge of nausea, that the people were dead. But she kept counting, because she couldn't stop, chanting out the numbers in a blur of terror, because the next body would be Mama or Papa. But she reached nineteen and, shaking with relief, saw that her parents weren't there. Four old women, an old man, seven younger women and seven children, girls and boys, three of them very small. She was aware of the crowd murmuring behind her. The word *cholera* meant nothing to her. As she stood there, two men dressed in white coats with bright red crosses on their white armbands appeared, carrying a stretcher, which they put down and with a few businesslike moves unloaded another body, which they laid out at the end of the row. She moaned and stood on tiptoe to see, not Papa's face but an older one, deeply lined and furred with white whiskers. The dead man's collar stud had come undone and the starched ends were pointing up like a soiled white horseshoe. His eyes, milky blue, were wide open. So was his mouth. *Two bodies in the water*, the man who looked like Venizelos had said. She hadn't understood him then, but as the white-coated men unloaded another corpse, she realised what he had said.

She didn't know that she was screaming until an arm caught her around the shoulders and she was pulled against the folds of a heavy wool skirt.

'Hush, little one!' a voice said, while a hand began, quite roughly, to smooth her hair. Zoë felt herself being led backwards through the crowd. 'Hush!' The hand shook her, pressed her face into the rough cloth, which smelt strongly of onions and sweat. She stumbled, blindly, her chest still heaving, her throat raw, until the woman holding her sat down abruptly on a packing case.

'You mustn't scream like that, little bird.' Zoë looked up into an older face, lined, a little heavy, framed by a printed cotton headscarf. Blue, white and black flowers on red. The woman smiled. Zoë opened her mouth again and the woman quickly pressed her hand over it. 'Don't be scared,' she said, gently. 'Everyone is scared. But you mustn't attract attention to yourself.'

'I want my mama!' Zoë croaked.

'Of course you do, *koritsaki*.' The woman took a deep breath. 'Was she there? With those unfortunate ones?'

Zoë shook her head furiously. 'No!'

'Good, good. Thanks be to God.' The hand began its stroking again. Zoë felt herself growing calmer. The wasps buzzing inside her started to be less angry. 'But you're alone, aren't you? You'll have to be clever, now. You'll have to be so, so careful. I've seen such things . . .' The woman began to rock, slowly, and the movement felt so soothing to Zoë. 'Holy Mother, such things. But as long as we're alive, we must be thankful. So no more screaming, *koritsaki*. Will you be a brave one? A brave girl?'

'I don't *want* to be brave!' Zoë said, letting the woman's skirt muffle the words. 'I don't want to be!'

'Hush now.' The woman's hand, large and rough, caressed her hair, played gently with the tangles. Zoë felt herself go limp, and then sleep came for her so suddenly that she didn't have time to say anything else, to beg the woman not to stop holding her, to reach up and take her hand.

She awoke to find herself alone, lying beside the packing

case, a neatly folded sack pillowing her head, looking into a thicket of bare legs, laddered stockings, dirty feet. She sat up and looked around wildly for the woman in the black skirt. But the woman was nowhere to be seen. Zoë had never felt more lonely. It overwhelmed her so that there was no Zoë Haggitiris, nothing of herself left at all. Terrified, she jumped up and fought all the way across the quay, trying to outrun the horrible emptiness she felt, until she came to the edge of the dock, the edge of the world.

Shaking, she dropped onto a coil of rope and, drawing her knees up to her chin and hugging them to her, she sat, rocking and moaning, staring down at the oily water between the moored boats, at the shoals of slender, silver fish that twisted and coiled through the rusty mooring chains and ribbons of weed. Had there been fish, when she'd been down there? The sea was full of fish. Why hadn't she seen fish? A thread of breeze caught the label tied to her scarf and flapped it into her face. She batted it away, and that made her remember the American woman and the man who had looked like Venizelos. She had wanted to ask him something, but she hadn't quite known what that was. But now she did. *Are my mama and papa dead?* He had looked at his papers and told the woman to write the label. *They're dead, aren't they?* The bodies in front of the church had frightened her so much that she had pushed them out of her head but now they came back, but this time laid out at the bottom of the sea. She fought, then, not to see but there they were: Mama and Papa, lying peacefully on clean white sand, Papa in his sailing jacket, Mama in her hat, smiling up at the beautiful fish.

She didn't even realise that she was singing until she felt a shadow slip across her skin. She looked up to find a gaunt woman standing over her. The woman's eyes were outlined with smudged kohl and her reddish hair was tied up in a grubby, once-bright silk scarf. She smiled down at Zoë.

'Where did you learn how to sing, my golden one?'

'What . . . ?' Zoë squinted into the sunlight. The woman had a wide mouth. Her skin was stretched tightly over her cheekbones and her eyes were sunken. Zoë thought of various witches and vampires in the stories that Cook had told her. But the woman didn't look much like a vampire. Too tired to be evil. And did vampires call you *golden one*?

'My papa takes me to the Cafe Trieste on Rue Medjidi . . .' The words felt so nice to say. 'He always buys me a cream cake. I like to listen to the music.'

'I bet you come from Bournabat. Yes? Or Cordelio?'

'My house is in Bournabat. I live at number 32 in the Street of the English Church,' she said.

'So, little doll. Where's Papa now?' the woman asked gently.

Zoë sucked her finger for a while, looking at the fish darting below the rainbow film of oil on the surface of the water. If she said it aloud, would it be true? 'I think . . .' She knew she must tell this woman, this stranger, the truth, but as she tried, she had began to cry instead. Rocking on her nest of rope, she pointed straight down into the sea. 'Mama too,' she managed, at last.

'Mercy,' the woman sighed. She used the same word, *aman*, which Zoë had just been singing. 'You're all on your own.' Zoë said nothing. What was there to say? She just fingered her label and wondered whether she was going to cry again, and how long it was until the foreign ladies in the funny uniforms started dishing out their thin, salty soup. Then she noticed that standing behind the woman's legs was a little boy about her age, with wavy dark hair and very black, piercing eyes. He was staring at her the whole time, so she made a face at him. He scowled back, and tugged at the woman's skirt.

'Mama! I'm hungry!'

'We're all hungry, Pavlo,' she said, patting him on the head. 'Shush, my love.' Then she squatted down on her haunches beside Zoë. 'Sing it again, *koukla*. Eh? It makes things better, to sing.'

Zoë pursed her lips. 'All right.' And she folded her hands across her chest and started.

A black stone on the beach, my Lula, my Xanthoula,
A black stone on the beach, my Lula, my Xanthoula.

The woman joined in. '*I will make a pillow there . . . Och*, too sad, little golden-hair. You have a lovely voice.'

'So do you.' Zoë was surprised at herself. She hadn't liked this stranger at first, but it was true, she had a good voice, deep and husky. When she had sung the *amans*, her voice had sobbed up and down the scale, just like the lady singers at Cafe Trieste.

'Mama!' The little boy started to wrench furiously at her skirt.

'All right, Pavlo, little devil! We'll find something.' She stood up, looked around her, and Zoë saw that her face had taken on the half frightened, half vacant look that all the grown-ups in the crowd seemed to have. She patted Zoë absently on the head and, before Zoë could say anything, she wandered off into the mass of people, the boy stamping along behind her.

Then she thought the boy had come back, because she turned at the sound of a strange voice and found herself looking at two skinny little legs, thick socks pulled up almost to the knees. 'You were on that boat.' Zoë blinked. She looked up and saw a boy, but not the child of the thin-faced woman. This boy had straight black hair, cut short all around but with a fringe that flopped over his forehead. His grey eyes were studying her keenly. 'You were on that boat. I waved at you,' the boy repeated, as if Zoë ought to remember. And she did remember, hazily, though she didn't want to, because it took her back to the ship, and the endless horror of being crushed against the rail, the sobbing all around her, the shame when she had soiled herself. Hadn't she looked up, and seen a little white figure on a gigantic ship that was a hundred times bigger than her own?

'Hello,' she replied, in English, and he stared at her in amazement. They talked – for how long, she doesn't remember now. He told her about butterflies; and now, trudging along this endless road, she thinks she saw one, a gorgeous creature bigger than a sparrow, fly up out of his hands. He told her about colours. Colours . . . there is no colour around her now. Everything is grey and brown and dust-powdered.

But, back then, she closed her eyes and saw the butterflies. Then she thought of the red colour she had seen in the sky behind *Thetis*, and that made her cry again. She was always crying, now. But the boy told her the name of the colour, and that made her feel better, somehow. He held her hand and talked about figs and ice cream. How funny. No one had held her hand since she had fallen into the sea, and it felt nice. The boy was her friend. Had she known him, before? He said something about Smyrna. He wanted her to sing again and she was going to, she wanted to . . . And then he simply vanished: one moment kneeling beside her on the edge of the sea, with butterflies around his head, the next moment gone. She opened her mouth to sing for him, and the air swallowed him up.

Zoë decided, because it seemed like the most sensible thing to do, that the boy had never really been there. But if he hadn't been, why did she miss him? If no one had left her, why did she feel left alone? She noticed that the water had a nasty smell, of fuel and rotten things, so she got up and followed the woman and the boy, because . . . She could not have said. Perhaps because she was almost sure that they, at least, were real. But the two strangers had vanished into the crowd. Besides, it was soup time. She thought she might see the woman in the queue, but she didn't appear again.

Zoë had only just woken up on the third day when she heard voices, amplified by megaphones, booming hollowly across the harbour. Pushing out from under the heavy, salty-damp tarpaulins, she peered out at the crowd, which at night transformed itself into something else, a dense, stationary maze, as if the people were heavy thread embroidered in strange patterns onto the fabric of the harbour, knots and circles and wheels of sleeping or fretting people. Now they were hauling themselves shakily to their feet and the pattern was unravelling. The tinny megaphones were shouting about children, as far as Zoë could make out. There were lots of children on the docks – hundreds, probably. Zoë had seen plenty of others like her, alone, with labels fluttering from their clothes. Some of them had formed themselves into little gangs, others wandered around, eyes huge and red with tears. None of them looked like the sort of children Zoë would have been allowed to play with back in Bournabat. None of them looked like the sort she wanted to have anything to do with now, because they seemed to belong there, in a way: ignored by the grown-ups, they slipped through the crowds in little packs, stealing any bit of food left unguarded, mocking the children who still held on to their parents' clothing or sat, protected, within the many little castles of piled-up suitcases and bags. She didn't want to belong here. She didn't want to play with children of whom Miss Butland would most certainly have disapproved.

She saw grown-ups, the clean ones, the ones with armbands and clipboards, walking through the crowd, pointing to children, beckoning them. There was already a crocodile line of staggering, sleepy children behind each grown-up. A stocky woman with round glasses hooked across her doughy face spotted Zoë, smiled perfunctorily across the heads of a group of huddled old women and summoned her with a brisk wave of her hand.

'Orphan!' she said, loudly, to the woman next to her, who reached out and grabbed Zoë by the collar. It was so unexpected, and so forceful, that Zoë didn't even struggle. She found herself at the end of one of the crocodile lines, behind a boy wearing a blanket and not much else. 'Where are we going?' she asked him, but he said something back to her in Turkish, and she didn't quite understand, though it sounded like *food*. They snaked through the crowd towards one of the tents, joining with other lines until they were a column of shuffling, sniffing, coughing children. Zoë's stomach started aching at the thought of what might be inside the tent. She imagined a feast laid out: ice cream and cakes and cheese pies . . . But then she remembered that the woman had said *orphan*, and Zoë felt a little spark of hope begin to glow in her heart. All the orphans, the ones who had lost their parents, were being told to go into that tent, and why would anyone make them do that, unless . . .

'Are our parents in there?' she asked a tall girl behind her, but the girl burst into angry tears and Zoë didn't dare to ask anyone else. So she shuffled on, too hungry to think properly and feeling much too small and frightened to consider stepping out of the line.

Each time a child went into the tent, the line came to a stop, then jerked forward a few steps, then stopped again. By midday, Zoë was getting close to the tent. She was starving and terribly thirsty, as she had missed the tasteless corn mush that was doled out by way of breakfast, and she had drunk nothing since the night before. Hunger and the beating sun had long since emptied out her head of anything except a stuttering parade of images: Mama and Papa, waiting patiently somewhere inside the tent, perhaps drinking tea from china cups, smiling when they see her. She wanted that at first, more than anything. But then that picture was replaced with the food stalls on the Smyrna waterfront: souvlaki hissing over charcoal braziers, plaited sweet breads, sugar-dusted Turkish delight. Nuts and dried fruit in great, wasp-invaded heaps. The pictures in her head made her stomach hurt so badly that once or twice she had to double over in pain.

Inside the tent she was just able to make out a desk, at which sat two bearded men and a woman with her hair done up in an almost fashionable bun. The dough-faced woman would take the child at the end of the line by the upper arm, lead them up to the table. There they would stand, then they would disappear towards the back of the tent. Zoë was not able to see more than that. But she was edging closer, so she supposed she would find out soon enough. She needed the lavatory terribly badly – children were just squatting or doing their business where they stood, but she could not bring herself to do that – and her thirst was been getting unbearable. It looked cool inside the tent. Maybe there was cool water in there? She would have some, before the cakes, before Mama and Papa. She had felt herself swaying, and let her mind drift into the tent, into the cool shadows behind the desk. There must be water there, surely. Or big glass jugs of lemonade, with chunks of ice floating in them, ice in jagged pieces, bumping against transparent rounds of lemon. Just a glass of water, though . . . She closed her eyes and there was the marble top of the big worktable in the kitchen at home, a glass of water beaded with moisture, and inside it a silver spoon holding a translucent jewel of grape jam or a nugget of *vaníllia* made from sweet mastic. She even heard Cook's voice, rough-edged because she came from the poorer part of Boudjah, away from the big mansions. *A submarine for you*, kopella mou. A submarine. How she loved those ice-cold, sweet-sour treats in the summer. Maybe there would be submarines inside the tent.

Kopella mou. Kopella! If only Cook were here now . . . Then Zoë realised that it wasn't Cook she was imagining inside her head, but a real voice. She turned, startled, to find a woman she vaguely recognised waving at her. Dyed red hair twisted up in a gaudy scarf, wide mouth, sunken cheeks. The woman who had sung with her at the edge of the water.

'Come here, *koritsa mou!*' The woman hissed at her like an angry goose, though she didn't seem angry.

'Ma'am?' Zoë said, though her throat was so dry that all she could manage was a squeak. The submarine was still drifting around in her head. But the woman was beckoning to her urgently and the little boy – there had been a little boy yesterday, hadn't there? She almost remembered him – was frowning so hard that his eyes looked like two raisins. 'I'm waiting to have a submarine,' she croaked. 'And to see Mama and Papa. You can . . . you can stand with me, if you like? Please?' She reached out her hand to the woman, the only person she had recognised in a whole, lonely day. Then the crowd moved, and the girl behind her shoved her, meanly, in the small of her back. She stumbled forward and as she put out her hands to save herself, she felt herself jerked off her feet, and when she opened her eyes, which she had squeezed shut in shock, she was inside the crowd, and the woman was dragging her by the hand away from the crocodile of children, away from the tent, from the cool water. From her parents.

'No!' Zoë screamed and tried to pull free, but the woman's grip was too strong. She walked quickly, threading through the narrow spaces between groups of people, her little boy trailing from her other hand. 'I want my mama and my papa!' Zoë screamed, but the woman took no notice. At last, they came to a place where the throng of people was thinner on the ground. The woman stopped inside a small circle made up of suitcases and Gladstone bags, cloth bundles, a cardboard box wound so tightly with twine that it looked like a ball of wool. There were a few other people sitting around. A small fire was burning in a square made of four bricks, and a hunched figure in black was heating a little copper coffee pot over the flames. The woman sat down heavily on one of the suitcases. At once, her fingers went to Zoë's sailor scarf. She pulled and tugged at the string of the label and in a few moments it was hanging from her hand. 'Here,' she said, handing it to the figure with the coffee pot. 'Burn it.' A wrinkled hand took the label and shoved it into the flames. It flared briefly, then was gone.

'What's your name?' the woman asked Zoë.

'My name is Zoë Haggitiris. It said so on that label,' Zoë added, goaded on by the fury that had been rising inside her since she had been pulled out of the line.

'Do you know what else was on that label?'

Zoë shook her head petulantly.

'And what you were queuing up for?'

'A submarine! And Mama! And Papa!'

The woman clicked her tongue. 'Your label said that you are an orphan. You know what that means?' She waited, watching Zoë intently. Zoë's chest began to heave. She stuck all her fingers into her mouth to stop herself saying anything bad. The woman smiled so unhappily then that Zoë, despite the misery that felt as if her heart was being crushed like a rotten peach, saw that she was kind after all. When the woman held out her hands to her, Zoë took them.

'Yes,' she whispered.

'Good. I'm sorry, little doll. But what they're doing is rounding up all the orphans and taking them off to a big, nasty place far away . . .'

'I wanted to go with them!' If Zoë had had the strength, she would have stamped her foot. 'I want water! I want to go to the lavatory!'

'*Lavatori,*' the person tending the fire chuckled, repeating the English word.

'Oh, little bird. I don't think you'll go to the *lavatory* again.' She squeezed Zoë's hands. 'This isn't Smyrna, my darling. Smyrna is gone. We're in Greece now, Old Greece, among the peasants.' She sighed, and her wide mouth turned down at the corners. 'Haggitiris. Did your daddy have a beautiful shop near Xenopoulo? Selling jewellery?' Zoë nodded. 'I loved that shop. I used to stare in the window every day. All gone now, all that lovely stuff. The Turks looted all those shops. I saw it.'

'Papa took all his jewels,' Zoë said, proudly, and the woman's eyes went very wide. 'On our yacht. In big boxes.'

'And what happened to Papa's yacht?'

'It sank.' Zoë found herself staring at the little boy, who had wound himself under the woman's arm and was clinging to her, staring back at her with big, hostile eyes.

'God. At the bottom of the sea.' The woman clicked her tongue. 'Well, that's not the worst thing that has happened. Now, Zoë. Are you really all alone? No brothers and sisters? No aunts? An uncle? Grandparents?' Zoë shook her head to all of that.

'My grandparents all died. My uncle Paul was killed in France. So was my uncle Nico. Mama . . . Mama was going to have a baby. A brother, she said.'

'*Po po po.*' The woman let go of Zoë and made the sign of the cross, then pulled the little boy, Pavlo, against her, and kissed his greasy black hair. 'It's the end of the world, little one, but we're still here. Isn't that the worst thing of all?'

'I don't know.' Zoë twisted her hands into her tunic. 'I don't know!'

'Listen, little doll. There are more people coming in every day. Haven't you noticed? The Turks are kicking everybody out of *Mikrá Asía*.' Asia Minor. Home. 'All the Greeks and the Armenians too, the ones they haven't slaughtered. We're refugees now.'

'What's a refugee?'

'A refugee is . . .' The woman closed her eyes and sighed. 'It's when someone has lost their home, and they haven't found a new one yet. Thanks be to God that we're still alive, I suppose. And now there isn't room for us in the harbour here, and people are dying like flies, so they're moving us to a camp in Athens.' The woman leant down, and the boy shifted with her, still glaring. She took Zoë's hands again. 'I'm going to take you with us. I'm not leaving you here. Do you want to know why?' Zoë shook her head hurriedly: she didn't want to know anything else, ever. But the woman just smiled. 'Because you used to eat cakes at the Cafe Trieste. The lady singer you liked to listen to was my sister. You were copying her, in your little voice. Your tiny little voice.' Zoë heard a catch in her throat. 'Holy Virgin . . . Look at us all here. Wallowing in our own filth. Didn't we all used to be so beautiful?

61

Your papa and your mama. My sister, may she be with God. No, *koukla*. I don't like to think of you going off to some orphanage. I'm going to take care of you.'

'Whah?' It had been less of a word than a strangled yelp. The little boy was looking up at the woman with horror in his face.

'It will be fine, Pavlo,' the woman said. 'The more the better. We have to stick together in this land of peasants.'

'I don't *like* you!' the boy shouted suddenly, his face red and twisted. Zoë opened her mouth to shout something back at him, just a reflex, because she wasn't feeling anything except despair; but then she had seen that it wasn't anger in his face. It was terror. *You're as scared as me*, a tiny voice inside her said. She looked at him clutching his mother's skirt, at the woman whose hands were very gently stroking hers. She didn't look like a vampire at all, Zoë realised: she looked like a mama. Not her mama, but the kind of mama who might have come out of that terrible wound of flames and smoke. Her big dark eyes reminded her of the old icon of the Virgin that Cook had kept in the kitchen at home: deep, full of loss and gentleness.

Zoë prodded the pavement with a toe, and looked around. Smoke was rising from countless little fires. The harbour stretched away, a graceful arc blackened with a rust of human beings. Flies rose and fell in clouds. She realised then, because somehow she had not realised before, that this was all quite real. There was no going home. Everything was going to be broken from now on. Everything would be strange. This woman and her scared little boy were no more nor less strange and frightening than anything else. And Zoë, who for all of her short life had been given choices – which dress? This cake? That book? – understood that she would be given no more choices. It was an awful realisation, but oddly she felt her heartbeat slow, her face grow less hot. She turned back to the woman.

'What's your name?' she asked.

'Katina. Katina Valavani. And this is Pavlo.'

Zoë felt her shoulders begin to shake. *I mustn't cry*, she tried to tell herself, but just as the tears started anyway, she was folded into strong arms and her salt-sore face was pressed against the black cloth of the woman's dress. She whimpered, and breathed in the smells of sweat and smoke, and, very faint, the ghost of perfume.

'It's all right, little doll,' the woman whispered into her hair. 'My poor little darling. I'll keep you safe. I promise.'

That had been this morning. Now, standing in the street on the outskirts of Athens, Zoë stares at herself in the window, stares and stares, fascinated and horrified at the same time, until Kyria Valavani touches her shoulder.

'We're moving again,' she says. 'We must be almost there, surely.'

But they are not. The line shuffles into other streets, past grander buildings. Trams and buses and motor cars pass them in the roads. Everything looks more modern than Smyrna here: the streets are wider, the buildings look foreign. But there is something grubby, down-at-heel about this city. Its people, staring at them through tram windows, from shops, from houses, look suspicious. They don't have the spark of people back home, the ready smiles. They hold themselves differently, as though the sky is pressing down on them. The refugees creep past squares lined with palm trees. Zoë looks up, and there is a sight so familiar to her from books that it seems like another dream. A white temple on a bare crag of rock. They pass into a zone of low white houses and narrow cobbled streets right up under the rock, past shops where bottles of lemonade and drinks of every colour are lined up on shelves, looking more beautiful than Papa's shop ever had. The smell of food is everywhere. But they creep on, skirting the houses now, through an empty place of rocks and dead grass squeezed between the city and the crag. They are stumbling over stones in the grass, past ruined walls and fallen columns. No one pays them any attention. Zoë has been staring at her feet for hours. The girl in front of her fell over again ages ago, and her mother – and that horrible boy – dropped out of the line. Zoë wonders what has happened to them. She remembers the line of dead bodies back at the harbour. When Mrs Valavani takes her by the hand, Zoë squeezes the unfamiliar fingers as if they are a charm that will make such thoughts go away. And they do, a little.

'Thank you, Holy Virgin,' gasps Mrs Valavani, after they have staggered along a dusty, churned-up path lined with trailing, thorny plants that catch their ankles. It is almost sunset, and the light is turning golden.

'What?' Zoë gasps. Mrs Valavani is pointing ahead. At first, all Zoë sees is another temple standing in a field of sunburnt grass. Then she sees bright white pyramids. They are so perfect, so pointed, that she thinks something has gone wrong with her eyes. But then she sees people milling around them, and realises they must be tents. There is a Greek flag flying above them, and a flag with a red cross on it. The smell of food reaches them along with the familiar scent of tobacco smoke, and the line lurches forward. Soon they are among the tents. Men in army uniforms are there to meet them. Women, like the women at the harbour, are going back and forth busily with clipboards. One of them comes up to Mrs Valavani.

'Names?' she asks, in French-tinged Greek.

'Valavani. Katina, Pavlo.' Her fingers tighten around Zoë's hand. 'Zoë.'

'From?'

'Smyrna, miss. Where else?'

'Husband?'

'Dead.' Mrs Valavani's fingers twitch. Zoë sees that she is biting her lip.

'Occupation?'

Mrs Valavani raises her chin proudly. 'I sold dresses, *mademoiselle*. In my shop, Katina Valavani, Maison de Modes et Confections. Rue Boyiadjidika.'

'Date of birth?'

'My God . . . the eighth of August 1890.'

'And your children?'

'Pavlo was born on the seventh of June 1917.'

'And the girl?'

'Zoë, tell the *mademoiselle* your birthday. She's very clever, you know,' she adds to the French woman.

Zoë stares at the woman's dress, follows the pale blue lines of flowers up and down. Her birthday? It was . . . It was . . . 'The twenty-second of January,' she blurts out. '1916.'

'Well done, *koukla*. Her daddy was so proud of her. You've spelt my name wrong,' she adds, tapping the Frenchwoman's clipboard.

'You are to be in Tent . . . Tent Fifteen,' the woman tells them. 'Blankets will be issued.' She looks down at the two children and wrinkles her nose. 'Clean clothing. We hope to have bathing facilities ready tomorrow. There will be dinner in an hour. Please go to your tent and do exactly what the officer there tells you.' She nods briskly to them. 'Next. You. Name?'

'Are you six?' Mrs Valavani asks Zoë as they walk to their tent.

'Umm hmm.' Zoë is thinking about food, and bathing.

'I thought you were older.' She coughs. 'That bloody woman. Like a machine. We're nothing to these people. Nothing.'

'Is it true? About your shop?'

'Is it true about your papa and his yacht? His jewellery?'

'Of course.'

'Well then, *koukla*. Yes, I had a shop. It was all real. Remember Xenopoulo? Remember the cafes at Punto? Swimming at the Baths of Daphne? It was life: *our lives*.' She squeezes Zoë's hand almost too tightly. 'Everything we tell each other will always be true. And these people, these Old Greeks, these peasants, they'll never believe us. But we have to believe each other. Understand?'

Zoë doesn't understand. But soon she is pulling on a clean dress, threadbare and clearly someone else's, but she doesn't care, because it doesn't stink of the lavatory. Dinner is like heaven: thick soup full of tripe and calves' feet. She eats more than she has ever eaten. She will burst, she thinks as she walks back to the tent behind Mrs Valavani. Pavlo is trying to keep up with his mother but he ends up beside Zoë. The camp is lit by strings of bare bulbs strung between poles and trees, and in their yellow light she sees his eyes, round and scared.

'Don't you like me?' she asks.

'No,' snaps Pavlo.

'Oh.' Zoë shrugs. 'Are you scared?'

'No!'

'I am.'

'You're a girl.' Pavlo almost trips over a piece of marble, and Zoë reaches out and catches his arm. He stares at her hand on his sleeve. 'Girls are always scared,' he says, and shakes her hand away. 'But . . . I'm scared too.'

Perhaps Zoë is thinking about the little boy in her mother's belly, down at the bottom of the sea. Perhaps it is just the comfort of having another child beside her. But she reaches out again and takes his hand, which is hot and damp. 'Don't worry,' she says. 'I'll look after you.'

Chapter Four

Devon, England, 1923

'I don't want to go!' Tom says this just loud enough for his mother to hear, though they both dart an anxious glance over to where Daddy is standing on the other side of the room. 'I don't want to, Mummy!'

'Don't be silly, Tommy. It will be fun. You'll see.' But Mummy's face contradicts her words. Though it is just past nine o'clock on a May morning, it is gloomy in the kitchen. A thick drizzle is falling outside, and the clouds are hanging so low over the house that if one had a long enough ladder, Tom thinks, one could climb up and touch them. Not that one would want to. Though he has only lived here on Dartmoor for a few months – they are renting a small, damp cottage near Moretonhampstead while the house they are going to live in properly is mended – he is quite well acquainted with clouds and what they are made of. At home in Kerala, the monsoon had brought clouds and mist, and rain so heavy that Tom had barely been able to stand up in it, but in Kerala, one minute it was pouring, the next minute the sky was blue and the wet was steaming off the trees and roofs. Here in

Devon the rain just sets in. It is like being sat on by a big, wet retriever dog. It is into this sort of day that Daddy intends to take Tom for his first riding lesson.

Sitting beside Daddy in his car, a rather smart Star 11.9 which isn't sporty enough for Daddy and which he complains about incessantly, Tom watches the wipers clack across the windshield, spreading rain like butter on hot toast. The car smells of leather polish and damp clothes, and the sharp rubber scent of Daddy's mackintosh mixed with his shaving soap: sandalwood and birch tar. Tom shifts uncomfortably. He is wearing a tweed suit – Norfolk jacket and plus fours – and it is horribly itchy. Mummy has tucked a scarf around his neck – a scarf in May! – but still he feels as if someone is going at him with sandpaper. He is holding Daddy's brown felt hat in his lap; holding Daddy's hat is supposed to be an honour. At least it is keeping his knees warm. The car bumps and jolts along a lane between grey granite walls. Tom looks out at miserable sheep and dejected cattle. They plunge down into a valley and through an oak wood, twisted branches trailing rags of greyish lichen. Daddy turns the car in through a gate next to a thatched lodge. The wood gives way to rough fields the colour of faded army uniforms, in which more dejected cattle stare at them, chewing stoically as the water trickles off their woolly black coats. A house comes into view, long and white, with a lot of peaked gables and tall chimneys.

'What a big house,' Tom says, to break the silence.

'It's a hunting box,' Daddy corrects him.

'Oh.'

Daddy steers the car onto a crescent of gravel in front of the house, stops, pulls up the handbrake, turns off the engine, lights another cigarette. The front door opens and a man appears, hand raised in greeting. 'Hat, Tommy.' Tom gives it to him. Daddy gets out of the car, adjusts the hat on his head, waves back to the man. Tom gets out as well, reluctantly. He notes that what had been actual rain higher up the valley is now a fine wet mist, what the people in the village call *mizzle*. Still, this is a distinct improvement.

'This is Mr Symington, Tom,' Daddy says. Tommy stands up straight and puts out his hand, the way he has been taught.

'Hello, young fellow,' says the man. He has a small nose and a carefully trimmed moustache. 'Come for some riding?'

'Yes, sir,' says Tommy.

'Jolly good.'

The two men set off around the house and Daddy signals with a perfunctory wave of his hand for Tom to follow. He does, trotting at their heels while they talk, ignoring him completely. Behind the house is a walled garden, which they skirt, and a patchwork of small fields divided by more granite walls. Further away, the thickly wooded hillside rises up into the mist.

'Over there,' the man says, pointing to one of the nearest fields. A young man is standing near its gate, putting a saddle on a small, shaggy creature. As they get closer, Tom sees it is one of the wild-looking ponies who live up on the open moor, though smaller than usual.

The pony's name is Vulcan, Mr Symington tells them, and he is an Exmoor pony, not a Dartmoor pony, something which the two men find quite funny. 'He's a bit of a stick-in-the-mud,' Mr Symington says. 'Fat as a lardy cake and lazy with it. My little girl finds him dreadfully dull. But he'll do for a beginner.' The young groom leaves them, and so does Mr Symington, promising to return with 'provisions'.

'Now, then, Tommy. Up you get, old chap.' Daddy is holding the pony's bridle. The beast has velvety fur the colour of dark caramel. Tom reaches out and strokes it, cautiously. It feels like the old sofa in the nursery at Da's house in London. He looks into the pony's eyes, hoping to find some comradeship or perhaps sympathy, but they are as unfathomable as two large, wet black marbles. Daddy is watching him from under the brim of his hat, and Tom can sense his impatience. Daddy is always impatient, except when he is laughing with his friends, or riding off somewhere, or cleaning his guns. But there are different levels, and Tom has become sensitive to them all. He can tell whether Daddy is mildly bored, irritated, or about to erupt in fury. Now, he is about to become irritated. Tom takes hold of the saddle, as he has seen Daddy and Mummy do. Daddy says nothing, but Tom knows his performance is being scrutinised. Everything he does with Daddy seems to be a test. He lifts his booted foot and puts it through the stirrup, which is wet and slippery. It takes him a few tries before he can get his weight onto it. His heart is pounding. But Daddy says nothing: no advice, no encouragement. He grits his teeth and pulls himself up. To his intense relief he manages to swing his leg over the pony's back and suddenly he is sitting in the saddle. He beams at Daddy, who merely gives him a satisfied nod. Tom sits, feeling the wet soak in through the seat of his trousers. So this is a saddle. He is surprised by how uncomfortable it is. Daddy lets go of the bridle and stands back, hands clasped behind his back. He raises his chin and narrows his eyes.

Tom does what he has seen cowboys doing in the moving pictures: he stretches his legs and kicks, hard, at the flanks of the pony. This is much less easy and as a result a good deal less satisfying than it appears in the pictures, but it has an immediate effect. Vulcan lurches forward and breaks into a sprightly canter, head down, heading for the nearest wall. Tom, taken completely by surprise, jerks backward. He still has hold of the reins, though there is far too much slack, and he almost goes over the back of the saddle. But the belly goes out of the reins just in time and now he is catapulted forward. His head meets the ridge of the pony's neck and his mouth is instantly stuffed with the thick, wiry hair of its mane. He can't see anything except hair and a blur of muddy grass. One of his feet is out of its stirrup. He wraps his fingers desperately into the pony's mane, lifts his head in time to see the lichen-speckled stone of the wall rearing up ahead. Daddy is yelling something at him but he can't make out any words. The reins . . . Where are the reins? He lets go with one hand, gropes around on the plunging neck until his fingers find leather. Gripping on, he manages the same with his other hand. By this time he is sobbing with fear and desperation, but there is only one thought in his head: *Don't fall off. For heaven's sake, stay on.* Moaning with fear, he gets himself upright in the saddle. The pony, directionless but weighed down with a useless passenger, is charging along the length of the wall. Tom's left leg is inches away from the uneven stones.

'Turn him!' Daddy is stalking across the field after them. Tom has no idea what he means. But he knows he should be doing something with the reins, so he shortens his grip and pulls back as hard as he can. Vulcan comes to an abrupt halt, and Tom finds himself weightless, floating in a cloud of horse-smell and mizzle. Then, with an awful thud, he hits the ground.

Tom is looking up from the nettle patch in which he has landed at Daddy's face, red with anger under the brim of his trilby.

'What the devil were you playing at?' Daddy barks.

'Sorry,' says Tom, biting his lip. The last thing he wants to do is cry, which always makes Daddy angry, but he can feel hot tears in his eyes already. His hands are smarting from the nettles, and there is a strong, dull pain in his left shoulder.

'Well, get up, get up,' says Daddy. He stands, feet apart, hands behind his back, an officer at ease. Except he isn't at ease. His lips are pursed and his moustache is bristling. Tom waits for a hand up, but Daddy keeps his hands where they are. So Tom has to roll over painfully, nettles pricking his hands and wrists, his face. His shoulder hurts. But he struggles to his feet.

'Now catch your damn pony,' Daddy snaps. Vulcan is at the other side of the field, tearing at a clump of sedge with his teeth. Tom limps over and, to his surprise, the pony barely looks up when he puts his foot in a stirrup. The pain in his shoulder makes it difficult to use his left arm, but he tries and then there he is, back in the saddle.

'Reins! Shorten your bloody reins,' Daddy snaps. He has crossed the field in a few angry strides. Tom does what he imagines Daddy means. But before he has got a proper hold, Daddy slaps Vulcan's backside and with an affronted toss of his head, the pony is galloping again. This time they are only halfway across the field when Tom, whose feet aren't even in the stirrups, slides sideways and finds himself with his face shoved hard into a clod of earth. Vulcan is a few feet away, grazing.

'Get up.' Tom knows that Daddy is speaking through clenched teeth. Although he doesn't turn around, he knows Daddy's jaw will have a bulge the size of a chestnut in it. He scrambles to his feet and staggers over to Vulcan, who again lets him mount, though the pain in Tom's shoulder is so bad that he can barely manage it. His face is streaming with tears, but he gets his feet set, shortens his reins and digs in his heels. 'Gee up!' he says, knowing how pathetic he sounds. 'Gee up, Vulcan!' Soaked to the skin, his tweed jacket caked in mud, skin burning from nettle stings, his shoulder feeling as if a giant dog has set its teeth into it, Tom kicks desperately at the beast, willing it to move before Daddy reaches them. He finally kicks too hard, and again Vulcan sets off, tearing towards the gate, where to his horror Tom sees Mr Symington, holding a thermos of tea in one hand and a couple of china mugs in the other. Worse, Mr Symington is almost doubled over with laughter. At this point, perhaps seeing his master, Vulcan stops dead. Tom feels the now-familiar sensation of weightlessness.

It is Mr Symington who grabs him under the arm – the right arm, thankfully – and heaves him upright.

'I say, you've had a bit of a tumble, old chap!'

'Yes, sir,' Tom manages through chattering teeth.

'If you can meet with triumph and disaster . . .'

Tom tries to smile. Why do grown-ups always throw bits of that poem around? Daddy has made him memorise 'If' and is always declaiming it himself, though Mummy says it makes her want to scream. 'Yours is the Earth and everything that's in it.' Which, he thinks, really couldn't feel less true at this moment.

'No dawdling, Tommy. Mount up.' Daddy is standing over him.

'I think he looks a bit done in, don't you, Jim?' says Mr Symington. 'Enough for one day, don't you think?'

'Nonsense. Tommy: quickly, please.'

Head down, clutching his shoulder, Tom trudges over to Vulcan, who lets him hoist himself up. The pony doesn't even bother to raise his head, but keeps tearing savagely at the grass. Tom listens to the powerful teeth rip and scrape. He kicks feebly but Vulcan just flicks his ears. 'I hate you,' Tom whispers, but he doesn't, and his words seem so unfair, and so mean, that he starts to cry, still kicking with his heels.

'I really think he's had enough, Jim.' Mr Symington sounds a little anxious. 'He's had a jolly good try and this rain really is a bit foul. Tommy can come back next week, and ride with Diana.'

'He'll bloody well ride now,' says Daddy.

'Oh, come off it, Jim. Let's go inside. I've got this tea but Cook can make us a proper pot and a sandwich or two. I'm sure Diana would like to meet Tommy.'

There is nothing that Tom wants less in the world than to meet another person his age, particularly a girl. He gives Vulcan another desperate kick and the pony lifts its head resignedly and begins to trot. Tom is upright, his feet are in the stirrups, his back is straight, but his left hand isn't working properly. In fact, it isn't working at all. Tom tries to gather the reins in one hand but as he is groping for them, Vulcan increases his speed a little and Tom finds himself slipping. He tries to hug the pony around the neck but Vulcan's coat is slick with water and he cannot find any purchase. Down he goes, until, still hugging the pony's neck, good hand wrapped tightly around bad wrist, he is being dragged along between the beast's legs. Finally he lets go, and watches the pony's shaggy, muddy belly pass above him, like a drowning sailor looking up at a passing ship. Then Daddy is bending over him. His collar is grabbed and he is hauled upright by the scruff like a naughty puppy.

'You're a disgrace, Tommy. A damned bloody disgrace. You've let me down.'

'Come along, Jim!' Mr Symington calls. Daddy waves cheerily to him, then turns back to Tommy.

'I'm ashamed of you. D'you hear? Ashamed.'

As things transpire, Daddy and Mr Symington go inside for

sandwiches and tea, while Tommy is banished to the car. He sits in the back seat, staring blankly at the steamed-up window, shivering. When Daddy finally appears, he gets in and starts the engine without a word. Tommy is not asked to hold Daddy's hat.

The car, heaving and rattling through bends and up slopes, is filled with an awful silence. It is as if there is a roll of barbed wire in the driver's seat instead of Daddy, which is uncoiling itself and filling the small, damp space with cold, sharp thorns. Tommy is trying to keep his shoulder still. It hurts when he moves his arm and there is a horrible grinding feeling which he might be imagining but seems quite real. They have been driving for half an hour with nothing but the thump and squeak of the windscreen wipers for distraction and Tommy has almost fallen into a sour doze when he feels the car slowing down. He opens his eyes and sees they are pulling into a lay-by. The car stops abruptly. Daddy wrenches savagely at the handbrake and turns off the car. Tommy's mouth goes dry. He has been waiting for his father's rage to boil over, and now it has.

But Daddy doesn't say anything for several long minutes. He lights a cigarette and draws on it so hard that half an inch turns to ash. When he inhales it sounds as if he is gasping in pain. In two or three more draws it is gone. Daddy grinds it out in the ashtray and puts both hands on the steering wheel. Tommy sees that his father's knuckles have gone white. He pushes himself into the angle of the seat and the door, bracing himself. But when Daddy speaks, he doesn't raise his voice. He just sits, gripping the wheel, staring out through the streaming windscreen.

'My battery . . .' He pauses, and hits the steering wheel softly with one clenched fist. 'We were in one of the big pushes around Cuinchy. Counter-battery fire. Very sharp business. The Huns were throwing everything at us and we were trying to support our chaps who were . . . You could see them in front, trying to take their objective and it was . . . Really, it was dreadful. One of my guns got hit: not badly, two of the men slightly hurt. We had to get it back into action. And there was this captain. Dreadful ogre but absolutely no nerves at all. Marching up and down with shells bursting everywhere. I got the men bandaged up and put them back to work. Then this captain – can't remember his name, he hadn't been with us long – sent me back to Brigade HQ with a message. Took me all of ten minutes, and when I got back to the guns . . . When I got back . . .' Daddy swallows, painfully. 'A German five-nine battery had found us. One of the guns – the one which had been hit before – was gone. Nothing left. Nothing at all. Crew, all blown to atoms. The other gun . . . The number three – nice chap – was in his place. But he didn't have a head. The sergeant was sitting there with one arm on, one arm off. The others were knocked about but still all right. And the captain . . . The blast had blown off most of his clothes, d'you see. Skinned half his body as well. But he was still upright, just as if he was on parade, still giving orders. And the men were staring at him with eyes like dinner plates but they were doing what he told them. And do you know what he said when he saw me? "Work your guns, Collyer." I could see his damn ribs. "Work your bloody guns." Then another five-nine came over and blew me right out of the position and as I was lying there, knowing I was wounded, that I'd got a nasty one, I was so unutterably relieved. D'you see? Because I . . . I had been so bloody *glad* it hadn't been me, but now I wasn't a shirker. *Work your bloody guns.*' Daddy takes a long, shuddering breath. 'Anyway.' He lights another cigarette and starts the car, eases it back carefully onto the road.

The rest of the drive is silent apart from the hiss of rain on the roof and the frantic rhythm of the windscreen wipers. There is nothing to distract Tommy from his father's words as they sound over and over in his mind. He has never heard anything like them. Most of them mean nothing to him, and the pictures they paint are so horrible that he decides he must have heard them wrong. They don't fit in the safe leather interior of a Star 11.9. And the story itself: had it been Daddy's version of 'If', with guns and swearing? *You'll be a man, my son* . . . It hadn't quite sounded like that, though. It hadn't sounded, really, as if Daddy had been talking to him at all. He decides to try and forget the whole thing. The thought of it makes him feel sick and his shoulder is hurting enough already. He stares at the back of his father's head, at the neatly barbered nape of his neck, too neat to ever have been in the same place as a man with half his skin ripped away, or a man with no head at all. He shivers, and feels sick, and listens to the wipers clatter back and forth.

When they get home, Tommy is not allowed to sit in the kitchen but is sent straight upstairs to his room, where he gets painfully out of his filthy, soaked clothes – his left arm is no use at all by now – and into his pyjamas, listening all the while to Daddy and Mummy arguing downstairs. His baby sister starts to scream. Tom pulls the quilt up over his head.

Much later, after Daddy has taken his gun and gone out to revenge himself on the furred and feathered creatures of the moor, Mummy comes into Tom's room. She has run a hot bath for him, and lets him lie in it for what seems like hours. As he clambers out, Mummy waiting with a fluffy towel, she notices his shoulder, which is bruised black and khaki.

'Does it hurt?' she asks, and he shakes his head, not wanting to be any more of a damned disgrace. He can't sleep that night, because every time he turns over, the pain goes through him like electricity. The next day Daddy drives into Exeter. Tom hears Mummy dialling the telephone and a little while later Dr Henderson, short and wide, stretching the buttons of his old-fashioned waistcoat which he decorates with an ornate watch fob, arrives. He takes Tom over to the window, examines his shoulder briefly and nods his head.

'You've broken your collarbone, old chum. How did you manage that?' he asks, in that kindly but distant voice that doctors reserve for children.

'I fell off a pony,' says Tom.

'Jolly well done!' says the doctor. 'Best way to do it.' He shows Mummy how to make a sling out of an old pillow case, and Tom is left tucked up in bed, his left arm splinted against his chest, dizzy with pain but beginning to feel the subtle warmth of vindication. After she has seen Dr Henderson off, Mummy comes back and Tom tells her all about Vulcan.

'Do I have to stay in bed for a long time?' he asks, when he is finished and Mummy is frowning.

'Only a few days,' she says, brightening. 'We'll have such fun, I promise. Daddy has to go up to London anyway, on business.'

'What can I do with one arm?'

'Hmm. You can draw. We can draw together. I'm horribly out of practice. Lucky for you, you're right-handed.'

That night, Tom wakes up to hear china smashing downstairs, Mummy's high voice and Daddy's clipped growl bashing against each other. They only stop when the baby starts to cry. The next day, Daddy leaves early for his business trip, and Mummy brings him breakfast in bed. On the tray is a box of brand-new German pencils.

'I've been saving these for an emergency,' she says. 'Do you think this is one of those?'

'Mummy, why is Daddy so angry all the time? With me?'

Mummy sighs. She slides a pencil out of the box and rolls it between her fingers. The sun, at last, is shining through the window and it glints off the band of gold at the end. 'It's . . . it's because of the War, darling. That's all. Nothing to do with you. Don't take any notice.'

'You notice.'

'I'm supposed to.'

'Is that what mummies do?'

Mummy smiles, a little sadly. 'Yes. Among other things. Now, what shall you draw?'

CHAPTER FIVE

Piraeus, Greece, 1927

'Is this it?' Pavlo is looking dubiously at a roofless box made from three panels of thick plasterboard. Another panel is propped up alongside. The box is about as long as a carriage on the Athens Metro, and perhaps twice as wide. It stands on one corner of a crossroads, the intersection of two rough tracks across a farmer's field. Other buildings in various states of construction – some just foundations of rubble, others almost finished, glorified sheds with half-tiled roofs, stand closely packed and stretching away in all directions. Behind the field, the ground begins to rise steeply towards the rocky slope of a low mountain. Wrapped around the mountain's feet, a dingy patchwork of fields has already been half swallowed by a grid of streets lined with more tiny, close-packed houses. Less than a mile away to the south is Piraeus Harbour.

The houses between where Zoë stands and the blue inlet of the harbour have all been put up very fast – half of them weren't here last year. The government is building whole new towns in Piraeus and Athens for the immigrants: Kaisariani, Nea Smyrni, Nea Makri, Nea Fokaia, Nea Chalkidona, Palaio Faliro. The planners have named their emergency settlements after the places their new inhabitants have been exiled from. Zoë has been to Nea Smyrni. Had the people who built the place ever been to the real Smyrna? How could they have dared name this crooked, matchbox town after her home? Where are the patisseries? Where are the goldsmiths? The beer gardens? Xenopoulo, with its escalators and the latest Parisian fashions? In New Smyrna, the houses may have roofs, but they don't have much else. Sewage runs down culverts in the middle of the streets.

'Beautiful, isn't it? The nicest one!' says Mama Katina.

Zoë shades her eyes with her hand and peers through the heat-disturbed air. None of the houses look very nice at all. She is dimly aware that two of them could have fitted quite comfortably inside the drawing room of her home in Bournabat. Zoë doesn't like remembering the house where she had lived with Mama and Papa. It isn't exactly real any more, just like Mama and Papa have stopped being much more than two words that make her feel sad. So she understands Mama Katina, who sometimes draws pictures of her own house in Boudjah, a French-style mansion with fretwork gables: *This is what we have. This will be ours, and only ours.* Katina always tears up her drawings with one of her sad smiles. 'What's the point?' she says. 'This is what we have now.' *This* is a partitioned few metres of a warehouse near Piraeus Railway Station where they have lived for the past four years. Before that, they had been camping in a cinema in Athens. But that is about to change. The Refugee Settlement Commission has notified Mama Katina that the Valavani family are to be rehoused, at long last. In a couple of months, maybe sooner. 'Before your birthday,' Mama Katina has assured her. Zoë will turn twelve in January. It seems funny to think that she'll be celebrating inside this odd little house.

'It'll be nice, you'll see,' Zoë says to Pavlo. 'You can play your bouzouki and no one will yell at you.'

'I'll yell at you,' Mama Katina says, and pinches both their cheeks. 'Don't worry, little birds. I know it looks like a shack but we'll have our own kitchen and our own lavatory. No more wading through other people's pee in the middle of the night!'

'*Aman!*' Pavlo says, cheering up. The communal bathrooms in their warehouse, with their overflowing toilets and slimy cement floors, are a constant source of horror to him.

'Can we get a kitten?' Zoë asks. There are a few cats in the warehouse and last week, one of them had produced a litter of tiny ginger and white kittens. All the children had been beside themselves, but then the overseer, a sour, balding Athenian, had taken them away in a potato sack.

'Let's see how much room we have,' Mama Katina says gently. 'Now, anybody hungry? I can smell food!' She puts her arms around her children and they begin to walk up the hill.

'Mmm! I can too,' says Zoë. 'I'm going to eat until I explode!'

'Come along, darlings.' They walk through the raw streets into open country. A church is being built a little way off. They pass by the whitewashed wall and freshly planted wisps of cypress trees that mark the new cemetery. Ahead, Zoë hears music: a violin, and the ripple of a kanonaki zither. A clarinet joins in, and Zoë's heart lifts. She grabs Pavlo's hand.

'Come on, old tortoise!' she laughs. Mama is going to sing today, and the thought of that is even more lovely than the thought of food.

'Will Batis be there, Mama?' Pavlo asks. Funny Mr Batis, who sells patent medicines and plays the baglamas, knows every musician in Piraeus. Mama says that he is a wicked man, but she always says it with a smile. Zoë knows he is wicked but she likes him anyway. She has never forgotten the time when she had been singing along to a gramophone record in the warehouse, and Mr Batis had squatted down in front of her and listened, nodding his head. To be heard, as a child in the refugee camps, is as precious as diamonds. When Mr Batis listened to her that day, it made her feel the way she thinks Mama must feel when she sings at a wedding or at one of the clubs down in Piraeus.

A little while later, they are standing in the middle of another dry, stony field, watching a wedding feast being laid out on long trestle tables knocked together out of planks and scraps from the building work which is going on a few yards further on. The daughter of Mrs Vlessas, their neighbour in the warehouse, is marrying a policeman's son. Mrs Vlessas is from Seydiköy, outside Smyrna. The policeman is from Athens – a Vlach, a shepherd, as the refugees call the inhabitants of this primitive country. Mountain people. Peasants. Salt fish eaters. The wedding is being held in this field because the Refugee Settlement Commission is going to build another few streets here and the newly-weds are on the list for one of them.

The wind changes – the Piraeus municipal rubbish tip is just to the south, and its stink has been wafting over them – and suddenly the air is rich with the smell of a goat roasting over an open fire, of steam from cauldrons of butter beans and bitter greens from the mountain, of snails – the little coffee- and cream-striped snails for which the refugee children scour the hillsides, in return for a few coins from the local tavernas – being fried with garlic, of fish being grilled alongside scrawny shanty town chickens. Zoë's mouth is watering so much she is afraid she must be slobbering

84

like a dog. She waves to her friends: Efi Sotirakis, Voula Mavrou, Marika Stavrides, Tula Hadjisava, Daizy Vassiloglou. People are milling around, gossiping and smoking, the men in suits and straw boaters, the women in their best dresses. Another gendarme and his young family. A soldier with a medal on his chest. Half-feral children crawl under the tables and chase the feral cats. Many of them have shaved heads stained yellow from being painted with anacryl to cure scabies. Yellow arms, yellow legs. She sees Pavlo down in the crowd, lurking by the cooking fires, and squeezes her eyes shut so that she can beam him a telepathic message: *Bring me a lamb chop.* Telepathy is fashionable among the grown-ups this year and Zoë has been trying to send her brother thought waves for months now, but so far she hasn't succeeded. Pavlo sidles past the grills, which are set up over brick-built troughs filled with glowing charcoal, and heads for where a burly man in an army shirt is wrestling a cask of wine onto another trestle table. Daizy is trailing after him like a puppy: he always seems to have a girl in tow.

Pavlo has a fascination for wine and the other strong drinks, Zoë has noticed lately. He'll make a pot of coffee and drink the lot, just to see what happens. He has taken to smoking tobacco scrounged from the dog-ends he collects up from the pavements. Little things that Mama Katina doesn't seem to have noticed – or perhaps she doesn't care. There are worse things happening to people in the refugee settlements than ten-year-old boys acquiring a taste for cigarettes.

He is an odd child, this boy she now thinks of quite naturally as her brother. Nervous and intense, he never seems to be quite touching the ground, because he walks like a deer in the forest: stiff-legged, always waiting for a hunter or a leopard to burst out through the trees. He would rather live in his dreams, Zoë knows.

Just this morning he told her of a princess he had met, a being made entirely from scraps of shimmering embroidery silk, the kind Mama Katina saves in an old chocolate box with a picture of Lake Geneva on the lid. He needs something to keep him from floating back into his dreams. Coffee, tobacco, wine and stolen drops of ouzo and tsipouro. But most of all it is his bouzouki that keeps him tied down here in the real world.

Already, at ten, his fingers dance up and down the frets, almost too fast for Zoë to keep track of. The instrument was a gift from a dying man, Mr Gounaris, who had owned a cafe in Ayvalik but who tried to find his feet here in Piraeus by playing in bars down by the harbour. Perhaps it had been going well, this new career; Zoë hardly saw the man: he slept all day in his screened-off portion of the warehouse, and went out in the evening, his bouzouki wrapped up in an old overcoat. But sometimes he would wake up in the afternoons, and if he did he would sit on his bed and practise. Zoë and Pavlo would always slip over to stand outside the curtain that passed for Mr Gounaris's door, and listen to the notes winding in and out, up and down. The roads, he called them, the modes that made the music sound one way or another, happy or desolate. Zoë loved the sound of their names: *sabah, ousak, hijaz, rast, minoure, piraiotiko. Houzam* and *karadouzeni.* They could have been streets in Smyrna.

Once, Mr Gounaris was arrested – Zoë never found out why – and when he came back after five months in Averoff Prison, he brought something for Pavlo. A miniature bouzouki, about the size of Mr Gounaris's forearm, with six strings and a bowl made out of a gourd. A baglamas, he called it: easy to make in prison, easy to hide. Look, you could slip it up your sleeve. It made a high, tinkling, tinny sound but Mr Gounaris could make it sound wonderful. Pavlo took it in his hands, eyes as wide as saucers, and just stood there, cradling it like a baby. Zoë knew that her strange, shy brother would never ask the important question so she did.

'Why him?'

Mr Gounaris tilted his head, the vaguest of shrugs. 'Because he listens,' he said.

'But I listen too.'

'I know you do. But you don't need an instrument,' Mr Gounaris said. 'You already have the voice of a nightingale.' Zoë decided this was just the typical meanness of grown-ups, though Mama was always saying the same thing. Then Mr Gounaris was taken ill in one of the typhus epidemics that often burnt through the refugee settlements. The morning of his death, he asked for Mama Katina, who came back from his bedside with the bouzouki. 'He wants you to look after it for him,' she told Pavlo. Mr Gounaris died in the afternoon and Pavlo became the bouzouki's owner.

The bride and groom appear. A priest blesses the party and the guests are called to table. Mama Katina is given a seat on the couple's table, because she has made the bride's dress. She has a dressmaking business in a shed behind a garage near the church of St Nicholas, and while it isn't quite a Maison de Modes et Confections, she earns a small but steady trickle of money from making up dresses in cheap fabrics. People will bring her pages cut from magazines which they have probably found in dustbins in the nicer quarters of Athens, film stars or debutantes posing in far-off ballrooms, and she will run up a copy in scrounged or stolen material. Or she will make her own creations. When she is feeling flush she will give Zoë and Pavlo money for a tram ride, and send them into Athens to lurk around Kolonaki or Vasilissis Sofias Avenue or the Hotel Grand Bretagne on Syntagma Square, where they spy on rich women. Back in the warehouse or in Mama Katina's workshop, which smells of oil and petrol fumes from the garage, they describe to her the fashions they have seen, Mama questioning them and questioning them until the tiniest details have been picked out. As they talk, she will be drawing with a stub of pencil on a piece of butcher's paper, and when she has squeezed everything out of them, she will hold up the paper.

'Like that?' she will ask, and they will stare at the women flouncing across the dun-coloured paper and nod. 'Like that,' they will say. 'Just like that.'

They are great fun, these raids on the kingdom of the wealthy. The children are amazed by the smart new cars, by the marble buildings, the shops – especially in Kolonaki – that are full of *things*. Mannequins draped in glossy furs, windows full of nothing but gentlemen's hats, or pens, or books. Restaurants. Cafes where men in linen suits sit at marble tables and read gigantic newspapers. It reminds her, of course, of home, though if she is honest with herself, Zoë isn't sure that she remembers what *home* really means. When she wanders through these streets, memories come to her in odd ways, and sometimes it is as if she is walking among ghosts. In turn, it is very obvious that Zoë and Pavlo are nothing more than ghosts here. They flit through the city, which is as unreal to them as a stage set, invisible to everyone, even the police. At least they aren't alone. There are a hundred thousand children just like them in the shanty towns around Athens and Piraeus. They all look the same: threadbare clothes darned and patched and worn out from constant cleaning; brown, stringy limbs; stomachs that are always growling; and hair cut short to make it easier to comb out the lice. Zoë can tell her kind from one quick glance: it is the eyes that give them away. Bigger than they should be, from what they've seen, and sunk just a little deeper in freckled, gaunt faces that have aged out of step with the passing of ordinary time. Her face, when she can be bothered to look at it in Mama's powder compact mirror.

If they are noticed, likely as not they will be jeered at. *Turks* is what they are called, or *dirty refugees*. Sometimes people throw them coins, especially when Pavlo is ferreting around on the pavement next to some cafe or other, picking up dog-ends. Enough, rarely, to buy themselves a small pastry or a piece of fruit. But they are always hungry when they ride back to Piraeus.

Zoë sits at the table, feeling uncomfortably full. She has eaten more in the past half hour than in the whole of the last two weeks, surely. Huge yellow butter beans stewed with tomatoes; a heap of the tiny fish called gopes that children fish out of the harbour with nets made of old stockings; a slightly over-charred chicken wing trailing a succulent rag of breast meat. Her hand had been slapped away from the lamb chops – for grown-ups only – but she has sawed her way through a stringy lump of goat and picked the slippery curls of flesh from more snail shells than she can count.

'I'm dying,' she groans happily to Mama.

'*Aman!*' Mama exclaims, and hurriedly spits to ward off the evil eye. Then she chuckles. 'What a feast! It reminds me of . . .' She stops, and shakes her head. 'I shouldn't say such things. Do you even remember the old days, *koukla*?'

'A little bit.' Zoë considers. 'Not very much. I remember our kitchen – the smells, mostly. It was always steamy and smelt like cinnamon and onions and baking. Will our new kitchen smell like that?'

'Of course!' Mama has switched to English, as she often does with Zoë. When she found out that the little girl she had found on the waterfront spoke both languages, she decided that she would not forget the language she herself spoke perfectly, with a soft, smoky curl to the words. 'We'll have to find the money for the cinnamon. And the onions . . . And the flour . . .' She makes a face and they both laugh. Like everyone they know, the Valavanis live on rice and beans and wild greens, a few eggs, with salt fish on Fridays and sometimes a scrawny chicken or some mutton feet or neck for a stew. 'What else do you remember?'

'Well . . . Oh, you know, Mama. I've told you before.'

'But tell me anyway.'

'It's the place with the cliffs.' Zoë closes her eyes and chases images she no longer really believes in. But it is a familiar memory: a little group of people are standing in front of a cliff that rises behind them. There are trees, thorny bushes. She knows there had been the sound of running water. Bright purple flowers are spiking up out of the brown soil. There is a woman in white, with a big, floppy white hat, and a man in old-fashioned tweeds.

'Nymph Dagh,' Mama says. 'We'd go there every spring for a picnic, just like you. I expect we saw each other there. Isn't that funny? If I'd waved . . .' She takes a sip of her wine. 'I wonder why I'm thinking like this?'

'Is it because of the new house?'

Mama looks at her, eyebrows arched. She takes Zoë's face in her hands and kisses the tip of her nose. 'You are so clever, darling one. Yes, of course it is. Remembering what we had, and having to be grateful for that little box of a house. But I am grateful. We must be grateful, Zoë. We have nothing, nothing at all, and now we're going to have . . .'

'A box to put it in!'

'If you were any sharper, Zoë, you'd cut clean through that dress,' Mama says in Greek, laughing. 'Except it isn't nothing, is it?' She hugs Zoë against her. 'It's you, and Pavlo, and me.'

'It's us!'

A little later, Zoë is slumped in her rope-backed wooden chair next to Efi, sipping a tin cup of lemonade and watching the bride, who is greeting her guests and relieving them of their gifts, mostly tiny envelopes containing, no doubt, even tinier sums of money. Despite the setting – the wind has veered round again, and the municipal dump is breathing over the parched field – Mrs Vlessas's daughter looks stunning in the dress Mama Katina has made her: a replica, in ivory damask curtains, of Greta Garbo's dress from *The Mysterious Lady*. She looks down at her own dress: expertly sewn together from an expensive shawl that Mama had found, tattered and stained, in one of the flea markets. It looks expensive – it looks beautiful, because Mama can make beauty appear from anything – but because Zoë knows it had once been a ball of dirty cloth, it still reminds her of what she is: a refugee girl.

Meanwhile, the musicians are setting up under an awning made, far less expertly, from faded, pink-striped bedsheets. She knows most of them: Mr Karagozi, the butcher, with his oud; Petro, who plays guitar; the square head and neat moustache of Mr Perpiniadis, who sings in church and has such a beautiful voice. There is Mr Batis, grinning and showing the big gap between his front teeth. Others she hasn't seen before: the clarinet player; another with a big round drum; and a thin man with a long, serious, almost saintly face especially catches her eye. He is taking a violin out of its case. The other musicians are all being very attentive to him, and Zoë wonders if he is famous, though what would a famous musician be doing at this wedding on the edge of the Piraeus tip?

'Who's that?' she asks Mama, pointing.

'It's rude to point,' says Mama. And then she points her own finger. 'Him? That's Dimitrios Semsis. Head of Recording at His Master's Voice,' she says, with a reverence Zoë doesn't hear very often from her lips.

'*Aman!*' Zoë breathes, impressed. Mrs Vlessas has a phonograph, an old one with a big trumpet like a dingy flower. Zoë loves the records, the heavy, shiny blackness of them, the way there is music hiding in the tiny grooves. 'Is that his dog, then?'

'Dog?'

'You know, Mama! On the label.' She loves the little white and brown dog, the way he is staring, confused but patient, into the trumpet of the phonograph.

'You're so sweet, *koukla*.' Mama chuckles and pinches Zoë's cheek gently. 'Can you imagine a dog in a recording studio? Bark, bark, bark . . . Well, they want me up there.'

Mama pushes back her chair, kisses first Pavlo, then her, on the top of their heads – Zoë smiles at the wine and garlic on her breath – and walks over to join them.

The band has set out a chair for Mama Katina next to the long-faced man, who kisses her hand and gives her a tambourine, which she taps and then listens to, expertly. Zoë waves but Mama is too busy talking to the men to notice her. *She is beautiful*, Zoë thinks. Tall, always very thin, she wears the black clothes of a widow, but not the shapeless weeds that so many of the refugee women – so many widows – hide themselves behind, growing stout and stooped long before their time. Mama has made her clothes herself and Zoë thinks they would not look out of place in Kolonaki. She has almost forgotten that Katina Valavani is not her real mother. She tries to picture her parents here, in the breeze from the rubbish dump, and for a moment she sees them, out at the edge of the field, the border between the waste ground and the ugly new buildings, quivering in the transparent ropes of hot air: a woman in a white dress, a man in a blazer and a sailor's cap. Almost solid, almost hers again . . . But they have no faces, because she no longer has faces to give them. And they are already fading. She can't keep them. They don't belong here.

There is a speech. The groom's father, rather overweight, strutting proudly in his khaki gendarme's uniform, makes some bad jokes. 'Will we get arrested if we don't laugh?' Pavlo whispers in her ear.

'You smell of retsina,' she whispers back. 'You *should* be arrested.'

The gendarme makes a toast and the party's cheers echo from the rocks of the mountain. The priest blesses them all again and everyone crosses themselves. Another speech. Laughter. And then the band starts to play. Mr Karagozi picks out a complicated skein of notes on his lute-like oud: swirling, mysterious, not quite happy and not quite sad. The road is the one called *kiourti*. The long-faced man with the violin breaks in, picking up the oud's tune, making it soar and dip. It seems to wind around the wedding party like a silk scarf or a flame, caressing faces, not staying long enough to burn. Zoë has never heard anything so beautiful. It falls, rises, falls and climbs, slows. Mama sways in her seat, her back arches and the muscles in her throat tense.

> *I'll break cups because of the words you said,*
> *And glasses because of the bitter words.*
> Aman, aman, *don't cry any more, my little girl . . .*

'What a voice,' says the woman sitting next to Zoë. Mrs Bakas is small, wiry, sharp-tongued. A widow, of course. 'I heard her when she used to sing in the cafes in Punta,' she goes on, reaching across the table to snap up a lonely square of kataifi that the children have somehow missed.

'Wasn't that her sister?' Zoë says, watching enviously as Mrs Bakas licks her fingers. She is stuffed to the gills, but even so . . . 'Mama had a shop that sold dresses, you know.'

Mrs Bakas shakes her head, concentrating on the kataifi which has left sticky threads of pastry on her chin. 'No, no. Katina was the singer first. Marika was much younger. Katina had the better voice anyway. She used to sing in that big cafe . . . What was it called? The Trieste! And in some of the others. The better ones, mind. She was respectable.' Mrs Bakas clears her throat and waves to a boy who is going around with a brass tray loaded with little cups of coffee. 'One of those! Thank you. Yes, she was respectable. Her father did something with the railway in Boudjah. She did sewing, too, but it was the singing she loved. Anyway, it was at the Trieste that she met your father, of course.' Mrs Bakas takes a sip of her coffee, and frowns. 'Not *your* father. Christ on the cross, I'm losing my memory. Pavlo's father. Import, export: the fig business. Lots of money. He took her out of the cafes. Married her just like that' – she snaps her fingers – 'and set her up on Frank Street in her own shop. Oh, God! You should have seen that place.' She shakes her head, drains the little coffee cup.

Zoë has never asked Mama Katina about her past, because she knows that if she hears the story of Katina's life, she, Zoë, won't be in it. She feels like stopping Mrs Bakas, but it is too late. So instead, she asks one of the questions she has never dared ask Mama.

'So, her husband . . . what happened to him?'

'Same as what happened to all of them.' Mrs Bakas signals for another coffee. 'The Turks rounded up all the men – boys as well – who were fit. The others . . .' She shrugs. 'The old, children, those they sent down to the waterfront to let fate decide. If they couldn't walk, dear God, they killed them there and then. Katina's husband saw a friend of his, a Turkish officer. He stepped out of line to go and talk to him, and the soldiers killed him with their bayonets, on the spot. Oh, my God . . . But I won't tell you any more. It isn't for the ears of children.' She sighs and rubs her eyes. '*Aman!* The pity of it all. What times. What times.'

Zoë shudders, trying not to think of her own daddy being shot or killed with bayonets. But then she sees him at the bottom of the sea, on the white sand, next to Mama. They are just bones now – she knows that, but this is how she thinks of them: laid out in the dappled, dancing light, with fishes weaving silver ropes around them. She closes her eyes and listens to Mama Katina, who is coming to the end of her song. Mama's voice trembles, drops down to a deep sob, a word that sounds as if her heart has flown out of her mouth. Zoë knows, suddenly, exactly what Mama is feeling: she is away from this world, somewhere on the roads that lead back to the sunshine before the catastrophe, and then, always, to the dead.

'What about Marika?' Zoë asks Mrs Bakas, who shuts her eyes and lifts her hands dramatically. Zoë waits for more horror but suddenly there is a shout and a chittering of children's voices from nearby. Recognising her brother's voice, Zoë turns around just in time to see Pavlo twisting in the grasp of a hefty boy with a head the shape of a potato adorned with brush-cut sandy hair. He is wearing a suit of grey cloth and, Zoë notes automatically with the instincts of the shanty town child, proper shoes. A Vlach, then: a local Greek. He has the shoulder of Pavlo's jacket in one meaty fist. With the other hand he is pointing towards the wine barrels and yelling something at the man in the army shirt. The man cups his hand to his ear, and the boy fills his chest to shout again. This is the moment that Pavlo chooses to kick him hard, right between the legs.

'Pavlo!' she shrieks at him, horrified but also admiring: it was a lovely move. He is already off, running towards the fringes of the new streets, which swallow him up in an instant. *He may be a dreamer*, thinks Zoë, *but my brother can still look after himself*. 'Who's that boy, please?' she asks Mrs Bakas, who glances over.

'*Po po po*,' she exclaims. 'What happened to him, the poor little puppy? Och, wait; it's *him*, the little shit! He's bound to have deserved it. Don't you know? That's Sólon. His father is the gendarme over there.' She nods towards the younger policeman. 'Corporal Pandelis isn't a bad sort, for a Vlach. But his sons are little swine, both of them. I shouldn't say such things, but . . .' As Zoë knows quite well that Mrs Bakas runs a small but definitely illegal drinking den in her house, she reckons that the woman's opinion is to be respected. 'Sólon pushes people about,' Mrs Bakas goes on, 'and his brother likes to look through keyholes. They'll be gendarmes too, soon enough. And then, watch out.'

Zoë is having none of it. She pushes her chair away and runs around the tables to where the boy, Sólon, is still bent over, his hands on his knees, his face white. Zoë marches up to him, leans down. 'What were you doing to my brother, you bastard?' she barks into his ear. Sólon looks up, wincing.

'Caught him stealing wine,' he pants. 'Thief . . . son of a Turk . . .'

Zoë knows just what to do next. Indeed, she has her foot drawn back, ready for the blow, when she glances over towards the band – a guilty conscience, perhaps? – and sees Mama Katina waving to her, beckoning her over. She sighs in frustration, bends down again and hisses in the boy's ear.

'If I ever catch you calling my brother a Turk again, you dirty pig, I'll do you in, hear me? I'll kick your fat arse all the way to Constantinople, and we'll see what the Turks think of you then.' She walks away, ignoring his strangled curses.

Mama is waving to her from under the awning. 'Mrs Vlessas wants to hear you sing, *koukla*,' she says.

'What, here?' Zoë stares at her in horror.

'She always says how much she loves your voice. I told her you would.'

'But I can't! Not in front of all these people!'

'Then sing with me. We can do "Elli, Elli". It's easy. You know it backwards.'

Zoë sees Mrs Vlessas looking at her hopefully. Oh, God . . . *Well*, she thinks, *I did* eat all her food. *I suppose* . . .

'All right. But I'm going to sing quietly.'

'Don't be silly.' Mama grins and takes hold of Zoë's hand, playfully but firmly. She says something to the band and before Zoë can change her mind, they launch into the song, which she has heard a hundred times and sung, yes, quite often enough to remember the words. It starts with a lurching figure, then drops into a little jog between octaves. Mr Semsis, the famous violinist, bends his head over his instrument and, looking up, winks encouragingly at her. She begins to tap her foot. Lurch, then jog. Mama nudges her.

Elli was shapely,
and her hair was black, her hair was black.

She's never sung with a proper band before. As she sings, she feels the music – the clarinet that wails on the edge of control, the demanding voice of the violin, the drum, the jingle of Mama's tambourine, all of it dancing inside her.

Elli, Elli, the soldier doesn't want you
Because you kiss with jaded lips.

She is singing the last chorus when she realises that Mama isn't singing with her, but she doesn't care. She slips her voice in amongst the instruments and lets the music fill up her chest. It feels like nothing she has ever felt before. So much feeling: she doesn't know what to do with it, so she lets it out in the song. Not happiness; not sadness either, but beautiful dread, as if the music is a window onto the real world, a vastness of pitiless beauty and desolation. She is walking beside her father in the laughing streets of Smyrna. She sees the red mouth swallowing the city. She thinks of bayonets.

CHAPTER SIX

Devon, England, 1931

There is no one to collect Tom on the last day of term. He has been expecting his father to turn up in his Riley Nine, a sporty little car done up in British racing green which, though a bit impractical for transporting Tom's trunk and assorted bags, always gets a look of guarded envy from the other boys. But after he has been lurking in the hall just inside the main doors for long enough to feel mildly embarrassed, the headmaster's wife bustles up, fiddling nervously with her beads, and tells him that there has been a change of plan.

'Your father has just telephoned us, Collyer,' she says, sounding slightly more flustered even than usual, 'to say that he's had an unavoidable engagement. It is a *little* inconvenient . . .' She winds the necklace around her middle finger. 'But we'll manage!' she continues brightly. 'A taxi's been ordered to take you to the station. Mr Frye says you should just catch the 11.52.'

'Oh.' Tom opens his mouth to say something else, but shuts it again.

'The bursar will provide you with funds for your ticket – your father to reimburse us,' she adds, firmly.

'It's ever so kind of you to go to all this trouble, Mrs Meade.' Tom pauses. He doesn't want her to see that he is upset. He clears his throat. 'What about my trunk, though? It's just that I have to change at Newton Abbot, and then there's a walk from the station.'

'Your father . . .' Mrs Meade frowns. 'We'll arrange with Captain Collyer to have it collected,' she says. 'At his expense.' Tom thinks he hears a hint of doubt in her voice. He isn't surprised.

'It must have been something jolly important for him not to turn up,' Tom says, hopefully.

'Oh. Yes, well, I'm sure it was. Now then, let's just go and see the bursar, shall we?'

Tom sits in the train, watching oak trees through the window. The engine is climbing up the valley from Bovey Tracy, trailing a thick cloud of smoke. He leans his forehead against the glass. The golden slope of the moor is bright in the sunlight – it has been raining, and the sky is still slate-dark in the east, but here it is clear and everything is gleaming, newly varnished. The train crawls into the cut before the village, a lush grotto of hart's tongue ferns, huge shuttlecock ferns, ivy and escaped rhododendrons, deep, shining green. Viridian. Hooker's green. All at once he is thinking about Kerala. There had been a sunken lane that had run across the plantation towards one of the hamlets. In the monsoon it had turned into a frothing stream and his ayah had kept him away from it, but when it was dry he would play in it, imagining that he was the last of the Mohicans. The details of his old life are almost gone now. The plantation makes him think of Daddy, and he growls with frustration.

Hawksworthy Station is a tiny village halt with a granite ticket office and an absurdly neat ornamental flower bed. Tom gets down, greets the stationmaster and climbs the creeper-festooned steps. The school bursar has given him two shillings – writing the sum down on a piece of notepaper which he slipped, ostentatiously, into an envelope marked *Capt. J. Collyer* – for travel expenses. Tom has incurred no such expenses in the couple of hours it has taken him to get here from Tiverton, so, reluctant, somehow, to go straight home, he wanders down into the village and buys a packet of twenty Gold Flake cigarettes and a penny bag of mint humbugs at the shop. He goes into the churchyard and lights up, thanking the bursar as he does so.

Leaning against a gravestone, Tom takes stock. He has got through his first year at Bishopstone, and it hasn't been all that bad. He happens to be rather good at cricket, good enough to be captain of the junior colts team. He is on the big side for his age, which keeps the bullies away. Not that there is a great deal of bullying at Bishopstone. It is Daddy's old school, and Daddy had remembered it, with great affection, as a citadel of Englishness, as hidebound in its traditions of institutional savagery as a nabob's elephant-foot trophy. But to Captain Collyer's dismay, the stories that his son has brought home with him in the holidays tell of a school into which dreadful fingers of rot are creeping. Rot in the form of modernity, of progress. Of kindness, even. In 1932 the school will be opening its doors to girls. Rot. Absolute rot.

To Tom, who has survived a stodgily old-fashioned prep school in Sidmouth, Bishopstone seems like . . . school. Hierarchy, discipline, ritual. Everyone in his place. But the fagging, the bullying, the beatings administered often and with relish by beastly but fair masters – the best involving a cane-wielding teacher taking a run-up the length of the school's celebrated Great Corridor – all this has drifted away quietly in the years after the War, much to

Daddy's regret. Perhaps it is because a good number of the masters are survivors of that War – the Old Shakies, as some of the crueller boys call them, boys who will drop a heavy book to see their teacher flinch or, with any luck, duck behind his desk. What larks. Tom can't believe that these boys don't see any connection between the Shakies and the twenty-one gold-leaf names on the board in the school hall. He doesn't dare say anything, though, which makes him feel like a coward, but anyone who would torment a shell-shocked soldier wouldn't hesitate to give a good pasting to a first-year boy, captain of the junior colts or not.

Well, I can tell Daddy that they caned me, Tom thinks. *That'll cheer him up. I'll need to talk it up a bit, though.* Because it hadn't been a proper caning. More a couple of distinctly apologetic taps on the hand in the headmaster's study. Tom's offence had been to draw an unflattering sketch of the maths master, John Hugo. He had overdone the man's nose, though not by much: Hugo has a nose like a goose's beak, fleshy and pointing straight out, with lavish tufts of black hair bursting from the nostrils. He might have overdone the eyebrows as well, and the beady eyes beneath them . . . His sketches, though they have got him into trouble this time, have made him popular with the other boys, so on the whole he thinks his caning is a small price to pay. Besides, he'd shown the drawing to Mr Dellal, who'd laughed and pronounced it 'excellent'.

Mr Dellal is the art master. One of the Shakies – he'd been a stretcher bearer, wounded on the Somme and again at Cambrai (this information delivered to a pair of sniggering book-droppers one afternoon by an enraged Mr Meade) – Gabriel Dellal is small, wiry, limping. Before the War, he was a student at the Slade. Mr Dellal is a proper artist, in fact, with a gallery in London. He has taken an interest in Tom's own work, though *work* is the last word that comes to mind when Tom thinks about art. There is nothing work-like about drawing, or painting with the watercolour set that Mum bought him a few Christmases ago, a small black tin box with the mysterious word *Cornellissen* printed on a gold label. It is . . . Tom doesn't honestly know. He throws away his cigarette end, pops a humbug into his mouth and stands up, stretches, feeling the sunshine on his back, the first day of the holidays. Drawing and all that stuff, that art, is just what he does. Why wouldn't you, if you could? Take a stub of a pencil and a bit of paper, and catch a bit of the world as it glides past like a big, gorgeous butterfly. It's no different, really, from cricket, Tom decides. If you could bowl a decent off-break, you'd do it. You'd more or less have to: like a duty, in a way.

Lake Cottage is a mile outside the village, up a steep lane that climbs between high banks towards the moor. Three steep granite steps lead to a lichen-encrusted wooden gate, and beyond it, a cobbled path winds between flower beds and shrubs to the front door. Tom loiters at the bottom step, chewing a couple more humbugs to mask the smoke on his breath. He has wandered slowly up from the village, enjoying the air, which smells of heather, sweet new bracken and the lanolin tang of sheep dung. Elderflowers hang their creamy umbels over banks of yellow gorse and purple heather, ragged robin, trailing vetch, herb Robert. It reminds Tom of the Monet landscapes that Mum had taken him to see at the Courtauld, the last time they had gone up to London. Not quite real, like the paintings, which shimmered like mirages from a distance, but up close were all thick paint and brush marks. He scrapes a sticky blob of humbug from his front teeth, climbs the steps and clicks the latch on the gate.

His brother and sister are playing in the garden, climbing in the huge old apple tree that guards the northern side of the house. When they hear the gate they jump down and run towards him, shouting his name in their reedy voices. Dora is nine, and Ivo is seven. They are both filthy: Dora's white pinafore is streaked various shades of camouflage from the bark of the tree, and Ivo is simply coated with mud.

'I fell in the brook!' he tells Tom, hugging him around the waist. 'You smell like mints. Give!'

'He fell in *again*,' says Dora, rolling her eyes extravagantly. 'He's always falling in. Mummy says we should tether him. Like a goat.'

'Goat yourself,' says Ivo good-naturedly. 'Anyway, if I *were* a goat, I'd eat everybody's underwear off the line, and serve you all jolly well right.'

'You're damp, Ivo,' says Tom, ruffling his hair. 'What were you doing? Looking for dragonfly larvae?'

'No, panning for gold,' Ivo says. 'Where are those mints?'

Tom takes out the crumpled bag of humbugs. Ivo and Dora dig into it, and their cheeks are soon bulging. 'Where's Mum?' asks Tom. 'Inside?'

'Yes,' says Dora. She suddenly looks a bit worried. Sucking pensively on her mint, her eyes drift down and to the side. 'She's upstairs. I told her Ivo had fallen in the brook, and she just, well, she just . . .'

'I expect she's just fed up with you both,' says Tom. He gives Dora the bag of sweets. 'Don't eat all of them at once, you two, or you'll be sick.'

'I want to be sick!' Ivo says happily.

'No, you don't. Anyway, I'm going to say hello to Mum.'

He thumbs the latch of the stable door, steps into the little stone hall with its ancient wooden bench set into one wall. The temperature is several degrees colder inside and it smells of damp plaster, but through the inner door, the house is homely, familiar. His parents' tastes fight for prominence on walls and shelves. An Augustus John painting of a group of half-dressed women; a set of framed Kalighat pictures (cat with fish in mouth, the black goddess complete with huge eyes and waist-length tongue, a musician, a monkey); a mirror in an inlaid frame: these are Mum's. Alongside these, defiantly, Daddy has hung his Snaffles prints: jolly huntsmen crashing through hedges on jolly horses; chaps in pith helmets riding after wild boar; a horse artillery gun train at full gallop. There is Daddy's own boar's head trophy, his mounted warthog skull, various tusks, teeth and claws, trophy shields for polo, rugger, point-to-point. Several fox paws. The tiger skin is in the sitting room, fighting it out with William Orpen's portrait of Mum, and the alabaster Mandalay Buddha.

'Mum?'

There is a copper pan steaming on the Rayburn stove, but the kitchen is empty. 'Mum?'

'Tommy . . .' Mum appears from the back room they call the brewery, though it is a glorified larder, filled, when Daddy is taken up with shooting, by curtains of fur and feathers, all dripping blood, all smelling not very nice. She is wearing an apron and her hair is slightly disordered. She smiles when she sees him, but . . .

'Mum? Are you all right? Dora said . . .'

'I'm fine, darling. Quite fine. Come here.' She wraps her arms around him and he is surprised by how stiff she feels through her summer dress. 'I'm making a rhubarb pudding,' she says chirpily, waving towards the stove. 'Mr Muggeridge brought up a great big trug full of lovely rhubarb from his garden, and . . .' She pauses, her face quite blank.

'Mum?'

'Rhubarb. Steamed rhubarb pudding. You like it, don't you? It's one of the things you like.'

'I . . . I think so. I'm sure I do,' he adds, seeing something happen to Mum's eyes.

'Oh, good! Good. Oh . . .' Abruptly, she folds at the waist and, hands on knees, sways gently in front of Tom, who watches, horrified. 'Oh, damn. I'm sorry, Tommy.'

'Mum? What's the matter?'

She straightens, and her face is red with tears. And yet, when she speaks, her voice is clear and steady.

'Daddy. He has left us, I'm afraid. He's gone.'

'Gone? What do you mean, Mum?' *Left us?* 'He isn't . . . isn't . . . ?' His mother's laugh, too loud, makes him jump.

'Dead? Dear God, no!' Mum sniffs angrily. 'Your father isn't the kind of man to just *die*! Not at all! Left. *Tout simple.* Gone.'

'So . . .' Tom finds he is fumbling in his pocket for the bag of sweets that isn't there.

'Gone off, that is,' Mum continues, through lips that have gone quite white. 'With someone. Some woman. Another woman. Another one.'

'But he was supposed to collect me from school,' says Tom, hearing the whine rising in his voice, finding that he doesn't want to understand what Mum has just told him. 'The head's wife said he had an unavoidable engagement.'

'Ha ha!' His mother fumbles with the knot of her apron, throws it viciously at the table. 'Ha! The bastard. Oh Christ . . .' She sits down hard on one of the kitchen's Windsor chairs. Tom stands in front of her, mouth wide but unable to say anything. Something rattles faintly, jauntily, in the copper on the stove.

Steamed pudding. He runs out of the kitchen.

Through the back door, up the path, over the granite stile. Beyond is a half-wild field, a newtake walled off from the moor centuries ago, in which granite juts out of the rough, yellow-brown grass and a small spinney of wind-bent hawthorn hides a busy rabbit village. One outcrop forms a sort of platform, a raised stone armchair from which the whole of the valley can be surveyed, the lower hills towards the coast, the straight edge of the sea. Though it isn't a private place, it is somewhere that feels intensely private, and Tom comes here often to think, to draw and daydream. His brother and sister haven't discovered the rock yet, so it is his own. Sitting on the rough granite, which is covered, like an old cheese, with a crust of yellow lichen, he can look ahead into empty space.

He sits for a long time, staring into the blue, watching a buzzard wheeling high overhead. He doesn't really know what to feel. Something is twisting in his stomach but the truth is that it is more like guilt than grief. Guilt, because there is a certain sense of relief. Daddy has gone. That should be an awful thing, he thinks. A shameful thing. He had been all too aware of the disapproval in Mrs Meade's face when she had told him that his father wouldn't be there to collect him. Daddy has that effect on people. They either like him a great deal – these are a certain type, horsey, county, loud – or they don't like him at all. People like the Meades. The vicar down in the village. His grandfather. Or Mum's friends. They all dislike Daddy with a passion, and Daddy returns the favour.

Tom sighs and lights another cigarette. When he closes his eyes he pictures Daddy, his smartly combed-back hair, his grey eyes, his neat cavalryman's moustache. Daddy standing next to some tall, beautiful horse, lost in his own world, one in which he has never made the slightest attempt to interest his son. He has never taken Tom riding except for that one awful day with Vulcan the pony. Tweed suit from Huntsman – 'I dread to think what that must have cost,' Mum says, whenever Daddy returns from London with a new item for his wardrobe – and shoes from Lobb's, always muddy. Tom has been getting a ha'penny to scrape horse manure off Daddy's shoes and boots for years, to pick it out of the broguing, polish them up to a slick toffee sheen.

Never having known anything different, Tom has generally been inclined to forgive his father for his distance, his loud, cruel jollity in which he and Mum are always victims, never companions. At least he has a father. Some of his friends never knew theirs – lost in France or Flanders. Or they have been sent back to England while their fathers stay with their regiments in India and Burma, or serve at sea, or plant tea or rubber, or help govern the Empire. It is the way Daddy treats Mum that upsets Tom. When he is happy, Daddy regards Mum as an object of mockery, and when he is angry he just goes at her. Not with his hands: Daddy isn't a violent man, at least not with his fists. But his tongue is clever and cruel and once he is in the mood, he will goad his wife until she locks herself in her dressing room, sobbing. Then he might start on Tom, who will have to stand there, listening to the litany of his failings past and future until Daddy loses interest. No, Tom doesn't feel any sadness over his father's leaving, though he wishes he did. He feels relief. And that makes him feel terrible. He sits and smokes, which makes him think of Daddy even more, because it was his father who presided, in a roundabout way, in Tom having his first cigarette.

It was at an afternoon party three years earlier, a society do at one of the big houses outside Exeter. The proceedings were dull and entirely predictable: Daddy holding court with his horsey friends, good-looking men and women whose clothes were never quite as fashionable as Daddy's, who told dull jokes and passed silver hip flasks back and forth; and Mum trapped in an orangery or a drawing room by older women in flowery dresses who talked at her while she wilted. There were always plenty of people who wanted to hear Daddy talk about racing, or hunting, or India, and no one who cared one crumb about the things that interested Mum, like Mrs Woolf's novels, or Matisse, or Rabindranath Tagore. On that particular afternoon, Daddy seemed to have been cornered by a tall, very thin woman with exquisitely sculpted hair and blood-red lipstick. Or perhaps he had cornered her. In any case they were standing rather close and talking very loudly. Tom wandered off. The house was old and filled with interesting things, and no one was paying any attention to him anyway, so he decided to explore. But this too became dull: all these houses seemed to have the same paintings on the walls – red-faced men in wigs, ladies with tiny mouths and almond eyes – and the same china on the mantelpieces. He decided to go outside, but as he made his way towards the front door he happened to glance into a room and saw, sitting on a chinoiserie table, his mother's handbag: crocodile skin, liquorice-black. Strange that it should be here unattended. He decided to take it to her, but when he went to pick it up, he paused. He had been very fond of Mum's bag when he was smaller. He had loved to rummage inside it when she was in another room, push his face right in between the gilded metal jaws and breathe in the strangely heavy air inside, the smell of powder, perfume, tobacco, lighter fuel and money. He had always taken out the cigarettes. His mother had favoured oriental cigarettes with ornate boxes. He would open the box reverently and run his fingertips over the sweetly rustling foil. Then he would lift it to his face and breathe in the cloying scent of the Turkish tobacco before putting it back, closing the handbag and slinking away.

Something about the stillness of the air in the room, that heavy, dusty air that only really exists in old country houses, made less for breathing than to carry the ticking and chiming of ancient clocks, made him stop and open the bag. Without thinking, he reached for the cigarettes – Murads, one of his favourite boxes, lime-green and orange, decorated with an Egyptian beauty guarded by two dog-faced statues – and opened the box. He let his fingers paddle across the cigarettes, enjoying the faint ribbing of the paper, the tiny, ornate gold lettering. He was quite oblivious until a fist closed around his hair and jerked him upright. The woman who had been talking to Daddy. She held him there, silently, on tiptoe, just about able to feel the parquet slithering under his shoes. Her narrow, pigeon-grey eyes bored into his. Not daring to move a muscle of his face, in case he started to blub, he held out the box. She accepted it with her free hand.

'You're Jim Collyer's boy.' Her voice was as cool and smooth as a silver letter opener. He nodded, terrified.

Her fist opened then, releasing him, and he lost his balance and fell hard onto his bottom. Through a film of tears he watched the woman stoop, pick up her bag (red fingernails vivid against the crocodile hide), extract the lighter. Not Mum's lighter after all. Not her bag. Almost the same, but now he sees . . . There was a rustle, the soft, crumpled *poff* of the flint and striker. Then red nails were in front of his face, and, between them, a lit cigarette.

'Take it then, you little shit.'

And he took it, sitting there on the floor beneath the inlaid chinoiserie table, on the waxy parquet. He took it between the first and second fingers of his right hand, the way you hold a

110

cigarette, though he had never even taken one out of the box before. He didn't dare to look up, but he felt the woman's eyes still on him. So, because he knew what she wanted him to do, he put the thing to his lips and sucked, hard, as if it were a drinking straw. His mouth filled with hot, burning smoke. He choked, retched. The woman's slender, stocking-clad leg flexed in front of him, the hem of her skirt rippling. He heard, beyond the cacophony of his own distress, the snap of the handbag clasp. He was drowning.

'Mrs Leeds? Where have you got to?' Daddy's voice. Heels clicked, leaving him alone. Fire lapped at his windpipe, blossomed in his chest. He sobbed, at last. Then he took another puff.

He has been sitting on the rock for a while before Mum appears below him, climbing up the path, an old straw cloche hat jammed onto her head, holding the hem of her butter-yellow dress out of the way of bramble and bracken. A little out of breath, she clambers up onto the rock and sits down beside Tom. A pair of ravens is mobbing the buzzard, diving and wheeling around him. The buzzard rises and falls, giving its harsh mew whenever a raven gets too close, and the ravens croak to each other in excitement. Tom can feel the same tension beside him in his mother. She is sitting on her hands, breathing deeply, her back rigid. She hasn't so much as glanced at Tom. He has the strange feeling that this is what it feels like to be a grown-up. The thought unsettles him, and he reaches into his pocket for his cigarettes. He has already taken one out when he remembers that Mum doesn't know he smokes.

'Honestly, Tommy.' He winces: Mum is regarding him from beneath the fraying brim of her hat, frowning.

'Sorry, Mum. I . . .'

'I think you'd better let me have one of those,' she says, and with a mixture of unease and elation he offers her the packet and lights a match for her. She inhales deeply, tilts her head back and blows a plume of smoke towards the buzzard, who has given up and is flying off dejectedly towards the high moor.

'What are we going to do?' asks Tom, finally.

'Do? I don't know. Yet.' Mum regards her cigarette as if she is surprised to see it there between her fingers.

'I'm glad he's gone,' Tom whispers.

'He's still your father, Tommy. You shouldn't think things like that.'

'Don't you think them?' Tom can't remember ever feeling so confused.

'What I think . . . No, I'm sorry. But then I suppose I'm sorry about a lot of things.'

'It will be all right, won't it?'

'Of course. Terrible things happen to perfectly decent people all the time. Every minute. Horrible tragedies.' She sighs. 'This one is very insignificant, I'm afraid.'

'So will everything be different now? What about school? Are we going to be poor now?'

'Oh, Tommy.' Mum leans against him, puts her arm around his shoulders. 'I wish I could tell you . . .' She throws her cigarette away into the grass. 'You mustn't worry. We shall be absolutely fine. It's Da who takes care of us. Your father is much too clever to spend his own money, you know.'

'Oh.' Tom considers this. 'What a beast,' he says, experimentally.

'I don't ever want to hear you say that again,' says Mum seriously. 'But, yes. An absolute, utter beast.' She looks up. 'I wish the ravens would leave the poor buzzard alone.'

'They have a nest in those pines over there,' says Tom. 'They think the buzzard is after their chicks.'

'Is he?'

'I expect so. But the ravens would eat his chicks too. Look, they're chasing him.'

'The world is such a dreadful mess,' Mum says, leaning back against the rock.

CHAPTER SEVEN

Piraeus, Greece, 1935

'Mama?'

Katina Valavani opens her eyes and Zoë feels an all too familiar sense of relief. Mama is lying back on the nest of pillows they have made for her against the iron bedstead. 'Hello, my darling,' she whispers. Her hand pats the quilt beside her. 'Sit. I'm still here.'

'How are you feeling?'

'I'm feeling fine.' Mama's voice is as thin as the skin on her hands, as delicate and papery as ancient silk. 'Are those old ravens here?'

Zoë sits and takes Mama's hand. 'No. Thank God, they've gone to pester Mr Deliyannides.'

'Is he still alive? Poor devil.' Mr Deliyannides, an old man who had been a conductor on the Bournabat Railway and lives two streets away, has had a stroke. The women of the neighbourhood must make their rounds of the dying and dead, and Katina Valavani has been left alone for a few hours. But ever since she took to her bed a few days after Christmas, the whole neighbourhood has known that she will never get up again. Women have been telling Zoë for weeks: your mother is surrounded by angels. Don't bother

her. She needs to make her peace. Katina was full of life, even then, though she was gaunt and her skin was almost transparent, as if she'd already coughed all the blood out of her body. But the women know the end is coming. They have started to drop by more and more often. Zoë seems to be boiling the coffee pot all the time, carrying the tray backwards and forwards, little cups of coffee to be filled, to be emptied of their sweet brown dregs, filled again. She knows them all, of course: Mrs Nasos, Mrs Kodjagas, Mrs Mouhtaris, Eleftheria Milionis, Mrs Zaifoglou. The old women, over the course of a few days, have made themselves quite at home. They don't even bother to knock at the door. Death is such a frequent visitor to Kokkinia that his arrivals and departures are just another social event.

'Is Pavlo here?' Mama asks, and Zoë frowns and shakes her head.

'He's out somewhere,' she says. The house has become a place of women, and Pavlo has made himself scarce. He is probably down in the streets behind the harbour, sitting in with one band or another in the *tekédhes*, the rough bars that drift across the line of legal and illegal, where men go to smoke hashish.

'At the Hanoum, I expect.' Mama sighs. The Hanoum is a club owned by a friend of hers, Apostoli Vikos, and for the last two years she has been singing there with Batis and his band. It isn't as rough as some of the *tekédhes*, but it is on one of the seediest streets in Karaiskaki, the red-light district just behind the harbour. Zoë has begun to sing there too. Six months ago Batis had begged her to sing one song, and now Mama lets her go with Pavlo, but only in the daytime. 'I worry. You know I worry. You'll keep an eye on him, won't you, Zoë?'

'Keep an eye on him yourself,' Zoë says firmly, and squeezes Mama's hand.

'Of course.' Mama squeezes back. 'But one day . . . You're a woman, Zoë, and I'm going to talk to you as a woman. I'll be gone soon. No, don't shake your head. I will. And it isn't so terrible. I'm not afraid – what could be worse than this world? – and you mustn't be either. You're strong. It is such a funny thing . . . When I saw you that day, on the waterfront, sitting there all alone and singing "Loula Loula", I thought you were so tiny and helpless. But you weren't, and you aren't now. I wish your brother had your strength. *Aman*, but he doesn't. He isn't tied to the earth, and one day I'm frightened that he will just drift away.' She closes her eyes. 'When I was a little girl, I had a cousin whose family owned a house right on the edge of the sea at Lidjia. One summer, when we were visiting, he went out swimming. He couldn't really swim – he must have been nine or ten, I suppose, and I was a little older. And he got into trouble. Went out too far, and sank like a stone. Thanks be to God, a fisherman saw everything and hauled him out. They brought him back to the beach and hung him up by his ankles until the water came out of him, and he lived, but only just. And for the rest of the summer, his mother wouldn't let him go swimming without a rope around his ankle. I had to hold on to the other end and pull him out if he did anything silly.'

'Is that true?' Zoë chuckles. 'You never told me before.'

'I swear. But you know, that's what Pavlo needs. I've been holding on to his rope all this time. Soon, someone else will have to. Zoë, dearest one, I'm afraid it has to be you. Until he finds a nice girl, gets married . . .' She shakes her head and her laughter is thin and rasping. 'But meanwhile, will you do that, Zoë? He'll sink, otherwise. Or float away, like a balloon. Will you promise me?'

116

'I promise. He's my brother, isn't he?'

'You have always been my gift, Zoë. My gift from the sea.' Mama takes a painful breath. 'Do you forgive me?'

'Forgive you, Mama? What for?' Zoë stares at her in surprise.

'For pretending to be your mother, all those years ago.'

'My . . .' Zoë's heart seems to stop for a moment. She takes Mama's hand and presses it against her face. 'You are my mother. You've never pretended.' She gulps, fighting tears. 'I've been very, very lucky. I've had two mothers. And both of them loved me . . . loved me just . . .'

'That makes me so happy. Shush, darling girl. I'm sorry I upset you.'

'Upset me, Mama? I love you!'

Mama struggles upright and takes Zoë in her arms. She is nothing but bone beneath her nightshirt and her skin smells powdery and sour, but Zoë doesn't notice. She buries her face in Mama's hair and sobs.

'Shush, shush, my little bird! Shush.' Mama strokes Zoë's back. She begins to whisper something into Zoë's ear. Through her crying, Zoë begins to make out a tune and then the words, low and achingly familiar.

Nani nani, my darling daughter
Sleep sweetly, Mama's here
She's going to bring you five white eggs
Five full baskets
To lay around your bed.

The old lullaby, the sweet nonsense of the words that Mama had sung her, countless times, in tents, in abandoned buildings, in

117

seething crowds, calms Zoë now as it had always calmed her then.

'One more thing,' Mama is saying. 'When I go, let me go alone. Do you understand? Everyone here is a widow or a widower, and so many are only half in this world. The other half is below, with the ones they've lost. With Charon. I want all of you to stay here. I'm not afraid of the boatman. I'm afraid of turning around on his boat, and finding you behind me. Don't cry for me. Don't yell and scream and all that nonsense. Let the old ravens do that. Let me go, Zoë.'

'I don't want to!'

'And I don't want you to. But you must. Do you promise?'

Zoë swallows and winds her fingers through Mama's hair. 'If I can't cry, what can I do?'

'You can sing for me, like the country women do. But later, later. Whenever you sing, sing for me. Can you promise that, my daughter?'

'Yes, Mama.' Zoë closes her eyes and thinks of all the songs that will be sung, all the songs already germinating in her heart. 'I do. I promise.'

It is freezing cold in Athens Cemetery Number 3. The wind is blowing down out of the north, and everyone has their overcoat collars turned up, their hands clamped down onto their hats. February is a bad time to die. Zoë, by the graveside, looks around at the people around her, shuffling their feet, dabbing their eyes with handkerchiefs. Her friends, just behind her: Efi, Marika, Voula. She catches Mr Georgiou, the mechanic, looking enviously at the hands of Mr Prokopiou, the baker, which are clad in a newish pair of capeskin gloves. The musicians – Stellakis, Batis, Iakovos Karagozi, Apostoli Vikos, Dimitrios Semsis the violinist –

stand in a gloomy huddle. Even Batis's gap teeth are hiding behind his moustache. Beside her, Pavlo is looking straight ahead across the grave, across the rows of white marble gravestones to the sea, which is bottle-glass green and fretted with white caps that look as if the graves continue on out into the bay, as though the cemetery has no limits and the sea itself is a part of it. She loops her arm through his and shivers.

Katina Valavani had not wanted to inconvenience her friends and her neighbours. She would have liked to stay until Easter, to hang on in this world just long enough to make sure her funeral was touched by the spring sunshine. The doctor, though, had not been able to manage even this small thing, though he had said plenty of useless stuff. If, years ago, Kyria Valavani had gone to a sanatorium, if the houses in the refugee settlements were less damp, if the bad air of the city wouldn't hang quite so low, then things might not be so hopeless. But everyone knew that tuberculosis didn't get cured in Kokkinia.

There had been some good days, some happy days. Mama had found some last reserve of strength, and the three of them had made her tiny bedroom a strange little oasis of laughter and music. The neighbourhood women were almost offended by this affront to the traditions of dying, but Mama waved them away.

'Ridiculous,' she said. 'I want to die of TB, not boredom. Sing to me. Play to me, my children.' So they sang her the old songs, the amanedes of Smyrna, and when she complained that they were too dirge-like – she, who had been the mistress of those songs for a lifetime – they sang her the ones that were being played now, down by the harbour, songs about booze, and hashish, and crazy love. A whole new music that people call rembetiko, that Mama herself had embraced in the last few years, always reaching for the future. 'That's more like it,' she said. 'I won't have anything to give Charon, but if I sing him one of these, the bastard will have to row me across.'

The priest is finished. As soon as the last words are out of his mouth, Mrs Bakas and Mrs Milionis fall to their knees at the edge of the grave and begin to wail, arms stretched up to heaven. The other women are weeping loudly. Zoë feels their eyes on her but, remembering her promise, she clamps her mouth into a line and steps forward with Pavlo. They pick up handfuls of earth, let them fall onto the varnished black lid of the coffin, onto the flowers, making them jump and scatter. Zoë stares at her hands, and at her brother's: long, pale, trembling as he rubs his fingers together, trying to dislodge the last crumbs of soil. He is an orphan now. *But I*, she thinks, *am twice an orphan. I have lost my mother for the second time.* She knows she ought to cry but her grief feels like sickness, not sadness. *I don't think I have any more tears left*, she thinks. *I wonder if they'll ever come back? Because I want to cry now. I want to climb down into the grave and beg Charon to take me too. But I promised.* Instead she takes Pavlo's arm and steers him away from the graveside, feeling his resistance, feeling all his thoughts and fears pulsing beneath his skin. He turns his face to her and his eyes are huge, staring out through the dark hollows around them. She notices that he is trying to grow a moustache.

They walk out through the gates, where more hearses are already waiting to unload their burdens. The plumes on the horses' heads are blowing in the wind. A white herl comes loose from one ragged ostrich feather and twirls through the air, coming to rest on Pavlo's lapel. He picks it off and stares at it, silently.

'Does it mean good luck, do you think?' Zoë says, to break the silence between them, which is starting to press down on her. She hates the way her voice sounds artificially bright.

'An undertaker's feather.' Pavlo closes his eyes and a faint smile stirs the corners of his mouth. Then it is gone. 'Sounds like a poem. Mama would laugh.'

'She would, wouldn't she?'

Pavlo takes out his handkerchief, folds it around the delicate wisp and tucks it carefully back into his pocket. 'We're alone now,' he says. He twists his hands together and moans. Zoë puts her arms around his shoulders and holds him tightly. He is rigid, but then he goes quiet. He puts his arms around her too, and rests his chin on the top of her head, looking back towards the gates. He is hardly there at all under his suit. Zoë takes hold of him and hugs him as tightly as she can. 'We're not alone,' she says. 'Mama said . . .' She stops. She wants to cry but she mustn't.

'What did Mama say?'

'That we'd always have each other,' Zoë says, brightly. She tries to smile and doesn't quite manage it.

'I don't want to go to the cafe,' he mutters.

'You spend your life in cafes.'

'Not like this.'

'You have to be there, Pavlo. I don't want go either, but this is the way it has to be.'

'Here they all are. God, what a crowd.' He sniffs, then waves. 'Thank Christ, Apostoli is here, Apostoli and the lads.'

'Of course they came, thick-head.' Zoë pinches his cheek gently, then steps back and straightens his tie. 'It's the band. Mama's band.' She tries to smile. 'Did you think they came for you?'

'Calm down, Zozo. *Aman* . . .' He shakes her off, but she can see the gratitude in his eyes. 'Where are we going, then?'

She leads him around the corner to a large cafe on Kafkasou Street, where the owner is expecting them. Mama Katina had put money aside for the funeral, but Zoë has had to make all the arrangements, going reluctantly for advice to the oldest and most experienced of the neighbourhood ladies. There has to be a little gathering after the burial, and Pavlo and Zoë must pay for coffee, brandy and a paximadi rusk for each mourner. Then they will go back to the house with Mama's closest friends for the traditional fish soup. Venetia Kodjagas, who is an encyclopaedia of all things funereal, has told Zoë exactly which cafe to book – 'Not him, he's a thief. Not there, the paximadi are so hard we'll all choke' – and has even ordered the soup from Dimitriou's Taverna, in obvious anticipation of a place at the meal. Zoë stands at the door with Pavlo, welcoming each guest, and then makes her way from table to table, making sure that everyone has their refreshments, muttering 'may God forgive her' in the traditional way. Pavlo wants to sit with his friends but after they have kissed him they shoo him away to do his duty. When the ritual offerings have been eaten and drunk, Zoë pulls her brother over to stand in the doorway again to shake hands.

'I hate this,' he mutters.

'I do too. But this is why we aren't alone, Pavlo. Look. The neighbourhood.'

'Christ, the bloody neighbourhood.' Pavlo sniffs. 'I suppose you're right, Zozo. Do you think it matters if we just pretend? Do you think . . . do you think it hurts Mama?'

Zoë squeezes his hand. 'Mama would be laughing her head off at all this. "You old vultures," she'd be saying. "Save some brandy for me!"'

'I can't do it.'

'You already have. I'm here. I'll always be here.'

'*Aman*,' Pavlo whispers, but he doesn't leave.

'Life to you,' they wish each mourner. 'Life to you.'

That night, when everyone has gone, Zoë sits alone in the little house. Pavlo has vanished. He slipped out before the last guest left, before the fish soup was all gone, the Soup of Consolation, as Mrs Kodjagas called it, though Zoë hadn't felt consoled. 'Where are you going?' Zoë hissed, following him to the door, knowing that the old women's eyes were following them. None of the musicians had come. Pavlo already reeked of brandy. 'To the Teké Hanoum. Batis and the boys are playing.' He glanced back into the house, at the dark figures hunched comfortably around the table. 'Fuck this.' And he went. He didn't even close the door behind him. Zoë had seethed with rage. *Abandoned already.* But then she realised: *You've already let go of the rope. You've already broken your promise.*

Mama's bedroom is empty. All the furniture has been carried out and stacked wherever it can go to make room for the vigil. Zoë takes a chair from the kitchen and sits in the middle of the floor, between the trestles that had carried the coffin. The few pictures on the wall – Mama's icon of St Polycarp, patron saint of Smyrna; an aquatint of Smyrna Harbour; another of Boudjah. A pencil drawing in Mama's crude, confident style of a large house surrounded by a walled garden. The cover of a copy of *Vogue* that Zoë found years before in Kolonaki, carefully framed – are all covered with black cloths, as is Mama's single mirror. The air still smells, faintly, of flowers and candle wax, of the wine the neighbourhood women used to wash the body, last night. And of the dull resignation of Mama's illness, milky and tainted, like cheap, rancid soap. The room is tiny but tonight, empty, it seems cavernous. Mama had only enjoyed her new house for five years. But then again, she hadn't really enjoyed it. The house in the drawing had been hers, back in Smyrna. She talked about it a lot in her last days, after

123

years of never mentioning it at all. Zoë had listened, holding her damp hand, as Mama moved through her memories, forwards and backwards, until, perhaps, she had brought every one out into the world. The last one was something about a cat, a big ginger tom called Alexandros, who one day had caught a raven. 'Just like those ones out there,' she whispered, pointing to the women in the kitchen. It must have been the last thing she needed to say, because by the next morning Mama had slipped into a coma. The image – the savage but lovable cat with the huge black bird, bigger than itself, in its jaws – had been a strange parting gift. In the days after, Zoë watched the old ladies take over the house and thought of the raven, how these old ravens had taken her life in their beaks.

'The old box,' Mama had always called their house in Kokkinia. She had been grateful for it – 'We should have an icon of the Refugee Settlement Commission,' she would say, and sometimes, instead of crossing herself she would trace the letters *RSC* on her chest – but Zoë understood that, over the years, it pained her to be so grateful for something so meagre. It was a home, though. A brutally simple one-storey building, four walls of panel board set up on a rubble plinth and topped with a roof of cheap tiles, it had a living room which opened onto the single bedroom, which in turn led to the tiny kitchen. A set of concrete steps led down into a little yard, and more concrete steps led up to the *lavatory*, as Zoë insisted on calling it, which was no bigger than a wardrobe. Within weeks of moving in, Mama had got one of the hundreds of unemployed workmen in the neighbourhood to slice the little box up into even smaller segments, carving off a bedroom each for Pavlo and Zoë from the living room and Mama's bedroom. For the first time in eight years, Zoë had been able to close a door on her own private space, though this space was little bigger than the single bed it held. Now it is full of Mama's furniture, not that there was much of that: a wire washstand, a chest of drawers, a straight-backed wooden chair, a rolled-up carpet. All of it stacked on Zoë's bed.

She sits there in the almost-dark. It is getting cold: she has let the stove go out. The house is silent but outside there are the usual noises: motorcycles, dogs, voices. Her ears prick, but the sound they are missing is Mama's laboured breathing, the paroxysms of coughing. It is good, surely, that those have fallen silent. It is God's mercy. That is what the old women have been saying. But Zoë doesn't believe them. God keeps taking things away from her. Mama hadn't really believed in Him either. 'Better to believe in Venizelos,' she would say, 'or the Commission.' She wonders whether the angels that Mrs Mouhtaris had said were gathered around Mama as she lay dying are still here. The thought makes her angry, somehow. 'You shouldn't have taken her, you angels,' she says aloud, and the silence of the house just grows more suffocating.

I can't stay here, she thinks. *I can't light the lamps, and drag the furniture around. I can't lie awake listening for her. All the love has gone.* She stands up, and the scrape of the chair against the floorboards is unbearably loud. The tap of her feet as she goes into the living room sounds like gunfire. She pulls on her coat and hat, opens the door and peers up and down the street, guiltily. What would happen if one of the old ravens saw her? A tempest of clicking tongues and gossip. But she can't stay here. Not tonight. Not alone. There is something she needs to do.

Karaiskaki is a slum. It sits back from the waterfront a little to the west of the church of Saint Spyridon, a collection of old, decaying houses and newer, cheap buildings strung between them. When Mr Moumdji turns his taxi off the broad waterfront esplanade and into the shabby street that runs into Karaiskaki, Zoë sees that even now, in winter, the whores are lounging in flimsy dresses. Laughing to each other, singing, wheedling the men who sidle past them. Dancing on the gangplank of Charon's boat.

Pyramids of rotting vegetables and discarded newspapers squat in boarded-up doorways. Broken bottles are sprayed across pavements. Mr Moumdji pulls up under the urinous glow of a street lamp. 'Are you sure you don't want to come back to Kokkinia, Miss Valavani? I'll take you for free.'

'I'll be fine,' Zoë says gently. 'I just need to find Pavlo.' She has known Mr Moumdji for half her life, but she finds she can't tell him the real reason she has come here. She pays the fare with what little cash is left over from the funeral, and watches as he drives away. *Would you understand?* she thinks. *I have to sing for my mother.*

She walks past cafes and tavernas spilling their yellow light and noise out into the street. There are men sitting at tables outside, smoking hookahs, leering. 'Little chicken,' they call to her. 'My tender little red mullet. Where are you going on such a night?' The street she is looking for is narrow and lined with shuttered businesses; it looks dead. Next to a cobbler's shop, she finds an old poster of the last prime minister, slowly coming unstuck from the nondescript door to which it has been pasted. She knocks, and waits. There is a rattle and the door opens a crack. A man's face appears, heavily stubbled, the points of his moustache lost in the shadows on either side of the narrow space through which he is glaring at her with bloodshot eyes.

'Zoë!'

The door swings open and the man's arm reaches out, hooks her around the shoulders and pulls her, gently, into the dim yellow light inside. The man leans against the door and locks it. 'Look who's here,' he growls in a tobacco-stained voice to a man coming up the stairs behind him.

'Zoë! *Kopella mou!* But what the hell are you doing here?' It is Apostoli Vikos, and the music is rising behind him, wrapped in a blast of tobacco smoke and the earthy musk of hashish.

'I didn't want to be alone,' Zoë tries to explain, but Apostoli puts a finger to his lips.

'What a day,' he murmurs, patting her hand. 'What a day. What a blow. Pavlo should never have left you, and just to play bouzouki with a bunch of villains like us . . .' He shakes his head. '*Po po po*, what a crime. But now you're here, come down and get warm. Have a little to eat. A little coffee. Listen to your monster of a brother for a while. Then we'll get you home.'

She follows Apostoli, descending into the middle of a small room whose low ceiling of unpainted beams and rafters is hung with a few old-fashioned kerosene lamps and criss-crossed with strings of bright triangular bunting, of the sort the big ocean liners are decorated with when they leave port. The brick walls are hung with Turkish rugs and kilims. Tables fill the room on either side, and in front of her is a low platform. There, sitting in an uncomfortable-looking chair, knee to knee with Batis on one side and Stellakis on the other, is Pavlo, bouzouki on his lap, staring straight ahead with wide, unfocused eyes while his hands move up and down the neck loosely but with intense precision. The tune they are playing is a tight, hard-edged zeibekiko dance. Dimitrios Semsis's violin skirls and Stellakis's guitar thrums out the rhythm. Someone Zoë doesn't recognise is playing another bouzouki.

Pavlo must have seen her. But he makes no sign that he has. The music seems to grow more tense. The cigarette hanging from

Semsis's lips has almost burnt down into his moustache. '*Aman!*' someone calls from the back. Zoë stares at her brother's unseeing face. She thought her fury at him had died down but suddenly it rages again. She stamps down the last two steps and straight up between the tables to the stage, where she plants herself right in front of Pavlo. Still none of the men look at her. Zoë can't bear it any longer. She takes her hand out of her pocket and slaps Pavlo as hard as she can across the face.

The band rattles to an undignified halt and there is complete silence in the basement. Pavlo's eyes come into focus and his brow furrows. Semsis takes the cigarette very slowly from his lips and drops it to the floor.

'Bravo!' Batis roars. Then Pavlo bursts out laughing. The tension in the room evaporates. He jumps off the stage and throws his arms around her.

'My sister!' he shouts.

'You're drunk!' Zoë says into his collar. She is melting with relief.

'I'm not drunk! Well, perhaps I am a *little* bit drunk. Why aren't you drunk? Come and sing with us!'

'Orpheus, but in reverse,' says Apostoli, who has appeared from a back room. 'Here, *koritsa*.' He puts a glass into her hand. 'Drink. It'll warm you up.' It is ouzo, watered down only slightly, and she coughs and makes a face. She isn't used to strong drink, but it does warm her, and she drinks some more.

'Come,' Batis says. He brings over a chair from one of the tables. 'Move over, Stellakis.'

Perpiniadis scrapes his own chair sideways to make room next to Pavlo. 'There. Sit with us.'

Batis picks up his baglamas and spins the little instrument between his fingers, grinning his gap-toothed grin. *He looks*, Zoë thinks, *like the Devil himself*. Still, she lets him help her up onto the platform.

'Ready, boys?' Batis nods, grins, raises the baglamas high over his head and plays a long, rattling note. Apostoli chuckles. Semsis bows at the waist, and when he straightens, his violin has picked up the note. Stellakis takes a breath. '*Ahhh! If your mama won't give you eighty shares, And the same in cash, forget your hopes.*' Pavlo begins to pick out the rhythm under Stellakis's words. Heavy, deliberate, another zeibekiko.

Dourou dourou, dourou dourou,
In the square at Koumoundourou . . .

She has sung here many times before but this is still Mama's place, her chair in the centre, and at first she feels uncomfortable. Little by little, though, the music wraps itself around her and she relaxes. Micho brings her another drink. As the ouzo sinks into her, she watches the water pipes go round the tables, the men smoking and flicking their beads. One of the women, much younger than the others, her round face white with powder and framed by stringy yellow ringlets, comes over to put a lit cigarette between Pavlo's lips as he plays. Zoë scowls at her but she just stands there, gazing at him, until the song changes.

'Who's she?' Zoë hisses to Pavlo.

'Her? That's just Anastasia.' Pavlo giggles. 'She likes me.'

'She's making me nervous,' Zoë says. The girl is pretty but she looks like a wax carving left on a sunny windowsill: her features are softened, blurry, except for her pale eyes, which stare, unblinking, at her brother.

'Don't be so stuffy, Zozo.' Pavlo takes her hand and lifts it to his lips. Zoë drops her head and smiles despite herself. She can never be upset with Pavlo for very long. But still she wishes that the girl would go away.

Now and again someone will get up and dance in the tiny space in front of the stage: arms out, eyes closed, head down or thrown back, they trace out the steps that the zeibekiko is showing them, steps of pain or pleasure but theirs and theirs alone. Hands fluttering in space or clamped against their hearts, they turn, stoop, kick and balance on the edge of collapse, of disaster, their friends calling out to them: '*Yiassou*, Dimitri! *Yiassou*, Vassilis!'

'I'm going to sing a song for our dear friend who took Charon's boat yesterday,' Batis says, when the night has slipped along and the *teké* has almost lost its strangeness. 'Our nightingale, Katina Valavani, the mother of Pavlaki here, and our dear Zoë. "San Pethano", lads.' 'When I Die'.

'Wait,' Zoë says. She hadn't intended to say anything, but she is reaching out for Batis, taking hold of his arm. 'Let me sing it.'

'*Aman*.' Batis takes her hand and kisses it gravely. 'Sing. Sing, little one.'

As she finds the words and lets them go, they cut into her like razors. She wants to tell the band to stop, to grab the bouzouki and the guitar and muffle their strings, but she can't move. Then she sees that the men sitting at the nearest table are weeping quite unashamedly. A man is standing between the tables, fists clenched, stepping out a dance that is no more than a cramped, swaying shuffle. *He's dancing for me*, Zoë understands, as the song flays her. *Those are my steps. I want to sway like that, in the freezing cold wind. My God. My God.* Beside her, Pavlo is playing with his eyes screwed shut, biting his lip.

When the song is over, Apostoli leans across her brother and taps her leg. 'Why don't you sing another one, *koukla*?'

'I don't think I can.'

'What? Of course you can, Zozo,' says Pavlo. His face is dead white and his eyes look bruised, but he is laughing.

'I don't want to!'

Micho has come over with one of the water pipes on a tray. He offers it to Batis, who takes a long, luxurious drag, letting a thick cloud of smoke out between his lips before sucking it in again with a theatrical gasp. He passes it to Pavlo, who sucks so that the coals glow orange. The smoke is heavy and alarming. Micho holds out the pipe to Zoë.

'Lovely Stambouli medicine for you, princess,' he says, but Zoë shakes her head. She has never smoked hashish. He shrugs and passes it on to Stellakis.

'You need some, Zozo,' Pavlo rasps. 'Honestly. It'll smooth you out like a hot iron.' He giggles.

'No thanks.' The neighbourhood women are always complaining about hashish smokers. She can just picture Mrs Moumdji and Mrs Kodjagas, the old ravens, clacking their beaks at her. *To hell with you*, she thinks suddenly. *Worming your way into our house to drink your Soup of Consolation.* 'Micho,' she calls. 'Come back. I've changed my mind. What do I do?'

He grins, and offers the pipe. 'Take a sip, as if it were the finest champagne in France,' he says.

But she has never drunk champagne. The smoke grabs her throat like molten lead. She coughs explosively and the whole *teké* cheers. 'Damn,' she croaks, pinching the bridge of her nose. 'This is shit, Pavlo! What's the point?'

'There is no point. That is the point.'

'God, I hate you. What do you want me to sing?'

'What about "Ta Hanoumakia"? We sang it to Mama last week.'

'"The Harem Girls" . . . Yes, right.'

They had sung it leaning on the end of Mama's bed, Mama laughing and coughing, waving them on even as she had been wiping blood from her mouth. Pavlo had whistled the introduction, and tapped out the measure on the sheet, on Mama's foot. Zoë closes her eyes. The song comes.

On the beach near Pasalimani you had your hashish den
And I'd come there every day to drive away my pain.
One morning I found them there, sitting on the sand . . .

On the sand . . . Is there a beach at Pasalimani? And the pain. It is ebbing away into warm, soft sand.

BOOK II

CHAPTER EIGHT

Vevi, Northern Greece, 11th April 1941

From where he crouches behind a narrow railway embankment, Tom looks out across a landscape of low, rolling hills dappled with scrub pine. The full moon, which is shining down from somewhere over his right shoulder, has not brought any magic to the scene. Instead it seems to have made it more dull, less sinister. To complete the illusion of humdrum familiarity, the Great Bear hangs over the ridge at a jaunty angle. He could be in Richmond Park. Tom stretches his legs and turns to look at the troop of four anti-tank guns mounted on the flat beds of Ford trucks, spaced out and dug in along the line of the wall. His troop, which he has been in charge of for less than twenty-four hours. Two days ago, he landed in Piraeus and was carried north in a series of convoys, jammed in with New Zealanders and Australians and a few Greeks. Then he hitched a ride with a regimental supply truck and found his unit here, strung out across this wide, low valley. The 121st Regiment, RHA (East Devon Hussars), in which he was, effective immediately, Gun Position Officer, Second Troop, C Battery.

Tom lights a cigarette and curls up against the cold. He is

still in tropical uniform beneath his scrounged greatcoat; the thin trousers and Aertex shirt are little better than pyjamas. Sergeant Duffield has promised to find him a woolly jumper but so far it has not appeared. The cold is savage. It has taken him by surprise – taken everyone by surprise, because it is meant to be hot in Greece. He keeps hearing these words muttered like a catechism: 'I thought it was meant to be sunny in Greece, sir, boiling 'ot,' over and over in Australian, New Zealand, Devon and Midlands accents, as if the mere dogged repetition will make date palms sprout up out of these frostbitten fields.

It has been snowing off and on for two days and there is a thin, hard crust of frozen snow on the ground. He stares at the ridge to the north, wondering at the familiarity of it all, at the village of Vevi on the crest, occupied since yesterday by a brigade of the Waffen-SS. So far, his war has been quite predictable. A few variations on themes of boredom and the drudgery: boarding school reinvented by one of Lucifer's minor secretaries. To pass the time, he tries to imagine how he would paint all this. *Landscape by Moonlight*, after Samuel Palmer. Tom shuts his eyes and tries to imagine it. But Samuel Palmer couldn't make this place anything other than it is: bland and freezing.

Just after dawn, Sergeant Duffield slides around the nearest truck and squats down next to him.

'All right if the men brew up, sir?'

'Of course, Sergeant.'

The sergeant shouts across the road and there is a muted, sarcastic cheer. The acrid smell of burning solid fuel, oddly comforting, rises over the dead grass and leafless almond trees. Duffield coughs and spits thickly into the bottom of the ditch.

'I expect it was colder in Norway,' Tom says through clenched teeth. His sergeant has been through it – Dunkirk, Norway, Libya. He volunteered this information yesterday over a cup of lukewarm cocoa in which the sugar had failed to mask the taste of petrol. He seemed to have decided to give the young subaltern the benefit of the doubt, though, after Tom had corrected the troop's field of fire and gone out for a reconnaissance on his own, a cautious stroll among the stunted trees that accomplished nothing except to chill him even more thoroughly. Tom hasn't told Sergeant Duffield that he used to be an art student, and that so far his war has consisted of nothing worse than an infected mosquito bite in Alexandria. On the other hand, Tom suspects all this is bloody obvious.

'Oh, yes, sir. Much colder,' agrees the sergeant. 'Much colder than this. Mind you, sir, you expect it to be cold, don't you – Norway? Not Greece, though. Bit of a swizz, if you ask me.'

'A swizz. That's exactly what it is.' Tom sighs, takes a pull on his cigarette and pulls his knees up closer to his body, shivering in deep, painful spasms. He is too cold even to be frightened of the SS, and that, he supposes, is a benediction. He pushes back the rim of his helmet and peers through a fringe of dead fennel stalks to where a faint haze of tobacco smoke marks a Bren gun position. Beyond, he can't see the Australians tucked in under the hillside. Besides the wind, the only sound is the hollow clank of goat bells from one of the lower slopes, and the occasional spasm of coughing from the ditches and shallow, scraped-out trenches that shelter his troop.

A thick, pearl-grey barrier of clouds rises behind the village on the ridge, swelling as it advances. All of a sudden the sun cuts through the gloom and a rainbow appears, startlingly bright. Without thinking Tom cranes his neck to look for its end, which hovers, tantalisingly, in the low pine scrub on the eastern slope of the gorge, tinting the dark green trees with hazy gold. There it is, his painting! He grins, and turns to see if Sergeant Duffield has seen the rainbow too, but he has just opened his mouth when it vanishes as suddenly as it appeared. It begins to sleet. The village drifts out of focus. The red tiled roofs lose their colour, and the trees on the sides of the gorge turn black, like the mottling of mildew on a damp wall. There is a sudden, rich growl of large engines coming to life beyond Vevi. And then, on the left, out of sight around the flank of the hill, the bright, insistent chatter of small-arms fire.

CHAPTER NINE

Attica, Greece, 26th April 1941

The road winds south like the bleached corpse of a snake, shimmering silver-grey with heat-haze, swarming with black shapes. Apostoli's old Citroën is crawling along this exhausted road through flat farmland. It has been a wet spring, and the fields are green and speckled with wildflowers: yellow, red, purple, white. Zoë, in the back, is leaning out of the window, away from the eye-scorching tobacco smoke that fills the stained burgundy interior of the car. In front of her, Vangeli is picking his teeth. Apostoli, his face slack with the tedium of driving, has just pulled off his tie and undone several buttons of his shirt. 'Fuck it,' he mutters to himself. Next to Zoë, Pavlo is hugging his new bouzouki as if it were his baby son; like a baby, the instrument is swaddled in a garish peasant blanket. The idea of Pavlo as a father would make Zoë smile were she not so tired and bored. And frightened. A little frightened.

The car lurches and rattles over the uneven tarmac. Zoë's backside feels as if it is fusing with the cracked leather of the back seat. With every pothole, the car's failing suspension punches her stomach up into her diaphragm.

'All of this, for a bloody bouzouki,' she says, wincing, glaring at Pavlo.

'What was that, Zozo?' Pavlo is fumbling in his waistcoat pocket for cigarettes. His grey trilby has slipped down over his eyes, so that when she glances at him, all she sees is his large, handsome nose and the swooping wings of his moustache. Zoë clicks her tongue in annoyance. It is impossible to be angry with her brother.

'I said, we should have left you for the Germans. But Semsis couldn't make his record without the great Pavlo Valavani.'

Apostoli lets out a bark of laughter. 'Semsis doesn't care about Pavlo! It's you he fancies, Zoë. And thank Christ for that!'

'Very funny.' Zoë looks out of the window at a landscape her city-bred eyes don't really understand. Yes, she is annoyed with Pavlo, but perhaps there are worse things than being out here, away from Piraeus, which is a saucepan about to boil over with the tension of the past few weeks. And with her, good friends. Her band. *I didn't have to come*, she tells herself. *I could have stayed in Kokkinia, stewing with everybody else. But these are the ones I want to be with now. We've been through it all together. This is no different.*

They have almost made it – perhaps they really have made it, though if this is success it doesn't feel like much. From singing in the Hanoum with Batis and the others, Zoë has moved up slowly but steadily. She left school and took a job as a weaver at the Madras Carpet Factory off Osia Xeni Square in Kokkinia, hard, back-breaking, hand-flaying work, but when Dimitrios Semsis asked her to record a couple of songs, two lovely Smyrna laments she had learnt from Katina Valavani as a little child, the band – Apostoli on the baglamas, Zoë, Pavlo with his bouzouki and Vangeli Karakassis, who plays bad guitar but writes good songs – became popular. Other musicians dropped in to play with them.

Batis – who is in the most popular rembetiko outfit, the Famous Quartet of Piraeus, with Markos Vamvakaris, Anestis Delios and Stratos Pagioumtzis – has been their champion. In true Batis fashion, he has been trying to coax Zoë to join the Quartet for years. Why would she, though? Markos is supposed to be the best bouzouki player in Greece, but Zoë knows that Pavlo is ten times the musician Markos is. The big clubs up in Athens are booking them. They have been on the radio. With Semsis recording them, they are going to be bigger than the Quartet soon. Last year, before the Italians invaded, HMV in America had been interested in bringing them to New York. America! The future had suddenly been worth living for. Or would have been. The war has knocked the needle off the record. The Greek Army has surrendered. The British are retreating. They are about to be occupied.

Vangeli leans back and the seat springs creak. 'Hitler's coming, no matter what,' he says. 'It's like old Semsis doesn't want to believe it's true.'

Zoë brushes aside Pavlo's fingers, which are still trying to find their way into his pocket. It has been a while since his last fix. She sighs, fishes out his cigarette packet, takes out two and lights them with his matches. She sticks one in her brother's mouth and inhales her own, thoughtfully. Pavlo's habit is getting worse. If only they could find a way to keep that girl Feathers away from him. She remembers when she first saw Feathers, staring at Pavlo in a trance, that night in the Teké Hanoum after Mama's funeral. The little dancer and part-time whore from the slums of Drapetsona. But Pavlo had felt sorry for her, and Zoë had too – why not? She was an orphan too, a refugee – until Feathers had given Pavlo some heroin to smoke one night. Had she known that it would take him over so completely? Of course, Zoë thinks now. Feathers had just wanted company. She's stupid and vain, but she was clever enough to see that Pavlo needed a way to escape. '*Aman*,' she mutters bitterly. Her brother is all need. A creature of needs and dreams.

'As long as Semsis keeps paying us, I'll keep rounding up his lost lambs,' Apostoli is saying. 'But what in Christ's name were you doing in Khalkis, Pavlo? It wasn't just for that bloody bouzouki?'

'A girl, what else! A girl, right, you little sod?' Vangeli reaches behind him, plucks the cigarette from Pavlo's lips and turns back, chuckling. He puts his garish co-respondent shoes up on the shelf in front of him.

'Mind the fucking veneer!' shouts Apostoli. 'It's walnut, you peasant!'

'Well . . .' Pavlo pushes the hat back on his head. He winces. 'No, not a girl. There's an old boy in Khalkis who makes these fantastic bouzoukis. Old-style. Beautiful . . .' He shrugs.

'So Hitler's just undone his fly to piss on Greece and you decide to wander up to Khalkis?' Apostoli clicks his tongue with exasperation.

'That's why Semsis got us to rescue him,' Zoë says. 'Because he's got soul. Eh, you old sods?' She pushes her knee into the back of Vangeli's seat. 'Remember what that is?'

They all laugh. 'Thanks, Zoë,' Pavlo mumbles. He holds his bouzouki just a little tighter. 'Wait 'til you hear this thing. She really sings. Really old-fashioned, Turkish, like Yovan Tsaous plays. The old boy that made it comes from Smyrna, you know. I asked him . . .'

'Och, Pavlo. No one remembers.' Zoë shakes her head, thinking that Katina Valavani had been right after all, that it's all gone, the past, as if it never existed; but she knows Pavlo means well, so she gives him a smile. 'So let's see this famous bouzouki that you had to snatch from under Hitler's nose.'

'Well . . .' Pavlo shifts the blanket-wrapped bowl of the instrument in his lap.

'Let's see it, then!'

He peels back a corner of blanket and reveals the instrument's head, which is shaped like a pointed leaf inlaid with curling mother of pearl tendrils.

'More! You're like a pimp with his tart,' shouts Vangeli.

'It does look beautiful,' says Zoë admiringly.

Pavlo wraps his arms around the bouzouki nervously. 'Let's . . . I'll get her out when we get to Athens. All this bouncing around – it might snap the neck.'

'Please yourself.' She sighs, exasperated. But she understands. She saw the look on her brother's face when his favourite bouzouki was smashed, the night the SS Clan Fraser blew up in Piraeus Harbour. They had been playing in Niko's club in Karaiskaki, the Cordelio, and the blast threw them all over the room and nearly flattened the place when a huge piece of the ship's loading boom landed in the alley outside. Half of Piraeus was destroyed, and Pavlo held his broken instrument like a dead child. *Aman*, she thinks now. There is a kind of beauty in her brother's soul that not everyone can see.

The car picks up speed. Zoë puts her head out of the window again. The air rushing past her face feels like spring water. She looks ahead; the road, miraculously, is empty all the way to the next looping bend, half a mile in front. They will be in Athens in time for lunch at this rate. But will they be serving lunch today? Everybody is waiting. The city itself, the buildings, the telephone poles with their sagging wires, the sparrows, all waiting for the Germans. People stand in little crowds, silent and still, on the street corners. The only people making any noise are the English

143

and the Australians, who are swarming over what's left of Piraeus, trying to escape. The people watch them, quietly. Greeks know what disaster feels like. It feels like this.

When she puts her head back inside the car, there is another layer to the heavy tobacco fug. Vangeli has lit his pipe. Tendrils of hash smoke are licking at the windscreen. Apostoli takes a lungful, then the pipe comes back, to Pavlo, who drags on it deeply and lets his head fall back as he passes it to Zoë. When the smoke hits her lungs she waits for the familiar rush and when it comes, she feels a strange sense of relief. At least something is normal.

'Zoë!'

The pipe is coming round again. Apostoli reaches under his seat and pulls out his baglamas, gives it to Vangeli, who grunts and picks out a chord, thumbs the two drone strings, runs carefully up and down the frets until his fingers slip into a pattern, chopping out chords as harsh and sharp as the edges of a tin can.

'*Inside the bath house in the city . . .*'

Apostoli's voice is hoarse and slippery all at once. 'A raven with honeycomb in his beak,' is what Semsis calls him, approvingly. Now the hash has grated his throat just a little bit more. Zoë throws back her head and joins the others in the chorus. Vangeli plucks and slashes at the baglamas. For such a tiny thing, its sound almost drowns out the engine.

'*He's smoking the hookah, with Turkish hashish . . .*'

Apostoli coughs and begins to laugh. Vangeli curses him, laughing as well, and chops out chords as they shriek the next chorus:

'*That's how they pass their lives, the pashas of this world . . .*'

So they don't hear the plane swoop down at the road behind them. They hear nothing but their own voices even when the car lurches and seems to leap up from the road. Zoë thinks she is still

144

singing as the world beyond the windscreen twists and she sees blue sky, black smoke and then a flash of even paler blue, yellow and a single black cross, like a reptile's eye. *It's seen me*, she thinks, and then the world smashes her against the roof of the car and pinches her out like a candle flame.

Someone has dragged her clear of the Citroën, which is lying on its roof in prickly scrub by the side of the road. The engine is burning lazily, and a patch of flowering broom is smouldering, yellow flowers shrivelling in the dirty flames.

'Zoë!' She blinks and a face snaps into focus, haloed by the sun. 'Are you all right, *koukla mou*?'

She sits up. Her back is sore but she knows at once that she is more or less unhurt. Looking down, she sees that she is only wearing one shoe, and that her stockings, her one good pair, are shredded. Beyond her bare foot, a pair of black and white shoes jut from the front door of the Citröen, ankles in black socks, trousers ridden up to reveal pale legs flecked with sparse hairs. Zoë looks up. Apostoli is squatting beside her. His shirt is soaked with blood and he is breathing hard.

'What's happened to us?' Zoë asks, knowing that she has the answer, but it has been mislaid.

'Those sons of bitches shot us up,' Apostoli says. Zoë puts out her hand and runs it down the slick cotton clinging to his chest. There doesn't seem to be a wound. 'It's not my blood,' Apostoli tells her.

'Oh, Christ . . . whose?'

'Vangeli's in there. They've killed him.' Apostoli glances towards the car and crosses himself. 'Pavlo bled all over me but it's just a cut on his face. I think his arm's broken, though. Vangeli . . . Don't look at him, Zoë. Promise me, little bird.' He puts a hand over his face and his shoulders begin to heave.

Zoë stands up, almost falls. She kicks off her one shoe. Resting her hand on Apostoli's head, she strokes his hair, which is matted with pomade and dust.

'*Aman, aman,*' she murmurs. *Aman.* The soul's own word. There is nothing else to say.

'*Aman, vré* Vangeli,' Apostoli answers, and begins to sob.

Pavlo is behind them, sitting with his back against a carob tree. His face is a bisected mask: half drying blood, half bone-white skin, and two blood-flecked eyes staring, horrified, at the wreck of the car.

'How are you, little one?' At twenty-four, Pavlo is a year younger than her, but she still thinks of him as a boy. *Aman* . . . 'Does it hurt?' she says, kneeling down beside him among the hard, shiny carob pods.

'I don't know. I don't know. Why did I have to go to Khalkis?' He screws his eyes shut and begins to rock. It is so quiet that she can hear the bark of the tree creak against his back. 'My arm's fucked. I'll never play again now.'

'Och, your arm is fine.' She takes his clenched left fist very carefully and makes him extend his fingers. 'Look, stupid. It isn't broken.'

'It hurts like a bastard.'

'A sprain. Remember what Mama said? A sprain hurts worse than a broken bone? How did she know that, eh?' She clucks soothingly as her fingers run softly under his jacket: everything feels as it should. But Pavlo yelps. 'I think you've broken a rib or two,' Zoë tells him. 'That's nothing. Now let me look at your face.'

Pavlo jerks his head away. 'Vangeli's dead.'

146

'Shush,' she says, but her lip starts to tremble.

'It's my fault. I had to have that bouzouki, didn't I? Why couldn't I leave it alone?'

She cups his cheek in her palm. 'Because you're the best bouzouki player in Athens. It isn't your fault there's a war.'

'Is it . . . is it broken, Zoë? Apostoli pulled me out. I don't remember what happened to it.' She frowns, but when she sees the look in his eyes, something between horror and pleading, she takes his good hand.

'What do you want me to do, Pavlaki?'

'Would you look for me, Zoë? Find it?' His hand squeezes hers, painfully. Zoë looks around hurriedly for Apostoli, but he is limping away up the road, waving his arms above his head. Another plane? No, he wouldn't be waving at the Germans. Zoë can't think properly. She sees Vangeli's shoes, the front end of the car burning quite merrily now, and stands up, begins to walk towards the smoke. Her body doesn't feel as if it belongs to her. Everything is too bright. She hears every dry leaf as they crunch under her feet. When she reaches the car she shuts her left eye so she can't see Vangeli's legs. There is a terrible smell of burning oil and spilt petrol.

The roof of the Citroën has become a small lake of Vangeli's blood in which things rise up like islands: her lost shoe, the hash pipe, a beer bottle. The dead man's arm is thrown out, the hand loosely holding Apostoli's baglamas. Something makes her take hold of the neck and pull it free. Vangeli's fingers drag against the strings and sound a hollow, ugly chord. She backs out of the car, puts the instrument down carefully. But she has to go back inside. Whimpering to herself, she ducks back into the shadows, into the noise of crackling flames and the tick of hot metal. The dark red leather seats loom over her like toothless gums. She retches, covers her mouth, hears herself whimper. *Aman, aman . . .* There is a flash of colour at the far side of the car, in front of the smashed window: the cheap, garish wool of a peasant blanket. She forces herself to put her knee on the lip of the roof and leans in, grabbing the underside of the front seat above her. Reaching, she just catches the edge of the rough weave and tugs frantically. A bundle shoots towards her, bumps over Vangeli's arm. The head of the bouzouki nearly hits her in the face and she jerks back, opens both eyes. For a moment, she sees the windscreen, a cobweb of cracks spinning away from a fist-sized hole, and in front of it, the dead man, lying on his back, dark suit jacket open, his shirt blackened, and where his head ought to be . . .

Zoë is crawling backwards as fast as she can, coughing bile. She discovers she still has hold of the bouzouki when she hears the hollow knock of its bowl striking the edge of the car's roof. It takes all her strength to pick herself up. Then she forces herself back to the car, where, eyes tight shut, she retrieves her shoe, staggers back to Pavlo and dumps the bloody bundle into his lap. He says nothing, but attacks the tangled blanket with trembling fingers.

'She's not broken, Zoë! Look!' He holds the bouzouki by its neck and jabs the head at the sky. The sun catches the mother of pearl and it flashes like lightning. 'Didn't I say I was worried she'd break her neck?'

'Oh, Pavlo. I love you.' Zoë slumps down next to him. His cigarettes are still in his waistcoat pocket. She pulls out the flat white Papastratos box with its gold circle and big red number one. Her hands are shaking so badly that she can hardly light one for Pavlo and one for herself. 'I saw Vangeli . . .' Suddenly, she begins to cry, great heaving sobs. 'Horrible, horrible,' she manages, between spasms.

'My God.' Pavlo leans against her. 'What have we done, Zozo?'

'We?' Zoë has managed to get herself under control.

'The world. This fucking world! Now I know why Mama never made us pray to the icon. God's a monster. Zoë . . . in my jacket pocket . . . inside.' His voice has changed. There is a familiar whine: the pain, she tells herself, but when she follows his instructions and slips her hand into the pocket, the little glass bottle she finds has *POISON* printed on the label in red, and in smaller letters, *morphine tartarate.* 'A New Zealand medic sold them to me,' Pavlo says, taking the bottle with trembling hands.

'This isn't why you went to Khalkis?' she asks, suddenly very tired. But Pavlo laughs weakly.

'Why would I bother? There's so much junk in Athens now, with all the soldiers . . .' He trails off, and studies the label. 'Half a grain . . . for fuck's sake,' he mutters, and shakes out a handful, nine or ten pills.

'Pavlo!' Zoë shouts, but he has already shoved them into his mouth. He chews, wincing, and swallows with difficulty.

'Five grains is hardly anything, Zozo,' he whispers, and leans his head back against the tree. He closes his eyes, then opens them again. 'I'm sorry,' he says. 'But you know, if there was a doctor here, what would he do, eh? Pills . . .' His eyes close again and his tongue, pale and flecked with half-dissolved white powder, runs slowly across his lips.

Zoë will never know what she is about to do – force his mouth open like a dog and stick her fingers into it, perhaps, dredge out the morphine sludge – because just then there is a low rumbling and she crouches, thinking it is another plane, but then she hears Apostoli yelling over by the road and sees that a small car is coming down the wide loop of road towards them. Pavlo's head keeps falling forward onto his chest. She has seen him nodding off many times before and she hates it: it terrifies her. 'Pavlo!' she says into his ear. But he just grins at her, sloppily, showing his pill-speckled teeth.

'Zoë! Pavlo!' Apostoli is yelling at them from a few yards down the road. 'Come here! Quickly!'

She gets up and starts to limp towards him. Dried leaves and twigs are sharp under her feet so she decides to put her shoes back on. Her toes squish into clotting blood. One strap is almost broken but she manages to cinch it tight. *I'm tottering like a whore*, she thinks, as she steps out onto the road. There, bearing down on them in a cloud of dust, is the car, small, green and open-topped. It looks like a toy, in which its three occupants barely fit.

CHAPTER TEN

'How long, do you think, Sergeant?' Tom peers into the smoking engine of the Austin 8. The oily castings and tubing are as interesting to him, and as meaningless, as Chinese calligraphy. The Signals sergeant is stripped to the waist and is rattling a spanner around in the depths of the machine. Arms glistening with sweat and grease, he looks like a vet straining to deliver an iron calf.

'Couple of minutes, sir,' he gasps. 'If you'll hand me that socket wrench . . . no, *that* one, please, sir . . .' He grunts, swears lividly, his New Zealand vowels echoing tinnily off the raised bonnet. Tom looks up and down the road. He watches the heat rising, the long view rippling to the north and to the south. *Two weeks ago*, he thinks, *it was snowing*.

Tom watches the sergeant's back, sunburnt pink skin contrasting with the dingy olive green of the car. He resists the urge to reach for the watercolours in his map case. Second Lieutenant Kerr is sitting on the boot of the open-topped car, feet on the passenger seat, scanning the sky. He works the bolt of his tommy gun, pulling it back, letting it snap back. Pull, snap. Pull, snap. He has been doing it since they left Kriekouki.

I was in a battle, Tom says to himself, *but I have no bloody idea what I did*. Two weeks – less – of fighting, of terrible roads, snow and bombs. Sleep, when it has come, has only brought the cold-sweat memory of Stukas. Daylight brings the real thing, and the hollow cough of mortars.

They were going to hold the line at Thermopylae. 'It's been done before,' said a jolly captain who was trying as hard as he could, and Tom didn't have the heart to tell him that it hadn't turned out particularly well the first time. This time, though, it went better than expected: the New Zealand and British artillery managed to hold up the German tanks long enough for the rest of the troops to withdraw south. Tom's battery were in action by a little stream that ran across a plain lush with olives and stands of reeds. Mountains rising on the left, the sea close enough to smell on the right. Then they pulled back through Molos. Tom was getting his guns into position again when his colonel sauntered over.

'Collyer. We've been told to send someone to HQ in Athens. They need a report, apparently. Bloody waste of time at this point but . . .' He sighed. The colonel, a middle-aged man with close-cut grey hair and a sculpted face that always reminded Tom of a pharaoh he'd seen in the museum at Alexandria, looked at Tom with eyes that hadn't been rested for days. He wasn't a bad type, Tom had decided. In fact he was a rather good type, always quick to encourage and not afraid to stand on the gun line, even when things were very tricky indeed. 'Can't really spare anyone but it'll have to be you, Collyer. I want you to take a car – ask the quartermaster.' The orderly officer, a red-faced man with a sparse moustache and a receding chin, jogged over at that point and said something to the colonel. 'And Collyer, you need to give a couple of Signals chaps a ride to Marathon. It's out of your way, I'm afraid.'

'OK, sir.' Tom saluted wearily. The colonel wiped his face with a sleeve and stuck his unlit pipe between his teeth. A flight of stukas was passing overhead. As the two men watched, they banked and their sirens began to screech. A few moments later, dull explosions rolled across from the direction of Thebes.

'Not quite a shambles, Collyer, eh? Not quite. Not *yet*. A bloody mess, but not a shambles.' He tapped his teeth loudly with the stem of his pipe, looking around at the portees and trucks. 'You're GPO of C Battery, aren't you?' Tom nodded obediently. The colonel knew perfectly well who he was. 'Seeing as you got thrown in at the deep end, and you should have been troop leader, not GPO, you've done bloody well. Anyway, can't have a second lieutenant as GPO, so I'm promoting you to lieutenant, effective immediately.'

'Thank you, sir,' Tom said reluctantly.

'You're a good officer, Collyer,' the colonel told him. 'Hate to use you as an errand boy, but if you have to be one, you may as well outrank the Signallers, eh?' The pipe went back between his teeth and he winked at Tom. 'Hope I'll see you on the beach at Rafina tonight. Best of luck, old man. Oh, and here's another order for you: scrounge up as much petrol as you can and get it to our muster points. Know where those are?'

'Roughly – around Markopoulon, sir.'

'Roughly.' The colonel chuckled bitterly. 'There are fuel dumps in Athens – probably a lot more on the docks at Piraeus. Find some Divisional Petrol Company drivers and get them to Markopoulon on the bloody double. Clear?'

'Clear, sir.'

'Good man. Well, best of luck, Collyer.'

'And to you, sir.'

Tom looks up at the sky again. 'How are things in there, Sergeant?' he calls. No answer except for more clanking. The country is almost silent around them. Now and again a bird pipes up and goat bells clank a little way off. *Strange that the quiet of the road, the birds singing in the trees, should be upsetting after the battle*, Tom thinks. He lights a cigarette, holds the packet up for Kerr.

'Oh, God, thanks,' the second lieutenant breathes. He looks far too young to be here. His hand is unsteady as he lights a match, sucks the flame into the tobacco. 'Where do you think they are?' he asks.

'Who?' Tom realises that he is thinking about the classrooms at Chelsea, of turpentine, of fleshy older women lying naked and bored.

'The Jerries.'

'Well, they're not here, and that's all that matters.' Tom looks up. The sky is terrifyingly blue. *Damn it*, he thinks. *He's got me at it now.* 'You know that isn't going to do a bloody thing against a Stuka, don't you?'

Kerr pats the gun. 'Psychological. Better than nothing.'

'Fair enough.'

'Righto,' says the sergeant, straightening up. 'I think that's done it. If you'd start her, sir . . .'

The engine turns over and fires at Tom's third push of the starter. The sergeant, whose name is Taylor, pulls on his shirt and battledress top and slides behind the wheel. 'We're off,' he says jauntily, as if he were driving his children to the seaside on a bank holiday. Tom hears the click of steel against steel behind him, and he knows that Kerr is looking up into the empty blue, his fingers working the bolt. Psychological.

Of course it is Kerr who sees the plane. He throws himself forward between the seats, pointing up and ahead at the long, thin shadow that has appeared against the blue.

'Bf 110,' says Taylor automatically. The sergeant's knuckles whiten momentarily around the wheel, then relax.

'He's going away from us, Kerr,' Tom reassures the young man – *Not much younger than me*, he thinks. He carefully slips his hands beneath his thighs so that the others can't see them shake. *Christ*, he thinks, *all the effort it takes just to look as if I'm in charge*. 'Marathon isn't far now, I don't think. What did that last signpost say, twenty-five kilometres?'

'You've got to drive to Athens as well. And back,' Taylor reminds him, too calmly.

Tom chooses to ignore this. 'Been in Athens before, Sergeant?'

'Landed there, sir. Had a nice picture taken of me and some mates up on the Parthenon.'

'The Parthenon . . .'

'Can't miss it, sir,' the sergeant says, kindly. 'Load of old stones up on a cliff.'

'Look! The bastard hit something,' says Kerr, pointing to where, a mile and a half away, a spiral of familiar, greasy smoke is winding up from the road.

Soon they are near enough to see that the smoke is rising from a wrecked car, which is burning upside down in a patch of flowering broom. 'Someone's still alive,' says Taylor. Sure enough, a man in a bloodstained white shirt is standing at the side of the road, waving his arms at them. 'Looks like another

155

one as well. A girl.' Tom shields his eyes to get a better look. The man, thickset and dark, with a heavy moustache, is staggering drunkenly, zig-zagging across the narrow road. Tom sees that, yes, there is another person, a young woman, crouching next to what looks like a body propped against a small tree. Hearing the car, she looks up and gets painfully to her feet. In the dazzling light she is a smear of dark cloth and a blurred, deathly pale face. Head down, she limps towards the white-shirted man.

'Poor bastards,' Sergeant Taylor mutters. *Can't be helped*, Tom thinks. They are making good time at last and, according to his map, they are only another half hour from Marathon. But the sergeant is braking. 'I'd rather not run this bugger over, sir. He's all over the place.' The man is staggering across the road, flailing his arms, and Taylor has to slow right down to avoid him, enough for the man to catch hold of the passenger door. He starts bellowing into Tom's face.

'*Inglesi? Inglis?*'

'English, yes,' says Tom wearily. 'Stop the car, then, Sergeant Taylor. I suppose we might be able to do something.'

Tom steps out. He has seen enough in the past two weeks to confirm that the man in front of him isn't wounded. Shocked, of course, quite badly, but the blood must belong to someone else. Not the young woman: she wouldn't be walking if she'd lost that much. The man against the tree over there . . . Strangely, he seems to be holding what looks like a sort of mandolin.

'Do you speak English?' he asks the man in front of him, who is blinking and licking his lips. 'Here, old chap,' he adds, holding out his tin of ration cigarettes. The man pulls one out and Tom lights it for him, holding the bloodied hand steady.

'*Efcharistó* . . .'

'How many of you are there? How many hurt?' Tom wants to be patient, he really does, but there isn't time for this. Something in the wrecked car's engine explodes with a small bang and he flinches. He sees Taylor flinch as well. 'Has anyone been killed?' he asks, louder. The man just shakes his head, disbelief in his face.

'Νεκρός,' he rasps. 'Νεκρός.'

Nekros: Tom knows that word at least, from the last days in the mountains, when his battery had been in action alongside a Greek unit. 'Dead?' Tom says. 'How many?'

'One.' The word, a perfect, round English word, takes him by surprise. 'In the car,' the voice continues. He realises that it is the young woman who is speaking to him. She has limped to the Greek man's side. Her face is streaked with dust and her dark blonde hair, cut just above her shoulders and parted fashionably to the side, is tangled. A damp lock of it is hanging across her face. She must be his age, more or less.

'Yes, one is dead,' the man says, as if the woman has unlocked his tongue. 'The other . . . he is hurt.'

Taylor has gone over to look at the pale man by the tree. He trots back. 'Young bloke, bit knocked about. Groggy but not much wrong with him. There's another one in the car. Dead as you please. Sodding mess,' he adds under his breath, glancing at the woman.

'You are going to Athens?' asks the man. Tom nods. 'You must take Kyria Valavani to Piraeus. Please. You take her. This one—' He points to the young man under the tree. 'This one and me, doesn't matter, we will go by ourselves. But you take her.'

'We'd better be going,' says Taylor.

'Right, Sergeant,' says Tom firmly. Kerr has already jumped into the front seat and is checking the magazine of his gun, whistling to himself through dry lips.

'Come on, sir.' Taylor climbs behind the wheel and starts the engine. Tom turns away but the man grabs his arm. Tom raises his hand to bat him away, but sees a watery gleam of pure desperation in the man's eyes. *He loves her*, he thinks. *Is it his daughter, or . . . ?*

'Please! You must take her with you. It is too dangerous for this lady here!'

'Apostoli . . .' The woman takes the man's free hand. The three of them stand there, a strained trinity. Tom looks from the man to the woman. She isn't looking at him but at her companion, eyes down, lower lip caught behind her front teeth, which are streaked with scarlet lipstick. Her skin looks unnaturally white but he sees this is face powder. Her face is a play of angles and ellipses: square jaw and straight nose, delicate heart-shaped chin, the lower lip, now released, a defiant horizontal slash, the upper a perfect half moon. Her eyes are large, hazel green, the shape of olive leaves. It occurs to Tom that this woman can certainly take care of herself. She is whispering to the man urgently. It sounds like water trickling over rocks: pattering, sibilant, but mournful. He thought for a moment that she must be English but she obviously is not.

Taylor clears his throat noisily from the car. Tom curses silently and looks down at the ground, willing the man to let him go so that he doesn't have to push him off, make an ugly scene that will just add to the world's misery. He sees crushed cigarette ends. He sees the woman's shoes. One is dusty cream and black patent leather. The other is a mass of clotting blood. Whether it is the ruined shoe that touches him, or the lock of amber hair hanging in front of those hazel eyes, or the soft flow of her voice, in which he can almost feel a deep, resonant echo, he comes to a decision.

'We'd better take her,' he hears himself saying. 'Climb in the back,' he tells the woman. 'Please be as quick as you can. We're in rather a hurry.'

'*Aman* – thanks be to God,' says the man. 'This one, she is a singer. Famous! She has many recordings. You must look after her, Kapetanios.' He pulls Tom to him and kisses him hard on both cheeks. 'You are a good man,' he says. Then he almost drags the woman over to the Austin. Her red mouth is open – trying to protest, or too stunned to react.

'You'll be all right,' Tom assures the man. He pauses, sticks out his hand. The other man takes it. 'Good luck.'

He has to put his foot on the rear wheel and vault in beside the woman in the cramped back seat of the car. As soon as he is in, Taylor stamps on the accelerator. One, two, three screeches from the gearbox and they are at the next bend in the road. 'Are you all right, miss?' Taylor asks the woman, shouting over the rushing air. 'There's some water somewhere.'

A canteen is found and passed back to the woman, who is sitting straight-backed and rigid, hands clasped, white-knuckled, in her lap. She takes a sip from the felt-wrapped flask, then a proper swig, head thrown back, and Tom can't help but notice the pulsing of her throat as she drinks, the soft blue outline of a vein in her long neck. Kerr has twisted around in his seat and is staring at her with a slack-faced intensity that suggests a child gazing at a large iced cake through a baker's window.

'Forgotten the Luftwaffe already, Kerr?' Tom asks, irritated.

'I say, look, how come you get to sit next to her?' Kerr is almost pouting behind his sparse, sandy moustache.

'Help Sergeant Taylor and look out for the Marathon turn-off,' Tom says, ignoring him. 'Should be just up ahead.'

The woman puts down the flask and wipes her lips. Glancing sideways, she sees him looking at her. Tom looks away politely, but not so quickly that he fails to notice the darkness around her eyes. He doesn't want to make her any more uncomfortable, so he squeezes himself against the side of the car, aware of his bare, dirty knees. He'd had to cut off his trouser legs yesterday: they had caught fire as he'd been dragging things from a burning lorry. He hadn't been badly burnt, though he had felt briefly ridiculous, and now he feels ridiculous again: his legs are alternately white and red, streaked with dirt and calamine lotion. Despite her ruined clothes, the young woman beside him carries herself like a lady, and she is . . . Tom presses his fingers into his forehead. He is horribly tired, and his thoughts are rattling. But yes, she's rather beautiful.

CHAPTER ELEVEN

Zoë sits huddled against the side of the car. She is hemmed in by the concertina struts of the folded-down roof, which are digging into her back. The seat itself is upholstered in ridges of hard green leather and the wheel wells jut up into it, painted metal curves that amplify every pebble that passes beneath the tyres. Zoë can't get her arm comfortably over the roof struts, and the wheel well is too smooth and hard to sit on.

They have turned off the main road onto a smaller, rougher one, winding through low hills towards the sea. The car bounces and rattles along, and with every bounce, the slippery leather slides her towards the middle. The officer has wedged himself into his own corner, one hand gripping a strut, the other hooked into one of the pockets of his filthy battledress tunic, which is undone to reveal a thin khaki shirt. His long legs are pulled up awkwardly, ankles jammed under the seat in front of him. He isn't wearing shorts, as she had thought, but trousers that have been clumsily sawn off at the knees, which are burnt raw and smeared with some dirty pink ointment. He has his face turned away, his peaked cap, with its badge of a crowned cannon, pulled down low against the sun.

The soldier in the front seat, the one with the machine gun, keeps leering at her in the rear-view mirror. He has sandy hair, slicked back with pomade, and a faint, boyish moustache. He is scared, she can tell: glancing at the sky, then back to the mirror, then back to the sky. His fingers are tapping a hard rhythm against the wooden stock of his gun. When he shifts his eyes to the mirror again, the driver raises his large hand and pointedly adjusts it so that the eyes disappear.

'I'd be ever so grateful if you kept your eyes on the map, sir,' he says evenly.

The man beside her shakes his head and mutters something under his breath. He arches his back, wincing. Since the crash, she has been numb, wrapped in the soft padding of shock. But now she realises that her own body is beginning to ache. Something clatters in the boot and it sounds like the bullets coming through the metal roof of Apostoli's car. Then it all comes back: the howl of the tyres, the abrupt silence as the wheels left the road and they were all weightless for a moment, rolling through air. Zoë presses her forehead against the cool metal of the roof struts. When she closes her eyes she sees Vangeli's ruined body. And the English voices – the men in front are arguing about something – are like long fingernails digging into her, finding much older scars, opening them up one by one. She doesn't want any of the memories, but still they come. Twisted against the roof struts, breathing in the scent of warm oil, they come.

She feels a gentle tap on her arm. Biting her lip, she turns enough to see a crumpled red and yellow pack of cigarettes held in long, oil-stained fingers. The hand shakes the pack so that a cigarette, bent and creased, rises clear of the foil. She takes it, not looking at the officer, trying not to snatch, trying to keep her own hand from shaking. A box of matches appears – *England's Glory*, she reads – and she manages to strike one behind cupped fingers. The cigarette tastes strange: thin and acrid. But she inhales greedily. She hears the officer light his own and feels him turn towards her again.

'Does it hurt?' His voice is polite and careful. She stares at the grass drifting by at the side of the road. She shrugs curtly, knowing she is being insufferably rude, that it isn't fair of her, that these men have helped her, saved her, maybe . . . 'You've had a bad time,' he is saying. 'Those bruises on your legs look nasty.' Reflexively, she jerks her knees towards the door and finds that, yes, they hurt.

'I am all right,' she says, not looking at him. She feels ill and full of guilty rage, guilty because she can tell that the man beside her is trying to be kind even though he is exhausted. He is talking to her partly to keep himself awake, she understands, and a little quiver of sympathy rises through her angry nausea. She shrugs again, face still turned away. She can feel him, too near. His hip is an inch away from hers. Her sympathy evaporates. Everything is too near. What would happen if she simply stood up and jumped into the smudged air beyond the car? But she's too tired to do that. She breathes out smoke, which vanishes into the dust cloud behind them.

'And – I'm sorry to be so curious – where did you learn such good English?'

Zoë takes a last drag and flings the cigarette end away. A heavy, scratchy blanket of nausea envelops her. She leans out over the blurred tarmac but she isn't sick. She swallows hard, forcing the sourness down, feeling tears burning in the corners of her eyes. She can't bear it, any of it. Pavlo, nodding off next to a burning car. Vangeli . . . She clamps her mind closed around that memory. The smoke rising above the sea, which they can see now, the hill cresting, the car speeding downhill towards houses, the jagged sweep of coast and the long back of Evvia across the gulf. She can't bear the jolly whine of the engine. More than anything, she can't bear the young officer with his scraped knees and his gentle, tired voice. But she feels him waiting for her to say something else, to perform. Anger stabs at her. The officer is watching her from under the peak of his cap. A lock of black hair has escaped and hangs diagonally across his forehead. His eyes are full of concern. She sees that his lips are chapped almost white. If she could, she would wave her hand and erase him from the world. But all she can do is speak.

'Who taught me English?' she says, drawing the words from her throat like steel wires. 'Well, obviously . . .' She forces her tongue to make the rudest imitation of every aristocratic Englishwoman who has ever graced the patched screens of the Piraeus cinemas. 'Obviously, it was my nanny.' *Nanny.* She draws it out, a sneer, three syllables, four, her eyes on him like razor blades.

The officer blinks and turns abruptly away. *Good*, she thinks. *Now leave me alone.* And then she starts, silently, to cry, and the breeze dries the tears into little streaks of cold on her cheeks.

A few minutes later she feels the car slow down. She raises her face from where she has pushed it into the crook of her arm, and sees that they are in a small town, almost a village, surrounded by British soldiers standing in groups, sitting against walls, in trucks, on motorcycles. The car judders to a halt and the two men in the front seat get out and walk over to a soldier with a red band around his cap.

She watches the officer – he is taller than she had thought – climb out stiffly. He shakes hands with the other two, walks quickly back to the car and swings into the driver's seat. He struggles momentarily with the gearstick, curses, then grins as the car lurches forward.

'Right, then,' he says, to the dust-filmed windscreen. They drive off, and he doesn't turn to look at her, not once, as they go past pine woods and clusters of half-built houses. Tentatively at first, then more confidently, she stretches out as far as she can across the back seat.

'Wait.' The officer brakes suddenly, and Zoë catches her breath, looking up at the sky for the plane that must be diving at them, but the officer is striding past her to the back of the car. He opens the boot and then a large coat is dropped onto the seat beside her. 'I'm afraid it's a bit barbaric,' he mutters. Then the door slams and they are off again. She bundles up the coat, which is made of thick, scratchy wool and smells of sweat and acrid smoke, and tucks it under her head. But the car is bouncing along and the seat is hard and slippery, and it is too much effort to keep herself braced between the doors. So she sits up and pulls the coat over her knees.

They are getting close to Athens now; the signs say Maroussi and Kifisia. The road is busier here: cars stream by in the other lane, filled with people and luggage. Horses pull carts. Donkeys trudge along. Men and women push bicycles festooned with suitcases. Children drag along behind their parents. There is a bus, even a couple of Athenian taxis. In the villages, the windows are shuttered. Outside one hamlet they pass a line of seven or eight people walking northwards, away from the city. Men, some women, one of them old, a boy of about ten. The man in front is leading a small donkey to which an oddly festive cart has been hitched: a milk cart or something like it, gaudily and freshly painted. The cart is piled with suitcases and carpet bags, and each person, even the old woman, is carrying something. The jolly little cart, the orderly clothes of the walkers: they could be on their way to a village fete, a saint's day, except for the wide, unfocused eyes that stare from every face. Behind them, in the direction of Piraeus, the columns of smoke are thicker. Zoë can't bear to look at those little figures. She can feel their fear, their confusion. Little stick figures, always shoved into someone else's story. But she sees the officer looking. His head turns here and there, his eyes darting, always avoiding her but seeing everything else. 'God,' she hears him whisper, once, as they pass a mother crouched at the roadside, head in hands, while her three children tug at her black shawl. There are soldiers everywhere too: every olive grove or clump of pines is hiding a clutch of trucks, tanks, guns and men huddled under camouflage netting which festoons the trees like huge, filthy cobwebs. Some men turn to stare at her, but there is no curiosity in their faces, just exhaustion and anxiety.

They have been rattling along at a good pace, but a mile or so after the officer has turned onto a wider road on the outskirts of Kifisia, the way is blocked by a soldier on a motorcycle. Beyond him, a short line of trucks and a crowd of soldiers, all stripped to the waist.

'Can't come through, I'm afraid, sir. There's a lorry on its side, and it's blocking the whole road.'

'Damn. Is there a way around?'

'Yes, sir, but it's chaos. We're trying to get everything clear for the evacuation tonight.' The motorcyclist is eyeing Zoë curiously. 'Going into Athens now, sir?'

'Yes. I have to report to Headquarters. Is it still in the Acropole Palace?'

'Was this morning, sir. I'd advise you to wait here. It'll save you time in the long run. Shouldn't be more than half an hour.'

'Half an hour! Christ . . .'

The officer gets out and walks down to the stricken truck. When he comes back he looks even more tired. He takes out his cigarettes, hesitates, and turns to her.

'I can't imagine that your nanny would approve of you smoking,' he says, and his mouth twists, almost smiling.

Zoë stares at the red and yellow pack, at the long fingers holding it, their nails stained black, worn jagged. Her mind slips sideways, to the garden, to hollyhocks and starched linen. Did Miss Butland smoke? 'I can't . . .' She stops herself. 'Thank you,' she says primly. She accepts a light, but then settles back in the corner farthest from him and turns her head away, though there is nothing to look at except a newly planted olive grove, lines of slender grey-green saplings enclosed by half-collapsed stone walls and a fence of rusty barbed wire. She finishes the cigarette and throws it out into the ditch, leans back against the hot metal of the roof struts and closes her eyes. The noises of the day drift around her: guttural foreign chatter from the army trucks, the occasional whine of machinery, a twittering of sparrows among the olives. Her head is pounding and her whole body feels dented. Perhaps, though, she should get out now and make her own way home. She knows where she is, roughly – there must be a tram from Kifisia or Maroussi, or a bus . . . Oh, God. The thought of walking makes her feel sick. But she can't stay here. She winces and rubs her face. The sparrows flutter and chirp. And there is another sound, a brittle *scratch*, *shush*, *scratch* much closer to her. It sounds like an insect. Why doesn't the Englishman get rid of it? She opens her eyes, unwillingly.

She finds the Englishman sitting with his back against the driver's door, boots propped on the passenger seat. In his lap is a flat leather case, on which is laid out a pad of white paper, a small metal paintbox and another flat tin full of pencils of various lengths and some delicate paintbrushes. The Englishman, to her utter amazement, is painting. A cigarette smoulders in his left hand, which holds the improvised table steady. His right hand moves delicately yet deliberately, the brush drifting and pecking. *Scratch*, *shush*, *shush*. Forgetting her pain, Zoë leans forward, watching in disbelief. The stiff leather of the seat creaks and the Englishman looks up and she sees him properly for the first time. He has a longish face, thin enough to show angular cheekbones, which are shadowed with several days' worth of stubble. The eyes are striking: large and dark – though puffy and bruised-looking with tiredness – under arched black eyebrows. A lick of heavy black hair hangs down over his forehead. He has a nice mouth, though his lips are badly chapped from the sun.

'Oh!' he says. Is that embarrassment? She looks over the seat at the sketchpad. What she sees under the wet point of the brush is, at first, a meaningless whorl of light and shadow: blacks shading into greys and browns, a blotch of yellow. The colours of a black eye. She squints and it appears: a car, Apostoli's Citröen, on its back like a dead fly, oily smoke boiling out of it. Beside it, shrubs of broom, their flowers livid, acidic. She breathes in sharply. The Englishman closes the pad hurriedly. 'I didn't mean . . .'

'What are you doing? What are you *doing*?' she demands.

The Englishman takes a drag on his cigarette; Zoë notices that his hand is shaking very slightly. He lets the smoke out slowly through his mouth and nose. 'I'm trying to see,' he says.

'What?' Zoë doesn't believe she's heard him properly.

There is a long silence, in which Zoë almost reaches out and grabs the sketchpad. She wants to throw it into the olive grove, destroy it. But then the Englishman closes the lid of his paintbox with a snap. 'I'm trying to see. The war. All of this . . .' He waves a hand, impatiently. 'It seems so meaningless. Painting' – he holds up the pad – 'it helps to make sense of things. I don't expect you to understand because I certainly don't.'

'You are a soldier.' Zoë tries to sound disapproving but instead she hears petulance.

He shrugs. 'I'm a painter. You're a singer – if you really are a singer?' He glances at her as he tucks his paints and brushes back into the leather case, but there is no judgement in his eyes, just curiosity.

'Yes, I am a singer!' she says indignantly.

'Well, then. Have you stopped singing, now there's a war?'

'Why would I?'

'Exactly.'

'But here, now . . .'

'We're in the middle of a disaster,' he says bluntly. 'And there doesn't seem to have been any point. At all. I suppose I believe that if I paint what I've seen, draw it, make a record . . . it'll make sense somehow.'

Zoë thinks of Vangeli's fingers curled around the neck of the baglamas. 'Did you know people who were killed?'

He sighs and wipes his forehead with the back of his hand. 'Yes.'

'Can I see?' Zoë says suddenly.

'What? Yes, certainly,' he says, and shifts his legs back under the steering wheel, wincing as raw skin scrapes against the gear stick. 'Here,' he says. He holds the pad out to her. She opens it carefully.

The first painting is a rough collection of blots and lines, but in a moment these resolve into a scene: a stone wall, a ditch and a pile of earth, a large tyre, a hunched shape that is a man in a tin helmet, turned away from her, a blanket around his shoulders, smoke drifting around his head. She turns the page. Here is a truck with a contraption on its flat bed – a gun. Men are sitting behind its shield, and another man, bare-chested, is handing up a crate to one of them.

'These are all Vevi,' he says quietly.

'What is Vevi?'

'A place right up under the Yugoslavian border, near Florina. We tried to hold up an SS brigade. Obviously we didn't succeed,' he adds, not quite smiling. 'I did these while we were waiting for it all to start.' She turns the page. 'This is afterwards.' Two trucks with guns on their backs, blackened by fire. Men lying next to them, wrapped in blankets. Zoë thinks they are dead but no, they are only sleeping. One man, propped against a tyre, is smoking a pipe. She turns the page again. A road, winding through a steep-sided gorge. A river, men stripped to the waist, pushing trucks through the water. Landscapes. Soldiers, studies of soldiers, several to a page. A tank, upside down by the side of a road. A man's face, close-up, tense with effort. A truck on fire, in the foreground a thing she realises is a boot and a leg with no owner. The colours, she sees, are changing. At first they had been pale, watery, which had made the paintings seem, in a way, innocent. But as the pages turn there is less water, more paint, and the colours are heavy, muddy. The drawings are more confident. She turns another page. Three men lie in a row. One is missing a leg. They are all very plainly dead. On the opposite page, a woman cries over the body of an old man. Then a stretcher inside a lorry, a pale, wide-eyed face.

'I'm sorry, I've been thoughtless. These aren't . . .' he says, reaching for the pad, but she holds it away from him.

'No, no,' she says, gently. 'Let me see.'

She sees a man's face lit by the light of the match he is holding to his cigarette. Soldiers huddled under netting. A beak-nosed man with a pipe clamped between his teeth. And then, the car. The burning car.

'That's all there is,' he is saying, and she feels him easing her fingers very gently away from the pad. 'I've been . . .' He clears his throat, and makes a business of fumbling with the buckles of his leather case. 'I've been too busy to do any more.' He stows the case under the seat and turns towards her. 'If you don't mind me asking, what on earth were you doing on the road in the middle of all this?'

Zoë rakes her fingers through her hair. Hanks of it are solid with dried blood. What can she tell this kind, serious young man that will not sound mad? Because it had been mad. 'It was my brother,' she says eventually. 'He is a musician – we are all musicians. Apostoli, the one who stopped you, and Vangeli . . .' She feels her mouth tremble.

'It's all right,' the Englishman says hurriedly. 'I don't need to know.'

'No, no. You were very kind. I should tell you. My brother, Pavlo – he was sitting under the tree – plays the bouzouki. You know what it is . . . You know what a bouzouki is?' He shakes his head. 'A Greek instrument. Pavlo is, really, maybe the best bouzouki player in Athens.' Zoë feels a small rush of pride. 'And we had a big, a huge explosion in Piraeus Harbour a few days ago. His best bouzouki was ruined.'

'That would have been the Clan Fraser,' the Englishman says. 'Yet another disaster.'

'So, you know. Hundreds of people killed, the whole waterfront of Piraeus destroyed, and my brother is sad that his bouzouki is broken. And then he disappears. Two days ago he calls on the telephone to our friend Micho: "I'm in Khalkis.

171

Come and fetch me, please!" Now, I would have let him go to hell, honestly . . .' She pauses, because that isn't true. 'But there is a man, a famous man, who makes records, and he wants to make one more record with us, our band, before the Germans come. There is some money, he says. But I need Pavlo. So we go to Khalkis. I was going to stay, but my brother has a girlfriend, very . . . It doesn't matter. But she was going to go and I didn't want her to. She is not a good person. I said no, you can't come, I'm going, there's no room for you. And there. We went. It seemed safe – no German planes, the war was further to the north. We'll go, and come back, make our record. There is Pavlo, in Khalkis. And why do you think he went there? To get another bouzouki. Only that. A very special one, yes, but in the end . . .' She feels something hot on her cheeks. 'Damn it,' she mutters.

'Here.' Long, dirty fingers are offering her a dirty handkerchief. 'I don't have anything else, I'm afraid.'

She takes it anyway and dabs away the tears. 'Thank you. You don't have to be so kind. I am a . . .' She searches for the word. 'A nuisance.'

'Rubbish. I haven't had this much fun in years.' She looks at him, knowing her kohl is all over her face, knowing her clothes are ruined, that her hair is stiff with blood. And he looks back. Unshaven, a cluster of scabs on one cheek, his black hair greasy and dull with dust, pushing the peak of his cap away from his face with an oil-stained hand. His eyes, piercing slate-grey, are streaked with red. She can't help it: she giggles, and puts her hand over her mouth. But he is laughing as well.

'Look,' he says, 'my name's Tom. Tom Collyer. And by the way, I never had a nanny. I thought I should say. Raised by my mother. Did you have one, honestly?'

172

'Don't you believe me? Miss Butland. From Hampstead. That was back home in Smyrna. There. I have told you a secret that no one else knows.' She laughs as if it is a joke but it is quite true and she suddenly feels strange because she doesn't know why she has just told him. 'I . . . Would you like a Greek cigarette?' she asks, to change the subject.

'Why not?'

'Here,' she says, finding the packet in her bag. He takes it from her. They are her favourite brand, Santé, in a scarlet and gold box with the face of a blonde starlet gazing seductively from a sky-blue circle in the middle. He takes one of the oval cigarettes but doesn't give the box back straight away. She watches him tilt it into the light. He glances at her and back at the box.

'She's a real person,' she says. 'Zozo Dalmas. An actress. Apostoli says she looks like me, to tease me – and she's called Zoë, that's my name. Zoë Valavani. In Greek, we make that Zozo.' *I'm rambling, she tells herself. I suppose it's because I haven't spoken English for so long . . .*

'He certainly is teasing. The hair, perhaps, but . . . no, she looks nothing like you,' the Englishman – Tom – says, handing back the packet.

'Oh.' Zoë thinks she might be offended. 'She's beautiful, isn't she? Notorious. She had an affair with Kemal Atatürk himself.'

The grey eyes pass across her face. 'Truly beautiful girls don't end up on cigarette packets.'

'Oh.'

'There's some, um, some water left,' he says. It is hard to tell through the sunburn, but Zoë thinks he might be blushing. She almost giggles again, but instead she takes the canteen and sips at the warm, slightly brackish water.

'And where are you from, Captain Tom Collyer?' she asks, when they have both drunk.

'I'm just a humble lieutenant,' he says. 'And I'm from a place called Devon, in England. Though I was born in India.'

'India! What is India like?'

'I can hardly remember. We left when I was five. Very hot. Very green. There were great big butterflies in the garden. I used to pretend they were angels.'

'Butterflies as big as angels!' Zoë says. There is something she can't quite touch, something just out of reach. Has she seen butterflies like that? Pictures in a book? No, someone told her once, someone . . .

But whatever it is vanishes in the whine of the starter motor. The engine coughs and growls. 'Looks like we're on our way,' Lieutenant Collyer says. He shoves the car into gear, then pauses. 'Would you like to sit in the front? Actually no, don't. This way I can pretend I'm your chauffeur.'

'But you mustn't! You're a . . . a lieutenant!'

'Believe me, Miss Valavani, I'd much rather be a chauffeur. Right. To the Acropole Palace. Then I'll take you wherever you need to go.'

It takes another half an hour to reach the centre of Athens, and Zoë has to guide Lieutenant Collyer to the hotel on Patission Street where General Wilson has set up his headquarters. The city feels, not deserted, but haunted, and Zoë keeps the heavy army coat tucked around her, even though the day is warm. Fear is hanging in the air like freezing mist. Trams are still rattling along Patission, though they are mostly empty. Soldiers are running in and out of the hotel, loading boxes onto trucks.

'Hope I'm not too late,' Lieutenant Collyer mutters, parking the car behind one of the trucks. He looks up at the white facade. 'Looks quite posh. I wish I could buy you a drink, Miss Valavani. But we live in unhappy times, so I think you'd better wait here. I shouldn't be gone long.'

Zoë spends a few minutes in the back of the car, but she doesn't like the way the soldiers keep looking at her, so she gets out and limps across the street to the trees in front of the polytechnic. It takes four cigarettes, smoked slowly, leaning against a eucalyptus tree in the shadow of a shuttered kiosk, for the lieutenant to reappear. As each one is finished, she leans, breathing raggedly, thinking that in a moment she will turn and walk away, down to Omonia Square and the metro station. Let the earth swallow her up. But each time she opens the packet, runs her finger across the silly blonde head of Zozo Dalmas. And finally the lieutenant comes jogging briskly down the steps, his cap under his arm. She watches him from across the wide, empty boulevard, sees him stop short when he finds the car empty. He stands with his hand on the door, his shoulders drooping, then he drags his hand across his face. *Ridiculous Englishman. Skinny boy with silly cut-off trousers and burnt legs. 'I can pretend I'm your chauffeur.'* Before she knows what she's done she has stepped out from under the tree, out into the street. She doesn't know why. Because she's alone? Because it is a long walk back to Kokkinia? And then he sees her, and smiles, walks around the car and opens the door for her. 'Sorry about that. Took much longer than I thought. Complete waste of time as well. Now let me take you home. I have to go to Piraeus . . .'

'But I live in Piraeus!'

'Fantastic. I need to scrounge up some petrol on the docks. If you tell me how to get there, I'll drop you off first.'

She settles into the seat beside him. 'My chauffeur.'

'At your service.' As they pull away, an air raid siren begins to howl and Zoë tenses, shivering, hugging herself. Trying to hide. *I'm trying to turn myself inside out*, she thinks. But then she hears his voice, gentle, foreign but not foreign. 'Don't worry, Miss Valavani. You're safe.'

'Nothing is safe,' she whispers.

'You're right. But you'll be OK. I promise. My word as an officer.'

'British soldier. You're leaving.' She sighs, without meaning to, and their eyes meet. She blinks in surprise: she will miss him.

The officer looks startled as well. He seems about to say something. But then he shakes his head and grins. 'My word as a painter, then. Means more. Not much, but a bit.' *That wasn't what you were going to say*, she thinks, and the sting of regret that she feels surprises her for a second time.

'All right.' His voice, oddly, does make her feel a little less scared. She dares to lift her head, in time to see the entrance to the metro station in Omonia Square slip by.

'But one thing does make me sad in all this.'

'What?'

'It's such a shame I'll never hear you sing.'

CHAPTER TWELVE

Tom parks the Austin beside a twisted black cage that has recently been a tram car and lopes across the rubble of Piraeus's waterfront. Petrol Company headquarters is supposed to be in the warehouse of G. Leoforos Bros, but there is no warehouse. There is barely a waterfront. The green-painted lorries and oil tankers parked as neatly as the rubble permits are all deserted. He sees pyramids of crates, abandoned cranes, a big 5.5-inch gun, its barrel neatly sealed with oil cloth. Out in the sea, the black smoke they have been driving towards all day is roiling up from an oil tanker which is lying on its side in the centre of a ring of blazing fuel. All around it, masts and cranes jut out of the water. Warships lie a little further out. Motorboats, lighters and dinghies are plying back and forth, avoiding the flames and the wrecks. His boots crunch through broken glass and he jumps over festoons of cables. The girl – Zoë – had been right: the whole waterfront area of Piraeus is completely wrecked.

The girl . . . In the end, she hadn't taken him out of his way at all. She had decided that she would be safer with friends near the harbour, which hadn't made much sense to him, but he couldn't argue with her. So she directed them through ever seedier quarters of Piraeus, past the railway station, which was half ruined and smouldering and down a narrow street lined with low buildings, some faced with grainy, crumbling plaster, some just rough brick. Telephone wires criss-crossed between tile roofs, tin roofs.

'Here,' she said, as they crawled along between two columns of Australian walking wounded. A blue painted door, a sign above it, ΤΟ ΚΟΡΔΕΛΙΟ. There was a hole in the cobbled street outside, and several men were sawing and hammering away at what looked like the remains of an old ship's mast. Tom pulled up outside, went around and opened her door, then blocked the pavement while the girl climbed out. A couple of bandaged Australians catcalled, weakly.

'Thank you, Mr Collyer.' That perfect voice. He didn't want to leave her there in the middle of this chaos. He didn't want to leave her at all. But he noticed that she was more confident, suddenly; more at ease. *She'll be fine without you*, he told himself. So he forced a grin and touched a forefinger to the peak of his cap.

'Goodbye, ma'am. It's been my pleasure.'

'Goodbye.' She stopped, and laid a hand very lightly on his arm. 'Please, be safe.'

'And you.' He watched her go through the blue door. Then it shut behind her, and though the street was full of noise and people, he felt, for a moment, quite alone.

Tom eventually sees a British officer in the stern of one of the ferries, sitting uncomfortably on the edge of a deckchair in front of a small cafe table, tapping on a portable typewriter. He goes up the gangplank, and salutes the unshaven captain in stained tropical dress. Behind him, wounded men are lying across the walkway or sitting propped against the bulkhead, sleeping or talking quietly. There is a tang of disinfectant and tobacco in the air.

'I'm looking for 4th NZ Brigade Petrol Company,' says Tom. The captain squints at Tom with red-rimmed eyes.

'Welcome to HMS *Arethusa*,' he says wearily. 'No Petrol Company here, I'm afraid.'

'Really? You don't happen to . . .'

'Christ.' The captain flops back in his chair and pushes his cap back on his head. His dirty khaki clothes and sunburnt skin look almost garish against the cheerful holiday stripes of the deckchair sling. 'Nothing's where it ought to be.' He sighs and pushes himself upright again. 'It's all a bloody tangle.'

'Yes, I know. My colonel detailed me to bring back as much petrol as I could to Rafina.'

'We've got plenty of petrol. Oceans of it. But all the trucks have been put out of action.'

'Why?'

'To deny the enemy. Completely pointless, of course. The Greeks have been siphoning off rivers of it but there'll be plenty left for Jerry.' The captain stands up. He leans over the rail and looks up at the sky. 'Bloody Stukas. Regular as a cuckoo clock. Should be another lot over any minute. Do you see that?' He is pointing to a long shape in the water alongside the harbour wall, a hundred or so yards to the north. 'Most beautiful bloody ship I've ever seen. Huge white steam yacht. The *Hellas*. Looked more like the *Cutty Sark*. She came in last night and started taking on a big party of New Zealand wounded. Then the Stukas came and . . .' He coughs and sticks his hands deep into the pockets of his shorts. 'Caught fire and rolled over with about five hundred men on board. The ones that got off: horribly burnt. It's a bloody graveyard, this harbour.'

'Captain Price!' A Rangers colonel with a neat grey moustache and a shirt half unbuttoned to show a vividly sunburnt chest erupts from a doorway behind them. Tom turns and salutes. The colonel ignores him. 'I have to go and see General Wilson,' he tells the captain. 'Have someone fetch the car, please.'

'The car bought it last night, sir,' the captain says laconically.

'Damn. Damn! So it did,' says the colonel. 'Well, find something else.'

'There are a couple of trucks waiting to take the AA batteries away. Everything else is buggered or disabled, sir.'

'For God's sake!' Then the colonel sees Tom. 'Who the devil are you?' he snaps.

'Lieutenant Collyer, sir. East Devon Hussars.'

'Just driven down from Thermopylae,' adds the captain.

'Driven? So you have a functioning car, Lieutenant?'

Tom hesitates, but it is too late. 'Yes, sir.'

'Stroke of luck. Have to borrow it, old chap.'

'My unit will be expecting me back, sir,' Tom points out as diplomatically as he can. But the colonel just shrugs.

'Overtaken by events. I need your car.'

'Of course, sir.' Tom is cursing volubly inside his head, but there is nothing to be done. Five minutes later, Captain Price has started the car – *his* car – and the colonel has climbed into the back. 'Shouldn't be long,' he says briskly. 'You're to wait here, Mr . . . Mr . . .'

'Collyer.'

'Wait here, Mr Collyer. You're in charge, in my absence. Got that?' He waves his hand. 'Let's get on, Price.'

'Wait, sir! In charge? In charge of what?' But the car has already veered around a pile of felled date palms and is disappearing up

180

one of the narrow streets. Tom can do nothing but watch it go.

He sits on a bollard, trying to understand what has happened. He is stranded. And the colonel's order had been nonsense. There is no order here at all. Downwind, the row of dead is creating a faint but unmistakably sweet tang. He smokes, and walks along the quay. The long, sculpted keel of the *Hellas* looks as sleek as a whale's back, too beautiful to be holding the cargo that must be drifting in its guts. Out to sea, warships are steaming away, past the low islands that drift between the harbour and the horizon. The sun leans westward and everything becomes flat, a scene painted roughly in two or three colours: grey, ochre, black. The Austin does not reappear.

Time for me to get out of here, he decides. There are plenty of abandoned trucks and Bren carriers. He chooses a Morris truck, the same type used by his troop. The thing won't start, though, and when he looks under the bonnet he finds that the distributor has been ripped out. He goes from vehicle to vehicle, but every one has been sabotaged or damaged by bombs. In one of them he finds bundles of clothing. He pulls out a pair of trousers in his size and a raincoat, all brand new, and he throws away his makeshift shorts and changes into his loot. As he pulls on the raincoat he realises how cold he is. It is an officer's coat, much nicer than the one he left behind in Alexandria. 'Fortunes of war,' he mutters to himself, rifling through the contents of a half-looted Catering Corps lorry and filling his pockets with biscuits, tins of fish, chocolate and cigarettes.

It gets dark suddenly in Greece. The sun is going down. Tom looks at his watch: it has stopped at 2.14. He remembers winding it this morning but then, perhaps it was yesterday? He hasn't slept for at least two days and time is beginning to slip and slide. And he is starving. He eats two cans of sardines, watching a gang of Greek children who have emerged from an alley to fish with pieces of string in the oily water. Tom waves and they wave back, but otherwise they ignore him. An air-raid siren starts to howl and a formation of German planes roars over, very low. They drop their loads out in the bay but they don't seem to have hit anything. There are more people moving around in the shadows: civilians quietly looting the trucks. They don't pay any attention to him at all. He wonders if any of them know the woman, the singer. Zoë. *I'm glad we parted as friends*, he thinks. *I hope she survives all this.* The thought that she might not hits him with surprising force. To escape it, he sets off again across the debris, his ruined kingdom.

In one of the abandoned anti-aircraft positions strung out along the harbour he finds a paraffin stove and a kettle, with mugs set neatly out on the ground around it. Ration boxes are scattered everywhere. Tom finds some tea and sugar, even a box of Huntley & Palmers digestive biscuits. The kettle is half full and he brews up. As he is pouring out the water, he hears an engine. Perhaps the colonel has relented – but no, there is a line of three ambulances coming around the long crescent of the harbour from the east. They stop in front of the *Arethusa*. Tom walks over. Wounded men, helped by medical orderlies and the ambulance drivers, are moving slowly down the gangplank. A medic is dragging a stretcher on which an Australian corporal lies, both legs encased in plaster. 'Steady, mate,' he is muttering. 'Steady, mate.' Tom picks up the other end of the stretcher. With the medic, he gets the stretcher case ashore and into an ambulance. They go back to the ship and carry off another stretcher, and another. A German fighter circles high overhead in the twilight and an anti-aircraft gun somewhere opens up at it until it turns leisurely away to the north. Tom finds he keeps glancing at the row of bodies from the *Hellas*.

'Someone should bury them,' he says to the medic, who just shrugs.

'But who?' The medic is making sure the stretchers are secure in the last ambulance. 'Everyone's left.'

'Where are you going now?' asks Tom.

'To the hospital in Kifisia.' The medic has a quiet, cultured voice. *He went to a better school than me*, Tom thinks. 'But we'll wait until it gets completely dark. We had some nasty moments on our way down here. The Luftwaffe have it all to themselves now.'

'North? But the Germans . . .'

'It was decided that the really bad cases should be left, sir. The Germans take good care of wounded prisoners.'

'What about you?'

'They're in my care. I'm going to make sure they get to hospital.' He raises his arms, clicks his fingers. 'You know, I haven't thought about what happens after that.' The medic shrugs again. 'And what about you, sir?'

'I'm HQ Evacuation. This is all mine,' Tom says, and starts laughing. The medic grins, and for a moment they are both laughing so hard that they have to lean against the ambulance for support.

'Is there anything more absurd than the British Army?' says the medic, catching his breath. 'None of the jokes really do it justice.'

'Would the men like a cup of tea? There's a kettle and some mugs over there.'

'I think they'd love that, sir.'

So they gather up the kettle and stove, scrounge more mugs from other gun positions and set up a tea station between two of the ambulances. Tea is served up by the light of a hissing Primus lamp. The drivers make grim jokes, while the wounded are calm and polite. To Tom, that seems to make the whole thing more sad, more unbearable, this stoical bearing of personal disaster.

The medic throws the stub of his cigarette into the sea and stands up. 'It'll be dark soon. Will you be coming with us, sir?'

Tom thinks quickly. Kifisia is near the turn-off for the evacuation beaches east of Marathon. There might be stragglers who could give him a ride. Or he'll simply be captured more quickly. If he stays here, he'll be captured tomorrow in any case.

'OK,' he says. 'I expect you could do with another pair of hands.'

CHAPTER THIRTEEN

Zoë limps into the Cafe Cordelio and finds Niko sawing at a piece of wood that is braced across the bar, Micho hanging on to the other end. The room looks different. She rubs her forehead. No, it is different. There are columns holding up the ceiling: elegant white columns.

'Zozo!' Niko looks up from his sawing, a cigarette dangling from the corner of his mouth. 'What do you think? Classy, eh?'

'Sure.'

He bangs a column with his fist. 'The loading boom that nearly killed us all. What do you think? It's turned this dump into the bloody Parthenon!'

'The Parthenon,' Zoë repeats. She leans against the nearest column, and it wobbles slightly. Nothing is quite real.

'Where are the *manges*?' Niko is still sawing.

'What?'

'The lads. Vangeli . . .'

'Vangeli's dead,' says Zoë. She sits down heavily in the nearest chair.

'Dead? Vangeli? What the hell are you talking about, Zozo

185

mou?' Niko looks up at last. 'My God! What's happened to you? Is that blood?' He comes round the bar and squats down in front of her. 'My God,' he says again, hands hovering over her ruined shoes, the blood on her legs and skirt. 'It's not true!'

'It is. It's true.'

'What happened?'

'It was a German plane. We were driving along. We were singing, Niko!'

'And the others? Apostoli? Pavlo?'

'They're alive. Vangeli . . .'

Niko takes her hands in his and squeezes them. 'It's all right, Zozo. Where did it happen?'

'I don't know. Somewhere out in the countryside. A British Army car stopped to see what was going on and Apostoli made me go with them. Him – I mean, I drove down here with an officer. He dropped me off outside the door.'

'Fucking Germans. Fucking Germans!' Niko stands up and slams his hand against one of the columns, which jerks sideways with a squeal of wrenched nails. 'And the British are leaving us to the wolves. I'd have had something to say to that officer.'

'His name was Tom and he was nice,' says Zoë. 'Could I have a drink, please, Niko? Some water?' Zoë's head is really starting to hurt. Niko softens immediately.

'Christ on the cross . . . I'm so sorry, my darling one. There. Have a cigarette. I'll get something for you to smoke. Micho! Fetch a water pipe! Make Zoë a coffee, you bastard! Bring some tsipouro!'

Micho, who has plainly just come in to help Niko with his carpentry, takes these orders with good humour. He puts a tray together and comes over, limping in his exaggerated *mangas* style. A bottle of tsipouro, a carafe of water, three glasses, an *arghile* water

186

pipe with a fresh clay bowl. A lump of black hash on a dented old silver saucer. Glowing nuggets of charcoal in a crude earthenware cup. Niko pours a glass of water for Zoë, and a good measure of tsipouro each for himself and Micho.

'Have some of this, my love,' Niko insists, pouring Zoë a slug when she has finished her water. She adds more water, though her hands are trembling so badly that Niko has to steady the carafe for her. All the hours she spent in the car with the lieutenant, trying to keep from going to pieces . . . But she can't do it any more. She watches the liquid swirl like opals, turn milky. She takes a mouthful, feels it burn her tongue. When she swallows, it begins to glow inside her chest.

'Vangeli. Vangelaki. I can't believe it,' Niko is saying. 'Did he suffer? What did those bastards do to him?'

'He didn't suffer,' says Zoë. She drains her glass, lets Micho pour her another. She closes her eyes as the tsipouro burns its way down, but opens them when Vangeli's mangled body swims out of the darkness. 'He was killed straight away. Apostoli is all right. Pavlo got a bang on the head and I think he broke some ribs. But he was more upset about his bouzouki. Took a fistful of pills and went on holiday.'

'What a madman,' Micho says admiringly.

'He had blood pouring down his face, but all he wanted was his precious bouzouki. Which he'd gone all the way to Khalkis to buy . . .'

'In the middle of a war,' Micho observes.

'Yes, but they're going to make a record,' Niko says, as if that explains everything. 'Stop interrupting.'

'And do you know?' Zoë watches the milky swirl in her glass. Her voice seems to belong to someone else. 'There wasn't a scratch on that bouzouki.'

'*Aman!* We'd better call Semsis!' Niko is busy with the hash, softening a piece that he has gouged onto the end of a thin knife, holding it over the charcoal.

'There won't be any record,' Zoë says. She catches the feral scent of the hashish in her nostrils. It brings her at once to the back of the Citroën, the pipe going round, Vangeli strumming ecstatically at his baglamas. 'We were singing "Bohemian Girl". We were all just having fun. Oh, Panagia . . . I can't talk about it,' she says, hearing panic in her voice.

'Of course not. Of course not, little bird. Now, let's have a smoke, eh?'

Zoë doesn't really want to smoke the *arghile*, but Niko is fussing over it so diligently that when he holds it out to her she closes her eyes and takes a drag, just to oblige him. Vangeli is there again, but the smoke runs through her body like amber and she takes another drag and hands the pipe to Micho. Her thoughts start to run. 'I'm so tired, Niko. Do you think they'll start bombing us again? I just want to go to sleep.'

'Of course you do, little bird. Don't worry about the Germans. Those pricks will never hit the Cordelio. They wouldn't fucking dare! But aren't you hungry? I'll send Micho out for something: a cheese pie? Some kataifi from Prokopiou?'

Zoë waves him away. She is beginning to feel awful. She gets to her feet and both men leap up to help her. 'Sleep, then!' says Niko. They each take an arm and lead her, cooing as if she were a child, through the bar and out to the little room at the back of the building. Niko keeps it free for her, so she always has somewhere to sleep when it is too late to go back to Kokkinia. It is clean, and the door locks.

'I'll bring you water so you can wash,' says Niko. 'Micho! Fetch some water for Zozo, you lazy bastard!'

Hot water is fetched in a big bowl, with a sponge and the cleanest towels that Niko has. A steaming jug is set down by the door. When the men have left her, Zoë slides the bolt on the door and kicks off her shoes. She undresses, shivering but glad to be rid of her ruined clothing. As she peels off her blouse she smells blood again. Tomorrow she will burn everything. Thank God she has a change of clothes here somewhere. She puts the bowl on the floor and steps into it. Slowly, she sponges off her legs, letting the water trickle down, threading red into the bowl. She has a nasty bruise on one shin and a network of shallow cuts across her thighs. Everywhere the sponge goes it discovers something painful. When her legs are clean, she throws the water out of the window, refills the bowl and finishes washing herself. By now she is rigid with cold, and the towels aren't big enough to wrap herself in. She has to bite her lip to stop her teeth rattling together. When she is dry she finds her nightdress, pulls it on and climbs slowly into the narrow iron bed.

Though she desperately wants to sleep, the chill has woken up her body. Her heart is racing; her mind is a movie screen and the projectionist has broken the projector. She lies there, staring up at the beams of the ceiling, the undersides of the roof tiles, the mortar. Cobwebs. An early gecko. Above the tiles, open sky. An air raid starts, sirens protesting, the rhythmic hammering of anti-aircraft guns, very close. She hears a mewing sound, thin and desperate. In the refugee camp below the Acropolis, the men had made snares to try and catch rabbits, and she had found one once, struggling, one leg half gone, mewing like a kitten. But the sound is coming from her. *I'll never be free of this*, she thinks. The pilots floating up there above Piraeus: they are all looking down, and they all see her. Everything fractures: she is the pilot, looking through the angled

189

crystal of her sights, watching herself on the bed, twisting her legs in the sheets, mewing in terror.

Don't worry, Miss Valavani. You're safe.

I'm not, she thinks, *I'm not*, and tries to push the Englishman out of her mind. But he stays, a calm, sunburnt ghost, as she hunches under the sheets, knuckles pressed hard into her temples, concentrating on the ragged throb of her pulse. *You're safe. My word as a painter.* And suddenly, it ends, the engines fading, the sirens working longest until their voices drop down through quarter tones to deep bass, to nothing. Footsteps in the street. Cars. The sirens start again. *It's real*, she tells herself, and, strangely, perhaps it is the reality of it that finally soothes her panic. She falls asleep as the engines of yet another flight of bombers fade away in the direction of Salamis.

CHAPTER FOURTEEN

The ambulance runs out of petrol in the middle of Athens, just south of the Arch of Hadrian. Tom has been watching the fuel gauge since leaving Kifisia but it still claims that the tank is a quarter full. The gauge is a dud, like everything else. He gets out and bangs it with his fist. It chimes hollowly. His watch, working again, tells him that it is half past five. The sky is a luminous Prussian blue, with the outlines of buildings and trees beginning to etch themselves onto its fringes. Ahead of him, the road branches: the wide, palm-lined avenue of Syngrou, and narrower streets heading east and south-east. South-east is where he is heading. The Germans have already cut the road between Maroussi and Marathon. It was already too late for that escape route by the time the ambulances reached 26 British General Hospital. As he helped unload the wounded, the officer in charge was preparing his staff for immediate surrender. So he took an ambulance with the blessing of a distracted RAMC captain.

He gets out and looks at his map. Porto Rafti looks to be about twenty-eight miles away. It is perfectly obvious to him that he hasn't a hope in hell of getting to the beach in time, or at all. He might as well stay here and wait for the Germans; there really isn't any good reason not to surrender. To wait out the war in some safe, dull camp with all his limbs still attached. He knows that he won't, though. *Why not?* he asks himself. But then he imagines his father's face as he opens the official letter, the look of disgust as he reads the word 'captured'. And then he remembers Daddy's hands shaking as he told him a story. *Work your guns, Collyer. Work your bloody guns.*

'Bit too easy,' he says aloud.

The points of the cypress trees lining the wall of a cemetery are getting sharp against the sky. He has been walking for half an hour. A large ginger cat with a sagging belly is walking along the top of the wall, keeping pace with him. 'Morning,' Tom says to it, and it blinks its sulphur-yellow eyes. Suddenly he hears an engine, a large one, coming down the street behind him. He whirls around, expecting to see a German armoured car, but instead, to his amazement, a large, dilapidated bus is approaching. *This is a dream*, he tells himself as he steps to the edge of the pavement and holds out his arm. The bus stops, and the door opens. The driver, unshaven but in uniform, nods at him. He says something in Greek and Tom has to shake his head.

'Do you speak English?' Tom asks. 'Where are you going?' The driver shakes his head and waves Tom aboard.

'*Ela,*' he says.

'No money,' Tom says, patting his pockets. The driver shakes his head again.

'*Den peirázei,*' he says. Tom understands: it doesn't matter.

'Thank you!' he says, and clambers aboard. The bus is empty. The driver closes the door and they trundle off. They rattle along empty streets, the driver pulling up doggedly at each stop, but there are no other passengers. The bus doesn't seem to be able to go much above ten miles an hour, but Tom calculates that they are heading towards the sea, and that is good enough. Eventually they come over the crest of a low hill and Tom glimpses the sea, not very far away. The bus slows down and creaks to a standstill. There is no stop, as far as Tom can see, but then the driver turns to him, pointing down the street.

'*Asfaleia*,' he says. 'Police. Maybe . . . not good for English soldier.'

Tom looks past him. There is a small company of men in uniform at the next crossroads, next to a military truck. 'Should I get out?' Tom asks.

'Yes. You go now.'

'OK. Thank you.'

'*Parakalo*.'

'Ah . . .' Tom hesitates in the doorway. He points towards the sea, hopefully. 'Glyfada?'

But the driver shakes his head. '*Faliron*. Glyfada' – he points to the left – 'very far.' Then he points to the right. 'Piraeus. Near.'

'Right. Thank you,' says Tom again. But the door is already closing. 'God go with you,' he hears the driver say. The bus trundles off.

Tom walks until the sun comes up, heading towards the sea, avoiding open ground, expecting to find other lost soldiers. But there are none. A large flight of German planes goes over at daybreak, heading for the Peloponnese. He is climbing a gentle hill, and from the top he sees the coast spread out in front of him. Smoke is rising from the east, with the sound of bombs. The beaches have been cut off. He looks in the other direction, and there is the sweep of Piraeus Harbour. *If I could just hide until it gets dark*, he thinks, *maybe I could steal a boat. The navy would pick me up*. It isn't much of an idea, and the only boat he has ever had all to himself has been on the Serpentine, but what else can he do? He is alone and everyone here is a stranger.

But he looks down at the harbour again, at the low, damaged streets leading down to the waterfront, and a thought – more of a sensation than a thought – begins to form. There is one person down there who isn't quite a stranger. The woman from the strafed car, with her perfect English and her nanny. Her hazel eyes. *I wanted to see her again*, he says to himself, *but don't be ridiculous. I'll never find her.* But somehow the world feels a little less vast.

He is never quite sure, later, how long it took to find the narrow street with its trailing wires and pieces of white timber propped against the walls. He walked for what seemed like hours, slipping from street to street, hiding behind an embankment and watching the first German patrol roll down Syngrou Avenue: two half tracks in convoy, trailed by three motorcycles with sidecars. The men inside were all smoking and laughing. *My troop would have had the lot of them*, he thought, and smiled at the absurdity of it all. Before climbing back out of his ditch, he decided that his cap made him too conspicuous, and shoved it into the mouth of a drainage pipe. But then he took it out again, pulled off the badge with its little bronze cannon and dropped it into a pocket. Sentimentality, perhaps. Or the thought of his father. *All right, you bastard*, he thought grimly. *All right.*

At last he turns down a narrow lane littered with discarded British packs, helmets, gas masks, rations. He steps over a shattered crate, its contents of light blue tubes spilling out over the cobbles. On an impulse he bends over to pick one up. *English Toffees*, says the wrapper. As he straightens he happens to glance to his right. There is a half-familiar door, and above it a sign, black letters on white. ΤΟ ΚΟΡΔΕΛΙΟ.

CHAPTER FIFTEEN

She wakes up to silence, though in the night she was twice woken by an unbearable roaring in her ears, only to find the dark room and its small, comforting emptiness around her. But now there is complete stillness. She has never known such a thing in Piraeus.

She splashes herself with tepid water from the jug to get rid of the smell of night sweat, and scrubs off every trace of yesterday's make-up. Then she dresses in the clothes she keeps here at the Cordelio: a smart, dark navy bouclé wool jacket with short leg o'mutton sleeves and a matching A-line skirt, which she got a local seamstress to make up for her. 'Spend everything you have on your clothes, my darling,' her mother always said. 'If the whole thing burns again, you'll have something nice on your back when you escape.' *None of this would have surprised Mama*, she thinks, as she puts on fresh make-up. When she walks into the main room of the Cordelio, she finds Niko standing in the half-open door. The room is empty otherwise, though the wireless is on. The boarded-up windows and dim lightbulb make the room feel as if it is underwater. The national anthem is playing. It stops, and after a short pause, starts again from the beginning. Hearing the tap of her heels, Niko wheels around, sees it is her and relaxes. 'My God, *koukla*. You look just like a goddess. You're the only good thing these eyes have seen today.'

'It's happened, hasn't it?' she says. 'The Germans are here.'

Niko tugs angrily at his moustache. The radio begins to play the anthem again. '*I shall always know you, by the fearsome sword you hold . . .*' Snarling, Niko runs to switch it off. 'Bastards: as if they hadn't surrendered. Yes, the Germans have come. Och, this fucking world.'

He makes a briki of coffee and they drink it together at one of the tables.

'I'm worried about Pavlo,' Zoë says. 'And Apostoli. What if the Germans pick them up?'

'Your brother can look after himself. He's clueless – for God's sake, with all the junk he puts into his arm! – but he's as lucky as any man I've ever known.'

'Lucky, Niko? Are you sure about that?'

'First, he had Katina Valavani for a mother. Second, he has you for a sister. And third, he has the Devil on his back, telling him where to put his feet. He walks through life like a blind man and yet he never steps in shit.'

'I have to worry. He's my little brother, and I promised to look after him.'

'Don't. Someone's looking after him, all right. Devil or angel. Both.' Niko turns on the radio again, but now there is nothing but static. Suddenly there is a loud crackle and a stab of feedback. Then a voice comes on, a man's voice, familiar like all radio voices are.

'*Attention: Athens' radio station will shortly not be Greek any more. It will be German! And it will be broadcasting lies. Greeks: do not listen to this station! Our war continues. And it will continue until the final victory!*' Another crackle, and the national anthem starts up again.

'God almighty . . .' Niko is walking out of the kitchen with more coffee. To her shock, Zoë sees tears in the corners of his eyes. 'They finally grew some balls, eh?'

Another burst of static, and another, different voice. Greek words, but not from a Greek throat. '*People of Athens! Your city has been liberated from the tyrannical occupation of the British by the armies of the Third Reich. The great German people respect the great history and peoples of Greece! Together we will resist Bolshevism and British Imperialism! Heil Hitler!*'

'For fuck's sake.' Niko bangs his hands down on the table. 'I have to go out. I promised Micho . . .'

'It's all right.' Zoë has never seen her friend so distraught. 'I can look after the place for a bit.'

'Thank you, Zozo. I just need . . . I need to see for myself. Do you understand?'

Zoë closes her eyes and nods. 'Go. I've seen it already.'

She is washing dishes in a zinc tub behind the bar when the English officer walks in. It is about ten o'clock in the morning. The Cordelio is empty except for two customers, a pair of elderly men who come in every day to gossip about some village in Asia Minor, though they pretend they are discussing politics, because they belong to the KKE, the communist party, and have spent half of the past nineteen years in prison. All she has to do is make sure they have coffee when they need it.

197

The officer is wearing a long raincoat and stiff, new-looking army trousers and he has tucked his rumpled shirt into the high waist, which makes him look oddly boy-like. She sees, with a strange stab of recognition, the slim map case hanging across his body under the coat. He seems to be offering her a small tube of blue paper.

'Miss Valavani?' he asks, uncertainly.

'What are you . . . ? You can't be here!' He seems to shrink before her eyes, and slumps against the doorjamb. His cheeks look more hollow than she remembers them, and darkly stubbled. The old KKE men have stopped talking and are watching the Englishman with interest. Feeling as if she is jumping into deep, dark water, she crosses the floor between the bar and the door in three quick steps, pulls the Englishman inside and kicks the door shut behind him. They stand, only a few inches apart, breathing fast.

'I should have bought you a drink at the Acropole Palace,' he says, trying to smile, which only makes him look more forlorn. 'So as I'm still in Greece . . .'

'This isn't funny,' she snaps. 'What are you doing here?' She locks the door and, grabbing his wrist, which is hard and roped with muscle beneath the rubbery sleeve of his coat, she drags him away from the door, feeling him stagger as he loses his balance for a moment. Then he lets himself be led to the table nearest the kitchen. 'Do you mind if I sit down?' he asks politely. Zoë sees that he is swaying on his feet.

'For God's sake!' she says again, furiously. She feels full of rage, rage at this man for coming here, bringing unknown dangers; rage at herself, for losing control. Because she has never been less calm. Her hands are shaking. Her body hurts. The Englishman smells like petrol and smoke, and yesterday's horror is coming back to her in a great, sickening flood.

'I'm sorry,' he says. 'This was the only place I could think of to come. After I left you . . . it's all so bloody stupid.'

'But what about your car? Why didn't you . . . why didn't you just drive away?' She waves her hand angrily, as if to fling him out of here, out to sea.

'Someone took my car. A colonel. He promised he'd bring it back.' He shakes his head. 'I expect people have been making a lot of promises like that recently.'

'Christ. Stay there. No, sit down. There, by the back door.' Zoë hurries over to the old communists, who are looking at her with a mixture of concern and delight.

'I apologise,' she says to them. 'This is an English officer – he helped me yesterday, and now he has come here.'

They both nod gravely. 'I saw their general fly away last night in a big flying boat,' the younger man, Christo, says. 'General Wilson.' He draws out the word with exquisite disdain. *Whi-i-i-lson.* 'But the soldiers have done their best.'

'Churchill fucked them all up the arse,' the older man observes. 'They came to help, now they are our guests.'

'Do you mind . . . ?' Zoë looks around the cluttered insides of the Cordelio, which suddenly feel much less safe, much less familiar.

'We will stay,' says the older man, whose name is Kosta. 'We'll keep a lookout.'

The younger man makes a pistol with his fingers and points them at the door. 'Bang, bang. Tell him we've fought the fascists too.'

Zoë doesn't know what to do with herself, so goes back and sits down opposite the soldier. 'I helped take some wounded up to Kifisia,' he says, though she has asked him nothing. 'The Germans had already cut us off from our evacuation beaches so I took an ambulance. I was going to drive to Glyfada but I ran out of petrol. Then I caught a bus . . .'

'A bus.'

'A bus. Going to Glyfada. But there was a roadblock. So I started walking. I suppose I should have just surrendered but I started walking. By that time the Germans had arrived. I shouldn't have come here – I can see that now. But I didn't know what else to do. This was the only place I could think of. And you.'

'Me?' Zoë frowns. Her hands are making soft fists on the oilskin tablecloth.

He tries to smile, but the effect is so sad that Zoë's heart gives a small, queasy lurch. 'Afraid so. Now that everyone's gone, you're the only person I know in Greece. And I don't know you at all, do I?' He begins to stand. 'I ought to be going.'

'Don't be ridiculous.' She stands up, almost knocking over her chair. 'Are you hungry?' she demands. 'You must be hungry.'

'I'm famished,' he says, with evident relief. She goes into the kitchen. There isn't much food left. *What do English officers like to eat? Cucumber sandwiches*, she thinks, and shakes her head. She is always reading about cucumber sandwiches. They sound disgusting. She cuts him a few slices of bread and fills a plate with some hard sheep's cheese, a leftover piece of fried salt cod and a scoop of olives.

'Eat,' she says, putting the plate down in front of him.

'Thank you,' he says. 'Thank you so much. Sorry.'

She rolls her eyes in exasperation. 'Must you English apologise for everything?' she says. 'You're in Piraeus now, Lieutenant. You will have to learn how to be rude.'

She polishes a glass and holds it up to the light, steals a glance at him over the rim. She can almost feel him trying to hold on to his dignity while his hunger is forcing him the other way. He has taken off his coat and underneath it, the leather case she remembers from yesterday hangs crosswise from one shoulder. A large pistol in a leather holster is dragging a dirty khaki belt down across his hips. He is trying to eat calmly, distracting himself from his obvious hunger by looking around the room, and his eyes, she notices, are caught by everything they encounter: the swords, the print of the harem girl, the photo of New York. She puts the glass down next to the plate and pours out some of Niko's sour yellow wine.

'Those two chaps over there. Are they . . . ? I mean, do you think . . . ?'

'Don't worry about them,' she tells him. 'Kosta and Christo are both members of the communist party. They want you to know that they have also fought against fascism.'

'Oh!' He almost doubles over in relief. The old men are looking over at him with unabashed curiosity and he waves a long hand in greeting. 'How do you say "good morning" in Greek?' he asks her.

'Καλημέρα.'

'*Kaliméra!*' the officer says, experimentally. The two old men raise their hands and nod their heads politely. He waves back shyly, takes a gulp of wine. 'I don't know how to thank you,' he says.

'Then don't. In any case it is just fate.'

'Fate?'

'You driving by when you did. You might not have stopped. Or I might have been dead.' She says it flatly, and his eyebrows go up. *I've shocked you*, she thinks. *You are easy to shock, you English.*

'Well, yes, that's true,' he says after a pause. 'But I'm very glad you're not.' He sighs. 'And I'm bloody glad *I'm* not, too. We're both lucky.'

'Forgive me for saying that no one in Greece is particularly lucky today. We have lost the war. And we have lost our freedom.'

'For now! But . . .'

'I look into your face and I see that you do not know what that means. We have lost, and you have not, Mr English Officer. You still have hope.'

'But that isn't bad, surely?'

'In England, no. Or Berlin. In Athens, even – in Kolonaki, where the nice houses are. But down here in Karaiskaki, everyone here learnt not to hope a very long time ago.'

'I can't believe that!'

'Really? We might have hoped that the Germans would be beaten. We might have been hoping the British Army would save us. Imagine the disappointment. Luckily, no one dared think any such thing. Do you understand?'

'That seems terribly grim.'

'But useful. Yes? Sensible. Learn to expect nothing, and you are never disappointed.'

'Christ. What . . . ?' He frowns. 'What on earth do you sing about, then?'

And to her surprise she finds herself laughing. 'Hope, of course. What else?'

'What else indeed?' The Englishman's face relaxes and for a moment, his eyes sparkle. He looks around again, brushing crumbs from the front of his shirt. 'This place. Is it . . . ? I mean, do you own it?'

'The Cordelio? No! What a mad idea, Lieutenant!'

'Call me Tom. You can't be a lieutenant without an army.'

'OK. *Tom*. No, the Cordelio is Niko's place. If you want to know if you can trust him, yes, you can. He's a . . . what we call a *mangas*. I don't know the English word, if there is one. Like . . . like George Raft. Scarface?'

'He's a gangster?'

'Gangster?' Zoë ponders this. 'No, not exactly. Tough, yes? Of course. Dressing a little bit . . .' She mimes putting on a snap-brim hat. 'A little Italian, a little Smyrna. But a gangster wants power. A *mangas* doesn't want power. He has *no* power, but he shows the rest of the world that he doesn't care. You understand? His power is his sad heart.' She puts her hand over her own heart. 'I can't explain it very well. Music. Sad, sad songs. Dressing in this way. Laughing at death. If you are not one of us refugees, if you have not come from Asia Minor, I don't think you will be able to understand.'

'Well . . . is it like the blues, do you think?'

'Blues? Hmm. My brother – Pavlo – knows about this. I don't know it. You must ask him. If . . .' She feels her skin grow cold suddenly.

'Your brother, who was sitting under the tree? He wasn't badly hurt. I'm sure he'll be fine. He's probably on his way back right now.'

'You think so?'

'I do. I expect I'll be gone by then, though.' Zoë watches him take another sip of wine. His eyes meet hers over the rim of the glass and she feels a little calmer. 'So this isn't your place. You live here, though?'

'No. But Niko keeps a room for me so I don't have to walk home late at night.' His eyebrows go up. 'I can assure you . . .'

'Please don't,' he says hurriedly. 'You don't need to assure me. Just ignore everything I say or do, Miss Valavani. I'm not usually this crass.'

203

'Crass?'

'Vulgar. Badly brought up.'

'Ah, yes. By your mother. Niko looks after me because he was a friend of *my* mother. This place is like my other home.'

'And your nanny?'

'I am afraid you will never forget that. *I* am sorry, Lieutenant. Tom. It was rude of me.'

'I am so completely in your debt at this point that you could have said anything and it wouldn't matter. But I suppose I am a bit curious: was your mother English?'

'My mother? No!' Zoë chuckles, picturing dark, exotic-looking Katina Valavani. But then she stops. *That isn't who we're talking about, is it*, she thinks. 'It's . . .' She sighs. 'Too much of a story.'

'You said you lived in Smyrna. That was twenty years ago. I'm surprised you haven't forgotten your English.'

'Nineteen.'

'Nineteen. Still, you must have been very young.'

'My mother didn't let me. She spoke it as well, you see.'

'Really?'

'You don't understand about Smyrna, Lieutenant,' she says, feeling a sort of anger rising in her chest. 'It wasn't like this miserable slum. It was like the Garden of Eden compared to here. Everyone spoke a different language. My mother had a dress shop in the best part of the city. She sold clothes from Paris and she spoke French, and perfect English, and Turkish of course. Her customers were women from London, even New York! So yes, she made certain I didn't forget. She used to find me English books to read, and I would steal English newspapers from the rubbish bins outside the Hotel Grand Bretagne . . .' She stops herself. 'We came to Greece, all of us, with nothing except what we had in here,' she

204

says, more calmly, touching the side of her head. 'The only treasure God left us with. That is what my mother would say. I wouldn't dare waste it.'

'Because of God?'

'What?' She can't keep the scorn out of her voice. 'No, because of my mother! She sewed dresses out of scraps until her fingers bled, and she sang songs, Smyrna songs, in too many cafes so that her lungs went bad. She had lived in a mansion, and died in a tiny paper house in Kokkinia. That's why I won't let it go to waste!' She notices that he is trying not to smile. 'What now? Is it so funny, listening to a Greek person speaking? Why did you come here anyway, you English? Just to leave us to the Germans?'

'I apologise on behalf of W Force,' says the officer, licking his fingers. He has just eaten the salt cod. 'If it's any consolation, I wish I was somewhere else too. I didn't want to come to Greece, Miss Valavani. I'd much rather have stayed at home in London and gone on painting pictures. But instead . . .' She watches his long fingers break off a piece of cheese and a piece of the bread, knead them unconsciously together. 'Instead, I'm in the artillery. You should be in a mansion and I should be in an artist's studio. This cheese, by the way, is delicious.'

'Oh. Good.' She glares at him, but his nicely shaped eyebrows are arching up behind his black fringe and he is looking at her with those large, intent eyes. Her anger dissolves. 'Don't call me Miss Valavani. It makes me sound like a teacher. I am Zoë.'

At that moment the door handle rattles. Their eyes widen. With the clarity of a nightmare, Zoë watches Tom's hand drop to the butt of the large, greasy pistol on his belt. Behind his shoulder, she sees Christo grin at her as he raises his fingers, cocks back his thumb, and points towards the door.

'Is there a way out?' she hears Tom say. She looks down and sees her hand gripping his wrist. Then a hoarse voice, muffled but familiar, booms through the door.

'Zozo? What the fuck is going on?'

CHAPTER SIXTEEN

When Tom sees the fear leave Zoë's face, he lets go of the pistol with an enormous sense of relief. He has never fired the thing in anger and he detests its weight and oily liquorice sheen. Zoë has already pushed back her chair.

'It's all right,' she tells him, smiling for the first time today. 'This is Niko! Stay here, please.'

She goes over to the door and peers quickly through a spyhole that Tom hasn't noticed before. The lock rattles and she opens the door just enough to let two people slip through. When she sees who it is, she stifles a scream with her hands. Then she takes the first man by the arm and whispers urgently into his ear. The man looks towards Tom, scowling. He is of medium height, wiry, wearing a sharp peak-lapel suit of navy pinstripe cloth, a white shirt and what looks to Tom's confused eyes like the red and yellow tie of the Marylebone Cricket Club. His moustache is waxed straight out and is almost wider than his face. Tom stands up, nervously, his hands half raised. *I'm surrendering to a man in an MCC tie*, he thinks.

The man, Niko, says something to Zoë. Then, in a couple of quick strides he is across the room. Tom notices that his movements are stiff but graceful, a dancer's, before Niko has grabbed him and hugged him tightly to his chest. He is surprisingly strong, and he is growling into Tom's ear with what seem to be words of endearment – at least, Tom hopes that's what they are.

'I'm so sorry,' Tom says. 'I don't speak Greek.'

'Then speak English! I speak English.' The man steps back and thumps himself over the heart with his fist. 'Working on ships, many years. I live in Cardiff.'

'Cardiff?' Tom blinks.

'One year. Tiger Bay. Lovely, lovely. The girls. *Aman.*'

'The Welsh . . .' Things are getting more surreal by the moment. 'I have a Welsh aunt,' Tom stammers. 'I'm really sorry to burst in on you,' he hurries on, 'but I didn't know where else to go. If I could just . . .'

The man grabs him again, by the shoulders this time, and gives him a shake. 'You fight?' he growls. 'The Germans? You fight?'

'Yes. Yes, I did,' says Tom. 'I'm in – was in – an anti-tank unit. Shooting at German tanks,' he adds, seeing the man's brows corrugate.

'Shooting at tanks? Ha ha!' His large hands flutter very close to Tom's face before seizing his cheeks and pinching, quite hard. 'All right, Kapetanios. You stay here. Lots of English running away, but not you, eh? Shooting at tanks!' He shoves Tom down into his chair. 'You eat?'

'I did,' says Tom. 'Miss Valavani has been looking after me.'

'Ah, Miss Valavani. Very good, very good! Zozo!' Niko bellows. Tom looks past him and sees Zoë over by the door, hands on hips in front of the other man. She seems to be scolding him, very loudly. Now that he sees the man properly, Tom recognises him at once: the man who flagged down his car yesterday. Was it yesterday? Now that he is clean of blood, Tom can see that he has a narrow face with high cheekbones and wide, hooded eyes. Even bruised, Apostoli – *I can't remember what the day is, but I remember that chap's name*, Tom thinks, amazed – is handsome. Now he is wincing as Zoë shakes him by the arms but he is wearing a well-cut dove-grey suit and a grey, wide-ribboned trilby and there is a certain, undeniable poise about him. He sees Tom, who raises his hand and grins ruefully.

'My God! *O* Kapetanios!' Apostoli raises both hands in joyful benediction. Zoë has him around the waist and is whispering urgently in his ear. Her face is tight but he says something and she relaxes. *Ah, of course*, thinks Tom. *She's with him*. Apostoli starts towards him, dragging Zoë. 'Kapetanios!' he says again. 'My Kapetanios!'

'He's a lieutenant,' Zoë says in English, glancing at Tom. She adds something in Greek.

'Ah! *Anthipolochagós!* Never mind,' says Apostoli, grinning. Tom stands up and offers his hand. Apostoli takes it and grips it between both of his own. 'I,' he says, '*dekaneas*. Corporal. Long time ago. But *kapetanios* means something else.' He hooks a thumb into his belt and sticks out his chest dramatically. '*Kapetanios* means brigand chief. Up in the mountains, fighting the Turks, the invaders. Lord Byron, yes? He was English *kapetanios*.'

'Byron?' says Tom. He decides to let it pass by. 'I'm so glad you're safe. But what about your brother, Miss . . . I mean . . .'

'Pavlo is fine, thanks be to God,' says Zoë. 'He went to the hospital and they wrapped up his chest. Now he is at Apostoli's house. Apostoli has a very kind wife who will come to regret having my brother in her care.' She is smiling, more or less, but Tom can't tell if she is joking. *Apostoli has a wife, though, does he? That is . . . well, that is good news, somehow.*

Meanwhile, Niko has gone into the tiny, rudimentary kitchen, nothing more than an alcove beside the bar with a couple of gas rings, a hearth or bread oven set into the wall, a brass tap jutting out beside it. He comes back a few seconds later with a large triangle of brownish pastry on a plate. 'Tyrópita. Cheese pie. Eat.' He steps away, comes back with a copper jug and refills Tom's glass. 'Drink.'

Tom looks around him. Everyone – the two old communists have come over to join them – is quite silent and they are all staring. He nods and smiles and gets no response, so he raises his glass to them. 'Cheers,' he says, politely, and drinks.

'Ελα, μανγεσ!' Niko turns to the company and holds up his hands, palms inward. 'Our brave guest!' He grabs another five glasses from the bar, splashes some wine into them and hands them round to the others.

'*Yiassou!*' he says '*Kalos orises!*'

The other men toast loudly. Zoë is watching, amused, from beneath lowered eyelids.

'They welcome you,' says Niko. 'Good. Of course. Now eat.'

The edge is off Tom's hunger and the cheese pie is more pie than cheese but the pastry is wonderfully greasy and in a few bites it is gone and he is brushing pastry flakes off his coat with buttery fingers. 'Thank you,' he says. 'Thank you so much.'

'It's nothing.' Niko refills his glass and sits down next to him. Zoë and Apostoli sit down as well. The two communists sidle back to their own table. 'Brave man,' says Niko, pinching Tom's cheek again. 'Our Greek Army surrender to the Germans but the English, they fight.'

'You did beat the Italians,' says Tom, licking his fingers.

'The Italians!' the man bursts out, scornfully. He slams his fist into the crook of his arm. 'Fuck the Italians! But now the Germans are here, it's going to be hard for us.'

'We'll beat them,' Tom says. *I don't sound very certain*, he is thinking.

'Of course! Churchill! Winston Churchill will send the Germans to hell. But for now . . .'

'I know,' says Tom, and rubs his face with his hands. He feels like crying. It's all been so useless.

'That's enough, Niko,' Zoë says. 'He's exhausted. He needs to sleep. Where can we put him?' Tom smiles. He is, suddenly, completely finished and he feels a rush of gratitude to the singer for having noticed. Niko is conferring with the singer and Apostoli. Then Zoë taps the table with a red fingernail.

'Tonight you sleep up in the roof. It's OK, comfortable. Someone lives there already.'

'Are they here?' says Tom, worried. He doesn't want to turf anyone out. He'd quite happily lie down under this table. Niko says something in Greek and Zoë shrugs.

'Leftheri is in the army. Apparently he is dead. Niko says his mother got the letter yesterday. So you can stay. It is lucky.'

'Not for Leftheri.'

She raises an eyebrow. 'No, not for Leftheri. But for you. Don't complain.'

'Will you show me?' Tom decides to stand up but he staggers and leans hard on the table. Immediately, Niko and Apostoli grab him under the arms. 'I'm fine! Just tired. Please.'

'Go with them,' says the singer. 'You will be safe.'

'Thank you,' says Tom, though the two men are already almost bodily lifting him across the floor. He starts to laugh: fatigue, the wine . . . how strange it all is. 'Will I . . . ?' But Zoë just raises her hand – farewell, or dismissal? She is already turning away. A door opens and the two men are pushing him up a ladder. He climbs unsteadily up and through a trapdoor, finding himself in a slant-ceilinged space that smells strongly of sun-baked dust and old sweat. Needles of sunlight point out a rough mattress jammed into the tight angle between roof and floor. There is a double sheet folded over to cover the mattress and to sleep under, and an army blanket.

'You can sleep there,' says Apostoli, but Tom has already dropped his coat on the floor and is wrestling with the laces of his boots. 'Wait.' Apostoli kneels down and deftly unpicks the knots and slips the boots from Tom's feet. 'Go to sleep. When you wake up, stay here until someone comes, yes?'

'All right.' Tom stretches out on the mattress, which is just hay stuffed into a sheeting bag, though it feels like paradise, and pulls the covers around him. 'Will she be here tomorrow?' he asks.

'Who?' says Apostoli, but Tom is already fast asleep.

CHAPTER SEVENTEEN

Niko thinks it will be too dangerous for Zoë to go home today. 'You can't go up to Kokkinia,' he tells her. 'Christ knows what's going on.' Micho has come in with the news that the Germans have hoisted a gigantic swastika flag over the Acropolis. A couple more regulars appear. Zoë can't believe how grateful she is for the presence of others, for the sound of their voices. By midday, the cafe is filling up. Zoë is full of nervous energy, so intense that it hurts if she keeps still. When she finally goes out, a short trip around the corner to Prokopiou's for pastries, she is shocked to find how normal everything is. People are out and about. Though she had expected to find the streets filled with German soldiers, there is no one in uniform at all, not even a gendarme. The bakery is full of people buying baklava, kataifi, squares of custard pie, all made from looted British supplies. People are expectant rather than fearful. She hears men telling each other that the Germans respect them for giving the Italians such a hiding, that Hitler worships the ancient heroes of Greece. Perhaps it won't be all bad for us this time, they say. Their voices, though: their voices betray them. Everyone seems to be listening for something, as if they can hear the alien flag snapping in the wind, up on the Acropolis.

In the end she does go home. The buses aren't running so she has to walk to the far end of Kokkinia. The shops she passes are almost empty, their shelves stripped. Prokopiou's is the exception, not the rule. *It will all get back to normal*, she tells herself, but she knows it isn't true.

As she walks through the narrow, rutted streets, she wonders if anything will really change. Life, surely, can't get much worse. A flight of bombers, the first she has heard all day, appear from the north, but they are very high, going elsewhere. She looks south towards the horizon. *That's the world, out there*, she thinks. *Here, it's become somewhere else.*

The house on Hozanitas Street welcomes her as it always does, all four walls rattling slightly as she opens the flimsy door. She walks straight in, expecting it to be empty, but instead she finds her brother and his girlfriend Feathers sprawled on the bench-like sofa in the front room.

'Pavlo!' Zoë shrieks, slamming the door, which makes a sound like a book being snapped shut, and stumbling across the floor to kneel in front of him. She grabs his hands, which as always are cool and dry. 'When did you get back?' she demands. 'How are you? What happened?'

'*Aman*, Zozo,' Pavlo drawls. 'I'm fine. Everything's fine.' His head is bobbing slightly on his long neck. The girl, whose head is resting on his shoulder, sniffs and lets out a loud, nasal snore. Zoë realises that they are both high. Sure enough, Pavlo's works, which are all too familiar to her – the glass and steel syringe, the spoon and sponge, the rubber ligature – are scattered across the small table that also holds Mama's old phonogram. Feathers snorts again and opens her eyes. Red-rimmed, the pale eyelashes slightly crusted, they focus on her momentarily and close again. Feathers has a high, rounded forehead, a small, upturned nose and an even smaller chin. A silver thread of spittle connects her lips to Pavlo's lapel.

Zoë lets go of Pavlo's hands and stands up. 'I told you not to bring her back here,' she says, furious.

'But it's just Feathers,' he protests. 'She wants to look after me, Zozo. She's so kind, isn't she?'

'Kind? She's a little junkie thief. And a whore. A Drapetsona whore.'

'She isn't on the game any more.' Pavlo tries to look affronted but his face keeps reforming into a rubbery smile.

'Do you believe that? For God's sake . . . You know she's a thief. She stole Mama's silver hairbrush and flogged it for dope!'

'How do you . . . ?'

'How do I know? Because she bloody told me! She doesn't think about anyone except her precious little self. She doesn't care about anything except heroin. And men. Think you're her only one? Open your eyes, Pavlo.'

'She cares about me.' Pavlo pulls Feathers, now snoring gently, harder against him. 'She loves me. And anyway, it was me who took Mama's brush. She wouldn't have minded.'

'You're lying,' Zoë says, furious. But even through their opiate haze, Pavlo's eyes are sad, almost pleading. She sighs. 'Why, Pavlo? Why do you protect her? She steals from you – from me, from everybody. She keeps you on the needle. Don't deny it: she can't stand the thought of you getting clean. It was her, wasn't it, who got you back on the shit when you came out of the army?' Zoë hears her voice rising. 'Can't you see how she drives people away from you? What about Daizy? She told so many lies about Daizy that the poor girl – she's my friend! – she had to leave Kokkinia!'

'Please, Zozo. The Germans are here. My ribs hurt. I just want . . .' His head wobbles and he blinks. 'Some peace. I'm sorry about the brush. I'll buy you another one.'

'What good will that do? It was Mama's!'

With obvious effort, Pavlo lifts his head and meets his sister's eyes. 'I know you hate Feathers. She likes you, though . . .'

'She bloody doesn't!'

'She likes you. She calls you her sister-in-law. Did you know that?' He chuckles wanly. 'But I . . . I need her, Zoë. Don't ask me to explain. I need the music. I need the junk. And I need Feathers. If I don't have them, I just . . .' He flutters his fingers. His eyelids are drooping again. 'I just fly away in every direction.'

'Christ, Pavlo.' She kneels and grabs his hands again. 'Are you OK, really?'

'Fine. Fine. Australians. Gave me a lift. They've all gone. Think they'll leave us alone?'

'Who?' says Zoë, confused.

'The Germans.'

'I hope so. But they won't. They've put their flag up on the Acropolis.' She looks up, and sees that his head has rolled against Feathers' washed-out curls. *He looks like a saint*, she thinks, *a dead saint*. She kisses his fingers gently. Then she goes into Mama's old bedroom, takes down the silver-framed icon of Saint Polycarp and puts it in her bag. In the lavatory, the loose brick behind which she keeps a roll of banknotes is undisturbed. She pads to the door and stands for a moment, listening to the

216

heavy breaths of the sleeping couple. Then she leaves.

At first she just walks but her feet and her sadness take her up to the cemetery. Mama Katina no longer has a grave but her children pay, every year, for her bones to rest inside the communal ossuary. So that is where Zoë goes. The cemetery seems unusually busy: she is not the only one who has felt compelled to come and talk to the dead. People are everywhere: couples walking arm in arm, carrying flowers; old men; old widows wrapped in black. It is the first place in the city today that has a feeling of purpose in the air. *We've all come to a place we understand*, Zoë realises, resting her forehead against the marble wall of the ossuary. 'Hello, Mama,' she says. 'It's happening again, I'm afraid to say. Everything's going to hell. But don't worry. Pavlo and I will be fine. You taught us very well, my dearest little mother. I'll never, ever forget you.'

When she turns to leave, she is crying, and she lets the tears run as she walks back towards the gate. It is getting dark – time for her to be back at the Cordelio. Black smoke is still coming up from the harbour. She brushes past a well-dressed older man in a banker's suit who is carrying a bunch of irises, walking slowly towards the middle of the cemetery, and his face, too, is wet with tears. A little further down the path she sees he has dropped one. She picks it up and holds it to her nose. It has no smell, just a faint coolness: farmed, not quite real, like most of the flowers sold outside the gate. 'I'm so sorry, Mama. I'm crying for you now,' she says, and doesn't even notice that she has slipped into English. 'I've kept my promise, but I can't do it any more.' She turns to look back at the ossuary. 'I was there when they dug you up, Mama. I washed your bones. I've sung for you: I've always sung for you. Remember when you told me not to follow you? What happens, dearest Mama, when the whole world is going down to Charon? The flowers don't smell any more. Nothing will be sweet.' She drops the flower on the crumbling tarmac of the path. 'Help me be strong, Katina Valavani. Wherever you are, help me be strong.'

Chapter Eighteen

Tom has slipped so far into a heavy, velvety sleep that he wakes to find Niko shaking him hard enough that his teeth are knocking together. He raises his hand to ward him off and Niko lets him go, a look of relief on his face.

'Thought you were dead, Kapetanios!' Niko says, crossing himself.

'Not dead. Sorry . . . how long have I been asleep?'

'All day. It is ten o'clock at night. It's good you slept. Feel better?'

Tom sits up. His skin feels brittle and his burns are stinging, but his head is clear. 'Whew! Much better, thank you.'

'Come down, then,' Niko says. 'It is safe. And you must eat, OK?'

'Are you sure?'

'Sure. We look after you.'

'OK. Wait a minute.' He does up his boots and follows Niko down the ladder. At the bottom, Niko looks him up and down and, apparently satisfied, slaps him on the back.

'OK! Now you come and sit down. The place is full—'

'Full?'

'Sure! But you don't worry about the people. They are all friends. My friends, your friends. You sit, eat, listen to music. Then afterwards, we take you to Zozo's house.'

'Where?' Tom rubs his eyes.

'To Miss Valavani's house. We have decided. You will stay there, Zozo will stay here. It is the best place. Here is too close to the harbour: the Germans are everywhere.'

'Where does Miss Valavani live?'

'In Kokkinia. Very nice. Not too far from here, but not too near.'

'That's . . . terrific. Thank you, Niko, for doing all this for me.'

'You help Greece, we help you. Let's go in.'

Niko is telling the truth: the Cordelio is packed. He takes Tom's arm and pulls him with friendly strength through the door. Immediately, every eye in the room is turned to him. Tom feels this collective gaze as a physical thing: it is like stepping into harsh sunlight, though the room itself is dimly lit. There is a low murmur as Niko leads Tom to a small table with two seats next to the bar. Tom notes that the way to the back door is clear, and the main entrance is screened by another three tables. 'Put your back towards the bar,' Niko whispers, and pulls a chair out for him.

Tom sits, looking around the room for Zoë, but he only sees men's faces: wiry, tough-looking men, all dressed to the nines. Suits, silk shirts, fine Italian hats. Bow ties, gaudy striped ties, boating blazers. Dark, hooded eyes, brilliantined hair, brigand moustaches. To Tom, it looks like Henley Regatta on the river Styx. He recognises the two old communists, playing backgammon near the front door. They nod towards him and go back to their game. A plate appears in front of him: British Army sardines. Then a glass of pale wine. He drinks the wine and begins, reluctantly, to eat the greasy fish. Almost everyone is watching him. He looks up, smiles, raises his fork. The wall of faces nods in approval. The man closest to him, short and wide with greying hair and a vast, straight moustache, nods and points to his plate. 'Good?'

'Oh, yes,' Tom says, grinning ruefully. 'Very good.'

'Ha!' The man laughs and claps his neighbour on the back. As if a signal has been given, customers get up and start to gather round Tom. 'You fight the Germans, yes?' they ask him. 'You fight any Italians?' 'British come back to Greece?'

Soon enough they begin to drift back to their seats. Tom drinks his wine, and Niko pours him some more.

'The . . . I think you say novelty? It has already gone.' Tom looks up. Zoë is standing next to him. She is wearing a short jacket in dark blue satin over a long, pleated skirt of the same material. Her blouse is black, and a long string of pearls is doubled around her neck. He fails to stop himself blinking in amazement. 'We have all seen English soldiers before. Thousands of you. So don't worry.' She frowns and looks down at herself. 'Do I look bad?'

'No!'

'Because you are looking at me in a . . . certain way.'

'It must be because the novelty of you hasn't worn off. Will you sit with me?'

'In a minute. Wait.' Zoë goes out through the back door. Tom fidgets with his cigarettes, sips at his wine, but after a few minutes she reappears with Apostoli and a tall, very thin young man with brilliantined hair and a waxed moustache. A young woman with peroxide-blonde ringlets framing a pale, unformed face is clinging to his arm. Her blue eyes drift over the crowd with a sort of detached hunger. *Her boyfriend would look like a caricature bounder*, Tom thinks, *if he weren't genuinely good-looking*. Because the young man is handsome, but there is something childlike, almost innocent about him despite the hair and the suit he is wearing, an Al Capone cast-off. He mutters something to the blonde woman and she walks off, submissively, and finds a seat in the far corner.

'This is my brother, Pavlo Valavani,' says Zoë, putting her hand on the young man's shoulder. Tom stands up and holds out his hand.

'I'm delighted to meet you,' he says. 'I hope your ribs are healing.'

'Yes, they are much better. Thank you.' The young man bows elegantly. 'An Australian ambulance came by later in the day. And I must thank you for bringing my sister home safely.' His English is perfect but, compared to Zoë's, sounds forced and slightly artificial.

'Go and help Apostoli. I will be just a moment,' says Zoë, giving her brother a peck on the cheek. She watches him limp through the tables, then sits down opposite Tom. 'We are going to play and sing,' she says. 'A special night. In a way it is a funeral for Vangeli, because . . .' Her face crumples for a moment, then she is composed again. 'They had to bury him there, by the road. And also we do not know what will happen so we will sing now in case we cannot sing later.'

'I understand,' Tom says. 'Zoë, I know this probably won't help, but I had to bury some good men too, in the last few days. Wherever we happened to be. It doesn't mean one doesn't care.'

Zoë reaches out and lets her hand rest on the tips of his fingers for a moment. 'I can see that you care, Tom. But tonight' – she looks around the room – 'the war is just beginning for us, and we remember Vangeli and the others who have died so far – hundreds just here in Piraeus – but in a year? Two or three years? Will we still remember then? So I think it's best if we do it now, while we still can.'

'Apostoli is waving at you,' says Tom. 'Surely your brother can't play, though? He must be in pain.'

'There are ways of dealing with pain,' she says, and he catches a sourness in her voice. 'But that is not the whole band. We have many musicians in the Cordelio tonight. The man with the violin is Semsis. We are very honoured: he is Director of Arts at HMV. The man with the big gap between his teeth is Batis. Stellakis will play the guitar. All very famous.'

'All these famous people, here in this little place?'

'You know, we call a place like this *teké*. There are not so many of them any more. These days we mostly play in the big cafes up in Athens. Men like Stellakis have made many, many records. They play them on the radio and then the songs become famous. Rich people like the music from the slums. But now the cafes will be full of Germans. So you know, this is like the old days for us.' She looks over. 'OK. They are calling me.'

'What will you be singing?'

'You'll see.' She grins, but he notices that as she stands up and turns away from him, her face changes. It is as though she has put on a mask. Every emotion has been smoothed away, leaving nothing but detachment and the smallest hint of disdain. Her back is straight; she is stalking between the tables like a statue come to life. And the men, who really do all look like race-track gangsters, watch her adoringly. *She is an actress*, he thinks, amazed. She glides through the cramped space and takes her place at the centre of a line of chairs that have been set up along the back wall. There is a tambourine on the chair and she sets it carefully on her lap. Apostoli is on her left with his bouzouki, Pavlo on her right with another bouzouki, a much more delicate instrument inlaid all over with mother of pearl. The man called Batis settles next to Pavlo. He leans and whispers something in Pavlo's ear and Pavlo giggles. The man with the guitar, thickset with a heavy, oblong face and sparse hair, sits down next to Batis and shares the joke. Semsis, the recording mogul, takes his place beside Apostoli, and beside him, a plump but funereal man is tuning an instrument that looks like a Renaissance lute.

The room falls silent. Apostoli says a word to Zoë, who leans forward and nods towards the man with the lute. She raises the tambourine until it hangs in the air in front of her, still and silent, all but hiding her face. The lute player takes a deep breath and bends low over his instrument. His hands shift suddenly, and a procession of notes slides into the air. Measured and with a deep, soft resonance, the individual notes begin to assemble into patterns. The notes slide up and down scales which Tom doesn't recognise; they hover and repeat themselves, shifting ever so slightly each time. Zoë strikes her tambourine and begins to sing as the other instruments come in behind her. She sings one word, *aman*, drawing it out as though tracing the lines that the lute has painted in the air. The music drifts behind her, the guitar picking out a slow, tripping bass, the bouzoukis trembling over the top. The words change: a lament, or an incantation. Zoë's voice winds its way inside him and finds a memory: another voice rising from the valley below Koovappally, from the Muslim village – the muezzin calling the faithful to prayer. He closes his eyes and remembers: lying in his little bed in a tent of mosquito netting, the bedroom almost dark beyond the netting, the sounds of dawn coming in through the shutters like a ribbon of gold. Zoë's voice trails the same golden ribbon around him.

The song is over. Tom opens his eyes and finds that they are wet. A bit taken aback, he lights a cigarette and looks around him, but everyone is looking at the musicians. The next song is different. Pavlo's left hand glides up and down the neck of the bouzouki, fingers trembling against the strings, then gripping them, then hovering above the mother of pearl flowers that shimmer between each fret. Even to Tom it is obvious he is a master. Then he nods and the band launch into a fast, jangling tune.

Pavlo leans forward and begins to sing in a high, cracked nasal voice that is the complete opposite of his playing. The words, whatever they are, sound knowing, wheedling. Tom guesses that there is some personal story being told, a boast, probably, though there is that same thread of desolation in Pavlo's voice that seems to run through all this music. Niko brings more wine. The song ends, and the band relax and start to retune. Conversations start up and the room quickly fills with voices. Above it all, Tom's ears catch something.

'Did you hear that?' he asks Niko, but Niko is already pushing his way towards the door, holding his hands up for quiet. There is another loud tap, a series. Niko frowns and peers though the spyhole. He curses loudly. The customers begin to shuffle and murmur. But Niko undoes the steel bolt and clicks some more locks. The door opens a crack. A low, rapid conversation takes place and then the door opens. A man in uniform steps into the cafe. A grey uniform with polished buttons and a shiny black Sam Browne belt that holds a black holster: a gendarme. The murmur inside the room turns sharp. Niko closes the door behind the new arrival, puts his arm around the gendarme's shoulder and whispers something into his ear. The gendarme frowns, and to Tom's horror he turns and stares right at him. Tom remembers that his pistol is upstairs, that he doesn't know if there is a back door to this place. At that moment, Zoë slides into the empty chair next to Tom.

'Don't worry about the policeman,' she says to him in a low voice. 'This is Sólon Pandelis. He is a . . . a good chap.'

'Are you quite certain he's . . . ?' Tom swallows: adrenalin has dried out his mouth. Then Apostoli shouts something. The newcomer sweeps off his peaked cap and grins, a little sheepishly. He has a pleasant, rather heavy face with a large nose and a bushy moustache that adds to his air of world-weariness. Everyone begins to curse good-naturedly.

'If Niko let him in, then you are safe. Sólon is a policeman but there are still some good policemen. If it had been his brother . . .' Zoë shakes her head. 'He's coming over. Try to stay calm.'

'I am absolutely calm.'

'Please. Don't worry.' Zoë lays her hand over his. Just for a moment, but it sends a shock through him. '*Ela*, Sólon!' She is beckoning to the gendarme, who is approaching. He smiles at Tom rather uncertainly and Tom smiles back. With a creak of leather the gendarme pulls up a chair and sits down opposite him. There is a tense pause. Every eye in the Cordelio is fixed on the three of them.

'Hello,' says the gendarme in heavily accented English. 'I am pleased to meet you.' He hesitates, then holds out his hand. Tom nods and takes it. The man's grip is reassuringly hard. The gendarme turns to Zoë and speaks urgently in Greek.

'He says – he doesn't speak good English – that he wants to help any man who has been fighting the Germans.' The gendarme speaks again; Zoë nods. Tom tries to follow the conversation but it is impossible. 'There is a soldier, Yiorgos, who is trying to escape. Sólon knows this man. He is going to try and help you leave Greece with Yiorgos and some other soldiers, but it is very dangerous for him.' She says something to Sólon, who shakes his head, smiling ruefully. He says something back, and looks at Tom. 'He says he would like to go with you to . . . to join the British Army, but he believes it is his duty to stay. I told you, he is a good man.'

'Tell him thank you,' says Tom, very touched. 'I would never have expected such kindness from strangers.' Zoë translates, and to Tom's amazement the gendarme takes his face between his rough palms and plants two bristly kisses on his cheeks. Then he turns to Zoë and says something else, laughs.

'He wants to know if I am going to sing some more,' she says.

'Are you?'

'Do you like it? Our music?'

'Very much. I don't understand it at all, but . . . what is it called?'

'The first song we played, the slower one, we call that Smyrneika. The songs we brought with us from Asia Minor.'

'It's funny, I thought they sounded Indian.'

'Indian!' Zoë's eyebrows go up. 'I've never heard Indian. Is it a good thing?'

'I think so, yes. What about the other songs, like the one your brother sang? They're different.'

'You liked them?' He nods sincerely. 'That is called rembetika. That is our music. Smyrneika is memory. Rembetika is our life now.'

'And what do you sing about?'

'Oh! Death. Murder, hopeless love, drinking, poverty,

227

hashish . . .' She chuckles at the look on his face. Taking a cigarette from his packet, she leans forward for a light. 'Now I must sing again,' she says, and once again her face transforms into a mask. She turns away and makes her way serenely to where the band are waiting.

She sings a song with her brother, the music snapping at their heels as they mix their pure and rough voices. 'Rembetika?' Tom wonders, aloud. Sólon grins and nods.

'Rembetika! Good, good,' he says. 'I . . .' He taps his chest. 'I like rembetika very much.'

'So do I,' says Tom, and leans back in his chair. He closes his eyes and listens. The song comes to an end and there is a sudden commotion. Tom sees Pavlo laughing and holding up a small dark object between a finger and a thumb. The audience is cheering.

'What's that?' Tom asks the gendarme, who is shaking his head, looking amused but slightly irritated.

'Hashish,' he says. *Hassiss*. Niko leans over the bar and says something to him, and he shrugs and mutters something in reply. Tom turns around, puzzled, but Niko seems happy.

'Pavlo, Pavlo the madman, he's got the last piece of hashish in Piraeus,' he says. 'And he says, let everyone have a smoke, because when it's gone . . .' He shakes his head. 'Good stuff too. The best: from Brusa.'

'Isn't it against the law?'

'Against the law? Of course!'

'Then what about . . . ?' Tom tilts his head towards the gendarme.

'Sólon? Sólon don't mind. He don't smoke but he . . . what do you say? He looks another way. Five years ago, hashish was legal. Well, not exactly legal. But nobody gave a damn.' He chuckles.

'Then the bastard Metaxas says it isn't Greek. Greek, Turkish, I ask you: what the hell? Sólon, he hates Metaxas, so he lets us do what we want. Bouzoukis, rembetiko, hashish . . . eh, Sólon?' He rattles off a burst of Greek and the gendarme sighs and rolls his eyes.

Niko has bent down behind the bar and come up with a tray full of crude water pipes, each with a wooden stem and a red clay bowl. He finds a pair of tongs and lights a piece of charcoal over the gas ring. When it is glowing he adds it to more charcoal in a clay bowl and blows on the pile until Tom can feel the heat of it from where he is sitting. Meanwhile, the band is playing a slow, lurching song with a high, lilting chorus. Batis's cracked voice takes the lead. Another smell joins the fug of tobacco and in the air. Niko claps his hands and Pavlo stops playing, digs in his pocket and throws something across the heads of the audience. Niko catches it deftly and holds it out to Tom. It looks disappointingly like a large, very dark Oxo cube. '*Brusiko mavraki*,' he says. 'Brusa black.' Niko adds the charcoal and the tongs to the tray, tucks the hashish into the pocket of his waistcoat and takes the tray out into the room. As he walks past a table, someone will nod or lift their chin, and Niko will give them one of the pipes. With the tongs he drops a piece of glowing charcoal into the clay bowl of the pipe, takes out the hashish, and, while the customers watch with eyes like razor blades, breaks off a piece and drops it expertly onto the ember. And on to the next table, as each customer sucks on the mouthpiece, inhales deeply, waits and lets out a plume of smoke. There is coughing and some restrained banter. A pipe reaches the band and is passed from hand to hand, each musician taking a couple of deep drags. Zoë only takes one, Tom can't help noticing, and barely inhales the smoke, which by this time is hanging thickly in the air and filling the room with herbal, animalic fumes which rather set his teeth on edge. Then suddenly there is a pipe on his table.

'You want?' asks Niko. Tom doesn't know what to do. He glances at the gendarme, who is staring neutrally at the far wall, and turns the mouthpiece towards him.

'Would you . . . ?' he begins. The gendarme smiles politely.

'Please,' he says, pushing it back towards Tom.

Damn, Tom thinks. *Everyone is watching*. Telling himself that he has the blessings of the police, he cautiously touches his lips to the roughly carved wood of the mouthpiece. Nikos drops a piece of the black, greasy stuff onto the charcoal. Tom puffs and his mouth fills with dry, hot smoke. *For God's sake*, he thinks, feeling a dozen pairs of eyes watching his every move, and breathes in. The smoke burns its way down his windpipe. Only the fact that he has spent the last fortnight in a fog of cordite fumes stops him from coughing up his lungs. He holds it in, as he has seen the others do, and lets it out gently. *It is better than cordite, but not much . . . No, it has a sweetish, piney taste. Salty as well . . . Perhaps it is an Oxo cube after all? In that case, why all the fuss? Surely it would be easy to . . .*

'Another?' Niko's voice slips him out of his reverie. *Why not?* he thinks. There's no effect at all. The policeman is smiling at him indulgently. He takes another drag.

It seems to be quite a bit later. Tom has been following the music where it has been trying to lead him the whole time, if only he'd noticed: into a half dream full of people, each trailing a story that he can follow all the way back to places that look, perhaps, rather like Turkish cigarette packets – but what, honestly, is more beautiful than a packet of Turkish cigarettes? He has been following the stories east, across the sea, back to where he is from, back to glossy green valleys and huge yellow butterflies. And now, he is here in the Cordelio but also out under the night sky, where the moon is rising, round as a tambourine . . .

She is singing. The night is the deep, sonorous drone of the violin. The stars are the trickle of sound from the lute. The moon is Zoë Valavani. He opens his eyes and sees a policeman's cap.

'What the . . . ?' he says, and Sólon the gendarme turns to him and pats his arm. 'Oh! Hello,' says Tom, politely. He blinks, and there is the night again, and the moon. He sails across another great expanse of time and place: a calm sea reflecting stars. Alone with the singer. The words mean nothing but he knows he is learning something unutterably sad: a terrible lesson given with such beauty, such love, alone with her in this dazzling moonlight.

He opens his eyes. The gendarme is helping himself to one of his ration cigarettes. 'Please go ahead,' Tom says, and takes one himself. His fingers feel like sausages wrapped in velvet. The cigarette traces a slow parabola towards his mouth, like a shell travelling across the firing range at Larkhill. 'Thanks,' he says, as the gendarme's lighter goes *poff* and he leans towards the flame. 'I dropped off,' he adds. 'Sorry.'

'Good?' Niko appears at his side. He puts a glass of beer down in front of Tom. 'English Army,' he says. 'Last one.' Tom finds that he is incredibly thirsty and drinks half the glass in one gulp. 'You liked the hashish?'

'Made me fall asleep, I'm afraid,' Tom says, taking another large mouthful of beer. He's never tasted hops quite this strongly before.

'Yes, yes.' Niko looks as if he's about to say something else, but just then Zoë comes in from the back and leans on the table.

'I think we should go. Do you think so?' she says. Tom takes a deep breath: there's something he's been meaning to say but he's completely forgotten what it might be. Her eyes . . . her eyes are extraordinary. 'Lieutenant Tom?' Niko whispers something to her. 'What . . . ? Christ and the Holy Virgin, what were you thinking?' She sits down opposite Tom and takes his hand. 'How are you feeling, *moreh*?'

'I'm absolutely fine,' he says, puzzled but deliriously happy. 'I was just . . . lost in your singing.'

'Umm hmm. Niko! For God's sake!'

'He is fine. Aren't you, Kapetanios?'

'Clear as a bell,' says Tom, smiling beatifically. He is, however, very hungry. And there is an argument in Greek going on over his head. Words are shooting back and forth between Niko, Zoë and the gendarme, who finally gets to his feet. He puts out his hand to Tom. 'Come.'

'Now?'

'If you can walk,' says Zoë, rather spikily.

'Of course I can walk! But aren't you going to sing some more?'

'Not tonight. Batis is just getting started. I can leave.'

'Oh.' The disappointment is crushing. 'If we're going, I need my case.'

'I have fetched it.' She holds it out to him. 'Paints, everything is in there. We will go out through the back.'

'And my gun?' Tom winces at the thought of it.

'I think it is better if we leave it with Niko.'

'Oh, thank God. Yes, you're right.'

The gendarme taps him on the shoulder. He almost bursts out laughing, and then he is overwhelmed by the knowledge that he will never see this place again. They lead him down a short corridor so narrow that Tom's shoulders brush the wall on each side. There is a heavy door made of rough planks at the far end. Niko opens it, looks around, and nods. The gendarme – he is coming too, Tom realises – steps out, and Zoë follows him. The cold air wakes Tom up, and then Niko is planting scratchy kisses on his cheeks.

'Good luck, Kapetanios.'

'Thank you,' says Tom, and hurries through the door. When he turns to say goodbye, it is already shut.

CHAPTER NINETEEN

They are in an alleyway barely wider than the corridor they have just been in. One end is blocked with rubble. They go the other way, and come out into a street that is familiar from his wanderings the night before last. They walk past heaps of broken glass and snaking telephone wires, the gendarme leading, Zoë last. As they take one turn, then another, Tom slows down so that he can walk next to the singer.

'I know you don't trust Sólon,' she says quietly, and indeed, he has been trying to find a polite way to say something along those lines, but his mind keeps presenting difficulties.

'He's the police,' Tom whispers back.

'So it's perfect if, God forbid, we are stopped. He will say he has arrested you.'

'Right. Supposing he hasn't, in fact, actually arrested me.'

'He won't. Sólon is half policeman, half *mangas*. He'd like to be all *mangas*, but he thinks about his duty too much. That is a good thing. We need decent gendarmes, not the Metaxas bastards . . .'

'You said something about a brother.' The world seems very heavy, somehow, as if the earth and all its weight is bearing down on him. Zoë's voice makes everything seem lighter.

'Sólon has a younger brother. Ioannis.' Zoë looks as if she might spit. 'He is a gendarme as well, but completely different.'

'How so?'

'When the Metaxas fascists came to power they made a youth movement called EON. With a black uniform, boots, white belts . . .' She shudders. 'Sólon wouldn't join. But Ioannis? *Och*. You see, their father was a gendarme. Not from Mikra Asia – from Athens. He married an Armenian refugee. Now he was a good man, fair, everyone liked him. When General Metaxas made his coup, there were a lot of strikes all over the country. Metaxas wanted all the gendarmes to fight against the workers, and Sólon's father said no. He wasn't a communist, he just didn't think it was fair. So he lost his job. He was disgraced, had to get a job on the docks. Ioannis was so ashamed of his father that he became the exact opposite. Everything Greek, nothing from Asia Minor, communists are devils . . .' She shakes her head.

'Poor Sólon. So is he a communist? Are *you* a communist?'

She laughs softly. 'Me? No. I'm nothing. Ioannis would call me communist because I hate the king. I hated Metaxas, I want a republic for Greece, democracy, equality. Most of us from Smyrna are like that. I don't know why. My mother used to say it was because we were more developed.' She laughs again. 'Everyone is always trying to get you to join something. Do you know? The EON, the KKE, the church. I just want to be Zoë Valavani.'

'Which is hard enough,' says Tom.

'Exactly.' She looks at him. 'How are you feeling, really?'

'Fine.'

235

'The hashish . . .' Her voice drops to a husky whisper. 'It was very strong. I just took a little and . . . *foof*! How much did you have?'

'Two or three smokes. It didn't do anything for me. I just got sleepy.'

'Two or three? *Po po po* . . . Niko is an idiot.'

They walk around the far edges of the devastation caused by the explosion of the ammunition ship. As they move away from the sea they enter a tight grid of narrow streets lined with new-looking, identical houses. Empty squares of ground open up here and there where a house has been taken down or never built. The gendarme walks steadily, confidently, though at each crossroads he pauses and looks up the streets before moving on. There is no one about. No one except the Piraeus cats, who are conducting their affairs as if humanity has ceased to exist. They walk for five or six blocks, and then the gendarme, who has paused as usual at a crossing, suddenly stiffens and draws back. Zoë slips to his side. They confer.

'It is a police patrol,' Zoë whispers to Tom.

'Damn.' Tom swallows. 'I'd better say goodbye, then.'

The gendarme turns and hisses something else. 'He's going to talk to them and lead them away. If they go, we'll carry on,' Zoë whispers. 'Quick. In here.'

There is an empty plot a little behind them. Zoë takes his arm and leads him, running on tiptoe, through a rough fence of palings and corrugated iron, and pulls him down behind a scrubby tree. He feels the singer next to him, her side pressed against him, thin and lithe. He can feel her heart beating. Greek voices, gratingly loud in the silence. Sólon, greeting his colleagues. There is a rapid exchange. Tom braces himself. He will simply stand up and walk out with his hands up, and hopefully the buggers won't notice the girl. But at that moment he feels her hand work its way nervously into his. He lets it in. Her skin is cold and he begins to rub it gently with his thumb, listening to the bantering voices in the street. The gendarmes laugh, the kind of laugh that comes at someone else's expense. *They don't care who they wake up*, he thinks. He hears the clack of boots, more laughter. The girl's fingers press into his palm.

The Englishman's hand is surprisingly strong and rough. When Zoë saw him painting, she thought his long fingers must be delicate, but then she remembers what he has been doing. The paintings of guns being heaved through rivers and out of ditches. The crates and the shells. That pistol. And then his thumb begins to caress the top of her hand, running back and forth, back and forth across the thin bones and veins. Although she senses that there is nothing more to it than a reflex of comfort or anxiety, she finds she is less afraid.

To Tom's amazement, the voices begin to fade. But they stay where they are, huddled together under the tree. Now that the gendarmes are gone they can hear each other's breathing, which is shallow and ragged. A large dappled cat with a belly hanging almost to the ground wanders past. Seeing the two of them, the cat stops in its tracks, backs away and hisses, before turning around and, with a certain sagging dignity, trotting off into the dry grass. Tom stands up and helps Zoë to her feet.

'Are you all right?' he asks. She nods and lets go of his hand. Tom feels a slide of disappointment. He signals for her to stay where she is, and peers out into the street. It is empty, and so is the cross-street down which the gendarmes have gone. He can still hear them laughing faintly, quite far away.

They carry on walking. The land is rising slightly. The houses are getting even smaller, and the roads are unpaved, just pale strips of compacted, chalky earth. It is a strange place. The tightly packed white houses, each one tiny, ugly, functional but just slightly neo-classical. The white roads. The occasional tree. *De Chirico would feel at home here*, Tom thinks. *Or Delvaux.*

'We are in Kokkinia now,' Zoë whispers. The responsibility of getting this man to safety is all hers now and it frightens her. At least they are on familiar ground. 'We are almost there.'

They stop in front of a house with a fading blue door that stands on a corner next to a spindly mimosa tree. It is indistinguishable from the other houses around it: a whitewashed single-storey rectangle with two windows and a shallow hipped roof of Roman tiles. A box, Zoë had said. *She wasn't exaggerating*, Tom thinks. Everything seems to be half scale up here. A couple of strides would take him across the street. Zoë takes out the key and unlocks the door. She walks in and Tom follows.

'Shut the door,' Zoë whispers. Tom closes it, the board walls give a shake and the tiny room is plunged into pitch-darkness. Hearing the cheap old catch snap into place, she finds her matches, strikes one and lights the kerosene lamp on the table. She adjusts the wick so that the light pools out over the old rug, the two chairs with their caning starting to unravel, the child-sized sofa. She feels the Englishman behind her, taking up so much room. A shiver goes through her: she is afraid, not of this man, Tom, but of his presence in Mama's house. This is her only place of sanctuary. The silence inside these walls is Zoë's only real treasure. But she is ashamed of it too. Lieutenant Tom didn't grow up in a house like this. He doesn't belong in a Kokkinia box. *But this is where I am*, she tells herself, watching the yellow flame of the lamp waver as she fits the glass chimney over it. *This is where we both are.*

238

Tom looks around. In the lamplight, the room they are in looks no bigger than a train compartment. *First class*, he thinks, but it isn't funny. There is hardly any furniture but what there is of it is taking up all the space. There is an ancient-looking treadle sewing machine with some neatly folded fabric draped over it. Nothing on the walls except a rather beautiful oriental hanging, and a fading sepia photograph of a low city strung out across the curve of a bay. The place is spotlessly clean and smells faintly of sweet Greek tobacco and Zoë's perfume. Then he notices the phonograph and the pile of records. Out of pure habit he steps over to them and picks up the top one. The familiar dog of His Master's Voice sends a little glow of comfort through him, though the writing on the label is all in Greek.

'Is this one of yours?' he asks, and his voice sounds frighteningly loud.

'Of mine?' Zoë spins around, sees Tom holding up a record. *He's touching my possessions*, she thinks. 'No,' she snaps. *I must not be rude*, she tells herself reproachfully. 'I mean, no. I don't have any of mine here.'

'Oh? Why not?'

'I . . . I don't like the sound of my voice when it has been recorded.' A man, *another thing I've never told anyone else*, she thinks.

'What a shame. I mean . . .'

'Please. Take off your coat.' Zoë holds out her hand for the greatcoat, which is heavy. When she hangs it from the wooden hanger on the wall by the door, the whole wall creaks. 'Sit.' She points to the sofa but he settles carefully onto one of the wooden chairs.

'I mean, it's hard to be an artist,' Tom goes on. The chair is uncomfortable and rickety but it would have been rude to take up the only comfortable seating. 'You don't like the way

239

you sing when it's caught on record. I don't like my ideas when I put them onto canvas or paper. I like my pictures when I'm making them, but the moment I step away, I think: that's not what I intended at all.'

'I am not an artist,' Zoë says. She considers the sofa but thinks it might be more polite to take the other hard chair.

'You are,' Tom says seriously. 'When I was listening to you tonight . . .'

'. . . you were high on Pavlo's black Brusa hashish.'

'Admittedly. But I'm pretty sure it's worn off now,' Tom says. It seems to be true. His mind has stopped sending him down lush paths of overgrown thoughts. 'I was listening, and it was very beautiful, hashish or no hashish. Now I'm thinking: if only I could paint like she sings.'

'You are very nice.' She gets up and goes into the kitchen. In the little curtained-off alcove beneath the basin she finds a bottle of decent tsipouro, a third full. *We'll have a drink and then he can go to bed*, she thinks. *I like listening to him talk. I like our conversation. Anyway, I have a duty.*

'What's this?' he asks as she pours an inch of clear liquid into a pair of small cafe glasses.

'Tsipouro,' she says, and holds up her glass. 'Cheers.'

'*Yassass!*' He takes a hearty sip. The stuff is strong and almost tasteless, like schnapps, but there is a subtle aftertaste. 'Thank you,' he says. 'It's good. It tastes like the Greek mountains.'

'Really?' She puts her head a little to one side.

'It tastes like the smell of the mountains.' He laughs. 'I'm not making sense. I didn't smell much in the mountains except burning lorries, but this was what I wanted it to smell like.'

'How sad!'

'Sad. Pointless.' He takes another sip.

'How long have you been a soldier?'

'Oh, months. They threw me in at the deep end. Can I tell you something?'

'Please.'

'I wasn't going to be a soldier at all. I was going to become a conscientious objector. Do you know what that is?' She shakes her head. 'Someone who refuses to fight on moral grounds. When I was at art school we all thought war was against everything that humanity should represent.'

'But sometimes it is proper to fight!'

'That's debatable. Anyway, if you'd grown up in my country after the last war, the Great War, as they like to call it, you'd have seen all the misery it caused. A million dead, and millions of other bodies destroyed, minds ruined. My father, for instance. Artillery captain. Horse trainer, society darling . . . perfect on the outside. Inside, he's a disaster, all because of the War. He made my mother's life hell. I thought, I'm not going to end up like that, and if enough of us think that way, there'll be no war. It didn't work, though, did it?'

'So you joined the army anyway.'

'Actually, my bloody father got me into his old regiment. Thanks to him, I was in uniform less than a month after the war started. But yes, I suppose I would have joined up eventually. Not the artillery, though. Something safe. Royal Corps of Zookeepers. King's Own Wigmakers.'

'That is funny.' She doesn't laugh, though. Tom senses that she finds his presence here in her home uncomfortable.

'So the upshot of it all is that I ended up in an anti-tank regiment. Straight out of advanced training onto a boat, two days

241

in Alexandria and onto another boat. And there I was, in the snow, in action.' He offers her a cigarette, watches as she looks for an ashtray. Her skirt swings gently as she moves around the little room. It is so . . . so domestic. He is terribly moved, perhaps because it has been so long since anything was this safe and ordinary, but also because it is as if a beautiful and terrible creature, an Indian goddess or a maenad, has manifested here to perform the most humdrum of tasks.

Zoë finds the ashtray and sets it on the table between them. She lets him light her cigarette and blows smoke at the ceiling. 'Pavlo joined up. When the Italians invaded last year . . . everyone went mad. Joining the army, waving their flags. I tried to stop him. Is that very terrible?'

'I don't . . .' Tom begins, but Zoë interrupts.

'I promised him I would look after him. And our mother . . . she lost her husband in 1922. You know, we also grew up without men around, Lieutenant Tom, because all the men had died. Half a million, maybe more. The Turks killed them on the docks of Smyrna or they marched them off and they never came back. So I knew, you see. I knew what would happen if Pavlo went marching away. He wouldn't have survived. He isn't . . .'

'You did the right thing,' Tom says. 'I didn't know that, about Smyrna. So you lost your father?'

Zoë takes a deep breath, and turns away from him. 'I lost . . . yes. You see why we sing those songs?'

'I think so. But Pavlo came back.'

'Yes. It's funny . . . actually it's sad. But yes, he came back.'

'I'm glad.'

'So . . . Tom.' She tries out the word again. 'I have told you two secrets about me. You must tell me one.'

'Is that a Greek custom?'

'A new one. Just for this house.'

'I don't have any secrets. I'm very dull,' he says. 'But . . . well, I think I told you that I was born in India. My father was there in the army, met my mother, and I was born in the hills. You could see the Himalayas from our bungalow, apparently, though I don't remember it at all. When I was tiny we moved all the way south to Kerala where my father had a go at planting rubber. He hated Kerala. Hated India. But . . . I suppose my secret is that I loved it there and I still do love it. We left when I was five – in 1922, in fact – and never went back, but I've never felt that I've belonged anywhere else. And I didn't belong there in India, so . . . there's my secret.'

'Why did you not belong?'

'Because I was British, you see. You – we – aren't supposed to like India. We're supposed to suffer it. You live amongst all that insane beauty, all that *life*, and you pine away for the drizzle of England.'

'I understand.' She does, keenly. She sighs, and pours another inch of tsipouro into their glasses.

'Do you know any happy songs?' Tom asks suddenly. He doesn't want to make this lovely woman miserable, and the little house is beginning to feel like a mausoleum.

'Do you?'

'Of course!'

'Then sing me one.'

'What? I mean . . . I'm a terrible singer.' He shakes his head, but she is looking at him from under her dark eyelids. In the lamplight, her face has taken on the quality of a painting: the more than real and the less than real. The curve of her mouth could only have come from an artist's mind, not from nature.

In the pass at Vevi, when the German tanks appeared out of the mist, he felt that every second of his life, every experience and sensation had come down to that one point: there, behind the wall, a drop of water hanging, reflecting grey, from the rolled rim of his tin helmet. He has the same sensation now, watching Zoë Valavani's mouth, seeing her lips gather in amusement. The whole of life contracts to the painter's eyes, the singer's lips. He takes a deep breath. 'Umm . . .' He can only think of the words to one song, and so that is what he sings.

If you were the only girl in the world
and I were the only boy
Nothing else would matter in the world today
We could go on loving in the same old way
A Garden of Eden just made for two
With nothing to mar our joy
I would say such wonderful things to you
There would be such wonderful things to do . . .

His voice cracks and he stops, raises his hands quickly to his eyes, which are wet with tears. 'Oh, God. I'm sorry. I can't sing . . . I've never been able to sing without crying,' he says, trying to swallow down all the feelings that are rising. 'There,' he adds hoarsely. 'That's my other secret.' But then he feels his hands being drawn away, and the singer's face is there. Her fingertips brush away the tears that are running down his stubbled cheeks and then she kisses him, hesitantly, and then again, fiercely this time.

Zoë stands up, her hands still on Tom's rough face. She has always left herself a way to escape, a place to hide, she thinks, looking down at him. *And now I've lost it. I've run out of luck. But it doesn't matter. The world stops outside this little paper box.* She takes his hands in hers. 'Come,' she says. 'Come with me now.' In two steps they are at the bedroom door. The lamp on the table casts a warm yellow fan of light through the doorway, which brushes the end of the white painted iron bed, the trailing corner of the white quilt. Beyond, it is quite dark.

CHAPTER TWENTY

When Tom wakes up he finds himself alone in the narrow bed. He sits up and looks around, but it is obvious that he is the only occupant of the tiny house. The bedroom is squeezed between the room where they sat last night and the kitchen, walls bare except for a mirror and a silver-framed icon. Both doors are open. *She's gone*, he thinks. *Perhaps she was never here*. But his skin smells of her perfume, and there is a red slash of lipstick across the pillowcase. Dim light is coming in through the slats of the shutters and there are voices outside, women's voices. Is it early or late?

His clothes are in a pile on the floor near the foot of the bed. Next to them, a blue pleated skirt spreads out like a giant cornflower. He gets up and dresses hurriedly, hating the feel of the rough battledress fabric against his skin, hating the idea that the coarse khaki wool is rubbing her smell from him, but he is still doing up his shirt when there is a creak of hinges from the kitchen and a moment later, the singer appears. Her face is damp and she is wearing no make-up. Her heavy dressing gown looks like a piece of costume from *The Firebird*, and her feet are bare. When she sees him she drops her eyes to the floor.

'Hello,' he says. '*Kali . . . Kali . . .*'

'*Kaliméra,*' she says, and raises her eyes. Tom feels his face grow hot.

'I was afraid you'd gone,' he says, and stands up to go to her. Force of a lifetime's habit makes him pause to straighten the bedcovers, and as he lifts the top sheet he sees, on the bottom, two dark red stains, one a neat circle, the other smeared. 'Oh. Oh, Christ.' He takes her in his arms and at once his body remembers the feel of hers, her narrow frame, its contradictions of hard and soft. 'I'm so stupid,' he says into her hair. 'So, so stupid. What can you think of me?'

She raises her head. He doesn't know what to expect: tears? Reproach? But her face is calm. 'Would you kiss me?' she says.

They sit on the bed, he leaning against the headrest, she sprawled across his lap, her head in the crook of his neck where if he turns he can find her lips in an instant. 'It didn't hurt,' she says, after a while. 'There was no way you could have known.'

'But I wish I had,' he says. 'I would have . . .'

'What would you have done? Something polite and English? I am very happy, Tom.' She glances at him, and he sees something like amazement in her face. 'I am so happy.'

'Then so am I. Unbearably,' he says, and stretches his legs. The bed is barely big enough for him, let alone the two of them. 'Zoë . . .' He closes his eyes and feels her name on his lips. 'Zoë Valavani. I don't think I've ever been this happy. You know, I don't think this was meant to happen.'

'No?'

'No! I mean, they had a war, and almost killed the both of us. We

247

meet, by the purest chance, and go our separate ways. Then I turn up again and cause all sorts of problems for you . . . The Fates have been trying to prevent this.'

'Hmm.' She thinks of something and giggles. 'The Fates set your trousers on fire!'

'Yes! Think how different things might have turned out if I hadn't managed to put them out.'

'I don't want to think about that. You shouldn't really joke about fate, Englishman. Greeks don't joke about fate.' She kisses him.

'No more jokes. I promise. I'll be serious. I feel serious.'

'Do you?'

'Well . . . I do. I feel serious about you.'

'Oh, *Panagia mou* . . . you shouldn't.'

'Why not?'

'The war. You don't know what will happen. Let's not talk about it.'

'But it's because of that: the war and everything else. It's as if the whole thing has been designed to kill us – us and everyone else – but instead it's brought us together. Something broke. Some mix-up. It's failed.'

'A mix-up.' She spreads her palm over his breastbone. 'Mistake. Or like a strike, perhaps? But I don't think the bosses will give us what we want, in the end.'

'This isn't the end, though, is it? We're here alone. We could just, I don't know, lock ourselves in until it's all over.'

'I only have some onions and a tin of anchovies. And a couple of glasses of tsipouro. Do you think that will last the rest of the war?'

'No. Probably not.' He kisses her and slides his legs over the edge of the bed. 'By the way, where's the, er, the lavatory?'

'The *lavatory*?' she says delightedly. 'I am the only person in the whole of Greece who says *lavatory*! And now you say it too.'

The lavatory proves to be a cement-floored cubicle not much bigger than an inverted sarcophagus, with a hole in the floor at one end, a tap with a length of half-perished red rubber hose protruding from the wall, a tin bucket with a wooden lid, a small iron washstand with a jug and basin. Like the house, it is immaculately clean. A light bulb hangs from the ceiling. Outside there is a narrow patch of earth separated from the yard of the neighbouring house by a board fence. His watch is inside but he guesses it is still early: around six in the morning. He stands in the doorway and listens. The chickens he heard through the window are scratching and conferring softly behind the fence. A cockerel starts to crow in the next street, which sets a dog barking. He can hear Zoë through the flimsy wall, filling the coffee pot, the trickle of water and the scrape of metal on metal. When he comes in she is standing in front of the gas ring. The absurd dressing gown is slipping off one shoulder. He bends and kisses her in the curve of her neck, brushes back the heavy curtain of her hair and breathes her in: warmth, the amber musk of her sweat and the ghostly iris and civet of her perfume. Her skin is startlingly pale, as white as the wild flowers beside the road down from Vevi. The pungent, oily steam of the boiling coffee swirls around them.

'They are saying that when this coffee is gone, there won't be any more,' she says, scooping a spoonful of sugar into the brown foam in the briki. 'And sugar. Is there sugar in England?'

'Not very much,' he says. 'England is pretty miserable, to be honest. Queues and ration books. My mother and sister seem to spend their entire lives standing in line outside butcher's shops. Or so I gather from their letters.' He wanders over to the bookshelf wedged into the corner between the kitchen door and

Pavlo's bedroom, bends and studies the titles. 'My God!' he says in surprise. 'P. G. Wodehouse! Hardy . . . Berenson? Mapp and Lucia, Zoë?' There are others: *Great Expectations*, *Zuleika Dobson*, *The Man Who Was Thursday*.

'My mother had a friend whose husband was a concierge in one of the best hotels in Athens,' says Zoë from the kitchen. 'The guests would leave books behind when they left and he would sell them to Mama for a few drachmas. She used to read them herself, so she wouldn't forget her English, and give them to me. Now I buy them when I can. There are Greeks there as well. Look.'

'Ah. But I can't read those.' He slips his arms around her waist and watches over her shoulder as she swirls the coffee expertly and pours it out into two minute cups. He reaches out and takes one, chin still resting on her shoulder. 'This is awkward,' he says, 'but I don't want to let you go.' He means it light-heartedly, but as soon as the words are out his mouth he realises that it is true. This is the happiest he has ever felt. Here, in this child's toy of a house with the enemy outside, watching this girl making coffee. He knows, more clearly than he has ever known anything else, that this moment contains the only real sense he will ever be able to make of the world. He will let go – he will have to let go. When he does, the merciless world will have no reason to show them any pity.

'Will you come back to bed with me?' he says. 'Please.'

Afterwards, Tom lies on his side propped on an elbow, trying not to fall backwards out of the narrow bed, and watches her. She is stretched out on her back, one leg twisted in the sheet, the other bare. Her arms are behind her head, fingers laced through the bars of the bedstead. He traces a rib gently with his fingertip, touches the beauty mark just below her left breast. Her skin is hot, almost feverish. He looks down at his own leg bent towards hers: sunburnt and singed below the knee, unearthly white above. He sees she is smiling.

'What are you thinking?' he asks.

'I'm thinking about what the old ladies around here say about men and women,' she says.

'And what do they say?'

'That a woman can hold out for a hundred years, but a man cannot control himself for a moment.' She chuckles happily.

'We don't have a hundred years,' he points out. 'Besides, you did hold out.'

'When you first saw me . . .' She turns towards him and rests her head in the crook of her arm. 'On the road. Did you . . . ?'

'I thought you hated me from the very first moment,' says Tom.

'Oh, no!' But she looks charmingly guilty.

'I wasn't all there, you know.' He shakes his head, remembering. 'We'd been in action for days and there was some bad stuff. My unit had only broken it off a few hours before. But even so, even so . . .' He brushes a breast gently with the back of his hand. 'I still noticed that you were extraordinary. I knew you were completely done in, obviously. But you just had . . . You were the most beautiful thing I'd ever seen. I actually thought you might be a hallucination. I'm glad you weren't.'

'I didn't hate you,' she says, reaching out for his hand. 'I just didn't want to be there. After what had happened. My head was going around and around. I was thinking about . . . things.'

'I understand. It must have been awful.'

'The car – Vangeli – that was terrible. But when I was driving with you . . . you don't understand, but I'll tell you so that you do.'

251

'Go on.' He slides next to her and pulls the sheet up over them. His hand finds the groove of her spine and rests there. She takes a deep breath.

'It was hearing you speaking English – you and your men. After the shock of Vangeli being killed, perhaps. But all sorts of memories began to . . .' She makes a claw of her hand and taps the side of her head. 'My parents are dead, Tom. My Mama Katina, who gave me her name, Valavani, and found Pavlo and me this house to live in, was not my real mother. No, that is wrong. She was more real than my mother.'

He brushes a lock of hair away from her face. 'I'm sorry I teased you about your nanny. I didn't understand.'

'You couldn't have known. My parents spoke English at home. Perhaps my mother was English. We were what they called Levantines. There were great merchant families in Smyrna – the Whittalls were English, and the Charnauds, and the Girauds . . . English, French, Italian, German. They had all lived there for hundreds of years, all married each other. I'm one of them, but I don't know how. My mother – I mean Katina, Pavlo's real mother, who adopted me – used to say that the Levantines were the most cultured, the most civilised people in the world.'

'Do you remember them at all, your parents?'

She closes her eyes. 'My father had a yachtsman's cap. White. That's all. I think my mother had curly blonde hair. But then I remember a book that I had. Little Blue . . . a girl. She lost her sheep.'

'Little Bo Peep?'

'Little Bo Peep!' she says delightedly. 'This book had lovely pictures, and I think . . .' Her face falls. 'I think I don't remember my mother. I remember this girl. Do you see? All these things were coming back to me, hearing you Englishmen. And it made me sad, which . . .' She sighs. 'Which made me angry with you. How stupid.'

'What happened?' Tom asks softly. 'If you want to tell me, that is.'

'My father had a yacht – that is why I remember his sailor cap – and we used to sail out into the bay for parties and things in the summer. So when the Turks came, he took everything from his shop, all the jewellery, all the money, everything, and put it all on the yacht. Then we sailed off, at night. I can remember looking back, Tom. At Smyrna, burning. The whole city.' He feels a shudder go right through her. 'But we were safe. Sailing towards Athens. We would have just started again here. My father would have had a lot of clients: rich Athenians used to go across to Smyrna to buy things you couldn't find in Greece. It would have been a little different, but it would have been fine.' She sighs. 'But instead, we were sailing through the night, and we were getting very near. And then . . .'

'You don't have to go on,' Tom says, concerned. Her skin has gone damp under his hand, and she is shivering.

'No. I want to tell you. I was asleep. But I have imagined this so many times. He was sailing along, through the Cyclades islands. There was a mist, but it was calm and he was a very good sailor. He had done this crossing many times. I was lying on the deck, by the . . . the bowsprit. It is strange what things you remember, and the things you do not. *Bowsprit*. In any case, my father is sailing along, and my mother is standing next to him. And a big ship, a warship, perhaps, is suddenly there, coming out of the mist. They haven't seen our little boat. And in a moment . . .'

'You were thrown clear.'

'I must have been. They found me clinging on to the bowsprit. It was a ship that was carrying refugees from Smyrna. A ferry, I suppose, or something like that, but packed, completely packed. They just pulled me out and put me with all the rest. And the next morning we came into Piraeus. That is where Katina Valavani found me.'

'Because she knew you?'

'No, by chance. She was a dressmaker and had a shop – very fashionable – and she always said that my mother had been one of her customers. It might be true. But I was all alone on the waterfront in amongst thousands of other people, and she heard me singing a song. She said it reminded her of her sister, who had died. I don't know if that was really true. I think it was just her kind heart. She had a beautiful soul.'

'So do you.'

'No. Not really. I worry about myself. Am I good? Am I happy? Do I have enough money? Mama didn't think like that. She didn't think about herself.'

'You risked your life for me last night,' Tom says. 'I know about selfish people – I would say I'm a bit of an expert – and you are not one of them.'

'Why such an expert?'

'Because I'm my father's son. My dear father is a monster of selfishness.'

'A monster? Really?'

'Well, perhaps that's overdoing it. He isn't Doctor Crippen or anything.'

'Crippen?'

'Someone who murdered his wife. My father didn't kill Mum, he just left her for another woman.' Zoë's face tells him that this

254

is not so unusual. 'Ah, but though he went off with this atrocious person, set up house with her in London and everything, he refused and still refuses to give my mother a divorce. My mother has the money, you see. Daddy had a small inheritance that he spent years ago and he doesn't have a penny of his own. So he's still married to Mum and bleeds her dry. The horrible thing is, he is absolutely shameless about it, as though it's nothing more than what he's owed. The last time I saw my father, after he told me he'd got me into the Horse Artillery, he spent the rest of the time complaining about how the war had stopped him and the ghastly Mrs Leeds from enjoying themselves in Monte Carlo.'

'Oh, dear.'

'I know, it's nothing compared to what you've been through. The trials of the English upper middle class . . . You're meant to pat my wrist now and say "you poor thing".'

'You poor thing!'

'Thanks.' He kisses her, and they lie like that for a while, under the sheet, limbs tangled, drifting.

'Do you think we should get up?' Time, in his gun troop, had been a torturer's rack. His body has learnt that drifting is not allowed. Right at the edge of sleep, it has propelled him into quivering, almost painful alertness. 'What time is it?'

'It is . . . How strange. I don't know,' says Zoë, stirring beside him. 'It is Tuesday, isn't it?'

'I have no idea,' says Tom.

'Mr Poulatoglou the vegetable seller comes to the corner every Tuesday at exactly eight o'clock. He is like our clock. But I think it is past eight. I must find my watch.' She gets out of bed and rummages naked through the clothes on the floor. 'Aha. It is . . . Holy Mother. Almost nine!'

'Are you expecting anybody?' Tom asks as he buttons up his trousers.

'Expecting? No, but this is Kokkinia. People come, if they are expected or not.' She has ransacked a drawer for underwear and is sitting on the edge of the bed in a pale blue slip, rolling on her stockings. 'Anyway, I'm sure Apostoli will be thinking about what to do with you, and Niko, and this soldier, this Yiorgos. Holy Virgin, and Sólon! And of course, the neighbours . . .'

'Yes, I meant to ask about your neighbours. Because they'll see me, eventually, if I nip out to use the lavatory. Are they likely to report you?'

'No, they won't. Mr Castanides is a communist. The government locked him up two years ago and he only got out after Christmas. His wife is an infernal gossip, but her son was wounded fighting the Germans last month – he is in hospital in Salonika. Since then, she has gone mad against the Axis. I don't think they will say anything. Actually, I'm sure they will help us if we need it.' She laughs, rather bitterly. 'They have always suspected me of having lovers, but an English officer trying to escape – this they will approve of.'

'I'm an English officer on the run *and* your lover,' he reminds her gently. She stands up and peers through the shutters and he thinks he must have said the wrong thing – it has always been bound to happen – but she comes back and kisses him hard.

'My lover,' she says, as if trying out the words. 'Mmm. My lover.'

'I've fallen in love with you, Zoë,' Tom says before he can stop himself. *Damn*, he thinks. *I'm such an idiot. But—*

'Of course,' she says softly. 'We have fallen in love. This is what has happened.'

'So . . . what are we going to do?' Tom feels a not unpleasant sensation of weightlessness. The world has shrunk down to the two of them again, and everything else is just space. 'Now, I mean. Because now I don't want to leave you.'

She sits beside him, buttoning up her blouse. 'And I don't want you to go. When we were lying here just now I was thinking that if you were Greek . . . if only you were Greek, you could stay.'

'Do you think I could pretend? You could teach me.'

'You, my darling Tom, could not be less Greek,' she says sadly. 'But you wouldn't stay anyway.'

'Wouldn't I?'

'You have your duty. You have your – what is it – your battery. Your men.'

'Perhaps. Damn. It's so ridiculous.' He puts his head in his hands. 'I can't help thinking about my bloody old father. The only time he's ever spoken to me as if he actually . . . as if I was someone he actually *knew*, he told me a horrible story about the War. The last war. I won't upset you with it but it was about duty. The man who's shirked every responsibility to the other people in his life is the one who ended up infecting me with a sense of duty. God, the irony.'

'*Eironeía*. I understand,' she says gravely. 'But I wish with all of me that it was different.'

'I'll come back,' he says. 'I will.' He takes her hands and holds them tight. 'I promise. I swear I will come as soon as I can and take you away with me.'

'If you promise . . .'

'I do. I mean it.'

'I believe you, Tom.' She holds his hand up to her face, and lets him feel her tears. Then she sniffs, and smiles. 'So. Where will we go?' She leans close.

'To London, if you like. Or Devon. You'd love it . . . or perhaps you'd hate it. All that rain. No, we'll go to India. I'll take you to Kerala. They have butterflies – I told you that. Like angels.'

'Then we'll go there.'

There is a knock on the door. They both jump. Zoë begins to curse in Greek. Then she collects herself. *She is wonderful*, thinks Tom, jumping up and pulling on his boots. 'Go into the lavatory,' Zoë hisses. 'Take this . . .' She skips silently around the cramped space, finding his map case, pushing it into his hands. 'And this.' His greatcoat. 'You slept in there. OK?' Staring at him, her eyes huge, her bottom lip caught between her teeth, she starts to laugh.

'OK.' He kisses her hurriedly and slips out of the kitchen door, two steps down and two steps up into the coffin-like lavatory. He shuts the door gently, clicks the bolt and slides down until he is sitting on the cement floor, his legs braced against the opposite wall. The light is off and he is surrounded by grey gloom. He listens to the chickens scratching next door. Nothing from inside the house, then he hears soft footsteps and the front door opens, which makes the whole house shake. He begins to hum nervously to himself. *Oh, dear, what can the matter be? Two old ladies locked in the lavat'ry . . .* There is the sound of voices. Zoë's and a man's, certainly Apostoli, but speaking quietly. There are footsteps, then a discreet tap on the door.

'Kapetanios? You are in there?'

'Ye-es . . .' Tom grimaces, trying not to laugh at the absurdity, but when he opens the door, Apostoli's drawn face takes away his amusement.

'You slept in this toilet?'

'Apparently so,' Tom says, feeling strangely bad about the lie.

258

'Oh. Hmm.' Apostoli ponders this. 'Good. Safe in there. Let's go inside. Zoë will make us coffee.'

They go back inside. Zoë keeps her head bent over the coffee pot. Apostoli seems to be berating her for making Tom sleep in the toilet. 'It was fine, honestly,' Tom says, taking out his cigarettes and offering one to Apostoli. 'Miss Valavani offered to sleep in there herself but I insisted.'

'Is true?' Apostoli asks. Zoë is biting her lip.

'What's going on in the city?' Tom says quickly. 'What are the Germans doing?'

'Taking over,' Apostoli says. He slaps his open hand down on the tabletop. 'But, Kapetanios, you must not worry. I have seen Yiorgos Karatsakis. His colonel says they are going tomorrow morning.'

'Really?' Zoë stops stirring the coffee and the briki almost boils over before she catches it.

'Yes. It is why I have come, Kapetanios. To tell you that Sólon – you remember him? The gendarme? Sólon is going to be escorting this lorry, with the colonel of Yiorgos and his men. They have official passes to travel on to Evvia – you know what it is, Evvia?'

'An island to the east of here,' says Tom, who has always liked maps.

'Exactly. This colonel and his regiment are from Evvia, so they have passes to go home and demobilise. They go to Evvia, they get on a caique . . .' He swoops one palm away from the other. 'To Turkey. With you too, Kapetanios.'

'It sounds terribly easy,' says Tom sceptically.

'Very easy. This colonel's brother, he owns many caiques. If you are just an ordinary person, very hard. If you are a colonel . . . easy.'

'Will it be safe?' Zoë asks, laying a cup before each of them. She risks a sideways glance at Tom and his heart glows.

'Safer than staying here,' Apostoli says, sipping his coffee and wiping his moustache. 'They are coming from the barracks in Haidari—'

'North of here,' Zoë puts in.

'So they will come down the road that goes past the cemetery, very early in the morning. You will be waiting there.'

'And we just drive away?' Tom stubs out his cigarette. Under the table, he feels Zoë's leg brush against his.

'Yes. You know, the Germans like Greek soldiers very much, because they make the Italians look stupid. So they are not making difficulties for them, not yet. It won't be hard to get out of Athens. Out of Greece, I don't know.'

'Apostoli . . .' Zoë frowns at him.

'I'm not God, Zozo! The kapetanios is a soldier. He knows about danger.'

'Here's to danger,' Tom says, and raises his coffee cup sardonically. 'Apostoli, I'm incredibly grateful to you and everybody. But if this scheme is going to put any of you at risk, I'll just go off on my own. It's my business, after all. If I was stupid enough to get myself left behind, I ought to be responsible . . .'

'You are a guest in our country!' Apostoli almost shouts. 'Greeks do anything for a guest. We would die for a guest! So don't say any more of that.'

'Thank you, my friend.' Tom reaches over and shakes Apostoli gently by the shoulder. 'What do I have to do?'

'I live a little closer to the cemetery,' Apostoli says. 'You will come home with me now, and in the morning . . .'

'You'll stay here,' Zoë says. Apostoli opens his mouth to say something but Zoë cuts him off with a raised hand. 'We can't move him in daylight. It is bad enough that the neighbours will have seen him. No, he is staying here. It takes ten minutes to walk to the cemetery. Tell me what time he should be there and I will bring him.'

'Hmm. You are right, though it doesn't . . . No, you are right. OK, OK, my friend. You will sleep in the toilet here, though! At my house, you would have had a bed.'

'It can't be helped, I suppose,' says Tom. Zoë's leg presses against his.

'OK.' Apostoli stands up. He comes round the table and embraces Tom, then Zoë. 'I should stay with you here, but Andromache . . . she never worries, but today . . . today, she is worrying.'

'Of course,' Zoë says. 'You should be with her.'

'Then you must bring Kapetanios Tom to the cemetery gate at . . . Sólon says six o'clock. Better if you are early.'

Tom walks him to the door. 'Bye bye, old chap. I won't forget you. I won't forget any of you.'

Apostoli smiles. Then Tom sees him look past his shoulder to where Zoë is washing the coffee cups at the other end of the tiny house. 'She is a brave little one, that one,' he says.

'I know.'

'Please . . .' But whatever Apostoli might have said, he thinks better of it. He pinches Tom's cheek hard and slips out of the door. Tom turns the key and the flimsy lock scrapes into place. *That wouldn't keep out a determined cat, let alone a German patrol*, he thinks. He goes back to the kitchen, to Zoë at the sink. The cups are long since washed, he sees; she is standing quite still, her hands wrapped around the single brass tap. Her knuckles are white.

'I meant every word, you know,' he says softly. 'About putting you in danger. I'm doing a dreadful thing just by being here.'

261

'Then what?' she whispers. 'Do you want to go?' She turns to look at him and her eyes are huge and red with tears.

'No.'

She is in his arms and he is kissing the tears from her face. The salt stings his chapped lips. 'Come back to bed with me,' he whispers.

'Oh, yes . . . but we can't! What if someone else comes? They will, you know.'

'I just want to lie with you beside me,' Tom says. He takes her hand and they go to the bed and lie down on the coverlet, Tom in his boots, Zoë in her shoes. But somehow, pressed against each other, his arm under her head, feeling each other's bodies through the thickness of their clothes, the hidden slide of skin against silk and cotton, the bump of bone on bone, they are more naked, somehow, than before. They watch the lines of light and shadow thrown by the shutters process solemnly across the wall. Time drifts in heartbeats. It drifts with the dust. It leaks, slowly, out through the cracks in the walls, under the doors, through the roof tiles.

Time runs on, bringing them a visit from Pavlo, who turns up with the pale girl with blonde ringlets. Her name seems to be Feathers. Pavlo sits on the narrow sofa, long limbs carefully arranged, looking like a Mayfair dandy in his elegant chalk-stripe suit, while the girl sits on a chair in the corner, hands folded in her lap, gazing at Pavlo with her washed-out, pink-rimmed eyes.

Pavlo has brought a flat parcel with him, a tablecloth tied with string which he unties to reveal three 78 records. Louis Armstrong and His Hot Five, 'Hotter Than That'; Django Reinhardt, 'You Rascal You'; Count Basie and His Orchestra, 'One O'Clock Jump'.

'You know?' he asks eagerly.

'Of course! Wow,' says Tom. 'I have this.' He taps the Louis Armstrong. 'But this one?' He holds up the Basie. 'Wow.'

'I will play,' says Pavlo. 'Which one first?'

Tom considers. 'This one,' he says, tapping the Django Reinhardt.

'Ah! OK.' Pavlo cranks the ancient gramophone and places the needle with exquisite care. The bass slaps tinnily through the trumpet, then the guitar ripples out. 'My God,' Pavlo says, sitting down opposite Tom, hands on knees, legs jumping in time. 'I love this man.'

'You could do this,' Tom says.

'I try! But my hands . . .' He holds them up. 'They are good for bouzouki, but the neck of the guitar is too wide.' He chuckles. 'I try. Eh, Feathers?' The girl nods primly. Tom notices that she never takes her eyes from Pavlo. 'But then, you know, I wonder: jazz bouzouki?' Tom winces and Pavlo chuckles again. 'Oh, God! That would be most horrible, no? I would never really do it. But this, this . . .' He gets up and replaces Django Reinhardt with Louis Armstrong. His eyes are shining. 'This blues: I want to play this.'

'You do, in a way,' Tom says.

Pavlo cocks his head. 'Thank you. What I want to say, though, is . . .' He searches for words. Tom notices again that his English, although it is excellent, isn't as fluid as his sister's. 'The music we play, rembetika, is out of style where we play mostly, up in Athens, the expensive places. What they want to hear is *light*.' He curls his lip disdainfully around the word. 'But things will change after the war. I think all old things will be gone. And I'm wondering what will be new, Tom: what will we play then?'

Count Basie goes on next. 'Where did you get this?' Tom asks. 'My London friends would be very jealous.'

'This is Piraeus,' Pavlo says. 'Sailors coming and going all the time. I tell them to bring me recordings from America. From New York. You have been there?'

'No. I'd love to see it, though.'

'Oh, me too! Niko lived there. I listen to him talk and, my God!' He bangs his chest with a clenched fist. 'I think it must be a wonderful place, America.'

They play all the music and then play it again. Pavlo is good company, though Feathers, silent as an owl in the corner, puts an edge on Tom's mood. When Pavlo gets up to leave, Feathers gets up too, and stands by the door like an expectant dog. Pavlo kisses Tom on both cheeks. 'I wish you very good luck, my friend,' he says. He looks past Tom's shoulder to where Zoë is sitting in the kitchen, reading. 'My sister does not like this music,' he says. 'But . . . she likes you.'

'Oh, I don't know,' Tom says hurriedly.

'But she does. And . . .' Pavlo's eyes look straight into Tom's. 'That is good. It makes me happy. When you come back . . .'

'I will.'

'I know. I believe. When . . .' He pauses, on the verge of saying something else. But instead he shrugs and grins. 'I will see you then.'

When they have gone, Zoë comes in and puts her arms around him, her back to the closed door.

'Do you like him?' she asks.

'Yes, a lot. An awful lot. Why didn't you come in?'

'I don't like the music. No, that's not really true. I don't like Feathers.'

'She is a bit of a strange one. She's not really called Feathers, is she?'

'No. Her real name is Anastasia. She is a refugee too, but not from Asia Minor. From Ochrid, in the north. There was a war, and her parents fled to Salonika. They died of plague, and Anastasia came to Piraeus. There was an aunt, she died too, and Feathers ended up living in the brothels in Drapetsona. It's a sad story. I feel sorry for her – I *want* to feel sorry for her. But she is bad for Pavlo. Terrible.'

'So why Feathers?'

'Oh!' Zoë chuckles for a moment, then stops herself. 'She used to dance in this club – it was really a brothel, but . . . I have played in places like that, so I shouldn't judge her for it. Anyway, she saw a film where a beautiful woman dances naked behind two big fans – was it *Bolero*? She went and bought two huge ostrich feather fans, but when she did her dance, the men in the club made a joke. You see, Anastasia was never very big, and she has been a junkie – you know what it is?'

'Christ. Yes, I do. Poor girl.'

'She started with heroin years ago. So she was pale and skinny. When she waved the fans, giving the men a little look here, a little look there, instead of whistling the men shouted "More feathers! We don't want to see! More feathers!"' Zoë laughs, though Tom sees she isn't smiling. 'It's funny, isn't it? But cruel. Anyway, she has been called Feathers ever since.'

'So why do you dislike her so much?'

'For what she has done to Pavlo.' Zoë makes a face and sits down on the little sofa, pats the cushion for Tom to join her. 'When she met Pavlo she was seventeen? Eighteen? But already on the junk. It was when our mother was dying. That was so painful for him, and he found a way to make the pain something he could bear. Feathers showed him how.'

'So Pavlo is an addict as well? That's awful!'

'Awful. I'm so scared for him, all the time. When he was a

boy he liked to drink, to smoke hashish. But now he just poisons himself. He tried to get clean over and over again – went away, went out with other girls. But always, Feathers turned up with a needle and a bit of stuff. I told you he joined the army when the Italians invaded? Well, the army took one look at him, skinny junkie boy, and decided he wasn't strong enough to fight. So they put him to work in a hospital. In the pharmacy. Would you believe it? But Pavlo wanted to stay clean. He fought the temptation so hard that he got sick from all the worry. The army thought he had TB and threw him out. And guess who was waiting at Goudi Barracks for him?'

'Feathers.'

'Of course. He had written to her, silly fool, and not me, to say he was getting out. And straight away' – she bends her arm and slaps the crook of it with two fingers – 'back on the needle. So that's why I hate her. It is bad of me. She is a fool, and weak, and her life has been rough, but I love my brother, and I promised our mother I would look after him.'

'He's a grown-up, Zoë.'

'I know he is. But one day something will happen, and I won't be able to help him.'

At that moment there is another knock on the door. It is Niko, and Micho, and when they finally leave, Zoë locks the door on the twilight street and they go into the bedroom and strip each other with almost brutal intent. And then, with the space that time permits them, they learn each other's bodies, giving and taking what they will need for the journey ahead.

It starts, that journey, when they step out into Hozanitas Street in next morning's darkness. Zoë takes Tom's arm and they walk up towards the cemetery. The dawn is coming but down in the narrow street it is still night. Cats drift across their path and watch from walls. The street lights are out and the city is completely silent. They don't speak: they have agreed not to. Everything has been said. In a few minutes they are at the cemetery wall.

'You'd better leave me here,' Tom whispers. He pulls her against him, breathes in the smell of her hair, kisses her upturned mouth. 'I love you, Zoë. I'll see you . . . soon.'

Zoë puts a hand gently over his face, letting the tips of her fingers brush his eyelids, his lips, feeling the roughness of his cheeks, the line of his jaw. Then she turns and walks away. Tom watches her, his breath catching in his chest. His hand slips into his pocket and finds, among cigarette packet and matches, emergency chocolate . . . a small, complicated shape. He pulls it out. His cap badge.

He runs after her. She has not gone far, and when she turns, the hope Tom sees in her face is almost unbearable. 'Here,' he says, holding out the badge. 'Give it back to me when . . .'

'Yes.' She takes the badge and tries to study it in the dim light.

'It says "*Ubique*", which means "Everywhere". Wherever I am, you'll be everywhere. My darling Zoë.'

'And you'll be here.' She holds the badge to her heart. 'Goodbye, painter.'

'It won't be goodbye.'

She smiles for the first time since they left the house. 'No.' Then she is hurrying away around the curve of the cemetery wall.

By the evening, Tom is looking out across the Aegean from the loop of a high road in the mountains of Evvia. Below, somewhere – he will find it soon – is the caique that will take him to a city strung out across a wide bay, mountains behind it, the waterfront an ugly cliff of new concrete buildings. 'Where are we?' he will ask the captain of the boat, who will answer: 'İzmir. Though we Greeks still call it Smyrna.'

But Zoë walks back down the hill through the city of little plasterboard houses, where everyone is dreaming of what they have lost: touching, in sleep, all the precious things that have been taken from them. As she walks she sings to herself, letting the words come out as smoke in the cool air, as ghosts. Her ghosts.

BOOK III

Chapter Twenty-One

Piraeus, February 1942

Zoë looks around at the other people waiting for the tram back to Piraeus. The line stretches a long way in either direction. She is somewhere near the middle. There are hardly any trams these days. She will be here for hours. It doesn't matter all that much. It isn't as if there is any food waiting for her at home. At some point in the course of the day she will hide somewhere and eat the little square of cornbread, the precious bobóta, the waxy yellow colour of a four-day-old corpse, which is hiding in her bag. That will give her enough energy to make her way back to the Ntama Koupa, the Queen of Hearts Club off Omonia Square, and sing with the band for another night. The grey sky – the sky has been grey since Christmas – lets out a sigh of northerly breeze and begins to drizzle.

There is an exclamation and a thin cry further up the queue. An old man is staggering and, as Zoë watches, his legs give away and he lands hard on his backside, his legs, so thin that his trousers look empty, stretched out straight in front of him. His head sags forward and his hat falls into his lap. The people nearest to him gather around, try and lift him, but he is quite limp. So he is dragged, as gently as can be managed, to the side of the pavement. A man and two women arrange him, face up, hands crossed over his chest, beneath the boarded-up window of a shop. Someone goes through his pockets and finds an identity card. Zoë crosses herself – everyone is crossing themselves – but it makes her arm ache with exhaustion so she stops. To die just like that. He will stay there now, she knows, until the municipal corpse collectors with their horse and cart come around and pile him in the back with all the others. The line settles. No one has the strength to do anything but stand still. Women whose stockings, if they have them, are sagging from their shrunken legs. Men who, when they gather their coats around them, seem about to cut themselves in half. *I'm no better*, thinks Zoë. She has not looked at herself in a real mirror for weeks, but whenever she catches sight of herself in a window, her stomach lurches. Her hands are like webs of skin, translucent bones and blue veins, and the skin where her stomach meets her ribs is beginning to bruise because it is stretched so tightly. Her insides feel as if they are withering. She hasn't had her period in months.

There hasn't been any food since the autumn. The Germans have taken all the food and sent it back to Germany. They have stolen everything: the factories cannot make cloth because the cotton has been stolen. There are no shoes because all the leather has been taken to Germany or Italy. The harvest has all gone north. She has watched soldiers in smart Wehrmacht uniforms stripping shops. Standing on counters in their polished boots so that they could reach the last bolt of cloth on the top shelf, the last packet of cigarettes.

The tram finally arrives but it is soon full and she has to wait almost another hour for the next one. Then there is a half hour walk to the house. She knows she ought to find somewhere to stay up in Athens, closer to the nightclub, but she is afraid that if she stops showing up at the house in Kokkinia she will lose it. Ownership has stopped meaning very much. Her fear is that she will simply turn up one morning and find the house belongs to someone else.

Her roommates are huddled together on the sofa when she comes in. Voula, Marika and Efi, shivering under one of the quilts. There is no fuel to burn in the stove, no gas for the kitchen. Voula was a weaver at the Madras Carpet Factory, but the Germans have taken all the looms. Marika has lost her job at a local bakery: there is no flour, no fuel. Efi is a nurse at the local hospital, but no one has paid her for months, though there are opportunities to steal food, the meagre rations of dead patients. The four decided to band together in the autumn. The idea was that Zoë would get some sort of rent, but there is no money. Instead they split what they have, and Zoë, as the mistress of the house, gets to sleep in the closet that was once her bedroom.

'Any food?' asks Marika. Zoë doesn't answer but staggers into the kitchen. She stands, staring at the cold gas ring, and imagines it burning with its jolly little blue and orange flame, sees the copper briki steaming, feels a man's strong arms slide around her waist. *Would you come back to bed, please?* She is clutching her bag to her chest, and she has to force herself to open it, take out the greasy square of paper, get a knife, divide the bobóta into four equal squares. Two inches by two inches of anaemic, gritty cornbread. She puts them on a plate and carries them, almost sobbing with disappointment, out to the others. *If they hadn't asked me,* she thinks, *I would have locked myself inside the lavatory and eaten it all, every repellent crumb. Surely I will go to hell . . . though there is no hell, because there is no God, even though I crossed myself when that old man fell down dead . . .* Her thoughts tend to fly around like this. One day they will just fly away out of the window and up into the drizzle, and then they will take her bones outside and leave them for the horse and cart.

'Here,' she says, and when they all grab for the pieces with their skeleton fingers, skeletons with painted nails, she feels a tear stinging the chapped skin of her cheek. There is silence as they eat, and chase every sandy crumb around their clothing, picking them off and licking their fingers like grooming monkeys. When the bobóta is gone, Zoë crawls under the quilt and falls asleep straight away in the meagre human warmth.

Chapter Twenty-Two

Cairo, January 1942

Dearest Zoë,

I have no idea when, or if, this letter will reach you, but there is the tiniest of chances that it will. I'll have to keep it short – what I need to say is that I love you and miss you dreadfully. You are with me every day, which is a benediction and a curse: benediction because your lovely memory has kept me more or less sane over the last few months, and curse because it is only a reflection of someone unimaginably more beautiful who lies very far away from me and, for the moment, quite out of reach. But I'll make do with the memory, for now at least.

That doesn't seem to have taken up *too* much room, so I will give you all the news from my end of things. If the writing is a little bit stiff and if you decide I'm not saying very much, well, I'm afraid this is an army letter and army letters, by definition, are cheerful and boring. But I'll do my best. Here goes! After I left you, we got to Euboea with no trouble at all, and then on to a big fishing caique which took us, by fits and starts, across to (unbelievably) Smyrna, which is now İzmir and as Turkish as any place I can imagine. There were other British soldiers there and we had to cool our heels for almost two months so I did a lot of exploring, but I'm afraid I couldn't find any real sign of the grandeur you described so lovingly. From there we got back to Egypt and the war. There was a big battle a little while ago and I managed to get myself wounded. Don't worry: I'm fine. I wasn't in the hospital very long and they treated me like royalty so, all in all, I've been quite lucky. I know you told me to be careful but it's rather difficult to be absolutely careful here (without people talking behind your back!) and of course it's my job. Meanwhile, it looks as if I will be going home to England soon for training. I can't tell you what for. But it is exciting and there is a chance that it might bring me closer to you.

There are lots of Greek soldiers here and it is clear that things are very bad in Greece. We hear of a famine in Athens and there seems to be a huge argument going on between the great and powerful about sending in food. I don't suppose you'll find it very amusing when I tell you it's even made the London newspapers. Lots of talk, not much action. It's terribly worrying to think of you there but not knowing what you are doing, what you are feeling, if things are good or bad. I hope so much, my darling, that they aren't too bad. But when I scan the newspaper for the word *Greece* and always find it next to words like *starvation* and *massacre*, I feel nothing but dread. I think of you singing, of your voice which I've never been able to describe in words and which I've tried to paint (yes, some people hear voices, I've been painting them instead), and then I think that perhaps there's nothing for you to sing about at the moment, not even those cheerful Piraeus songs full of doom and terrible behaviour (as your nanny might have said). I want to picture you sitting at that funny kitchen table in the sunshine, reading Mapp and Lucia. Maybe Pavlo is in the next room, playing one of his 78s – Count Basie? No, because you don't like it. I don't want you frowning when I walk in on you. There's light slanting in across your shoulders, your hair. The chickens are scratching out in the neighbour's yard. You look up from your book and give me the priceless gift of your smile. I'd fight the entire Afrika Korps with a penknife just to see that. But then we'd have to send Pavlo out on an errand, pretty damn quick.

Well, my dearest, I'd better sign off. I know that if this does by some miracle come into your hands, it won't be possible for you to reply. But if you happen to be somewhere looking south, blow me a kiss. Send it flying across the sea like one of those butterflies I told you about. I can see it now: dodging the Stukas, whizzing past battleships, fluttering over the heads of all the stupid, angry men who are keeping us apart, until it's here brushing against my lips. Be safe, dear Zoë. Be careful (I know I'm a fine one to talk). Try to hope – if your Greek side can't manage it, enlist the English side.

With all my love,

Tom

CHAPTER TWENTY-THREE

Another day. It is April. The trams have stopped running altogether and Zoë has spent the night on the floor of the cloakroom at the Ntama Koupa, wrapped in a man's raincoat, as she has done for the last three nights. This engagement was the band's first job in a fortnight. She wakes up early, feeling the bruises on her hip bones, and walks back to Kokkinia in the thin morning light. At least the sun is shining.

She walks down Stadiou Street. Stacked against the marble walls of the buildings, brass bedsteads glint in the sun, their owners standing next to them. These are the rich, the ones who live in Kolonaki and Thissio, and they are selling their beds because they have sold everything else. Their clothes hang from the beds, English suits, Italian scarves and shoes, arranged so carefully and with such genteel desperation.

A convoy of German Opel trucks full of soldiers passes her on the long, straight avenue down which she is walking. She stares at the soldiers' faces, her fist around Tom Collyer's badge in her coat pocket. They look bored, or peevish, or sleepy. No one so much as glances in her direction. Last night the club was full of German officers and their well-fed Greek mistresses and Zoë had to look at them, all right. She always has to look at them, to smile and flash her teeth and wave her tambourine so that the ribbons dance and the bastards keep applauding, so she can bring something home for Voula and Efi and Marika. No, not Marika. The cart has come for Marika. They found her one morning, blue and stiff on the kitchen floor.

Zoë can't help thinking about Marika as she remembers the food she ate last night at the club, some garbanzo beans cooked in black market oil. Not olive oil – there hasn't been olive oil since last summer – but some sort of industrial lubricant. Still, it was a feast, especially as there had been nothing but a few crusts of black bread for the two nights before that. And before the black bread? She can't really remember. She can only think of the little mound of beans, no bigger than a newborn baby's hand, swimming in its little pool of colourless oil. It was paradise, though her guts are rebelling horribly now. Twice she has to duck into a ruin to squat down and relieve herself, and each time she is more exhausted when she staggers back to the road. *Only another mile and a half,* she tells herself. Her shoes have become too large for her and she has had to pad them with newspaper.

There is a small German outpost up Grevenon Street, near the church, and someone is mending one of the Opel trucks, revving it again and again, sending exhaust fumes billowing up. There hasn't been a drop of petrol available to most Greeks since the occupation began, and still the mechanic revs away. It is a nice day, but the streets are almost empty. Emaciated figures plod here and there. There are beggars on the corners but before the winter there were many more. Last April, the place would have been bustling away to its usual rhythms, but the only rhythm now is wake, sleep, wake. And when that breaks, the horse and cart. The cats who should be sunning themselves are long gone, trapped and butchered, sold as rabbit when people cared enough to be squeamish, as cat meat when they ceased to care.

In the taverna on the corner, two gaunt men are sipping cups of acorn coffee for which they have paid several thousand drachmas, and playing backgammon. Money is meaningless. Zoë's stomach contracts agonisingly and she has to stop and lean against a telephone pole. It has taken her an hour longer to walk here than she planned. She rested in a doorway somewhere in Korydallós and the sun felt so warm that she let her eyelids droop, and only opened them again when something jabbed her hard in the side. A woman was standing there, raising her umbrella for another poke. She gave a start when Zoë's eyes had opened.

'What are you doing there?' the woman demanded. 'I thought you were a corpse! Get up, for God's sake. If you let yourself fall asleep like that, you'll be finished!' She sounded furious, but put out her hand to help Zoë up. 'There, there, pretty one. Keep walking, wherever you are going. Don't stop.'

She leans against the pole, watching the men sip their coffee. She can taste it, bitter as earth, but she'd like some, even so. Pushing herself away from the pole, she totters across the rutted street and towards her house. She can see it, and the stump of the mimosa tree, long since cut down for fuel. No longer feeling the ground beneath her blistered feet, she makes it as far as the front step, and she sinks down onto it with a sense of infinite gratitude. She clasps her handbag to her breasts – *Where have my breasts gone?* she thinks. *They used to be nice. Tom loved them. He loved me. When we lay in bed and the air smelt of coffee, sweet coffee . . .*

'Zoë! Zoë!' Her head is jerked back and someone slaps her hard across the face. She opens her eyes and sees grey. Hands are tugging at her ankles, stretching her out across the step. The grey is cloth. A gendarme's uniform. She looks up and Sólon's face is hovering close to hers. 'Wake up, *koukla*! Thank God, she's alive,' he mutters. 'Can you hear me, Zoë?'

She nods. 'Stop yelling, Sólon. Leave me alone.' She winces at his rotten breath. They all have this corpse-like stink now: they are dying from the inside out. She looks past him and sees it is Efi who has hold of her ankles. They carry her inside and lay her on the sofa. Efi kneels down beside her.

'When did you last eat, my darling?'

'I . . . Last night. I had some beans last night,' Zoë mutters guiltily. 'But my stomach . . . *och*. It hurts.'

'She has dysentery,' Efi tells Sólon. 'If she's had beans they'll have been ancient and full of rat shit, and God knows what else. Have you walked from Athens?' she says loudly to Zoë, who nods weakly. 'I haven't seen you for days.' Efi pulls off Zoë's shoes, and winces at the blisters.

'I've been at work.' Zoë can't manage anything more than a rough whisper.

'Have you heard about the strike?' Efi asks brightly. Zoë shakes her head. 'The postal workers have gone on strike for more rations. Now EAM have come in on their side. It looks like the government are going to cave in. More food for civil servants like me. I'll have more to share. You'll have more, eh, Sólon?'

'I do all right as it is,' Sólon mumbles, clearly embarrassed. Zoë knows he spreads his meagre ration around his large extended family and the way his uniform is hanging off him he plainly isn't getting much of it himself. 'But I support the strike,' he says, and looks at Mr Castanides. 'And I support EAM too.'

'*Po po po.*' Mr Castanides shakes his head. 'You should go to the mountains, Sólon. Join EAM. Fight with the partisans. That's where you belong.'

'I know,' Sólon says bitterly. 'But if I did, what about my wife, my boys? The Germans would send them straight to Dachau.'

Mr Castanides and Sólon are not natural friends. Castanides the old communist and Sólon the gendarme. But the times have whittled away their differences. 'It's good you stay here with us,' says Mr Castanides, generously. 'You help keep a balance against the bastard fascists.' He doesn't say more, but they all know who he means. Sólon's brother, Ioannis.

Zoë listens to this conversation as though from a great distance. Though they are all standing around in her house it seems to have very little to do with her. She rolls over to get comfortable but a spasm of pain in her guts cramps her into a ball. 'I have to go to the lavatory,' she gasps, and starts to cry.

'You need to drink,' says Efi. She has brought a tin mug of water and holds Zoë's head up so that she can sip. 'Drink it all. We're going to make you some soup.'

'With what?' Zoë is feeling a little clearer. She has just had a bad turn. A couple of hours' sleep and she'll be ready to walk back into Athens.

'With these,' says Mr Castanides, who has slipped out and reappeared with a bunch of young nettles and dock leaves. 'They've started to come up where we had the chickens,' he says. 'There were only a few, just enough for the missus and me,' he adds, apologetically, 'but what with the sunshine . . .'

'Thank you,' Zoë says, and tries to sit up.

'You must do nothing, darling, for at least a week,' says Efi, pushing her down again briskly. 'I didn't realise you were so weak. You've been hiding it from us.'

'It's my business and no one else's,' Zoë mutters. She has never accepted help from anyone. Why should this war make her change?

'For fuck's sake,' says Efi genially. 'I'm not going to have you end up like Marika. We'll boil these up with some salt from the sea—'

'What are you going to boil it with? Your breath?'

'Voula found a few pieces of coal last night, up by the Germans.'

'*Aman . . .*' Zoë closes her eyes again.

'Yes, we'll make it and you'll drink it all, do you understand?' Efi snaps. 'Or I will kill you myself. Hear that, Sólon? I'll murder her.'

'I hear. Do you want to be responsible for that, Zoë? It'll be your fault when I lock Efi up for killing you.'

'Go to the devil,' Zoë tells them, but she is chuckling. 'I'm going to die anyway.' It makes her feel better, oddly, to say it aloud. What a relief. *I'm sorry, Tom*, she thinks, *but I won't be here when you come back for me.*

But she doesn't die. She sleeps, and dreams so sweetly of Tom Collyer that when someone slips a hand behind her head and raises it gently so she can smell the rank soup, she thinks he has come to feed her, so she drinks the broth of weeds and seawater. She wouldn't have woken for anyone else. In the days that follow, she lies in bed under the folded-up carpet while Efi and Voula force her to drink, and take her to the lavatory, wash her and bring her back to bed. Voula, who is sturdier than the others, has enough strength to go foraging in the hills, and comes back with meagre bundles of greenery: dandelions, vine shoots, bramble shoots, the odd wisp of wild asparagus. The hills are being picked bare, she reports. Only by breaking the curfew and slipping out before dawn does she manage to find anything at all. Even so, it keeps them alive. The local church opens a soup kitchen and they queue for hours for cups of vile-tasting broth. They do whatever they can, they use every ounce of strength, every last spark of intelligence, and it all adds up to just enough. And then there is Pavlo.

In the last days of her illness, before it stops being serious and is just something to put behind her, Zoë's brother makes an unexpected visit. He sits on the edge of her bed, on the fraying carpet.

'You look like a ghost,' she tells him.

'Thank you,' says Pavlo. 'That means I must look better than the living.' He takes out a packet of cigarettes and offers her one. She takes it almost reverently. She hasn't smoked since last November.

'Where did you get these from?' The smoke is delicious but dangerous, as if it could burn her up entirely.

'Wait.' He pulls out a flat, circular tin with a bright red pattern on the lid. Opens it, and takes out a triangle of something black and gleaming. 'Voula,' he calls. Voula is scrubbing the kitchen floor, the kind of useless chore they have been doing for a year now, just to pass the time. Pavlo takes out a switchblade – Zoë hasn't seen that before – and cuts the little triangle into three equal slivers. 'Here you go.' He holds one out to Zoë. She sniffs it.

'Christ and the Holy Virgin!' she hisses. 'Chocolate!' Before she can stop herself she has jammed the piece into her mouth. The deep, earthy sweetness bursts inside her mouth so powerfully that she thinks she is going to be sick.

'Chocolate?' Voula snatches the piece Pavlo is offering her and holds it under her nose for a whole minute before slipping it slowly between her lips.

'Where did you get it?' Zoë demands, as Pavlo divides up the other triangle in the tin.

'Do you remember the Italian Army surgeon from the club?' Zoë can vaguely picture a nice-looking, grey-haired man in a tailored uniform. 'Well, he was there with one of his men. A junior doctor. You know, I can spot a fiend from a mile away . . .'

'A fiend?' asks Voula, who is still licking her lips ecstatically.

'On the needle. Anyway, I found him in the bathroom in the interval. Didn't take much to get it out of him.'

'Is this another story about buying heroin?' says Zoë testily. 'Because I'm sick of those. Write a song about it instead.'

'Patience, Zozo. I wasn't buying – I didn't have to. You see, *il dottore* wanted to go into business with someone.'

'Business . . .'

'He works in the hospital. So he takes what he needs for himself, obviously. But, turns out there are a few bad boys in the German garrison who are looking for a fix. *Il dottore* wanted to find someone to be a go-between. If he was caught selling junk to the Germans, it would be all over for him, but if a Greek . . . you get it? With connections?'

'You're dealing drugs to the Nazis,' says Zoë in disbelief.

'My God! How exciting!' Voula breathes.

'Shut up, Paraskevoula. He's an idiot.'

Pavlo shrugs his narrow shoulders. 'Sure, I'm dealing,' he says. 'We're not talking about much, unfortunately. A few ampoules of morphine, some heroin tablets. But only to the Bosch.'

'And what do you get out of this?'

'Just some treats like these, which they throw me as if I was a talking dog. The money all goes to *il dottore* and I'm not in a position to ask him for a cut. If anything at all goes wrong I get shot, basically, even if everybody else gets away with it. But listen: I'd never, *never* sell to a Greek, Zoë.'

'Like hell.'

'I mean it. I hate the shit with all my heart, but it's my life. You know how many times I've tried to get clean. If I can fuck some Nazis up a bit, then at least some good will come from it.'

'How are the others?' she says, to change the subject. The thought of Pavlo's habit always makes her feel that she has failed Mama Katina, and she had promised . . .

'They're hanging on. Lountas has promised us another gig. You've got to get well. I'll bring you some more chocolate. Some soup. Bacon!'

'I don't want it if it's come from selling junk,' snaps Zoë, though of course she does, desperately. Besides, she can see Voula giving her brother the kind of look she knows all too well. *Why can't girls resist him? He's a junkie bum, and he always will be. But, damn him, he is beautiful, and charming, and his heart, though it is pickled in heroin, is a good heart.*

They survive. Lountas books the band again and again, and Zoë grins and waves her ribboned tambourine for her conquerors. Sólon introduces Mr Castanides, very discreetly, to a black marketeer, who turns out to be the son of Mrs Vlessas, and who remembers Mama singing at his sister's wedding. Because of this, he gives Zoë good rates on beans and oil and chickpeas, good being 10,000 drachmas for a little bag of chickpeas, rather than 15,000. Mostly they live on nettles and carob pods and Efi's rations, and whatever Zoë can scrounge at the club. German treats from Pavlo, which Zoë refuses to his face but takes after he has left. She doesn't have the power to resist. Perhaps this is what it is like to be on the needle: this dreadful, all-consuming hunger.

Then the Allies lift the blockade, and there is a tiny ration of bread again, and news. Rommel has been defeated at El Alamein. Zoë thinks of a man with a floppy black fringe and sunburnt knees blowing up German tanks. Then she pictures crosses in rows, stretching away across the desert. *It isn't hope that's got you this far*, she tells herself; *it's bloody-mindedness. Don't think so much. Don't hope. For God's sake, don't start hoping now.*

CHAPTER TWENTY-FOUR

London, August 1942

Dearest Zoë,

Please forgive my silence but I've been on a boat for what seems like decades, and I've only just got back to England. If I'd swum the whole way I would have got here faster. We chugged down Africa, round the Cape and up the other side. We had to stop in Lagos for a week, which became a fortnight, and I did a lot of painting and absolutely nothing else – luckily I didn't catch malaria, though everyone else seemed to manage it. Hooray for gin and tonic! And now here I am back in London. Half of the place is in ruins and yet people are going about their business as if everything were perfectly normal. It is impressive but also a little bit frightening: it feels *haunted* in a way, the people most of all. Unnatural. Everyone is so chirpy, always finding the bright side of everything. I have a horrible suspicion that you would hate it. And actually, I'm beginning to understand your suspicions about hope. Understand, mind, darling;

not subscribe. You are my hope. Without hope, I don't have you. I expect you'd raise those wonderful eyebrows at me for saying that, and dish out some of your delicious disdain, but, well, I'm afraid you're stuck with it.

I managed to get down the country, to Devon (remember I told you all about it: rain, rain, rain) to see my mother and my sister. My little brother is still at school but he'll be called up next year and he wants to be in tanks. I keep telling him that, as an anti-tank gunner with strong opinions on the subject, I wouldn't recommend it, but he won't listen. He's always liked loud things, machines. I'm worried but there's nothing I can do, I suppose!

I'm pretty sure that you won't get this letter. I somehow don't think you got the last one either. A friend made the arrangements, but the chap who was going to deliver it was killed, unfortunately, and I'm trying to find another way to get things through to you. So perhaps it doesn't matter what I write. I'll tell it to you in person one day, one day *soon*, and you can tell me everything that's happened where you are. But I'll write anyway, just in case, and because when I write, I feel as if I'm talking to you.

I'm writing this in a wooden hut on the edge of Salisbury Plain. How to describe Salisbury Plain, except that, if you're training to be a soldier, it's a place you come to loathe. Which is a shame, as it can be rather beautiful. I am training, too. I'm going to be a parachutist. I can imagine you giving me one of your looks: well, all I can say is that it started out as a good idea. While I was in Cairo, I met an old acquaintance – the chap I gave your letter to – who was training for some secret stuff: jumping into Greece to

289

liaise with the partisans. I thought – instantly, in less than a heartbeat – that I had to do the same thing. So I went along to my colonel and told him I was going to volunteer for special services. To cut a long story short, he refused. 'I won't have one of my officers joining that mob of amateurs playing at pirates,' was the gist of it. 'But seeing as you have the urge to do such a damn stupid thing, they're forming some new units of airborne artillery.' He signed me up there and then. This particular colonel isn't someone you argue with. But I felt as if he'd just stabbed me through the heart.

I realise that jumping out of aeroplanes doesn't fall under the rubric of 'be careful', but, well, nothing makes much sense any more and this makes about as much sense as anything else. And it is rather spectacular. At first you are winched up in a barrage balloon, not very high but quite bloody high enough. You can see the curve of the horizon and the light . . . You know I can talk about this sort of thing for hours, and write about it too. I'll just say that the light, when you are up high, is clear and buoyant and seems to hold the promise of release. Of escape. And then you jump, and the ground comes up very fast and very solid. No escape after all. Yesterday I jumped out of an aeroplane for the first time. It should have been frightening but it actually felt rather ordinary. Like being on a crowded Tube train at rush hour and then suddenly pushed out onto an empty platform. I should have been more worried, I suppose. The day before, my unit was watching another lot make their first jump. The plane flew over the drop zone and one chap's parachute failed to open properly. He hurtled to earth with his parachute streaming up above him. Rather poetically, the instructors call this a 'Roman candle'. We ran across to him: he looked perfectly peaceful, as if he'd left himself behind in the light.

This is all a bit morbid, but it's all quite happy here. I worry continuously, though: not about the parachuting business, but about you. There hasn't been anything in the papers about Greece since we heard that the supply ships were getting through. It's so hard not knowing if you're hungry, or in good health, let alone good spirits. I imagine you singing – I can't imagine you *not* singing – but then I worry that there might really be nothing, at all, to sing about. That will change, my darling.

With all my love,

Tom

CHAPTER TWENTY-FIVE

London, 9th December 1942

My darling Zoë,

Tomorrow, or the day after, I will be a little closer to you. At the wrong end of the Mediterranean Sea, but it isn't a very big sea after all, is it? I've had to spend a lot of time looking at maps lately, and the Mediterranean, if compared to a proper ocean, like the Atlantic, isn't much more than a big lake. So I'll be at one end and you'll be at the other. If you stand on the harbour at Piraeus, you'll be looking at the same water I am. Perhaps I should put a message in a bottle, a nice brown army beer bottle, and give it a shove eastward. Keep a lookout!

I'm glad to be leaving England again. Training is over: they gave me a nice red beret and a badge with wings as a souvenir. I'm being flip: actually I'm startlingly proud of myself and the other men. I never thought I'd be the sort of person to be talking about doing my bit, but I see now that one has to do just that if the world is to be prevented from ruining itself completely. There's so much to do out there. I rather despise myself for writing this. I never wanted to be a soldier. I believed that soldiering was a moral outrage. But not very long ago I was here in London on leave and I ran into some old friends from art school in a pub. It's the place we all used to drink, a narrow, dingy little place with none of the passion and energy of the Cordelio but packed full of artists and poets and writers – and a good few tarts and scroungers. My friends are in the army too. They'd tried to be conscientious objectors – do you remember me telling you that I wanted to be one? – and though they hadn't quite managed it, they haven't been sent into the fighting. Quite the reverse: they're painting stage sets for a production of *Macbeth*. They took me down to have a look. Beautiful, beautiful work. I was so impressed, and so envious, that I almost cried. After I left them I wandered around a bit, through the smashed-up streets. I didn't want to be a gunner any more. I wanted to paint strange oak woods and magical starlight for the Piccadilly Theatre. I wanted to paint, which is to say, I wanted to be myself again. Before I met you I'd never found something I loved more than my work.

I walked some more, and ended up in Hyde Park, down by the Serpentine, which is a sort of pond where Londoners go boating and throw bread at ducks that look like mad tramps. I caught sight of my reflection in the water, which was, as it always is, a frightful pea-green colour, and it was such a shock to see that I *was* myself. Uniform and all. One is always oneself. Up until that point, even with everything that had happened, I realised that I had still been seeing it all as a bit of a joke, something I'd been going along with, but which wasn't really anything to do with me. I'd been an actor playing Tom Collyer. But all that fell away in one uncomfortable moment. Straight afterwards I felt . . . well, I felt an enormous sense of relief, as you feel when you pull the cord of your parachute and the silk hisses out and opens with a great, final *whump*. All the work is done. All you have to do is drift. I could have gone another way, been like Johnny and Michael, painting scenery – I could have done it quite easily. I don't blame them at all. They're being true to themselves. But I chose this. I have to be honest, Zoë: I chose to be Lieutenant Collyer, and I suppose that means I thought it was more important than being a painter, even though I couldn't admit it to myself. Now I have, and I can just get on with the business of soldiering. Perhaps that's where the relief comes from. I hope you don't think I've gone mad with all this cod psychoanalysis. You'll have to cure me. I'm not sure that anyone else can.

There's more to write but I have to go. We lift – such an elegant way to describe being crammed into a plane – at an ungodly hour tomorrow and I have to get back to my unit. More later.

CHAPTER TWENTY-SIX

Algiers, 10th January 1943

My dearest Zoë,

I'm looking out over a beautiful blue and silver sea. I've calculated that you are a mere one thousand, one hundred and thirty miles away from me, as the RAF flies. That's almost nothing, isn't it? I'm tempted, very tempted, to go down to the docks, take one of the little fishing boats and start rowing east. They are beautiful, those boats: blue and red, green, egg-yolk yellow. I can't quite believe that there are things like them left in the world, where everything seems to be reduced to the gloomy shades of mud, brick dust, grease and dirty cloth. I loved the boats in Greece, with their painted eyes that made even the dingiest craft look like something from the *Odyssey*. The boat that took me over to Turkey had eyes, big, swooping eyes from a pharaoh's coffin. I would have felt like Odysseus himself if I hadn't been so bloody miserable, leaving my Penelope – that's you, in case you nodded off over my strained classical analogy. Actually, you're Circe and Calypso as well, so there. There's a sort of magic, here around this sea, in the ordinary things. I'm pretty ordinary: surely it would give me safe passage across to you.

But I'm stuck here, I'm afraid. Lots to do. We arrived in North Africa almost a month ago and it's been a slog, a bloody one, almost since we landed. We've been pulled back now and are cooling off in Algiers. It's calm here, untouched by the war if you don't look too hard. Very French. I came across a stall in the old souk yesterday piled high with old copies of *Vogue Paris*, and I thought of your mother, what you told me about her. Algiers is cosmopolitan in a minor key, faded sort of way, and I wonder if I might catch a glimpse of old Smyrna if I sniff around enough. There is a small community of posh French ladies here, trying terribly hard to keep up appearances. Succeeding, too, for the most part. But they couldn't hold a candle to your effortless beauty, or your style. I bought one of the *Vogue*s and painted your face over the cover, but it wasn't a good effect and I chucked it away. Remember when I told you that you were too beautiful for a cigarette box? Turns out you are too beautiful for *Vogue* as well.

Something I wanted to put in the last letter but ran out of time: I was invited out to dinner with my father and his mistress – I suppose she's his mistress, as she lives with him but he's still married to my mother. Normally I would have wriggled out of it but I hadn't seen the old man for some time and I decided to go along. We went to some dreadfully – and dreadful – posh place in Mayfair. Mrs Leeds is a genuinely ghastly woman and ordinarily she dominates things, but I felt, in spite of the surroundings and the proximity of La Leeds, that Dad was making an effort to be, well, nice. We actually had a conversation. At the end of the meal he somehow contrived to get rid of Mrs Leeds and we ended up at the bar, drinking whisky and just talking. He wanted to know about the war, but as a soldier, and he was fascinated by the minutiae (which are unbelievably dull) of anti-tank gunnery. We ended up drawing diagrams and arcs, fields of fire and falls of shot, in spilt water on the bar. When Mrs Leeds came to find him, he hugged me, rather stiffly but still a hug, as we said goodbye. I left not knowing quite what to make of it all. Now he's taken to writing me rather sweet letters.

Zoë, here we are again, under the same sunlight, but *only* a thousand miles apart. I'm whittling the distance away, bit by bit, mile by mile. That's why I've ignored your orders to be careful, my love. I'll only get closer to you by pushing. Pushing away at the bloody enemy, helping to push him right out of our lives. Maybe next time I write, I'll be a few miles closer. I can't wait. I love you.

Tom

CHAPTER TWENTY-SEVEN

Near Foggia, September 1943

Dearest Zoë,

I'm writing this in Italy. Italy! I've always wanted to come here, ever since I first saw Botticelli's *Venus* in a book. Venus, the lady on the scallop shell, bobbing ashore in all her naked glory. Now that I come to think of it, doesn't Niko have a repro of her pinned to the lavatory door at the Cordelio? And now I'm wondering whether the Cordelio is still open. Still standing, even. God, I hope it is. I'd hate to think of the world without the Cordelio.

It has to be said that Italy hasn't quite – yet – lived up to my expectations. It's been pouring with rain and I've been spending most of my time in various holes in the ground. I have a nasty (sneeze!) cold. We landed at Taranto, behind the heel of the Italian boot and now we're inching up the leg – not, admittedly, much higher than the ankle at this point. Before that, I was in Sicily. Quite an exciting time it was too – 'exciting' in the unpleasant sense, unfortunately. But there were a few moments that were less exciting and more enjoyable, such as when I almost literally ran into an acquaintance of mine, an old teacher in fact, riding a bicycle (unbelievable but true) down the main street of a little mountain village, a couple of bottles of wine in the basket in front of him. Edward Ardizzone is a lovely, portly chap who looks distinctly comical in uniform, but he turns out to be quite fearless. Apparently he captured another village almost single-handedly – by accident, he assured me – which isn't bad going for an illustrator of children's books. We sat in an abandoned chapel and drank some of the wine, and he told me he was there as that most extraordinary of beasts, an official war artist. I should write that with capitals: Official War Artist. The army pays him to draw pictures. I showed him some of mine, of course – I'm still carrying my old case around with me everywhere – and he was nice enough to say that I should ask the Commission for a job myself. Funnily enough, that had never occurred to me before. I know a couple of chaps who have gone down that path. In fact one of them, a man I knew and admired very much was killed when his plane went down near Iceland. But I don't think I'd get the job. The army needs artillery officers more than it needs artists. If it were the other way around, I don't suppose we'd have as many wars, would we?

I was in an abandoned school yesterday – we've been using them as field hospitals and I went to get some aspirin for my cold – and I found an atlas. With a piece of string – highly scientific – I was able to work out that you are only 495 miles away from me! That's walking distance, my darling. And a bit of sea, although that looks swimmable. So near. I can't help thinking that the fact that we're *here* now means we'll be *there* sooner rather than later.

More soon.

All my love,

Tom

CHAPTER TWENTY-EIGHT

Devon, 20th March 1944

My darling Zoë,

I'm back home – my actual home, that is, down in Devon.
I've been here for a couple of weeks, but I've only just got the
use of my arms back, otherwise I would have written sooner.
Before I came here I was in a hospital outside London. I
was wounded – as you've probably guessed by now – just
before Christmas, but I'm OK. Actually I'm going out of my
mind with boredom, though my family – Mum, sister and
grandfather – are doing their best to cheer me along.

It looks as if I'm out of the fighting for good, which
I expect you'll be glad to hear. I won't tell you how it
happened, because it would only bore you. My left arm
is a bit of a mess, and my right arm was broken but seems
to be fine otherwise. I have some shrapnel in my left leg
and a bit more in my head, but not enough to excite any
doctors. All the best people are full of shrapnel these days.
As soon as I showed that I could count to ten and wiggle

my fingers, the doctors lost interest. That must be good, mustn't it? I admit I was worried until the cast came off my right arm, but although it's a bit stiff it works a treat. I can hold a brush and a pen, which is the main thing. I still get frightful headaches but apparently they will go away with time and meanwhile, I have some extremely strong pills to help things along. I rather think Pavlo would approve.

I had some bad news while I was in hospital. My father died around the time I was being shipped back to England. Apparently he had a heart attack and died in his sleep. In the end I heard about it from, of all people, Mrs Leeds, who managed to get to me before Mum. She was dressed in black and looked even more terrifying than usual, though she was genuinely upset – at least I think she was. She sat on the edge of my bed and smoked my cigarettes and seemed almost motherly, stroking the cast on my arm. She started to cry, and I did too, though afterwards I wondered if it was all the drugs they'd given me which had done that. But I loved my dad, in a peculiar and complicated way, and I find myself grieving for him, for a man I never really knew because he'd made himself deliberately unknowable. He was only forty-nine. So very young. It turns out that he'd been gassed in the last war and it had damaged his heart. I never knew: he'd never told anyone.

I wrote to a man who'd known my father: a general, the chap who'd actually signed me up for the regiment in '39. He very kindly wrote back to me and told me all sorts of things: that my father had been one of the best-loved young officers in his brigade, that he'd been recommended for the DSO but that there had been some sort of mix-up. He'd ended up in India because of the gassing: it helps me to think of him as a racehorse put out to pasture, not as someone running away from responsibility, which was how he always seemed to appear. I'm afraid that was how he felt. How ghastly. I do need help to think about him. It's awful knowing there are things one will never be able to straighten out. At times I think I'd give what remains of my arm for just one more conversation. At least we had that evening last year. Not enough, but something, at least. While I was in hospital I heard that I'd been promoted to captain, his rank, and I want to tell him, because he'd have been happy, I think. I *hope*.

Almost as upsetting, in a different way, was my realisation that Mrs Leeds, who I'd always thought of as a mercenary harpy and a gold-digger, actually loved him very much. Where does my poor mother stand in all this? I don't know. She was still his wife, but she hadn't talked about him, except briefly and bitterly, for years. Unfortunately, she's always loved him too. This is all rather typical of Dad, come to think of it. Years of absolute bloody-mindedness, of being horrible to everyone who came close to him, and still we all, in our different ways, loved him. Why? Perhaps that isn't really the point. Thanks to you, I understand love. I know not to question it.

It's been raining, and hailing, and sleeting pretty much non-stop since I arrived here, and because the cottage is built on a steep hill, I can't really walk anywhere. I can get around the house reasonably well with a stick but I tire very quickly, so I've been sitting in an armchair in front of the fireplace, watching damp oak logs smoulder, and listening to my mother's phonograph. Do you remember, by any chance, my telling you that she has a collection of Indian music? Just a small pile of records that she brought back from India. The one I've been listening to the most is by a singer from Hyderabad, I think, called Gauhar Jaan. She reminds me terribly of you. The music is similar to yours but also very different. I can hear the same threads run through both. There's a quality in her voice, though . . . When I listened to you singing, it made me imagine that I was standing on the edge of a high cliff, a sheer drop into nothing, but in front of me, in a sky full of stars, was the full moon, so close you could almost reach it, but if you did, the drop . . . I reached, you know. Gauhar Jaan's voice has a bit of that in it. Stuck here in this chair, I have nothing to do except pine for you. Music makes it a little more bearable.

I've been talking about you rather a lot, I'm afraid. Apparently, when I was stuffed full of morphine and God knows what else, I babbled about you incessantly. My sister insists she caught me speaking Greek, but she has no idea what Greek sounds like, and I can't speak it anyway, so it can't have been true. Now I am back to my normal self, whatever that means, I need to talk, and my family are always asking me about everything. 'Everything' means the war, but I won't talk about that. Even if I wanted to dwell on it, which I don't, I wouldn't want to inflict anything on them. Perhaps I'm turning into my dad. So I chatter away like a Thomas Cook tourist, a sightseer, and in a way it's true, because on the face of it I've had a cruise-ship itinerary: Suez, Cairo, Alexandria, Athens, Piraeus, Algiers, Palermo. And I talk about you – very discreetly! *Tommy's friend*, they call you, which is discreet of them as well. Only my grandfather, Da, has really taken the plunge with me. We were sitting by the fire one night, drinking and watching the flames. He suddenly leant over and slapped me on my (good) leg. 'Zoë, eh? Means "life". You're in love, my boy. Lucky fellow. Lucky fellow.' You would like Da. He would like you. I think he would get up and dance in the Cordelio if he ever had the chance.

I did the atlas and string trick: I'm one thousand, six hundred miles away from you now. Do you know the game called Snakes and Ladders? A game for children, based on the Hindu law of karma (what child-hater dreamt that one up?). You struggle towards your goal, up the ladders, only to take a wrong step and be whooshed back down on the back of a snake to where you started. I don't know what the hell to do now, Zoë. They won't let me back into combat, which was my only chance of getting to Greece – not much of a chance, but something. Da tells me not to worry. He was having sword fights with naked mountain tribesmen long before I was born, so I suppose he knows what he's talking about. But it's dreadfully, dreadfully hard to sit here, doped up and missing you so very badly, knowing I can't climb the ladders any more. I won't lose heart, though. You're in there, and that is all I have left.

All my love,

Tom

CHAPTER TWENTY-NINE

London, May 1944

Dearest Zoë,

I'm writing this in a flat I've rented in London, near the British Museum. I came up because I was at a bit of a loose end: still in the army, but jobless. I would put on my uniform and go and talk to people in various government offices, each of whom simply passed me on to someone else. I was going a bit mad, probably. I'm still taking pills for my headaches, which are becoming much, much rarer but really lay me low when they come on. My bad arm, though pretty well healed, can't do all that much. I can hold a packet of cigarettes, or a book, or my paintbox in my left hand, and I've taught myself how to get dressed without help. I'm not crippled, thank God, just maimed . . . I'm joking, Zoë, but there's a streak of self-pity in me now which I absolutely despise. It's far worse, and far more disfiguring, than my various wounds. That, of course, was what was sending me slowly round the bend.

But it turns out that my grandfather was absolutely right when he told me not to worry. I've ended up on a ladder again. Karma? I'd like to believe in karma but I don't think the world could ever make that much sense. Anyway, I was having a cup of coffee in a French cafe in Soho – yes, we have coffee here, but none of that posh coffee bean stuff: pure dandelion root, my dear – when I saw an old friend of mine crossing the street. It was the same chap who tried to arrange for my first letter to be delivered to you (I'm afraid that one never reached you). He's Greek, from Smyrna, in fact – name's Christopher Dimitriou. His parents brought him to London in 1922. I've known him since art school. He looks a bit like a Greek icon, and that's the style that he paints in as well: huge, gloomy, mystical canvases. To cut a long story short, we went out for lunch and when he heard I was at a loose end, he promptly took me round the corner to a rather notorious private club called the Gargoyle (I've always wanted to see inside, because they're supposed to have two beautiful Matisses – alas, they've sold them). He introduced me to none other than the head of the War Artists' Advisory Committee, Mr Kenneth Clark. We had a sort of impromptu interview there and then, which I thought I'd failed spectacularly because I'd had a couple of glasses of wine on top of a headache pill. Turns out I passed. Clark sent me a telegram the next day, telling me to report to him at the National Gallery. So I am, as of this moment, an Official War Artist. I'm going to draw and paint the war, and get paid for it as well. My contract does say that everything I produce will belong to the Crown, which is fine by me. Now I'm just waiting for my first commission. It's all quite extraordinary.

I think, when we see each other again, I'm just going to sit and listen to you tell me about everything. For days, and days. I could listen to you speak for ever, and it will take a long, long time for you to give me all the news, the things you've seen, the things you've done. Meanwhile, I'll try to describe London so you have some idea what it's like these days. When I first left in 1941, the Blitz was still on, and when I came back a year later the city was all smashed up, all the wounds still very raw. Rubble everywhere, dangling wires. Now all that has been tidied away. The biggest bomb sites in the middle of town are hidden behind hoardings with adverts pasted all over them. You look up from a gigantic image of the Bisto Kids to see half a building, or the side where a neighbouring building collapsed. Sometimes you'll see a house with no front wall but with the floors still intact and stairs zig-zagging up to nowhere. The streets are full of the injured: soldiers with one leg or one arm, men in wheelchairs, women on crutches. I passed a shop window the other day on Wigmore Street: a medical supply shop with a display of prosthetic limbs. One of the legs had been cut away to show the inner mechanism and it looked just like one of those eviscerated houses: springs zig-zagging like a ghost staircase. So that's London: empty sleeves pinned across chests, ersatz coffee, ghosts of buildings. And life going on regardless.

To pass the time – no, so much *more* than that! – I've been taking Greek lessons. Can you believe it? Dimitriou found me a teacher here in London. She's called Mrs Karavangeli and she's the wife of one of the deacons at the Greek Orthodox Cathedral (we have a Greek cathedral, you know: just to confuse matters, it's on Moscow Road). I sit in her kitchen in Bayswater and she talks to me in Greek, and then we read her children's picture books and Greek newspapers, very old ones from her attic. She says I'm coming along but she's a very kind (plump, grey-haired, so don't get any ideas) lady and even if I studied for the next ten years my Greek would never be half as good as your English. But we can have lively discussions about Athenian construction scandals from 1932 when next we meet.

I'm not sure where my new job will take me. It's quite possible I'll just end up in Scotland or Cornwall, painting ships or munitions workers. But I've told the WAAC that I want to work where the fighting is, so with a bit of luck I'll be on my way again. If so, and only then, I'll get out the atlas and the string . . .

With all my love,
Tom

Chapter Thirty

It is 14th April 1944, Zoë's name-day, and though no one has celebrated her day since the Germans came, she has given herself a couple of hours to enjoy the luxury of sitting in the kitchen, reading an ancient copy of British *Vogue*, September 1937, that she has found stuffed into a cavity in the wall of her bedroom. Efi is at work and Voula has been in the mountains with the partisans since last summer. She stretches her legs under the table and stares at the cover of the magazine. A coincidence: it is *Vogue*'s 21st birthday edition, and today is what passes for Zoë's birthday as well, since she has long forgotten the actual date of her birth. January 1916 is all she remembers. And a spring birthday is – used to be – so much nicer than a winter one. The cover is vaguely surrealist: a purple curtain flaps to reveal blue sky, across which a white unicorn is trotting towards a white birthday cake held aloft by a slender hand. Candles are detaching themselves from the icing and drifting away through the blue. *Many Happy Returns*, says the writing on the cake. 'Thank you,' Zoë murmurs, sighing in anticipation of PARIS FASHIONS from seven years past. It sounds almost normal outside:

people coming and going, neighbours sitting on their front steps, chattering, gossiping.

But the lightness is an illusion. Partisans – fighters of EAM who now call themselves the Greek Peoples' Liberation Army: ELAS – are operating in Kokkinia. There is fighting all the time, some of it against the Germans, some of it Greek against Greek, because there are new Security Battalions made up of Greek collaborators, some of them fascists, others fanatical royalists. Graffiti – slogans, political diatribes, the hammer and sickle – has changed the look of familiar streets completely. It is as though the city itself is sloughing off its skin like a snake and revealing its true nature. Just last month, ELAS fought the Battalionists up and down the streets of Kokkinia. The SS took over the school next to St George's church, only a few short streets away, cordoned off the whole area and arrested three hundred men, who were all marched off to the concentration camp at Haidari. They heard, days later, that fifty of them had been shot. Zoë had known two of them: a young teacher, and the son of the man who owns the kiosk in Osia Xeni Square. Now the neighbourhood wears new clothes: bullet holes, the black starbursts of mortar explosions, the darkening blood in pools on the pavements or running in thick streaks down the walls. Efi slips out at night with a German medic's bag to help wounded fighters. Zoë isn't sure if Efi has joined ELAS or not. Sometimes she wonders if she ought to, but instead she keeps her distance. They can kill her, she has decided, but she won't fight. She won't add to the misery of the world. What had Tom said? He'd wanted to object. Conscientious objector. Is that what she is? She has these thoughts, and then she takes out Tom's cap badge and stares at it. *You fought, though*, she thinks. *Did they kill you, or are you still alive? Can you feel me here, thinking about you?*

There is a knock at the door. She curses, drops the magazine onto the table. Opening the door, she finds Pavlo standing there grinning, and behind him, to her dismay, is Feathers. And, her dismay rapidly turning to horror, Zoë sees they are both holding suitcases and Pavlo, of course, has a bouzouki in a bag slung over his shoulder.

'Hello, sister! *Xronia polla!*'

'*Xronia polla*,' Feathers echoes, in her too-loud voice. 'Sister-in-law,' she adds slyly.

'Come in,' Zoë says, eyeing Feathers suspiciously.

'We need a place to stay,' says Pavlo. He drops his suitcase and looks around. *You don't look well*, Zoë thinks.

'You can have your bedroom back,' she says curtly. She grabs her brother by the sleeve and pulls him into the yard, kicking the door shut behind them. The whole house rattles. 'What in the Holy Virgin's name is Feathers doing here, Pavlo?' she hisses.

Pavlo rolls his eyes sympathetically. 'I know, I know,' he says, his voice heavy with apology. 'But since Drapetsona got bombed, the poor thing has been drifting around the city. We can't just leave her on the street.' *God, he is so charming*, Zoë thinks. *But* we? 'I thought she was quite at home on the streets,' she says icily.

'Yes, exactly, the poor little doll,' says Pavlo, as if he hasn't understood, but he has, Zoë knows. He's understood perfectly well.

'She will pay rent,' she says firmly.

'She's my guest!' Pavlo raises his hands in perfectly acted horror. Then his shoulders slump. 'Listen, Zozo, I know you don't like Feathers—'

'Don't like?' Zoë hisses. 'Don't *like?*'

'I can't let her die, Zozo. She'd be on my conscience for ever. It's my fault she's like this.'

'What?' Zoë exclaims so loudly that Mr Castanides' face appears in his window. She forces a smile and a wave, and he waves back. 'It's *your* fault?' she says, barely in control of herself. 'She got you back on the needle after you got clean, and she's kept you on it ever since! She's a . . . a vampire!'

'You don't know her, Zozo,' says Pavlo sadly.

'Thank Christ!' Zoë growls in frustration: how can Pavlo really believe what he is saying? 'Well, that's that, then,' she says, and storms back into the kitchen, where she surprises Feathers, who is sitting in her chair and leafing through *Vogue*.

'I can't read this,' says Feathers, peevishly. Zoë snatches it away from her.

'That's right, you bloody can't,' she says, and runs into the front room where she sits, her whole being throbbing with anger. But there is nothing she can do. She listens to Pavlo and Feathers talking in the kitchen, Feathers' grating voice that always seems to be flapping between suspicion and protested innocence. *I'll move out*, she decides. The band is getting a lot of bookings from the posh clubs on Ermou Street in the centre of Athens. Their pay, hundreds of millions of drachmas per night, is enough for small necessities: a pint of olive oil here, some rice, a loaf of bread. Apostoli and his wife have a room to rent. She lights a black-market cigarette and considers. Yes, that's what she'll do. She'll move out.

The next day, Zoë is sitting on Venetia Kodjagas's step, chatting with the old lady in the summer sunshine. 'How could your brother bring that whore into your home?' Mrs Kodjagas is saying. 'How you must suffer.'

'The neighbourhood knows how I have suffered, Kyria Venetia,' Zoë says, making the ritual response. The neighbourhood is the judge: this is the inviolable law of Kokkinia, and now it has judged Zoë and found her wronged. She is puzzling on this strange reversal of fate when there is a commotion from the cafe down the streets. Zoë stands up to see what is happening. She sees two Battalionists dragging a man out into the street. They are screaming at him, then they take their pistols out. Zoë braces herself for the shots, her hand making a fist around the artillery badge in her pocket, but instead they begin to beat the man with the butts. In a moment, the man's face is red with blood and he has dropped to his knees, trying to shield his head with his hands, but they keep beating him. The whole street hears the man's fingers snap. When he has collapsed into the gutter they start kicking him, roaring with laughter. They give him one last kick, and one of them bends down and roars into his ear, 'You fucking red queer! Can't take your medicine?' The two Battalionists put their pistols away. But then the one who yelled pivots around, pulls his gun out again, leans down abruptly and shoots the man in the back of the head. There is a bright jet of blood, the body jerks and one shoe flies off and lands in the doorway of the cafe.

'Fucking swine.' The man is buckling his holster. He turns to look up the street and Zoë sees who it is. Ioannis Pandelis. Captain Ioannis Pandelis of Security Battalion Four. Sólon Pandelis's brother. Their eyes meet.

'What are you staring at, you two whores?' he shouts, throwing back his shoulders. 'This—' He bangs his chest. 'This is a Greek patriot! Why do you fear me? Are you a couple of reds?' Pandelis struts towards them. He still has the pistol in his hands, and he waves it at them. 'Up! Up!'

Zoë's skin turns to ice. 'Don't move, Kyria Venetia,' she whispers, and stands up.

'Come here!' Pandelis roars. Biting her lip, Zoë walks over to him, keeping her head up, though the effort is painful. Pandelis reaches out for her. His fingers dig into the muscles around her collarbone.

'Let go of me!'

'Zoë Valavani. Still singing your Turkish songs with your queer of a brother?'

'I still sing,' Zoë manages to say. 'The songs my mother taught to me.'

'Your mother!' Pandelis laughs in her face. His breath stinks of brandy. 'Who keeps you safe so you can grunt your foreign shit, eh? The Battalions, that's who! Patriots, giving their blood so that red whores like you . . .' He swallows wetly. 'You know, *Tourkala*, you should thank your protector,' he rasps. 'Go on, then! Thank me in the name of Greece.' He grabs Zoë's wrist, pulling her hand down, twisting it until her palm is pressed against the bulging crotch of his trousers. 'This is your house, isn't it, this little refugee kennel? Let's go inside.' He leers, his face even redder. 'You dirty little Turk. I bet . . .'

'Get away from me, you pig!' Zoë struggles, but his grip is too strong. He stares at her, breathing heavily. 'No, no, no,' he says, but just as she feels she can't fight against his grip any longer, the other Battalionist appears behind him. 'Come on, Ioannis, you arsehole! We'll be late!' the man says, as if Zoë isn't there at all. 'I don't want Plytzanopoulos giving me any shit.'

Zoë feels Pandelis's grip tighten until it is unbearable. He growls. Then he throws his head back and spits in her face.

'Don't think I'll forget you, Zoë Valavani. One day I'll make you sing for me, all right. We'll be back for you. For all you reds.' His companion, plainly bored with the proceedings, claps him on the shoulder and begins to pull him away down the street.

Zoë stands, shaking but unable to make her legs obey her, watching the two men walk past the dead body outside the cafe and disappear around the corner. Her wrist aches from the man's fingers. She realises that her other hand is still clenched around Tom's badge.

Mrs Kodjagas is crossing herself and muttering the prayer for the dead. Zoë takes a deep breath, goes back and sits down beside her.

'Are you all right, Kyria Venetia?'

'Yes, but are you, dear one? My God, my God . . . what a curse, to see this madness for a second time in one life,' the old woman says, tears gathering in the creases of her face. Zoë opens her hand. The cap badge has dug into the flesh, leaving a perfect imprint of itself. In the exact centre of her palm, the spokes of the wheel radiate like a red flower.

'The English boy?' Mrs Kodjagas is looking down at the badge. 'The *kapetanios*?' A tear is trembling at the end of her nose.

'Yes,' says Zoë, slipping the badge back into her pocket.

'You were in love with him?'

'I . . . I mean . . .' Zoë stammers, but the old lady is gazing at her with an expression she doesn't quite recognise. 'Yes, I love him,' Zoë tells her, and the old woman's face creases with happiness. Just for a moment, hope visits them both.

'A good-looking boy. A *gentleman*.' Mrs Kodjagas uses the English word. Zoë blinks in surprise. 'What was his name?'

'Tom. Lieutenant Tom Collyer.'

'God keep you safe,' says the old lady. She takes Zoë's hand and presses it to her face. 'You and . . . *O* Kapetanios. God keep you both.' Her eyes are shining, but already, whatever has spread its wings over them is leaving. It can't stay here, after all.

Zoë gets up and walks nervously towards the place where the body lies. Men are crouching in the door of the cafe, looking down the street. One of them is holding the dead man's shoe. She looks around the corner and sees the two Battalionists in the distance, strolling along, arm in arm down the middle of the dirt roadway. She runs across and crouches down. The man's face is nothing but meat and splinters of bone, but she recognises him by his clothes: Christos Vlessas, the black marketeer, long since retired from that and now a postal clerk.

'What happened?' she asks Mr Savas, the owner of the cafe.

'Christ in heaven . . .' Mr Savas is kneeling in the road, stroking the dead man's back as if it might comfort him. His hands are trembling violently. 'Pandelis came in, stinking drunk. Christos just happened to look around. Pandelis must have thought he was giving him the evil eye, because he orders Christos to stand up and give him the salute. So Christos stands up, good as gold, and gives him an army salute. And Pandelis goes berserk. He wanted the fascist salute, see? Starts calling him a communist and a faggot, starts slapping him, and the next thing, they've dragged him outside . . .'

'But Christos wasn't a communist!'

'For fuck's sake . . .' Mr Savas is weeping openly. 'I'm a communist. Every other bastard here is a communist. But not Christos! Oh, the bastards, the bastards!'

They have to borrow a wheelbarrow from Mr Castanides and the men of the street take turns pushing Christos Vellas through the neighbourhood, up the hill to the cemetery, a terribly small procession of mourners following. Mrs Vellas, screaming in the throes of her grief, has to be held upright by Mrs Kodjagas and Mrs Castanides. The dead man's stockinged feet, toes poking

317

through, bob with every rut and dip in the road, the men from the cafe having decided that Charon won't be interested in Christos's nice Italian shoes. Zoë follows, trying to remember more about Christos than the beans and oil he sold her. But, she decides, that might be good enough. The first olive oil she had tasted for a year. She had paid for it, but what a gift it was. The priest from St George's is persuaded to come and say the proper words, but there is no coffin and the men dig a hurried, shallow grave in a patch of empty ground that is already mounded with fresh earth from other burials. When they slide him into the little slot in the chalky earth, Zoë can't bear to look down at his smashed face, so she throws in a sprig of wild basil flowers and walks back home as fast as she can, hugging herself for warmth, even though the sun is still shining.

CHAPTER THIRTY-ONE

France, 7th August 1944

My darling Zoë,

I'm writing this in a cafe on one of the main streets of Caen. That is to say, I'm sitting on a pile of bricks in front of a rough table made of a sign that once said *Cafe de* something or other, in the middle of a vast sea of rubble. Caen cathedral is a little way in front of me, not much more than a collection of stumps. The Canadians finally took the city yesterday and there is almost nothing left. The air stinks of death: there are uncountable bodies under the rubble. I've seen some terrible things recently. Fields full of dead cows. German soldiers, a lot of them not much more than boys, reduced to clods of meat by bombs. The bombing has just mown everything flat. A hundred yards or so behind me, down the street, there is the corpse of a woman lying on a pile of bricks and timbers. She is smartly dressed, as if she was on her way to church, handbag over her shoulder, stretched out, toes pointed, arms above her head. She doesn't even look injured, apart from a trickle of blood coming from her nose. When I saw her I just automatically reached for paper and paints, but as I was licking my brush I looked up and she had become you, just for a moment. I was almost sick. It must have been the smart black suit she is wearing. It's much better in the Cafe Something, apart from the dead SS man in spotty camouflage who is propped up just over there. I'm in the middle of painting a line of ambulances which are trying to get into the middle of the city: the red crosses and white circles are the cleanest things I've seen for days.

I shouldn't be telling you these things. I shouldn't be writing them at all. But you'll never read this, will you? I've been sending these letters to an address in Cairo, which is the only address I have for the SOE chap who told me, two years ago now, that he could get letters into Greece. And they have all come back, sooner or later. They always find me. *Me*, not you. But I'll send this one off as well, because there is nothing else I can do.

Zoë, if you are alive, do whatever you can to stay safe. I often think, these days, that the conscientious objectors had it absolutely right after all: humanity has turned on itself, and being a soldier just perpetuates the horror. I'm not really a soldier any more, but I am in uniform. What does that make me? A professional voyeur? I write this, and the corpse of the SS man – a corporal, probably eighteen or nineteen, stares at me through his filmy eyes. I don't mind him at all. I'm so used to the dead that I give him no more thought than someone behind me at a bus stop. But you would say that this has all happened before. You saw it, didn't you, my darling, when you were a little girl? And you survived. So I hope – I would pray if I had anything to pray *to* – that you will survive. ~~The dead woman in the black dress has~~ There are so many dead around here that sometimes one finds oneself talking to them. The dead are quite solicitous: they listen, and they don't scrounge your cigarettes. I think that is what my job is, to some extent: a dialogue with the dead. I can't bear the thought. We have to keep talking to the living, though. We have to keep writing.

I am going to get out of here. I'm almost at the end of this commission and there must be something further east for me. What, I don't know. This world has no love in it, Zoë. But I still love you. More than life itself: certainly a thousand times more than I love my own life. I am going to go east. I'll tell you more when I have my new orders. Keep yourself as safe as you can, my darling. Surely to God this is almost over.

All my love,
Tom

CHAPTER THIRTY-TWO

Cannes, 25th August 1944

Dearest,

My Thomas Cook itinerary continues. I'm writing to you from, of all places, the Croisette in Cannes. Beyond the palm trees is the beach, currently empty of Hollywood starlets and minor European aristocracy, but honestly, it doesn't feel as if there's been a war here at all, and all the bright young things have just slipped into their hotels for a quick siesta. The Croisette itself is an endless parade of Citroëns and Renaults filled with young French men and women waving sten guns and flags: Stars and Stripes, the Union Jack, but most of all the lovely old Tricolour. Liberation is a word that makes sense here, as it didn't in Normandy.

I came in with my old crowd, 2nd Parachute Brigade. Perfect glider landing, and I found myself more or less immediately being offered red wine and salami by a dazed but happy farmer. There's been some light fighting – the

Americans and French are doing most of the heavy stuff – and the Germans are retreating north. We liberated Cannes yesterday. As I said, it seems untouched, though it isn't, of course: the Gestapo shot eight people in the cellar of their headquarters before running away. I had a look this morning (documenting this sort of thing is part of my commission): belle époque, palm trees, stunning view. And in the cellar . . . I went down to make a drawing. How many places like this are we going to find, I wonder? Smell the same. When I went back outside, I might have been stepping back ten years, when my father and Mrs Leeds came here to gamble with my mother's money.

Yesterday I realised that I'd spent an hour painting a bowl of tomatoes, simply for the pleasure of using the brightest red in my paintbox. That should be a good thing, surely: if anything could be called a blessing these days it ought to be a terracotta bowl filled with fat, ripe (cadmium red), ridged tomatoes, warmed by the sun, the green starbursts of the stems smelling of cat piss on new-mown grass. I picked each one up and held it against my face: in fact I felt – and probably looked – like an old peasant man venerating a holy relic. Paint: that cadmium red, undiluted. I let it stain the paper, deeper and deeper. My eyes have been famished.

But the sheer normality itself is disturbing. When was the last time you ate a tomato, Zoë? How many years has it been? I read in *The Times* a few days ago about the EAM partisans allying themselves with the Greek government in exile. People are saying that the Germans are finished in Greece and that it's only a matter of time before we push them out for good. The newspapers are starting to write quite a lot about Greece, though mostly about the government in exile, who don't seem to be able to make up their minds about anything. One wonders what that means for Greece after liberation. But it is coming. Freedom for Greece. I can't believe I've even written that. Should I start to hope again? Are you daring to think such things, where you are?

This little splinter of comfort on the Riviera is nothing more than a weird Shangri-La and quite honestly, I feel disgusted with myself for sitting here in the sunshine. But my old outfit, to which I've vaguely attached myself, is leaving for Italy tomorrow and I am going with them. The fighting has moved north and I'll go and find it. I seem to have gained a reputation with the WAAC for recklessness, which I do nothing to deny. I can't stand being safe while you're in danger – the guilt of it. It's pretty useless, what I'm doing: I'm not under any illusions about that. Recording what people are already calling *history* is, I suppose, valuable but I'm an artist, not a photographer. When people look at war artists' work when this is all over (*if* they ever look at it), will they see anything except art? They will be concerned with aesthetics, with my talent, or lack of it, and not what I'm trying to show them. I mustn't think like that, though, must I? I must be a witness, not a painter. I must bear witness without flinching.

Tomorrow we sail for Naples. Eastwards again, my darling: the map will show me how close we are. But

I'm going to try not to *think* too much any more. I'm just going to work. You were right: hope is unbearable. But so beautiful.

With all my love,

Tom

CHAPTER THIRTY-THREE

Athens, October 1944

Past midnight, and the club on Ermou Street is still packed. There is an edgy, almost hysterical feeling in the air, an end-of-the-world fever. The tables are full of junior German officers and NCOs, black marketeers, a few low-ranking civil servants. All the Germans of influence left Athens days ago, along with most of the government, slipping away on special trains to what remains of the Third Reich. Zoë and the band give them what they want to hear: love songs, fake rembetiko with all the hashish, the knives and the *manges* ironed out of it. She is happy, though, because for the first time in years, she sees some faces she knows from before the war: people who bought the records she made with Semsis, Athenian intellectuals who would come down to the *tekés* in Piraeus for the thrill of it. She likes the way they are deliberately staking out their portion of the room, the way they are staring at the Germans with open contempt. Because the Gestapo are leaving. The SS are leaving. It will soon be over.

She grins at Apostoli. It is a good band tonight: along with Apostoli there is a young bouzouki player called Manousalis, and a friend of Batis on guitar. Strumming away on a baglamas is none other than Niko, who arrived out of the blue from Salonika. His sudden appearance feels like an omen of spring. It didn't taken him long, though, to find out sad news. His old friend Micho is dead, shot by the Germans. The two old KKE men have both died in Haidari. Of the old crowd from the Cordelio, half are dead or disappeared.

'Will you rebuild it?' Zoë asked.

'No. It wouldn't be the same. I think I'll go back to sea. Back to New York, maybe.'

It is very late. They have packed up and are sitting around, drinking brandy, talking to the owner about another engagement, when a man comes in through the back. He has his cap pulled down over his head and is wearing a long, dark coat. Zoë doesn't recognise him. She is just wondering if he is with EAM, because the owner of this club has connections, when he comes and stands in front of her.

'Are you Zoë Valavani?' he asks. There is something in his voice that she doesn't like.

'Who wants to know?'

'I'm a friend of your brother. Can you come with me, if you please?'

'A friend of Pavlo? What are you talking about?' says Zoë, the night and the brandy making her dismissive. 'Why should I go with you?' Apostoli is on his feet, and the stranger holds up his hands.

'I'm not here to make trouble, *mangas*,' he tells him. 'I have . . . some news, but I don't want to tell you here, Kyria Valavani.' He gestures towards the door.

'I'm coming with you,' says Apostoli. They follow the stranger to the back of the room. He takes out a cigarette with unsteady hands, cups his hands around the flame of a lighter. As the light flares it picks out his wasted cheeks, the *mangas* moustache only emphasising the way his skin is stretched tight over his skull. Heroin skin. Zoë already knows what he is going to say because she has been waiting for this moment, this messenger, for years.

'Pavlo's dead,' he says. 'I'm sorry you've got to hear it from a stranger. He's dead. God help him.'

'What do you mean?' Apostoli growls, but Zoë touches his sleeve. 'Tell me,' she says, looking the man in the face, trying to get him to meet her eyes.

'We were at the Teké tou Elefantás. It's in Metaxourgeiou . . .'

'I know where it is,' says Zoë. The place where Pavlo plays when he's not with them.

'Of course, of course.' The man winces. 'We'd finished – I play fiddle – and we'd gone into the back for some food, you know, something to drink . . .' His eyes slide away from hers. His face seems to be getting more hollow as he speaks. 'So we notice that Pavlo isn't with us. I go back out front, no sign of him, but the door's open – the street door. I go to shut it . . .' He shakes his head.

'Go on.'

'And there he is. On the step. Just . . . leaning over, with his bouzouki across his lap. I think he's just nodded off, right, so I give him a shake. And . . .' The man covers his face with an almost translucent hand.

'What was it? What had happened to him?' demands Apostoli.

'Overdose,' the man says at last. 'The needle was still in his arm.'

Zoë totters and Apostoli catches her just in time. The other band members rush over. Someone brings a seat and Apostoli lowers her into it. A glass is put into her hand and raised to her lips. She fights the burn of the cheap brandy as it goes down, and when she opens her mouth she hears a terrible moan that surely can't be coming from her throat.

'An accident,' she is saying. 'Was it an accident?'

'I thought so, but he was holding this,' says the man. He reaches inside his coat and takes out a clean yellow envelope. 'He addressed it to you. I think it means . . . you know. He'd been down,' he adds, 'but we've all been down, haven't we? I didn't think he'd go and do something like this.'

Zoë starts to open the letter but Apostoli kneels in front of her. 'Not yet, *koukla*. Not here in front of everybody.'

Zoë forces herself to look at the stranger. 'Where is he now?'

'He . . .' The man squirms where he stands, legs and arms twisting against each other. 'The owner didn't want trouble, you know, so he got us to carry poor old Pavlo down to the square at the end of the street. We put him on a bench and I went to the all-night kiosk in Koumoundourou Square and phoned for an ambulance. They came and took him away.'

'Holy Virgin,' roars Niko. 'You left Pavlo on a fucking *bench*? Our Pavlaki? Your friend?'

'It's all right, honey.' Zoë takes hold of his sleeve and shakes it. 'It was always going to end up this way. He'd have done the same for you, wouldn't he?' she adds to the stranger, who sniffs.

'It's just the life,' he says, as if that explains everything.

'And Feathers? Have you told her?'

'Feathers wasn't there,' says the stranger.

'Fuck! Where is she? I don't want her anywhere near . . .' And then she remembers. Pavlo will be in the morgue by now. 'Oh, God. It doesn't matter.'

'I'm sorry. Pavlo talked about you all the time. He loved his sister, he always said. And he was going to quit.'

'No, he wasn't, my friend. What's your name?'

'Dimitri.'

'My brother was good at love, Dimitri. Good at loving people, bloody terrible at being loved. You don't have to come here, after dragging my brother's corpse out of the way of your precious *life*, to tell me he loved his sister.' She puts her hands on Apostoli's shoulders and stands up to face the man. 'He was never going to quit, because he went through life like a man with his skin on the wrong way round, and everything hurt, and he didn't understand anything except heroin and the roads.' She sucks in air; her lungs hurt. 'I'm glad he's dead, because he doesn't have to waste his love on this shit any more.'

'He was a real *mangas*,' says Niko. His shoulders are quivering.

'*Yiassou*, Pavlaki,' says Apostoli. He splashes brandy into his glass and drains it.

'*Yiassou*,' shouts Niko.

'*Yiassou*, Pavlaki *mou*,' the others echo. Zoë notices Dimitri edging towards the door. She slips away from the men.

'Thank you,' she says. 'I know you can't help it. He'd have done the same to you if it was your turn. Or to me. Jesus, why . . .' She looks down at the letter in her hand and stops herself. 'I mean, thank you for bringing me this. That was a good thing you did.'

'It was nothing. I'm sorry.' Dimitri wraps his arms around himself, and for a moment he reminds her of Pavlo. 'It was that good German shit, you know,' he says, distantly. 'With the war and everything, the famine, it was like he'd found a seam of gold. Kept us alive.'

'Until it killed him.'

Dimitri hesitates, then shrugs. His eyes are desolate. 'True. But why are any of us still breathing?' he mutters, and slips out through the door.

Zoë spends the rest of the night on Apostoli's sofa. He lives not far away now, since his house in Piraeus was bombed last year. His wife Andromache's sister had died in the famine and she had inherited a little house in Psiri, near the Temple of Thession. Andromache is a warm, forthright woman who knows exactly how tight Apostoli's reins need to be to keep them both happy. Now she bustles around in her dressing gown, making Zoë a herb tisane which Zoë doesn't touch and making up the sofa as comfortably as she can. Zoë, though, is numb. She can't sleep, and lies awake, listening to every creak and rodent scratch in the old house, every snore and mutter of her hosts, staring into the darkness. The next morning she is getting dressed as the sun rises. She slips out without waking the others and walks through the dingy streets of Psiri, where the walls are daubed with graffiti she hasn't seen before: ORGANISATION X FOR THE KING! The black X, topped with a crown, is everywhere, painted over the red and white EAM slogans. The streets are empty. She supposes she must be up before the curfew but she doesn't care. She crosses Stadiou Street, trying not to look at the man hanging from one of the lamp posts. But as she walks past she sees his face anyway: young, so young. Massalias Street, narrow and tree-lined, is tucked away behind the university. She knows she has found the right place because there is already a small, forlorn queue outside the entrance to the Athens morgue.

'Name?' intones the small, untidy man behind the desk. He looks as if he hasn't left his post for days and perhaps he hasn't.

'Pavlo Valavani,' Zoë says quietly. Her fingers close around the cap badge in her pocket.

'Speak up!' says the clerk impatiently. Zoë repeats the name and watches while the man runs his finger down a long list.

'Not here,' he says, and looks up at her. His face has been so deeply scrubbed by fatigue and misery that it is almost featureless. Zoë takes a deep breath, her throat tightening, but what would be the point of crying, in this place?

'He would have come in last night from Metaxourgeiou,' she says slowly. 'About twenty-eight years old, black hair, tall. Light brown eyes. He was probably wearing a pinstripe suit.'

'Metaxourgeiou,' says the clerk mechanically. The people behind her in the line begin to shuffle their feet. It has taken an hour to get to the front of the queue and the silence of her companions has been slowly crushing her. The clerk is looking at another list. 'Wait here,' he snaps, and leaves through a side door. In less than five minutes he is back, accompanied by an orderly in dirty hospital whites. One hand is covered in a large elbow-length black rubber gauntlet, and the other gauntlet dangles from it like a dead raven. The orderly crooks his finger at Zoë and turns without a word.

'Thank you,' she whispers to the clerk, but he is already turning his crater-like eyes on the next person in the queue. The orderly leads her down a long, dirty corridor. Steel trolleys are pushed up against the wall and a filthy mop stands in a bucket of grey water. The air is almost spongey with the smell of disinfectant but it isn't strong enough to mask the undercurrent of decay. Through a pair of double doors and into another corridor, and there, on one of the steel trolleys, a young man in a pinstripe suit.

'You haven't covered him,' whispers Zoë.

'He just came in,' says the orderly, baldly. 'Is it who you're looking for?'

'Yes.' Zoë goes to the side of the trolley. Pavlo's face looks carved out of powdery chalk and his lips are blue, but he looks absolutely peaceful, like a marble statue in the First Cemetery. *He's been practising for this his whole life*, she thinks, and almost laughs. 'Why did you do it?' she whispers.

'Hurry up,' says the orderly. Zoë leans down and kisses her brother on his strange blue lips.

'I love you. You know that, don't you? I love you, Pavlaki.'

'What happened to him? We don't see many in such a nice state these days,' says the orderly, pushing the double doors open for her.

'He was worn out,' she says simply. The orderly nods. It seems as good an explanation as any. 'Did he have anything with him?' Zoë remembers to ask when they are almost at the end of the corridor. 'A watch? Things in his pockets?'

'People who come in like that never have anything in their pockets. Let alone a watch.' He laughs, a short and humourless sound that echoes from the tiled walls. 'Get your paperwork from the man at the desk.'

Zoë takes the bus back to Kokkinia, getting off late so she doesn't have to walk through Osia Xeni Square. The street she walks up is the street she came down all those years ago, on her way to find Pavlo in the *teké* in Karaiskaki after Mama's funeral. She felt more alone then than she had ever thought possible but today is worse.

333

She is as alone now as she was on the dock at Piraeus when they tied a label to her little sailor suit. She is floating in the empty sea, and there is no bowsprit to catch on to.

In the house, she lights the gas ring – there is gas, today – and makes a briki of German ersatz coffee. She has drunk two cups before she remembers the letter. After Dimitri left, she slipped it into her bag, intending to read it at Apostoli's house, but she didn't dare light a lamp in case she woke her hosts, and in the morning she was in too much of a hurry to leave. The envelope is there, a neat oblong of expensive yellow parchment paper. She finds a knife and slits it open, carefully. Inside, a neatly folded letter.

My dearest sister,

I am so sorry but I cannot live in this way any longer. I have tried to keep going but I find it more and more impossible. If you are reading this and saying to yourself that I have been hiding my state from you then I am glad, because that was my intention. I'm afraid I have been coming to this point since the dreadful winter of our hunger. My nerves are completely destroyed, and every day is a new torture. I cannot find the music the way I used to be able to find it. My fingers are not working properly and I do not hear the roads in my head. People will start to notice if they have not already and I am horribly afraid of that.

I know that I am a coward and what I am going to do is a cowardly thing but I am being torn to pieces, slowly, and I don't want people to see me come apart. I don't want you, my dearest Zoë, to see your brother go mad. I don't want to think what Mama would do and I am glad she is not here to suffer this, but I am sorry, again, that you are. I hope it is not too dreadful for you, but alas we are all very used to dreadful things and this will be better than madness for all of us. I do not believe the world will ever be right again and weak men, such as I am, will end up being crushed. You have always been brave, my dear sister, and I don't think I have ever seen you be afraid. Please forget all about me as I do not want to be remembered at all.

> *Goodbye,*
> *Your loving brother,*
> *Pavlo*

The letter is written out in Pavlo's neat handwriting. 'You will write like a professor at the university,' Mama always insisted as she stood over them at their exercise books. The thought of Mama reading these words bring the tears racing down Zoë's cheeks. She almost misses the much shakier, scrawled line at the bottom of the page.

I liked Lieutenant Tom very much, Zoë, and I thought he was a good man and a brave man. I expect he will be coming with the English soldiers. Please tell him I would have liked to talk to him more about Mr Louis Armstrong and when you see him again please tell him

The words meet the edge of the paper and stop. *Were you very near the end, here?* she asks her brother, silently. *Had you already opened your little case and taken out the needle? What made you think of Tom Collyer, last of all? Why did you never speak to me about any of this?*

She goes outside and sits on the cement step by the kitchen door, watching the Castanides' two chickens scratch in the dirt. Her fingers trace the lines of the Artillery badge: they know the tiny bronze landscape as well as they know the contours of her own face. The wheel, the crown, the letters that spell *UBIQUE*. *Everywhere. But not here*, she thinks. *Not here with me now*. The little bronze wheel turns. Just a toy. She drops it back into her pocket and goes to Pavlo's room. There is a slim black case in his suitcase. She opens it. Nestled in black velvet, steel and glass twinkle like strange jewellery: her brother's spare works. The syringe, a silver teaspoon, a carefully coiled length of rubber. She picks up the single ampoule of colourless liquid. Caught between her finger and thumb it looks so pure, so clean, like a diamond. Or a chink of light shining through from another place. She can slip through to where there isn't any pain, and no more longing. It will only take a moment. Then she remembers a voice. It comes to her without warning, clearer than a memory. *If you were the only girl in the world, and I was the only boy.* 'I'll stay,' she says aloud, and drops the ampoule back into the case. Then she takes a deep breath. She needs to find the priest. There is a funeral to be arranged.

Pavlo is buried in the cemetery at the top of Koutasi Street, with the priest from the Church of the Annunciation officiating. It is a proper funeral, too. Pavlo knew a lot of people, far more than Zoë imagined, and they have all chipped in and come up with enough to buy him a coffin of black painted wood, and a ride to his final resting place strapped to the front of a car belonging to a Piraeus municipal engineer. Pavlo lies there at the bottom of his hole, dressed in his best suit and surrounded by flowers. A set of amber komboloi beads hanging from his right hand, a cigarette next to his cheek. His baglamas on his chest. Black lips, black eyes. *God, you look dreadful*, Zoë thinks. The musicians smoke and scowl, the junkies fidget, Mrs Kodjagas and the other widows of Hozanitas Street dab ostentatiously at their dry eyes. There is one blessing, at least: Feathers has not been seen since the night of Pavlo's death, so the thing that Zoë has been dreading most, seeing Feathers at the edge of her brother's grave, does not come to pass. She watches in silence as the men lower the lid of the coffin. Then she begins to sing.

> *As you go to be with strangers, my love,*
> *Do not be long, because I cannot bear the pain.*
> *Take me too, take me along for company.*
> *Remember me so far away, remember me forever.*
> *As you go to be with strangers, take me too, take me along*
> *for company.*

They go to a cafe further down the hill, the only place that has enough watered-down brandy and paximadi to give everyone their ritual mouthful. Then she goes back to the house with Efi to cook the fish soup, the thinnest fish soup in the world, for the widows. *That's it*, Zoë says to herself, after the old women finally leave. *I'm completely alone. I am my whole family: Haggitiris, and Valavani too. They both live inside me now, and when I'm gone* . . . She sits on the front step in the last purple light of sunset, turning the painter's badge over and over in her hand. *If you could have heard me singing today*, she tells the man she doesn't entirely remember any more, a collage of thoughts and memories in a box marked Tom Collyer: floppy black fringe, long fingers – *like my brother's,* she thinks suddenly – a calico pattern of cuts and burns on bare arms. Trousers cut off ragged above the knee, trailing threads. Eyes, the colour of which she doesn't recall, but were perfect, gazing into hers that morning when they woke up. The Germans had only been in Piraeus for two days then. There had still been an inch of coffee in the jar.

CHAPTER THIRTY-FOUR

Rimini Airport, 16th September 1944

Dearest Zoë,

I'm just south of Rimini, and I am writing this letter surrounded by Greeks! I spied an artillery battery and wandered over to the command post – 8th Army is clearing the approaches to the city, which are full of paratroopers and dug-in tanks – only to be met with a lot of yelling and screaming. Apparently the field I'd just strolled across was in the sights of a German machine gun. I suppose they must have been having a nap. The bloke in charge, a captain, was pretty cross with me, especially when he discovered I was, of all things, a painter. But then it turned out we'd been in different parts of the same battle in '41, up in the mountains. After that we got on like a house on fire. They have reasonably good coffee and a splendid view of the German lines. Lots of chat about Greece. It turns out that Captain Leventis and his men are all diehard royalists. They seem to think they're fighting for the return of their king, and that all this other stuff is just a distraction. The captain even told me, with a rather unsettling gleam in his eye, that EAM were as bad, 'no, worse, than the Germans'. I asked if they knew any rembetika songs and they looked at me as if I'd turned into Stalin himself. Instead they sung me something that sounded robustly patriotic, though I couldn't understand the words. That sort of music all sounds the same, somehow. I think they've forgiven me now. I'm going with them when they attack tomorrow. I want to fight beside Greeks, just once.

To get here, I drove up and across country from Naples. I'd almost forgotten that I'd been in Italy before. The main road goes quite near Monte Cassino, and the air still reeks of corpses. Finally made it to Florence, but all the museums are empty: looted, possibly. People are starving, ragged children begging in the streets, prostitutes with the eyes, and the patience, of the dead. I had to leave. I kept driving until I got to the Adriatic. In the Upper Tiber valley there are fresh graves everywhere beside the roads. In some places the landscape is quite haunted. In others it's glorious, just like I'd imagined it from the paintings. Funny: tangles of wrecked machinery are so ubiquitous here that they seem part of nature. It wouldn't surprise me to find a burnt-out Tiger tank in the background of a Leonardo next time I look at one. When I got to the coast I walked down to the sea and stared east, but then a flight of American bombers took off from an airfield behind me, these great silver shapes roaring just above my head. They flew out to sea and then wheeled sharply to the north, as if they'd run into an invisible wall. I sat down and drew the exhaust trails. Some

New Zealand gunners came by and invited me to their mess, otherwise I think I would have sat there all night.

21st September

We are in Rimini. The Greeks – 3rd Mountain Brigade – came in early this morning. I've just done a quick portrait of their commander, a General Tsakalotos. When I told him it would belong to the Crown, he practically salivated at the word. I don't understand these royalists at all. It's like being back in the 17th century. But while I was sketching he told me that the Allies will be going into Greece as early as next month. My old brigade is supposedly going to be the spearhead. The general seems to think the work ahead will be in securing the country from what he called 'subversive elements'. I thought he meant collaborators, but he actually meant EAM. I don't think he has a very high opinion of the provisional government. He isn't involved in any planning, though, as he told me, rather bitterly. It's amazing what people tell you when you're doing their portrait. When I'd finished, I slipped off and wrote a letter to the WAAC, begging them to send me to Greece. I gave it to the postal service chap and my hand, dearest Zoë, was shaking like a leaf.

We'll be pushing north again tomorrow and I will go too, but I'm going to write to the OC of my brigade and beg *him* to take me with him if and when he goes. We're all beggars these days, but some of us are luckier than others. The children in Rimini were pitiful. I'm not eating much at the moment – a little piece of shrapnel is working its way

out of my head and I feel slightly sick most of the time –
so at least I was able to give away my rations to a few of
them. Is it worse in Greece? It must be. General Tsakalotos
didn't strike me as the sort of chap to worry very much
about ragged children. But I'm going to try and think more
positively. At some point, things have to start going right.

With all my love,
Tom

BOOK IV

CHAPTER THIRTY-FIVE

Sorrento, October 1944

The only oil paints Tom can find in Naples are dark, gloomy, oppressive. He has a single tube of *giallo primario*, a slightly acidic yellow, and two of cobalt blue. The rest are dark browns, ominous reds, blacks (there is a selection), sinister greenish blues. He wonders, as he lays them out on the sun-warmed table, if this is because the only artists who came to Naples before the war wanted to paint those hackneyed views of the bay, the kind of thing you can find in every Italian restaurant in London. The sinister colours suit his purpose, though. He begins slowly. His palette is a broken dinner plate and he has scrounged his easel from an abandoned school. The hotel has sold him a small can of white house paint as primer. It is a long time since he has worked in oil and he has to remember how to do it. But he knows exactly what he wants to get onto the canvas.

Dear Major Collyer,
In reply to your last letter of 21st September, the Committee
agrees to extend your present contract to cover the expedition
to Greece . . .

'Thank God,' Tom said aloud as he opened the letter from Mr Gregory of the WAAC. That was been over a month ago, in a dug-out somewhere near the Fiumicino River.

> . . . *with the stipulation that you proceed first to Naples and cover the negotiations for the Greek provisional government, making your way to Greece with them* . . .

'Oh, for God's sake.'

And so, although Greece has been liberated by his old unit, Tom has been forced to wait in a small town outside Salerno for almost a month for the government of national unity to be given the all-clear for their return to Athens. Cava de' Tirreni would, under normal circumstances, be a delightful place to spend an enforced and rather highly paid holiday. But he is going slowly mad. He has drawn all the Greeks several times. He has painted them in conference and strolling through the grounds of their digs, the impressively turreted Villa Ricciardi. Bored to distraction, he has wandered about in Naples and clambered over the ruins of Pompeii, which reminded him, unpleasantly, of Caen.

He lightens brown with house paint, blocks out a trapezoid of interlocked squares on which he paints a line of dark shapes, all receding to a horizon of concentrated blue. Below this, a smooth white shape, a pod or a pregnant belly tapering to a point at one end, floats in a bath of green-blue. He starts another canvas. This time, the pregnant pod is an upright slash in a deep field of black tempered with brown, the white made livid with green.

'An African mask?' Tom, startled, twists round and finds a man standing behind him, looking at the painting. One of the Greeks, a diplomat who is staying at the hotel along with his wife. Tall, dark hair going thin above a slightly pear-shaped face. Large dark-ringed eyes behind black-rimmed spectacles; he looks like a great, solemn child. *I haven't drawn you yet*, Tom thinks.

'No. It's a . . . it's a capsized ship,' he says.

'Really.' The man comes closer and studies the canvas. 'Powerful. Frightening, in fact. Do you mean it to frighten?'

'It frightens *me*,' says Tom. 'That is, it's something I see more often than I'd like.'

'The curse of our times,' says the man, and smiles gravely. 'To walk through these terrible dreams not knowing if one is asleep or awake. I should think it would take a brave man to be a war artist.'

'I don't know about bravery,' says Tom, surprised. 'Anyway, this wasn't a dream. I saw it.'

'Did you?'

'In Piraeus in 1941. The *Hellas*. She'd been dive-bombed, and capsized with something like three hundred men still aboard her. I saw her the next day.'

'When I first looked at it I thought it was one of those fertility masks from Africa, the ones that mimic a pregnant belly. But now I see that this is pregnant with something quite different.'

'Pregnant. Yes, I suppose that's my intention.'

'Well, I shall leave you to your work.' The diplomat turns and walks away, hands clasped behind his back. *Well*, thinks Tom, *that was interesting*. Not the sort of conversation he has come to expect from the Greek contingent, who are so fixated on their goal, and so much in disagreement with each other over how to achieve it, that they don't seem to be able to think, let alone talk, about anything else.

The next day Tom is working again. He has intended to start another version of the *Hellas*, but he finds that, instead of the swollen leaf shape of the floating hull, he has outlined a face. He closes his eyes, listens to the parliament of sparrows in the olive trees, and sees a woman crouched beside him under a canopy of shadowy fronds. A pregnant cat picks her way across a litter of bricks. The woman turns to him. They are in her house, two rooms, walls no thicker than a cardboard box. She stands up and holds out her hands. In the uneasy, gin-clear light of early morning she turns to him, her hair webbed across a lace pillow.

'Very Byzantine.' The diplomat is there again. Tom sees his wife reading at a table in the shade near the hotel. 'I mean that as a compliment, obviously.'

'Byzantine? I'm not sure . . .' Tom looks at the half-finished painting. The beloved face, emerging from or – the thought makes him shudder, but he considers it – sinking into heavy, textured black. The man is right: the face has the huge eyes and transfigured seriousness of an icon.

'Yes, there is that quality to it,' the man says. 'A modern icon.'

'I'm not sure what I've done,' says Tom, truthfully. He realises what the face he has painted reminds him of: Arnold Böcklin's *Medusa*, beauty ruined, staring out of darkness with blue lips and dead eyes, mouth open to curse or to plead.

'Another dream?'

'I'm not sure,' Tom repeats, half to himself.

'The Orthodox Church believes that an icon painter, if he is doing his job properly, is actually making his subject incarnate. Making the spiritual into touchable reality. So the worshipper is gazing, not at a piece of painted wood, but at the soul, if you like, of the saint depicted.' The diplomat chuckles drily. 'I am not sure of the implications of that in the context of modern art.'

'I've never thought of myself as a modern artist,' Tom says, dropping his brush into the jar of turps. 'They used to laugh at me at Chelsea because I loved Samuel Palmer.' He glances at the diplomat, who surely can have no idea who Samuel Palmer is. But the man is listening intently. 'The function of the artist is to disturb – that was the big idea then. But I've always been drawn to beauty and mystery – hence the laughter. These days, though, I make things like this, even though I don't want to. The horror just seeps out. Perhaps artists have rediscovered the ability to – what did you call it? – to incarnate.'

'Yes. I wonder.'

'Because I'd love to have the ability, the . . . the *power* to do what you said: to paint her just as she was; not just her, but her soul. Instead I've just disturbed us both.'

'Is this what they talk about at the War Artists' Advisory Committee?'

Tom laughs. 'I think their conversations run mainly to invoices. I'm Tom Collyer, by the way.' He holds out a paint-stained hand.

'George Seferis,' says the man, shaking it warmly. He nods at the painting. 'Who is she?'

'Oh. A friend.'

'Hm,' Seferis says. 'I wonder: would you care to dine with my wife and me tonight? We are both rather starved of interesting company. The talk here is so utterly circular.'

'I'd be delighted.'

That night they eat bad food and drink good wine. The diplomat's wife is called Maro. They talk, inevitably, about Greece and what is likely to happen when George Papandreou and his government finally land. 'It will be a disaster,' says Seferis. 'It is already a disaster. These men . . . they are being led around by a bunch of

349

utter fools and incompetents in, I am afraid to say, your British government. They couldn't even sell peanuts to children, half of these men, and yet they are deciding the future of my country for me. Not just Britain. Russia as well. I am afraid that the heroes – I call them that, yes – of the resistance have been betrayed from the very beginning. And this rabble cannot agree on the smallest thing amongst themselves. They are all professional politicians, you see.' His lips curl in distaste. 'It is all personal spite and vendetta and not a thought for our poor country.'

'And do you tell them this?' asks Tom, fascinated.

'Maro and I dine, most nights, at the table of the Foreign Office in the hotel across the street. Where I am treated like Judas Iscariot at the Last Supper. But I've had enough of this tragedy. Let us talk about art! Do you know the paintings of Nikos Ghika? I feel sure you would like them.'

That night, Tom learns that Seferis is a poet as well as a diplomat, who has lived in London and translated T. S. Eliot's poems into Greek. Tom is able to tell him that his grandfather knows Mr Eliot – 'he's an old soldier, though, and somehow I've never been able to imagine him reading *The Waste Land*.'

'Have you?' asks Seferis, amused.

'I have. *"Unreal City / Under the brown fog of a winter noon / Mr Eugenides, the Smyrna merchant / Unshaven, with a pocket full of currants . . ."*'

'"*C.i.f. London: documents at sight, / Asked me in demotic French / To luncheon at the Cannon Street Hotel / Followed by a weekend at the Metropole.*"' Seferis finishes the stanza. 'Curious thing to memorise.'

'I knew someone from Smyrna. And . . .' He shrugs.

'You knew someone from Smyrna? I am from Smyrna!' says Seferis.

'Unreal city.'

'Alas, yes.'

Tom dines several more times with George Seferis and his wife.
'You've both saved my sanity,' he tells them one night, after the
prime minister and his cabinet have finally left for Athens. It is
already 16th October. Tom has not been able to wangle his way
onto the ship, and it looks as if he'll have to wait until the 22nd
to find himself a place, along with the Seferises and the other
diplomats and functionaries. The disappointment is crushing but
he tries to hide it as best he can. His mood isn't helped, though,
by the bug he is coming down with. His skin is crawling and his
body is swinging wildly between hot and cold, but a few aspirin
and some wine will surely set him straight. Maro Seferis has just
asked him about the life of a war artist, and he is trying not to
sound too bitter.

'The WAAC – they're the hand that feeds me, of course, but
I'm dying to bite it,' he tells her.

'We are all impatient,' says Maro. 'Though I am intrigued: why
are you so keen to return to Greece? It is more than a painter's
interest, it must be. But you are not Greek.'

'Tom is in love,' says Seferis.

'Rubbish, George,' says his wife. But Tom must look guilty,
because then she laughs. 'Heavens, I think you are right! Can we
enquire, Tom? Or is it something deep and secret?'

'Oh, Maro. Don't torture the poor boy. This is a serious
business.' Seferis takes a sip of his wine. 'Can I guess? Your
lover is in Greece, of course. Perhaps in the refugee settlements,
yes, those unreal cities? Because she is the one you know who
is from Smyrna.'

351

Tom makes a face. His fever, or whatever it is, has just given him a good shaking but it is also the effect of being found out.

'You shouldn't tease him,' Maro objects. 'He isn't enjoying it, George.'

'No, I don't mind,' says Tom weakly. 'It's just one of those things – foolish things. Like the song.' He really isn't feeling well. 'I don't know if she's even alive. I've had no way to get in touch with her. The news . . . the famines. I can't help thinking . . .'

'Then don't,' says Maro firmly. 'People have survived, you know. Our family is waiting for us in Athens. It hasn't been easy, of course, but if your . . . your friend?'

'Her name is Zoë,' says Tom. His teeth are starting to chatter.

'Zoë! Well, there you are!' says Seferis brightly. 'Zoë means life! What could be more auspicious than that? But Tom, are you feeling quite well? You look rather shaky.'

'I'm fine. George, would you mind very much if I asked – you of all people must know – if, honestly, she's likely to be OK?'

'I'm sure she is,' Seferis says firmly.

'And what's going to happen now? You don't seem very optimistic.'

'To be honest, I am not. There has been too much meddling – both from malice and sheer incompetence – that I am afraid our prime minister's dream of a sudden return to normality is, well, quite impossible. Churchill has the king waiting in the wings, EAM-ELAS have already, in essence, been double-crossed. But there is always hope. You see, I have contradicted myself. I have been infected by those damned politicians. And now, Tom, I think you should take yourself off to bed, my dear chap. There is a nasty flu going around. You'll want to be fit for the voyage.'

But the ship leaves without him. He doesn't have flu at all but malaria. Seferis comes to say goodbye, and leaves a small book wrapped in brown paper. Έρημη Χώρα: *The Waste Land*. When 22nd October comes, it finds him in a field hospital outside Naples. Shivering under thin army blankets, he imagines the ship coming in to Piraeus Harbour without him. *She won't be waiting for you*, he thinks, but even so he sees the singer waiting, waiting until the last passenger has come ashore, then turning away, back to those strange, low streets. Unreal city.

CHAPTER THIRTY-SIX

Athens, October 1944

Zoë is getting ready for bed when there is a loud knock on the door. She groans. 'What now?' she mutters, while Efi, still dressed, goes to see who it can be. Sólon Pandelis comes straight in without asking permission, without saying anything, shuts the door and leans on it. It takes Zoë a moment before she recognises him, because he isn't in uniform, and she can't remember ever seeing him in plain clothes, and yet here he is, in an old tweed suit with cycling breeches instead of trousers, his calves in army gaiters, a satchel slung across his back and a flat cap pulled down low over his face. She hasn't seen him since that day in August, when he helped so many escape the round-up.

'Sólon!'

'I'm sorry to intrude, my dear ladies,' he says, his voice strained, as though he has been running. 'But you have to come with me.'

'Whatever is the matter, Sólon?' Zoë asks.

'It's about my brother.'

Efi plants her hands on her hips. 'What about that bastard?' she snaps.

'He's coming to arrest you.' Sólon pulls off his cap and almost twists the peak in two between his fists.

'My God . . .'

'Where can we go?' Efi says. Zoë shakes her head in disbelief at her friend's calm.

'Are you in EAM?' Sólon asks. 'Because I am. I've been in EAM for two years. I think you are too, Kyria Efi. You, Zoë, I don't know.'

Efi takes a deep breath. 'I am; she's not,' she says. 'What do we do?'

'Please trust me,' Sólon says. 'My friends will take you to a safe house.'

'How?' Zoë has sunk down onto one of the rickety chairs. 'It's long after curfew.'

'In a gendarmerie van. There's a group of us, mostly serving gendarmes. Which I'm not, any more. I've deserted, I suppose.' He shrugs, as if the confession pains him. 'We must go right now.'

'Can we take anything?'

'If you hurry.'

Zoë rushes into Pavlo's tiny room, dumps the contents of his suitcase out on the bed and stuffs her own clothes into it, realising how few she has left. Then she looks around. Everything else except for the kerosene lamps and the icon have been bartered off long ago for food: Mama's sewing machine, the gramophone, the records. She goes to the lavatory, pulls out the loose brick and takes Mama's icon and her roll of banknotes. Efi is already packed: she has even less to take than Zoë.

'Damn.' Zoë unhooks the bouzouki from the wall of Pavlo's room and gives it to Sólon. 'We can't leave it here for those sister-fuckers,' she says, grinning at the sight of Sólon holding the instrument. 'You look like a proper *mangas*, Sólon. Pavlo liked you. I know you sometimes couldn't tell with him. But he did.'

'Do you remember the time he kicked me in the balls?' Sólon mutters, bending down to pick up their cases.

'At that wedding! I thought you two would be enemies for life.'

'I caught him a couple of days later and gave him a real thrashing. So after that, we were even. But do you know what? It was Ioannis who never forgave Pavlo. Strange, isn't it? He felt the family honour had been humiliated. By a Turk. That's how he thinks: Greeks and Turks. Greeks and communists. Right. Let's go.' As Sólon straightens up, Zoë sees the butt of an automatic pistol jutting from the waistband of his trousers. *I've always thought Sólon was a bit ridiculous, with his glum face and his uniform*, she thinks. *But there's nothing ridiculous about him at all.*

'You keep saving me, Sólon Pandelis,' she says.

'The neighbourhood is my judge,' he mutters. His face is turned away, so she never knows, afterwards, what she might have seen there.

Sólon opens the door, leans out and gives a low whistle. Zoë hears the rumble of engines further down Hozanitas Street. She recognises the sound of German trucks, the sort the Security Battalions use. Sólon hears it too. 'Right. We're going over one block. Run. When we get to the van, climb in the back and get down.'

They race through the alley to where a police van is parked. The two men in front are uniformed gendarmes. They greet Sólon in whispers and he opens the back doors. The two women scramble into the small, musty space. 'You'd better cover yourselves up,' Sólon hisses.

'Aren't you coming, Sólon?'

'I can't. But I'll see you later.'

There is a tarpaulin and they wriggle under it. The sound of the Battalionists' trucks is much louder, and Zoë can hear drunken yelling. The smell under the canvas is nauseating: evidently, the last people to travel like this had been dead for some time. As the van, an old pre-war Ford, grumbles and jolts down the unpaved streets of Kokkinia, Zoë wonders whether, in fact, she is dead herself, whether this is all an elaborate joke being played on her by Charon. But when they bounce over tram lines and the tyres start to hum against tarmac, she has a different thought. What if this is a trick, not of Charon's but of Ioannis Pandelis, and they are heading for Stournari Street, to the Security Battalion torture chambers? She squeezes Efi's hand and listens to their breathing, amplified by the stiff canvas above them.

'I'm frightened,' she whispers, though she can't say how she really feels: hollow with fear.

'Me too,' Efi whispers back, and Zoë hears the echo of her own terror. Then the road gets bumpy again. They are bouncing over cobbles. The truck stops and the handbrake screeches. Then the doors open.

'Here we are!' a young man with a pox-scarred face says, smiling, and she takes his offered hand and climbs out of the van, Efi sliding out behind her. He is wearing an Italian Army tunic, civilian breeches and army boots. His companion, coming round from the driver's door, is even younger, a boy of about eighteen, and similarly dressed; and they both, Zoë notes, have German machine guns under their arms. The scarred one leans into the cab and there is a ripple of quiet laughter, then the van drives off. The street they are standing in is a sloping, unpaved track lined with single-storey hovels even smaller than the RSC houses of Kokkinia. EAM-ELAS has been painted in large, dripping red letters across two of the nearest ones. 'You're safe now,' the scarred-faced one says, while his friend fishes around in his jacket pocket and finally produces a key.

'Where are we?' Zoë asks.

'Kaisariani,' says the one with the key.

'Just around the corner from the clap hospital,' says his friend, grinning toothily.

'Do make an effort, Kosti.' The boy has walked over to a particularly ramshackle hut and is rattling the key in the lock. 'Better get inside, ladies. Don't worry . . .'

'Don't worry?' Efi demands. 'Who in Christ's name are you two peasants, anyway?'

'Shh. I'm Evangelos and this is Kosti. Third Battalion, 26th Regiment ELAS. You're a medic, aren't you? Welcome. We need you. And you too, of course,' he adds, nodding to Zoë. 'But right now, let's get out of sight.'

Inside, Evangelos strikes a match and lights an old oil lamp. The yellow light fills a square, rough-walled room, empty except for two crude, narrow plank beds, the oil lamp and a large tin chamber pot. Small enough so that the beds take up most of the floor, it smells of damp whitewash and mice. An empty rice sack is nailed across both tiny windows. 'A palace, isn't it?' Kosti says in a low voice. 'We need to talk quietly: the walls are like rice paper. But you'll be safe. No one on this street is going to turn you in.'

'Is this your house?' Zoë goes over to the window in the far wall and lifts the curtain. She looks out on a deep, stony ditch, more of a ravine, down which a runnel of dark liquid glints unpleasantly in the moonlight.

'I grew up here,' Kosti is saying. 'It belonged to my aunt and uncle. Now it's mine, I suppose, because they both died in the famine. My parents died when I was ten.' He looks around. 'There were six of us in here . . . But don't worry, comrades.

It's empty now. One of our safe houses. All yours. The two of you won't know what to do with yourselves in all this space.' He chuckles grimly and the two women join in despite their lingering fear. There is something familiar here after all: the humour of refugees. Kosti has taken a bottle of wine, a loaf of bread and a greasy paper package from his bag.

'I'll leave this for you,' he says. 'Do you have any money?'

Zoë hesitates, but what is the point? 'A little,' she says.

'Good. Petrakis – his shop is up by the church – will give you fair prices for food. He's a good comrade. Where are you from?'

'Smyrna. I was born there. So was Efi.'

'Me, I'm from Tsanakkale up the coast,' Kosti says proudly. 'This one' – he nudges Evangelos – 'is a Vlach. From Psychiko, no less.'

Efi whistles. 'That's more posh than Kolonaki.'

'We're all Greeks,' says Evangelos. 'All comrades. Are you with us, sisters?'

'With you?' Zoë mouths, suspiciously.

'EAM.'

'Yes,' Efi says.

Evangelos turns to Zoë. 'What about you?'

'No, I'm not in EAM.'

'Why not?' Evangelos folds his arms and frowns.

'I'm a singer,' says Zoë. She sticks her hands in her pockets to hide her unease and her knuckles bump against Tom Collyer's badge. 'What good would I be to you?'

'The struggle . . .'

'I've been fighting since I was six years old, little one,' Zoë says, feeling suddenly ancient. 'Twenty-two years. I still don't know what victory looks like.'

'Oh, give over, comrade,' Kosti interrupts. 'They aren't in the mood for a lecture. Neither am I, at this time of night. Don't take any notice of him, sisters. He's just joined the EPON—' He sees them both frown. 'Our youth organisation. Last year he was an engineering student . . .'

'And you were a road sweeper,' says Evangelos, shaking his head. This seems like a familiar, friendly routine to Zoë. *I don't care*, she wants to say. She closes her eyes for a moment and sees Pavlo's collapsing face in a halo of dahlia blossoms.

'I was a road *builder*. But we're still comrades, and that's all that matters,' says Kosti. 'We'll leave you now, sisters. You'll be quite safe: this neighbourhood belongs to us.'

'How long will we have to stay here?' Efi asks.

'Not long,' says Evangelos. 'The Bosch are leaving, any day – might even be tomorrow. After that we'll settle up with the quislings and the Battalionist scum. And then . . .'

'And then what?' Zoë feels bludgeoned with exhaustion. She drops down onto one of the beds and finds it as hard as a paving stone.

'And then *laokratia*, of course. People's democracy.'

'See? Everything's settled.' Kosti grins. 'Someone will come and check on you in the morning. Goodnight!'

The next day they are woken by gunfire, only a street or two away. The two women dress quickly and go to the door. The street outside is even more ramshackle in daylight. It runs down a shallow ravine, and square shacks are piled against the rocky sides without any seeming order. They all seem to be built out of daubed mud; it looks like a place built by giant wasps, not humans. Women are gossiping and pegging washing to lines that stretch back and forth across the narrow space, oblivious, apparently, to the shooting and to the red and white graffiti that every house seems to have acquired. The more Zoë looks, though, the less alien the neighbourhood becomes. The houses are rougher, but they are only a little smaller than the RSC houses in Kokkinia, and in the voices of the women she hears the familiar rhythms of Asia Minor. A few are speaking Turkish, and the sound cheers her. A man comes around the corner and jogs down the street, ducking under the washing lines and laughing as the women scold him. Kosti, his gun slung across his shoulder. He sees Zoë and Efi and waves.

'Sleep well?' he asks when he reaches them. 'Sorry if we woke you up. We're having a bit of fun with some Special Security arseholes. Now then: Kyria Sotirakis?'

'Good morning,' says Efi. She has put on trousers and a man's sweater, and she is tying an old scarf around her hair. Kosti is looking her up and down with approval.

'Morning, morning.' He pushes his cap back from his damp forehead. 'You couldn't give us a hand, could you? We have a few wounded.'

'Is that an order?' Efi says, spikily, but Kosti just grins.

'I'm as bad at giving orders as I am at taking them,' he says. 'No, but if you aren't doing anything else . . .'

Efi sighs. 'Wait. I'll get my bag.' Efi ducks inside the hut.

'You know, I've heard you sing a few times,' Kosti says to Zoë. 'Before the war. It was the right thing to say – what you told little Evangelaki. Should be good enough for anybody, to be a singer. And your brother is Pavlo Valavani, right? What's he doing now?'

'He died,' says Zoë, and turns away.

'Damn. I'm sorry.' He crosses himself. 'That *mangas* could really play.'

At that moment Efi reappears, the German medic's kit over

361

her shoulder. 'I promise I'll look after her,' says Kosti.

'She can look after herself,' says Zoë, and hugs her friend tightly. She watches them run back through the billowing curtains of laundry and vanish in the direction of the smoke.

Zoë waits all day for Efi to come back. A couple of women come to the hut with a piece of fresh bread and some cheese. They are both from near Smyrna. The fighting, they tell her, is over a block of flats taken over by a unit of the Special Security. 'But in broad daylight?' Zoë asks, amazed. 'What about the Germans?'

'The Germans have given up,' they say.

It is true. Efi comes back to the hut early next morning, her pretty, round face rosy with excitement. It is the twelfth of October.

'It's over, Zozo! They're going! They're really going!'

'I don't believe you.' Zoë has been preparing to be angry with Efi since yesterday evening, when she didn't come home. 'So you're not dead?'

'Of course I'm not! And it's really true! They're leaving Athens right now. Come with me!'

She drags Zoë out into early morning streets already swarming with people. Everyone seems to have a blue and white flag. They fall in with a squad of partisans all wearing ELAS caps and armbands. They carry their weapons quite openly: German and Italian rifles and machine guns, bandoliers packed with ammunition. Kosti pushes through the crowd and hugs them both. Zoë sees Evangelos with a can of paint, splashing a huge 'EAM' onto the side of a church.

'Where are the Battalionists?' Zoë asks warily. The air still smells of cordite and burning petrol.

'If they've got any sense they'll be halfway to Berlin, the shits,' he says. 'Don't worry so much! Don't you get it, my sister? We're in charge now. We've won!'

362

And Zoë forces herself believe it, as they march into Athens, into Syntagma Square, and run over to Ippokratous Street to watch the German convoys rolling out of the city in perfect order, each truck moving at exact speed, full of neat, expressionless soldiers. After all the terror and misery, the day feels like one of the American cartoons she sometimes went to see at the Cineac Theatre, because the Germans, through a flaw in their inscrutable logic, didn't object to Mickey Mouse. Watching the Germans leave has that flat, jerky, too-bright quality of a cartoon. The Greek flags are so thick that the street looks like a carpet of forget-me-nots, but the crowd lining the street is completely silent. The only sound is the chug of the Opel trucks as they edge their way out of history.

And then they dance. All of Athens dances. Somehow Zoë finds Apostoli and Niko in a cafe on Ermou Street and they sing every song they can remember, standing arm in arm in front of the university and later on at some fancy hotel where some Nazi general's wine cellar has been liberated. Oh, it is wonderful. But somehow, it is too bright, too flat. She has to force herself to believe, but it feels like a cartoon. When she saw the swastika flying from the Acropolis that day in 1941, it felt terrifyingly real. Liberation feels like Mickey Mouse.

She spends that night on Apostoli's sofa in Psiri. 'I'm going home,' she decides next morning, as Andromache is heating up the coffee: German ersatz, but the real stuff will be back soon now that there is peace again. Peace. Walking through Psiri, she realises how much she has missed Kokkinia these past few days. *There are worse places than Psiri*, she tells herself, but the quarter is the kind of place where weeds grow sideways out of the crumbling stucco of the houses and people don't know their neighbours. Still, everything feels more real today. The city is coming back to life. There is a sense of buoyancy, almost as if the Germans had been affecting the force of gravity. Even the tired October air, as she waits for the tram in Omonia Square, tastes like champagne. Two days ago the trams weren't even running to Piraeus because of the fighting. Now the Battalionists and the Special Security units have melted away or turned themselves in to the police. Prime Minister Rallis has been arrested. British paratroops have landed and are driving towards Athens. The government in exile is sailing from Taranto. People are reading the newspapers and finding things that make them smile. She hasn't seen such a thing in years. When she gets home she will stand in the close silence and tell Mama everything that has happened. *At least I have my ghosts*, she thinks, and then her hand touches the cap badge in her pocket.

'What does it say about the British?' she asks the man opposite her.

'They've parachuted onto Megara Airport!' he says, sweeping off the shiny straw boater he is wearing – *He must have been guarding it like dragon's gold this whole time*, she thinks – and waves it happily, to the consternation of the elderly women on either side of him. 'It says here that some are going north to chase the Bosch, and the rest are coming here.'

'Is it the Royal Artillery?'

'Artillery? No, it's the . . .' He squints. '2nd Parachute Brigade.'

'Oh.' She doesn't let the man see that the news has deflated her a little.

'It's over,' the man says, settling the boater at a defiant angle on his carefully combed but thinning hair. 'We'll have a proper government. We won't need artillery!'

'Yes, you're right,' says Zoë, and laughs. It feels beautiful to laugh. 'We'll be ourselves again, won't we?'

Back in Kokkinia, she falls into the embrace of the narrow streets, the tiny, orderly refugee houses. And the people, hanging out their laundry, selling this and that from their front steps, gossiping: the refugees have survived once again.

She turns into Hozanitas Street. There is the cafe. The lamp post knocked crooked by a German truck in August, the sagging overhead wires, still carrying nothing since the Germans blew up the power station. The brown flank of the mountain at the end of the street, the bright tiled dome of the church of the Annunciation. *I've only been away for a week*, she thinks, *so why does it all look so different?*

Then she sees. The corner. Her corner. It is gone. The house has vanished. All that is left is an impossibly small space, a black rectangle. enclosing a low, angular heap of blackened timber. She is still walking. Her mind and her legs are refusing to believe what they are being shown. Because it isn't possible. Then she sees Venetia Kodjagas sitting on her front step, left stranded by the emptiness beside her. Standing in the middle of the street – her legs understand now, they won't carry her any further – she flings out her arms, but there is nothing left to catch hold of, not even ghosts.

'How?' she whispers. 'How?'

She feels a hand on her arm. 'Come here, my darling. Come on. Sit down next to Venetia.'

Mrs Kodjagas is leading her gently but firmly past the black absence of Katina Valavani's home. The old lady, who is herself shrinking, fading into the black folds of her widow's costume, lowers herself onto the step and pulls Zoë down beside her.

'How?' Zoë whispers again.

'Oh, my dear. It was the night you left – and thanks be to God you did leave. Ioannis Pandelis and his thugs did it. I looked out when they kicked down the door, and then I saw flames. My God, what a sight! Haven't we all seen dreadful things, my dear one, dreadful things, all our lives? That God should still be testing us . . .' She waves a hand in the air, the fingers clawed with rheumatism. 'It has happened often enough, the Lord knows, but next door, and to Katina Valavani's daughter? God rest her soul, that poor woman . . . And you, dear one. But at least you are alive. When we saw the house burning, we believed you were inside, that Pandelis had murdered you and the Sotirakis girl. Dear God! We woke the neighbourhood with our screams. If Mr Castanides had not arrived – he's been in Haidari, the poor man, the martyr, but they let him out last week – and told us that EAM had saved you, we would be mourning still. Sólon the gendarme, wasn't it, Zoë *mou*? Who took you away?'

Zoë nods her head. It feels alien, a mannequin's head on a gimbal. 'It was Sólon,' she rasps. 'Was there anything ? . . . I mean, did you save anything?'

'Nothing. People came with buckets and water and put out the flames, thanks be to God, otherwise Kyria Castanides and I would have been homeless as well. We poked through the ashes but there was nothing, my dear, except what you see.'

Zoë forces herself to turn and look. The heap is being given what form it has by the blackened lattice of Mama's iron bedstead. Behind it, a shape that might be the kitchen sink. 'I had nothing left,' she says at last, and takes the old woman's hand in her own. 'So I suppose I have lost nothing. Isn't that a blessing?'

'Here.' Mrs Kodjagas holds out a spotless white handkerchief for her, because the tears are starting to pour down her face. 'Cry. God knows that we have learnt how to do that.' The old woman sighs and leans against Zoë, and her slight weight is more comforting than Zoë will ever be able to explain. 'Cry, Zoë Valavani. But not too much. Something will turn up.'

'Will it?'

'I don't know. But we can say that. Fate has taken everything else, but she's left us our tongues, eh, to say foolish things?' She chuckles hoarsely and threads her arm through Zoë's. 'You can build another house. That one was just boards and mud. Perhaps there will be bricks now. Brick houses for everyone! When the Turks killed my husband, I was sure I'd been left with nothing. And now the government is going to build me a brick house to die in.' She chuckles again. 'Something always turns up.'

'Thank you, Kyria Venetia.'

'You never got married, Zoë.' Mrs Kodjagas turns her lined face up to Zoë's. 'If you had been married . . .'

'My husband would have died in the famine, or in Osia Xeni Square.'

'Oh, dear.'

'Well, isn't it true? Why else do all the refugee women wear black? Mama taught me that. The whole neighbourhood did: that you give your heart to someone else and they leave you wearing black.'

'There was the English boy.'

'Do you remember him, Kyria Venetia? Because I don't think I do.'

'Really?' The old woman squeezes Zoë's wrist, just a ghost of pressure.

367

'All right. I do remember him. But I'm afraid he died a long time ago. So many battles. So many ways to die. Sometimes I think that the British Army will come into Athens and I'll see him riding on a tank. He'll jump down and then . . . you know, Kyria Venetia. These are our dreams, aren't they? Our Kokkinia dreams.'

'You still think of him?'

'Always.'

Mrs Kodjagas sighs and pats Zoë's arm. 'You're very like your mother. Gloomy but so passionate. She would agree with me, you know.' They both turn and glance at where the bedstead rises from the debris like the door of a vanished cage. 'She'd tell you, like I have: something will turn up.'

CHAPTER THIRTY-SEVEN

It is nearly two months, because the anti-malarial drugs gave him jaundice, before Tom can make the calm, dull crossing from Taranto to Piraeus. The Mediterranean is safe now, the last U-boat long since sunk. He has hitched a ride on a tank landing ship full of armoured cars. There is fighting in Athens: the provisional Greek government, all those argumentative, balding men he drew in Cava de' Tirreni, have failed after all. On 2nd October they ordered EAM-ELAS to disarm, the next day there was a demonstration and the police opened fire. After that, ELAS attacked the police stations and the monarchist bases, and British troops were drawn in. Now, in Athens, there is civil war.

They round Cape Matapan before dawn. Tom is awake, staring out into the darkness to port, feeling his blood shifting with excitement. He has been waiting for this for so long. The sun rises as they come up the east coast of the Peloponnese, past Hydra and Poros and the mountains of the Argolid, carrying a roof of heavy grey cloud. They clear the island of Aegina and there, in the distance, a white haze resolving from stacked shades of greys and blues: the city. Athens. It is 19th December 1944.

Tom has found a place to sit wedged between lashed oil drums outside the wheelhouse. Even with his paratrooper's smock zipped up over the oily submariner's pullover he has had since Normandy, it is still chilly. He shivers and remembers the pass at Vevi. Cloud-swathed mountains like these, the same cutting wind and the smell of snow. As they come closer to Piraeus they are joined by a tug flying a large Greek flag – the royal flag, with a golden crown in the centre. It takes the lead as they steam past Salamis and a motley fleet of ships riding at anchor: Greek Navy, Royal Navy, rusty merchantmen. He has borrowed a pair of binoculars from another officer and through them he watches the dun-coloured hillsides to the north of the harbour, the lattice of low white houses spreading up their flanks. *That must be Kokkinia: where is Hozanitas Street?* He squints and adjusts the focus but the geography tells him nothing. When he sleeps, more often than not he finds himself in front of the little corner house with the blue door. Sometimes it is like Wonderland: he is far too big to fit through the door. Sometimes he can't find Zoë's house amongst endlessly replicated, cube-like huts. But sometimes the door will open and he will step inside. It doesn't matter now. She's there, inside the blurred circle of the binoculars. They are just a couple of miles apart. But as he gazes, puffs of smoke blossom among the houses, and above the hiss of water and the thud of the LSTs comes the sound of small arms fire and artillery. He winces. *Probably looking in the wrong place*, he tells himself.

Tom has been prepared for ruins in Piraeus, because it had been half destroyed when he left it, but the scale of the destruction around the harbour shocks him. There is almost nothing left of the waterfront or the docks. The grain silo that guards the western

370

entrance to the harbour is still standing, but not much else. He walks down the ramp, the sound of engines deafeningly loud behind him. Three years, seven months and twenty days. He walks away from the noise of the disembarkation, looking for familiar sights. There are almost none except for the curve of the quayside. And then his memory meshes with the scene in front of his eyes. That was where the *Arethusa* was moored. That, surely, was where he sat with the wounded and talked with that medical orderly. He lights a cigarette and walks along the quayside. Yes, he went aboard the *Arethusa* here. The anti-aircraft guns were here, and here. There was a row of corpses laid out here, on this innocent-looking patch of concrete. He looks over the edge, but where the upturned belly of the *Hellas* had rolled, the water is filled with brightly painted fishing dinghies. He feels a small prick of dread.

There is a military policeman watching the unloading of the LST. 'I need to go into one of the Piraeus suburbs,' Tom informs him. 'Where can I find some transport?'

'Out of the question, I'm afraid, sir,' the red cap tells him politely, though his expression suggests he feels himself confronted by an imbecile. 'ELAS are in charge between here and Athens, sir. You wouldn't want to be wandering off into no *suburbs*.'

'Bloody hell.' Tom takes off his beret and drags his fingers through his salt-stiffened hair. *You knew this*, he tells himself. *You read it in the paper.* But when he was sitting, blanket-wrapped in a deckchair with Capri twinkling in the blue distance, he didn't imagine this reality. There aren't any Greek civilians around at all, he realises, only sailors and gendarmes. There are columns of smoke everywhere. A mortar round goes off very close by, and everyone on the dock flinches. 'I'll take a car, then. At my own risk. I'm a . . .' He hesitates, and points a thumb at the green

371

flash on his shoulder. 'I'm an official war correspondent.'

'Sorry, sir. If you were Monty himself I couldn't let you do it. You wouldn't get far anyway.' The MP lowers his voice. 'Rumour has it that one of our lot got dragged out of a police station just around the corner from here. When they found him, ELAS had skinned him alive.'

'That sounds like utter rubbish to me, Sergeant,' says Tom.

'Still can't let you go off on your own, sir,' the MP says apologetically, but he draws himself up to his considerable height and Tom knows there's no point arguing.

Not even a villainous pair of Greek commandos, whose jeep is bristling with weaponry, will take him to Kokkinia, even though he all but implores them. 'Kokkinia is full of *commounistés*,' they tell him, not bothering to keep the suspicion from their sun-lined faces. The only way open to him is into Athens by tank or armoured car. A friendly dragoon sergeant offers him a lift, and soon he is half standing, half sitting in the turret of a Humber, trembling with frustration and enveloped in a fug of sweaty socks, tobacco and petrol smoke, armpits and old sardine tins. When they set off, he wonders if they are turning into the street where the Cordelio was, but the buildings are mostly rubble. There is destruction everywhere, and graffiti, great dripping reams of it. They pass a large bloodstain spilling down the front steps of a little house, on which someone has dropped a now-wizened bouquet of wildflowers.

As they drive along Syngrou Avenue, ruler-straight and terminally shabby, they keep passing Sherman tanks and armoured cars. The fighting seems to be going on in small pockets on both sides of the avenue. Machine guns are firing not far away in the direction of the Acropolis and there is the familiar flat thump of mortar rounds exploding. The tin cup of strong, sweet tea the crew have made him tastes strongly of petrol, but he sips it dutifully. Once or twice a bullet pings off the armour. 'Not trying very hard,' is the verdict from the crew. There is not much ambiguity inside the armoured car about ELAS: murdering gangsters, the lot of them, says the driver. Communist thugs working with German deserters, the wireless operator agrees.

'You can't really say anything good about either lot,' says the commander, an older man from Yorkshire. 'Say what you want about ELAS, at least they gave Jerry a run for his money. The ones on our side prancing around in Jerry uniforms . . . no, they're all bloody savages, sir.' The turret traverses while the commander and the gunner decide whether or not they've seen an ELAS mortar team or women with baskets full of laundry. 'The people stuck in the middle, though, the ordinary Greeks: they're lovely people who don't deserve all this bloody nonsense. I was in Normandy and I've never seen so many dead civilians.'

They drop Tom off outside the Hotel Grande Bretagne – the Fortress, as the commander calls it. Like most soldiers he doesn't quite know what to make of this scarred and limping paratrooper captain with the purple and white ribbon of the military cross and a green *War Correspondent* patch over the wings on his sleeves. 'It's where they're all staying: photographers, correspondents, the top brass. I've heard,' he adds, as the armoured car pulls up in Syntagma Square, 'that ELAS don't shoot at the Yank journalists. Everyone else is fair game, though, sir . . .'

'Thanks for the words of encouragement,' Tom says. As he jumps down with his rucksack, an RAF plane, a twin-engined Beaufighter, roars over them flying low and slow, and begins to circle the Acropolis. Sandbags and concertina wire guard the approaches to where the Hotel Grand Bretagne spells out its name across its roof. More concertina wire, and a line of armoured cars parked along the front. *I'm here*, he tells himself. *I'm here with her, and we're breathing the same air again.* He sees a cafe further down the street and starts towards it, crunching through the broken glass which lies everywhere, jaggedly reflecting the blue sky and the graffiti-covered walls: ΖΗΤΩ Η ΕΘΝΙΚΗ ΕΝΟΤΗΤΑ! *Long live national unity*, he translates, thinking of the verger's wife on Moscow Road, how patient she was with him as he puzzled through her children's books. He needs to sit and think, surrounded by Greek voices. He crosses the wide, deserted road, but as he steps onto the pavement on the other side in front of the hotel, a military policeman runs over to him. He looks Tom up and down, noting his paratrooper's smock and beret, his rucksack and his lack of a sidearm. But he salutes smartly enough.

'Sorry, Major,' he says apologetically. 'There's a sniper about. You wouldn't mind stepping inside for a minute while he's dealt with, would you?'

'I'm going over there,' Tom says, pointing to the cafe, but just then there is a whine and a sharp crack, and the MP winces.

'Honestly, sir. For your own good.'

'Pretty dreadful shooting,' Tom observes, but he catches a look of pain in the MP's face. *The poor sod will have me on his balance sheet if I catch one*, he thinks, and relents. 'All right, Corporal. I'll just go in and have a quick cup of tea.'

'Very good, sir,' the MP says, with obvious relief, and heads for the doors of the hotel, Tom following him more sedately. There is a surge of gunfire from several streets away. 'Sure those aren't just spent rounds?' Tom asks, but the MP shakes his head.

'I think he's aiming for the police building next door, but we can't take the risk, sir. Not with all the brass around.' The MP salutes and leaves Tom inside the lobby, which is full of military personnel milling around: staff officers, orderlies, a senior Air Force officer, all of them trying to look indispensable. Tom wonders how much a cup of tea is going to cost him among all this marble and cut glass. He decides to have a drink instead, and wanders about until he finds an elegant panelled bar. A curved sign proclaims FORTRESS BAR in not very neat black paint. He orders a bottle of Egyptian Stella beer, because that is apparently all that is on offer this afternoon, and finds a place at the end of the bar. His plan has been to find a small hotel in some quiet district like Kolonaki, but the Greek barman tells him there are no quiet districts at the moment. So he reluctantly takes a room upstairs, which is small, clean and has a narrow view of Mount Lycabettus. He throws his rucksack onto the bed, washes his face in the tepid, rusty water in the bathroom sink, takes his map case painting kit and goes out.

The sniper has given up or been dispatched. Tom walks through the line of armoured cars and into Syntagma Square. He can't help but notice that the pavement is dappled thickly with large black stains. The blunt snout of a Vickers machine gun juts menacingly from a sandbagged position at the top of the steps leading to the Tomb of the Unknown Soldier. Paratroopers are manning other positions in the corners of the square, watched by Greek policemen in black uniforms, looking shifty. There are garlands of decaying flowers propped against some of the trees, and a few civilians are standing around, looking lost in their own city. When they see him coming some nod and smile politely but others turn their backs. *I'm sorry*, he wants to say. *This is nothing to do with me.*

But it is. The fighting started here, two weeks ago. He stops in front of a bloodstain, a faintly human shape bruising the marble pavement. A black-booted policeman watches him idly from across the road. So much blood, over the past three years. He has become utterly used to it. But now, as he lights another cigarette, he finds that the defences he has put up to deal with the carnage to which his profession demands he bears witness are no longer enough. Because there is a chance, however small, however improbable, that one of these blurry outlines might be the imprint . . . *Impossible. She wouldn't have been here.* But as he watches the smoke from his cigarette drift up into the green fluting of the cypress, he knows that isn't true at all. There are countless ways in which Zoë Valavani might have died.

He sits down on the nearest bench, feeling all his certainties, all the beliefs he has demanded of himself in order to stay alive and sane evaporating into the Athens air. The air that smells of pine trees, burning houses, tank exhaust and cordite. Athens is just another battlefield after all.

CHAPTER THIRTY-EIGHT

Andromache is not well. She has had diarrhoea for two days and is too exhausted to get up from the bed. Apostoli, gaunt with hunger and lack of sleep, stays slumped on the floor at her side. There is cholera in the neighbourhood and shelling has disrupted the water supply. Burst sewer pipes leak out into the street. No one has left the house for a week, maybe more, except to run to the standpipe on the corner to fill jars and buckets with water, or to one of the Red Cross stations where volunteers risk sniper fire to hand out cans of soup and slices of jaundice-yellow bobóta. The sickly taste of the gritty corn bread, though it is keeping them all alive, never leaves her and sometimes she wakes in the night after dreaming of it, only to gag on its oily ghost in her mouth. The three of them have retreated to the cramped upstairs rooms of the house since an artillery round came in through the kitchen window and destroyed the icebox. Though there has been no ice for years, it was one of their stores of tinned food and now they have very little left to eat. At night, the sky is criss-crossed with tracer. Spent bullets lie so thickly in the streets that even the little boys are tired of collecting them. They huddle together in the bedroom for warmth and for company. They barely talk, but being close to one another is just enough to stave off despair.

Psiri is on the front line between ELAS and the monarchists. Occasionally a British tank will grind through the narrow streets, and the Royal Air Force is constantly overhead, but it is a small though deadly civil war that is raging through this part of Athens. Further off, in the direction of Omonia, they have heard the sounds of a much bigger battle, which has been going on for days now. The year is at its pivot point. Outside, everything is grey: the light, the buildings, the faces of the people she sees around the standpipe. They gather news in hurried, breathless snatches. Churchill has been and gone. Someone says he brought the king with him, others say that is nonsense. ELAS still hold much of the city but more and more British soldiers are coming in every day and they can't last much longer. Is any of this true? No sooner has someone delivered a scrap of information than they will be ducking or running for cover as a sniper opens up or a Spitfire begins its dive. The graffiti is thicker than ever, huge EAM-ELAS slogans, hammers and sickles, lengthy diatribes that take up entire walls. Young men and women run from doorway to doorway, ruin to ruin, carrying rifles and wearing German helmets. Propaganda is shouted through paper funnels. But at the ration tables and the standpipes, people no longer cheer for the partisans. Every day, Zoë hears that someone else has died, someone's brother, uncle, granddaughter. The snipers don't seem to care who they target, and no one knows who they are: ELAS, X, the British. There will simply be a *crack!* and a body will go sprawling. In some streets, unclaimed corpses have become landmarks: the old woman stretched out beside a lamp post, the boy slumped on the doorstep of an abandoned shop. And the rumours are worse every day. Men rounded up by the British for no reason whatsoever and taken God knows where, bodies with their throats slit by X, or hacked to death by KKE assassins. ELAS fighters executed by Rimini Brigade soldiers, X-ites shot by ELAS. Men and women who have survived the famine and the *blokos*, who don't care who is in government so long as there is bread and oil in the shops, blown to pieces by rockets fired from RAF planes. Tracer arcs from the distant crag of the Acropolis. A woman drops dead in the middle of a quiet street, and children run and snatch up the cornbread that has slipped from her outflung hand.

Zoë sees Efi sometimes, always with her German Army medic's bag. These days she follows Kosti and his team of ELAS fighters who ambush the patrols of British paratroopers that dare to venture between the gasometers and burnt-out factories of Gazi. Sólon is leading his own group in the alleys and shopping arcades around Omonia. One day when they are both sheltering from a sniper, in the alley next to Aghia Kiriaki church, Zoë sees that her friend is agitated.

'What's wrong?' she asks. Efi takes a deep breath. 'You should stay away from our group.'

'Why?'

'Evangelos has gone a bit crazy, I think. He says things. Now he's carrying an axe around and says it's for the neck of any traitor he captures. It's all shit, probably, but . . . he doesn't like you. He says you're a reactionary.'

'Because I won't fight?'

'Well, that. And . . . I'm just saying what I've heard, Zoë.'

'Oh, for God's sake. You're like a sister to me, Efi. Whatever it is, just tell me.'

'He's saying that you didn't go out to fight because you love the British. There.'

'But that's . . .'

'Someone – one of those EPON kids – saw you playing with your lucky charm at the demonstration in Syntagma. You know, your cap badge. So now some of them are saying you have a British boyfriend, that you're bringing him information.'

'My God! They can't really believe that!'

'No one who knew you from before – that's me, and Sólon, now – they know the story. My darling Kosti understands. But the others, they're kids. It all happened such a long time ago, and for them, the world began last year. And Evangelos . . . he used to be so sweet, but now he terrifies me. So please, Zozo *mou*, just stay away.'

'Christ.' Zoë presses her face into her hands.

'*Aman.* Forget about it. Hey, listen, this'll take your mind off Comrade Evangelos. You know Feathers?'

'What about her?'

'She's only gone and joined the X!'

'Now you *are* joking!'

'One of Sólon's team saw her riding in one of those little British things – Bren carrier? – with one of their commanders.'

'Maybe she was a prisoner.'

'She was wearing an X armband.'

'Well, she was always rotten, right down to her soul. It's a terrible, terrible thing to say.' Zoë crosses herself. 'But I'm glad Pavlo didn't live to see all this.'

'He killed himself, didn't he?' Efi says gently. When Zoë doesn't answer, she puts her hand on her friend's arm. 'I guessed a long time ago. He knew his dose, down to the molecule. He'd never have overdosed by accident.'

'He couldn't take the world any more, Efi *mou*. It was like he foresaw all this. And he said that the rembetika was leaving him. Maybe he knew about Feathers – she'd have betrayed us all . . .' A thought jerks her back against the wall, as though the sniper has found his target. 'You don't think it was Feathers who put Sólon's brother up to having us arrested? Sólon told me that Ioannis joined the X the same day the Germans left.'

'Holy Virgin! But why would she do something like that?'

'She's always known what I think about her. Because . . . oh, my God. To get the house? No, that's too horrible.'

Efi whistles. 'It makes sense to me. She thought Pavlo belonged to her, so his property did too. Burn it down, build it up again in her name.' They look at each other. There have been plenty of stories, over the past two years, of collaborators turning friends or even close relatives in to the Gestapo so that they could steal their property, or to settle old scores, or just out of sheer malice.

'I don't think it can be true,' Zoë says. 'Feathers is a bitch and a schemer but none of her schemes have ever come to anything. She only cares about smack.' A boy starts shouting that the sniper has been killed, and long live EAM! Zoë hugs Efi and runs the short distance back to the house, feeling the back of her head tingling. She feels like that all the time: skin prickling, the sensation of being watched, of an eye, a finger, a trigger, a mind deciding whether she is to live or die.

CHAPTER THIRTY-NINE

Tom wakes with a thin, whining hangover. He doesn't get up straight away, but lies under the stiff sheets, stretching the pain from his limbs and taking stock. After his grim epiphany in Syntagma Square he hitched a ride in a tank up to the Acropolis, where he found his old colonel conducting business from his HQ in the museum. They looked out over the city, at the rising smoke and the diving planes. A machine gun nest between the Caryatids of the Erechtheion was firing down onto the neighbourhoods to the north, shabby streets bisected by railway lines and bracketed with factories and gasworks. Tracer, pale sparks in the sunlight, sprayed over the roofs like water from a garden hose.

'General Alexander wants to flatten the whole city, like the Luftwaffe did to Rotterdam,' the colonel told him. 'We won't, because there would be riots in London and I'm pretty sure my men would refuse. But it's a mess here, Tom. Your timing is impeccable.'

'I'd hoped I could get into Piraeus.'

'Hitch a ride with a convoy.'

'No, I mean the suburbs. Kokkinia.'

'Not a chance.' A Beaufighter screamed low overhead and wiggled its wings, and the soldiers around them cheered. 'The navy is shelling Piraeus, Tom. ELAS captured a whole platoon of our chaps there last week. Plenty of things to paint closer to home, I should've thought.'

'Are you manoeuvring for another portrait, sir?' Tom asked, laughing to mask his disappointment.

'No, just trying to save your skin. I don't want a pack of bereaved art critics out for my blood. They can be vicious, I understand.'

'I don't think I'd be missed,' Tom said.

'We're surrounded.' The colonel swept his arm around the horizon. 'We have Omonia Square and Syntagma, Mount Lycabettus and Kolonaki. We did have Kifisia but obviously we don't any more. Everything else is ELAS. We're on an island here, Tom.'

'Outnumbered as well is what they tell me.'

'In Athens, yes, but not by much. We're being reinforced: by the end of the week we'll have superiority. We outgun them already in the city. But if the divisions out there' – he waved at the mountains, not so far away – 'if they had committed those men even a couple of days ago, we'd have been done for.'

'I wonder why they haven't.'

'So do we all. For what it's worth, my feeling is that, despite a lot of evidence to the contrary, ELAS don't want to fight us.'

'Why not?'

'They think they're fighting for justice, and they seem to think that we, even after all this, are their best hope. They don't trust the new government and they certainly don't trust the king.'

'Are they right?'

The colonel shrugged. 'That's none of my business, old son.'

But it is, Tom wanted to say. The colonel was striding back to the museum, and Tom followed him inside. A generator chugged somewhere nearby, and a trickle of electricity cast a dim light, yellow and waxy as the fat on hanging beef, over the marble walls and the huge statues that reclined, armless, headless, more beautiful than the corpses on the roads around Caen and Falaise but still, in this light, just as dead. One giant, legs amputated at the thighs and with half a face, wore a paratrooper's red cap at a jaunty angle. A rifle dangled by its strap from a Nereid's arm. A section of pediment was draped in laundry: grey soldiers' underwear festooned like a century's worth of cobwebs. Their footsteps echoed in the cave-cool space, the colonel stopping to bend over a desk on which a radio sat, its dials glowing amber and red. A plane roared just above the roof and almost immediately the building shook with two, three, four concussions. Dust trickled from the ceiling in fine silver lines.

'Rockets. There's an ELAS unit just below us, in the police station at Makrygianni,' the colonel said over his shoulder. 'You should see the Spitfires on their strafing runs: we look down on them from up here, you know. Quite spectacular. Make a cracking painting, I should think.'

'I can't believe we're strafing Athens.'

'Have to dislodge the buggers somehow.'

'They thought we'd be on their side. Isn't that more or less what you said just now, sir?'

The colonel lit a cigarette, his face flushed by the light he held in his cupped hands. Then he looked up, and blew a plume of smoke through the last trickles of dust.

'It was a reasonable assumption,' he said. Another plane went over and again, the close detonations of rockets. 'Perfectly reasonable. But they were wrong, I'm afraid.'

384

Soon afterwards, Tom found another tank commander heading back to Syntagma. Bullets pinged against the armour of the tank he rode back in, and twice the commander stopped to give cover to platoons of soldiers trying to get across sniper-ridden avenues. He ate a passable supper of chewy meat – goat, he guessed – and went upstairs to paint what he had seen during the day. The pale guts of the tanks; ammunition stacked inside the Parthenon; the stomach of the plane that had buzzed them, so low Tom had been able to see the rivets holding it together. Robin's egg blue. He worked in the wavering electric light until his eyes hurt. Once, he got up to pour himself a glass from the bottle of Greek brandy that the colonel had given him as a welcome present, and when he went back to his desk, he saw that he had painted the dead woman in Caen. He tore out the page, tore it to pieces. When he opened the window to listen to the night sounds of Athens – an armoured car idling in the street below him, the clotted thump of mortars a long way off – the winter air on his face told him he had been crying. It was late, but he knew that sleep would be impossible. Sleep has been an uncertain prospect after his wounding in Italy, and after Caen, he has often wished he hadn't needed to sleep at all. The dreams that come every night are vivid, horrible and rigidly predictable. So he went downstairs to the Fortress Bar, where he found a loud party of journalists, press officers and photographers. The only booze on offer was Egyptian Stella beer, pale, weak and tasting of stale toast. He drank rather a lot of it while talking to an American, Earl Something-or-Other, who worked for the *Chicago Enquirer*. Then he went to bed and dreamt, as he always did, of the sleek, plump belly of the *Hellas*, splitting elegantly to reveal her cargo; Driver Tomlinson, gone from the waist down but still beckoning from his burning truck at Sidi Rezegh; a boy in SS camouflage, his guts in his lap, propped against a motorcycle near Falaise; a young woman in a neat black suit, perfect save for the line of blood drawn as if with a ruler from her nose across her powdered cheek.

He stares for a while at the ceiling, then gets up and washes in the marble basin of the once-sumptuous bathroom, the water now rust-brown and banging in the pipes. Going downstairs, he is chewing without enthusiasm on a stale breakfast roll and sipping black coffee that has all the appeal of peptic acid when he sees the journalist from Chicago negotiating blearily with a waiter on the other side of the dining room, which feels as big and as redundant as some hall in Versailles. Tom waves, and the man picks his way through the tables towards him.

'Mind if I join you?' he asks Tom. 'Earl McCall – Mac. Pleased to meet you, again.' He is young-ish, dressed in a loose brown tweed suit, Clark Gable moustache and eyebrows grafted uneasily onto an angular, knowing face. The waiter comes over with a shot glass and puts it in front of the writer, who picks it up and studies it blearily. To Tom it looks like the eye of some large reptile: an orange orb suspended in hazy golden liquid.

'This creature is an Amber Moon,' says the writer. 'Turns out one of you Brits was holding out on us, hiding a case of Johnny Walker up in his room. The Fortress People's Court decreed that he donate half of it to the bar.' He tips the contents of the glass down his throat and shakes his head like a wet dog. 'Ever had one? Prairie oyster with whisky. Damn functional.'

'No,' Tom says, laughing despite himself. 'Never tried that. The coffee's functional enough for me. And equally disgusting. Where are you from, McCall? You told me last night, but I've forgotten.'

'Originally? From Kansas City, Missouri.'

'Home of the Kansas City Blue Devils.'

'That's the Oklahoma City Blue Devils, buddy. But yeah, we got jazz. Last thing I did, before I shipped overseas, was go see Jay McShann at the Reno.'

So the conversation turns to music, and then to life stories. McCall has been in Athens since October. Before that: Italy, Normandy, the South Pacific. The other correspondents Tom has known have all worn military uniform, usually a little over-tailored, and Tom asks him about his tweeds.

'ELAS don't shoot at Yanks,' McCall says. 'They love us. It's you guys they're after. I got a big Stars and Stripes on my jeep, and I look like a college professor. Snipers blow me kisses.'

An idea forces itself through Tom's hangover. 'Been down to Piraeus recently?'

'Sure. Day before yesterday. One of your Indian regiments did an amphibious assault across the harbour – I got myself a ringside seat.'

'What about the outskirts? The refugee settlements?'

'Like Drapetsona? That was where the assault went in.'

'Like Kokkinia.'

'Never heard of it.'

'About two – two and a half miles north of the harbour. On the slopes of the mountains.'

'Kokkinia . . . wait a second. You mean Little Moscow?' McCall pronounces it *moss-cow*. 'That's the Badlands, chum.'

'Little Moscow . . .' Tom frowns.

'That's what the Rightists call it. Just next door to Little Stalingrad. Yeah, I know where it is.'

'Do you think you could get me in, with your Yankee charm?'

'Powerful stuff, that old charm. Hmm. What's your interest, anyway? Professional?'

Tom takes a sip of his coffee, already tepid. He winces and lights a cigarette instead. He studies McCall through the smoke. The journalist is waving at the waiter for another Amber Moon. Tom decides, on the spur of the moment, to trust him. McCall strikes him as one of life's romantics: something about the way the man studied the globe of yolk hanging like a setting sun in its whisky sky, perhaps? Or the way he fell silent, shaking his head, at the memory of Ben Webster's tenor saxophone.

'There's a girl . . .' Tom sighs. The warp and weft of his life, reduced to that ripest of clichés. He starts again. 'I was in Greece before. In 1941. You know about our Greek adventure?' McCall nods. Tom lays out the bones of the story. 'Then I managed to find the club again and they took me in. I stayed with . . .' He takes a deep breath. 'With Zoë. Until her friends got me on a boat. Not for long, only a couple of days.'

'But long enough.' McCall's drink has arrived. 'She was a singer, right?' He contemplates the liquid sunset again, then raises the glass to his lips and throws back his head. The sun vanishes. He winces. 'Sure,' he says. 'Let's go to Little Moscow.'

'Really? I wasn't going to ask . . .'

'Yeah, you were. And if you hadn't, well, I'd have been disappointed. That's some story you've been dragging about with you. And you've been busy, too.' McCall gestures with an unlit cigarette towards the medal ribbons on Tom's tunic. 'You didn't get that for doing pretty pictures, Major. April 1941 . . . you've had plenty of time to forget about your singer. But you haven't. I like that.'

'Thanks.'

'Sure.' McCall lights up and sighs, smokily. 'I've been chasing this war almost as long as you, Major Collyer.'

'You'd better call me Tom.'

'OK, Tom. So I'm the kind of guy who wants to do the best he can. They pay me to write about the war, so I get as close as possible. You know exactly what I've seen, Tom. And you know that isn't what I write for the folks back home. If every war correspondent actually did his job and wrote about what he's seen, or heard, or – Jesus Christ! – smelt, there'd be world peace tomorrow. Anyhow . . . you're alive. You're back here. You've got a medal. There's a girl. That's the first thing I've heard in a fucking eternity that hasn't made me want to climb into a warm bath and slit my wrists.'

'I don't know if she's still alive.' Why is he whispering? Careless talk costs lives, but who is there to overhear? And then he remembers lying in bed next to Zoë, listening as she talked about chance, the goddess, Tyche. Is this tempting her?

'Well, let's find out,' says McCall. 'If you want to, that is.'

'I do. God, yes, I do. She's why I'm here. Here at all, maybe.'

McCall stands up. 'Let's go, then. But you'll need to lose the camouflage. Got any civvies?'

'Some trousers.'

The journalist looks him up and down. 'The sweater looks OK. If you ask the concierge, he'll let you scrounge something from the cloakroom – the Krauts left a whole lot of stuff behind. A coat would be good. Meet you back here in fifteen?'

'OK. And thank you, Mac.'

'You're doing me a favour. It'll be a scoop: first correspondent in Little Moscow.'

The sky is a flawless, seamless tissue of blue reflected in the sea towards which they are driving down Syngrou Avenue, straight

389

and wide as a runway. Tom sits in McCall's jeep, wrapped in a beautiful tweed overcoat, watching the sagging telephone wires and the shattered date palms pass by. McCall is driving slowly, because the road is full of obstacles: burnt-out cars, shell holes, fallen poles. *Can't you go any faster?* Tom wants to shout. It is freezing cold. The label in his coat reads *Scheer – Wien* and it plainly cost someone a fortune. He chose it because it seemed to be the one least likely to have belonged to a Gestapo man. But it could have, or to someone just as bad. No one from Vienna has come here with good intentions lately. 'You'll do,' McCall said. But Tom wasn't so sure.

'I feel like a Nazi spiv,' he muttered. 'I don't want to show up after all this time, looking like this.'

'You really think she'll be there?' McCall pulled a stained porkpie hat down over his brow and turned away without waiting for an answer.

The jeep has a big American flag tied across the bonnet, WAR CORRESPONDENT stencilled in large white letters across the top of the windscreen and a smaller flag tied to the aerial. Tom has a pre-war motorist's map and he thinks he has worked out a route to Kokkinia which avoids the main trouble spots. McCall glanced at the map, at Tom's finger pointing out Zoë Valavani's house, said 'OK' and shrugged. The journalist has become a different person: cool and soldierly.

Keeping to the wider streets, they drive through a battered industrial area, much damaged by German and Allied bombs, its graffiti-encrusted walls pocked by much more recent gunfire. There are almost no adults about, but they pass groups of children climbing over rubble heaps and throwing spent shell cases at each other. As the jeep passes they stop and stare with vacant eyes sunk deep in dark, hunger-mined sockets. Eventually they cross a railway line. Tom looks at the map and sees that they have crossed into the kingdom of the refugees. They are in Kokkinia. A few streets further on, a man steps out into the street. He is carrying a German rifle, the barrel pointed a yard or so above McCall's head. McCall brakes, not too hard, and props an elbow casually on the top of the door. More men step out from a ruined house, all holding guns and wearing ELAS armbands.

'They won't shoot us,' McCall whispers out of the corner of his mouth. 'They'll just take us hostage.'

'That's a comfort,' Tom mutters back. One of the men, not far out of his teens, has just cocked an Italian machine gun that could turn them into meat and scrap metal in a few seconds.

McCall holds up a friendly hand and, to Tom's surprise, greets the men in Greek. The oldest man steps forward. McCall reaches under his seat and pulls out a carton of ration cigarettes – American Pall Malls – and hands them around. Safety catches click back on. There are smiles, and a short conversation. Tom can follow it: all those hours in that steamy kitchen on Moscow Road were worth it after all. McCall is asking directions to somewhere, to a church or a square. 'Really?' the ELAS man says. 'I could tell you . . .'

'We're in a hurry,' McCall says. 'Is it safe up there?'

'The fucking British are shelling Drapetsona and Keratsini. But north of Petro Ralli you should be all right. Let me send one of my boys with you.'

'No, no, comrade. Thank you, but we'll manage.'

'Here.' The man pulls off his armband and tucks it under one of the jeep's windscreen wipers. 'If anyone gives you trouble, tell them Captain Mavromichaeli of the 23rd Battalion says to leave you alone.'

They drive off. 'You can speak Greek?' Tom says, when the ELAS band is out of sight.

'Sure,' says McCall. He drives in silence for a minute or two. Then he takes out a cigarette and lights it one-handed. 'My wife was Greek.'

'You're married, then, Mac?'

'Was. She died in '42. Cancer.'

'Christ. I'm sorry.'

'Yeah, well.' McCall changes gear savagely, and throws the cigarette, unsmoked, into the street. 'She taught me the language, because we were going to go back to the old country. Her folks were from Salonika – her pop was some kind of big shipping guy but he lost his business in the Crash. Came over to Chicago and became a shoe repairman. But he sent Athena to college, and that's where I met her. Then the war started. The paper sent me overseas and while I was in New Guinea she got sick. I, ah . . . I never saw her again. Kind of why I got this assignment. I thought I could find her grandparents, you know, talk about stuff. I guess that ain't going to happen.'

'You never know.'

'They were old. I doubt they survived the famine. All kinds of bad stuff went on up in Salonika. I'll try and find them, but . . .' He shrugs.

'And yet here you are,' Tom says. 'And so am I. It's the curse of the observer.' He watches a skeletal, caramel-coloured dog digging in a pile of burnt timbers.

'Tom? Collyer! Are you ready for this, old man?'

Tom looks up. They have crossed Petro Ralli Street into the landscape of de Chirico and Delvaux. *Ready? No, I'm not*, Tom thinks. *But now I've jumped. I'm falling, like the man with the failed parachute dropping down onto Salisbury Plain, trailing useless silk. A white flame. A Roman candle.* 'Go left here,' he says aloud.

The jeep lurches into Hozanitas Street, and into the landscape of Tom's dreams. Tiny square houses, their rough stucco making them slightly shapeless, slightly out of focus. The narrow street, sloping upwards to a shoulder of mountain the brown of a dead fox's fur, is deserted. It was deserted that night, too, but then he'd known that the houses had been full of sleeping people. Now, in the sunshine, the place has no feeling of occupation at all. He notices at once that the trees, the young planes and spidery tamarisks, are all gone. Graffiti, the now familiar slogans of EAM-ELAS, cover the white walls like wounds. All the street's life has drained away. It is as empty as a body on a mortuary slab.

'What number are we looking for?' McCall asks.

'317.'

'We're just a couple of blocks away.' *I know*, Tom is about to say, when there is a huffing sound above them, like giant wings being flapped. A second later the jeep's tyres leave the road and a moment after that there is a huge explosion. 'Jesus Christ!' McCall bellows, wrestling with the steering wheel. 'What the hell was that?'

'It was a bloody big gun,' Tom says. 'Look over there.' A roil of smoke and dust is rising a few streets to the north-east. 'Must be the navy.'

'I'm not going to be blown to bits by the Royal fucking Navy, Collyer,' McCall says. The jeep has come to a stop in the middle of a crossroads. There is another flap of invisible wings, and both men duck. The explosion is a few yards nearer. 'But that's number 209. Let's go.' He guns the engine and the jeep hurtles on to the next block.

'It's the next corner,' says Tom. He has just noticed a shuttered cafe that he thinks he remembers.

393

'Oh, shit.' McCall brakes. Tom stands up to see over the dust-caked windscreen. The crossroads ahead is flooded with sunlight and shadows cutting in from the west. Too much light. Tom swings out of the jeep, though it is still crunching slowly over a carpet of broken glass and tiles, and walks forward. The air spirals above him and there is another crash and a fountain of smoke and rubble near the point where the settlement fades into the slope of the mountain. He notices the neat little cupolas of the church for the first time, and further on, the needles of cypress trees marking the cemetery. But where number 317 ought to be, there is nothing but a square patch of burnt earth. Two tiled steps lead up from the narrow pavement into thin air.

In the centre of the scorched ground is a low heap of charred timber, from which a grid, a piece of iron railing, is protruding. Beyond it, a narrow strip of dirt. Chickens once scratched there. In the house beyond, a man and wife lived. Mr and Mrs Castanides. The lattice of iron comes into focus. That blistered paint was cream. His hands gripped those bars as she moved above him. His fingers traced the moulded shells on the bedposts. There was coffee boiling in a copper pot. She turned in the morning light, and let the robe fall from her shoulders. She sang to him. He blinks, and reaches for the flap of his case: in his mind he is already seeing the wet brush dragging black across the paper, blotting it into a flattened square, the lines of the buildings, the perfect blue. Ultramarine. The holy colour. He bought it, didn't he, to paint the sky above her house.

'Come on, Tom.' McCall has his arm around him. Another six-inch shell from the cruiser in the harbour huffs overhead and bursts, shaking the ground. 'It's a shitty thing.' Tom lets himself be steered back to the jeep. 'But we've got to go, old man. OK?'

The jeep heads south and west, through the empty streets, past smouldering factories and abandoned barricades. McCall steers away from machine-gun fire, and once a mortar bomb explodes close enough to them that a piece of shrapnel tears a gash in the flag stretched over the bonnet. Finally they reach Syngrou Avenue, and pull in behind a small convoy of armoured cars, driving fast towards Athens. McCall has pulled the ELAS armband from behind the windscreen wiper and tucked it inside his coat.

'She might be OK, you know.'

'What?' Tom has been somewhere else. Dreams and memory . . . has he been living here, or there, these last years? The line between has become so thin. Thin as a film of paint or a scrape of pencil lead. He remembers Caen, how quickly the dogs came to dig in the ruins, dragging out bones and charred meat.

'Your singer. She might . . . I mean, she'll be all right. The ELAS guys in the carpet factory were telling me that a lot of people are camping out in the hills. I guess a lot of houses are wrecked – I mean, they've been fighting up there since March. If she was smart, she'd have left a long time ago. She'll be fine.'

'There's nothing left, Mac.' Tom sucks in freezing air and petrol fumes, and pats down the Nazi coat for his cigarettes. 'Before, I thought: what if she's gone? What if I knock on the door, and no one opens it? Or a stranger . . . but there's nothing.'

'I thought you were looking for a girl, Tom.' McCall takes an offered cigarette. 'But it was more than that, wasn't it? I could have told you: people like us, I don't think we get to go home.'

Tom tastes sulphur from the match as he sucks the flame into the tobacco. He lets it scorch his tongue. 'You're right. I was going to stay.' He shakes his head. 'With her. In that ridiculous little house, which she hated. That's all I wanted. Just to stay.'

'What will you do now?'

Tom looks at the armoured car in front of them, the young men in the turret, very young, pale and English. The Acropolis rises in the distance, coming closer, a white cage. He thinks of the machine gunners pouring out arcs of fire onto streets where they've never walked. Of ash and cinders, and what so often lies beneath them, these days.

'I suppose I'll do my job,' he says.

CHAPTER FORTY

'It would be nice to sing again, wouldn't it, Apostoli?' Zoë says. It is somewhere around Christmas. Perhaps: the calendar is gone. Andromache has fallen into a shallow sleep; she is no better. Zoë and Apostoli are sitting on the floor next to her with their backs against the wall, listening to gunfire crack and echo through the streets. Apostoli takes a drag on his cigarette. They have both been chain smoking all morning, and the British Army jam tin they are using for an ashtray is filling up.

'There's no music any more, Zozo,' he says.

'Don't be ridiculous, Apostoli! What do you mean?'

'Just listen. The war. This has been going on for ever. Hasn't it? Who's to say it will ever end? There's hardly any air to breathe, let alone for singing.' He reaches up and strokes his wife's limp hand. 'It's gone. I can't feel it any more. If this does end, I'm . . . I'm not going to play again.'

'Apostoli, dearest . . .'

'I can't. I'm finished. Did you know, Zozo, when I was

quite small I was apprenticed to a roofer? It was when they were building the first houses in Kokkinia. I had to run up and down the ladders, bringing the men nails and drinking water. And when the men had gone home, I'd go up and just sit on the roof we were building. Above all the mess. I'm going to go back to that.'

'A builder? For Christ's sake!'

'It's all done for, Zozo. When I was sitting on my roofs I'd see these guys walking past, with the swagger and the clothes – the *manges*. That's what I wanted to be then, not a nail carrier, a monkey working for a couple of drachmas a day. And I was a *mangas*, and it was good. But that's all gone. There won't be any *manges* now. There won't be any Greece left after this, or Greeks. We'll either be Russians or Americans.'

'Or English.'

'The English are done for. They can't even beat a few children.' As if to prove his point, a mortar round bursts close by. They both flinch. Andromache half wakes. She raises her head and moans. Apostoli squeezes her hand and she falls back into her uneasy sleep.

'Americans and Russians need music too,' Zoë points out.

'Yeah, but what music? The rembetiko is finished. No more *manges*, no more hash, no more *tekédhes*. You've heard the stuff they want in the clubs now – *light*.' He practically spits the word. 'Do you want to sing that shit? Do you think they'll want to hear Smyrneika? No one will want to remember the Catastrophe, or the slums, or . . .' He shakes his head. 'People will want to forget. Christ almighty, *I* want to forget. Don't you?'

Zoë bends her head to light her own cigarette. A fighter plane roars overhead, low enough to make the windows rattle. The guns up on the Acropolis are firing again. Sometimes spent bullets fall onto the roof. 'My mother taught me the songs from Smyrna because she didn't want the old world to be forgotten,' she says. 'Do you remember Smyrna, Apostoli?'

'Sure. I was ten in 1922. My father was a baker . . . We've talked about this a hundred times, Zozo.'

'I know, but . . .' There is a long burst of gunfire very close to the house, then yells and the sounds of running feet in the street below them. More gunfire: a tense, measured *tat tat tat* from the corner, a shouted order, an ear-splitting burst from a heavy calibre machine gun. A tank's engine growls at the opposite end of the street, clashes its gears, recedes. Zoë draws her knees up to her chin and clasps her shaking hands together. 'If I die—'

'You're not going to die.'

'But if I do, then . . . I have to tell you something, so it doesn't get lost. Apostoli, Katina Valavani wasn't my real mother. My mother died with my father: they drowned together. Her name was Mary. Mary *Hurrell*.' The word sounds shockingly foreign. 'And my father was George Haggitiris. Apostoli . . .'

She never finishes, and she will never remember, afterwards, what she was going to say. A plane swoops overhead and there is a whoosh and an explosion only a few yards away. The house shakes and something falls off a table in the next room and breaks with a crash. Andromache startles awake.

'Toli!' she moans.

'I'm here, sweetheart,' Apostoli says, squeezing her hand.

'My head hurts so much . . .' The sick woman curls up and begins to sob into the stained cushion.

399

'She has cholera,' Zoë says, stroking Andromache's forehead, which is cold and slick with sweat. 'She needs a doctor.'

'Of course she needs a doctor. But where is there a doctor, for God's sake?'

CHAPTER FORTY-ONE

Tom is walking with a platoon of paratroopers behind a Sherman tank as it grinds along a street near the gasworks of Gazi District. The Division has been pushing out from its bases on the Acropolis and around Syntagma now that Churchill's promised reinforcements have arrived. Although the fighting has not let up – if anything, it has got worse – since Christmas, something has shifted. Tom believes that the Greeks have, at long last, reached their breaking point. After the occupation, the famine, the round-ups and shootings, this new horror, this civil war that is destroying the city that the Germans at least left intact, has been too much. People say, 'We just want the king to come back,' even though the words sound like they are choking them. The hated king is at least a known quantity. The British Army have become a necessary evil. Just yesterday, Tom was out with a patrol probing north into Metaxourgeiou when one of the men was hit in the leg by a sniper. While the rest of the patrol took care of the gunman, the wounded man was left lying in the road with the platoon's medic and Tom. A middle-aged woman ran out from her house with a basin of hot water and a roll of bandages and began to dress the wound with a sort of angry efficiency which took the medic, and the wounded man, by surprise. The woman seemed furious – with the sniper, with Tom, with the man who had been shot – but also confused. One minute she berated the poor man while wrapping his thigh with bandages, the next she was clucking over him as if he were her own son.

'Why are you doing this?' Tom asked her.

'Because God cannot stand it any longer!' she snapped at him, and crossed herself angrily. The war is no longer just a fight to stay alive. It has become an offence against Heaven itself. The woman tied the bandage with a viciously tight knot, then burst into tears, her trembling hands stroking the wounded man's cheek with a tenderness that was almost unbearable to watch. She was going to ask Tom something, he was sure, but she didn't say anything else. He could imagine her question, though: why are *you* doing this? But he has no answer to that any more.

The tank expels a gout of black exhaust and stops. The commander calls down to the platoon leader. 'There's a report of civilian bodies in a courtyard near here, sir. Orders from HQ to investigate and collect identification.'

'Right-o,' says the lieutenant. This has happened before: a report of dead civilians, soldiers sent to confirm, and to gather anything that might identify the dead. Directions are given, and the platoon leaves the tank and turns up a street of small, crumbling houses, moving slowly, watching for snipers. Next to a tiny church is an abandoned garage. A metal door at the far end opens onto a small square of waste ground, once a paved courtyard formed by a high wall and two other houses, long since overgrown with weeds and littered thickly with oil cans, food tins, lamb and chicken bones. Against the far wall, a line of bodies, heads twisted at horrible angles against the plaster, faces already beginning to turn black. Men, a couple of teenagers, an older man in overalls, and the stockinged legs of a woman wearing a dark skirt and jacket. His mouth goes dry. *There's no reason to think . . .* he starts to reassure himself, but since Hozanitas Street there has been a shadow where his certainties had once been. He forces himself to go and look. The woman lies on her side, her face almost hidden by the jacket of the man next to her. Permed hair, a sharp chin, the bruise-dark skin taking the first deep lines of middle age. Thank God. Thank God! He turns away and automatically reaches for his painting kit. He squats in a corner of the yard, painting the soldiers at their grim task of searching the bodies. *How surreal it is,* he thinks. *I've come through the war to find this at the end of it all: a ruined city and a ruined people.* For the last few days he has been wondering whether he is witnessing a beginning here in Greece, not an ending: that a new world is being born. He blows on the painting and stares over at the dead. Did he really think that poor dead woman was Zoë? Surely not. But he did. His heart is still thumping with relief.

That evening he is trying to read the London newspaper in the Fortress Bar, but the effort of sorting the depressing news from the cheerful filler is too tiresome, so he is sparring half-heartedly with the crossword when he hears someone call his name. Walking through the door to the bar is George Seferis. Delighted, Tom jumps to his feet, arm raised, when he sees another man following the poet, a wiry figure in an army officer's service dress uniform. His cap badge says *Intelligence Corps.* Dark brows, a falcon-like nose, narrow chin, curly black hair parted and combed back severely. A black, sweeping moustache.

'Mr Seferis!' Tom shouts. 'And my God! Chris Dimitriou!'

'I have been wondering when we would meet again,' Seferis says, shaking Tom's hand warmly. 'And I take it you know this fellow already?'

'Of course! We were at art school together. Dimitriou! How are you?' The two men grab each other by the shoulders, and both of them wince.

'Sorry, old man,' Dimitriou says. 'Forgot about your bad arm. When did we last see each other?'

'It was that night at the Wheatsheaf, before D-Day.'

Christopher Dimitriou was one of Tom's best friends at art school. He was a brooding, intensely serious young man, who favoured junk shop business suits that slowly, over the course of a few terms, would become encrusted with oil paints. He painted large, forbidding works, heavy slabs of glossy black, orange and pink, beautiful but haunted faces emerging from, or being swallowed by fog. Everything suffused with a rich, pessimistic Byzantine glamour. His digs near the river in Fulham were dingy in the extreme and thick with the fumes of turpentine and tobacco. He was reputed to be so poor that he had to drink the poppyseed oil they used for thinning paint. So it came as a surprise to Tom that Dimitriou came from a wealthy family who lived in a stucco-fronted house in South Kensington. To their mutual surprise, they both joined up in 1939, but it wasn't until the end of 1941 that they met in Cairo, where Tom was recovering from the wounds he'd got in the battle of Sidi Rezegh, and Dimitriou was a military liaison with 1st Greek Brigade. They spent a lot of time together in London in 1944, both convalescing from wounds, waiting for postings and drinking in Soho.

'It was Chris who got me my job as a war artist,' Tom explains to Seferis. 'What are you doing in Athens, Chris?'

'I'm a press attaché, God help me.' Dimitriou makes a face. 'George and his lovely wife have adopted me, otherwise I'd have jumped out of a window by now.'

'That's Maro and George's speciality, saving lost souls,' Tom says. 'They did the same for me in Cava de' Tirreni.'

'I shall order some drinks,' says Seferis. 'Might we join you, Tom?'

'Please!' Tom watches Seferis wander across to the bar. 'I can't tell you how good it is to see some friendly faces at last. But the press office? There's an American journalist, McCall, who says the press office is like a seance, with Churchill's line coming out of you like ectoplasm. Except he was a lot ruder than that.'

Dimitriou bursts out laughing. 'I love Mac. He's got it absolutely right,' he says. 'It's really . . .' He shakes his head. 'Anyway. I would have run into you sooner, but I've been with the Winston circus on HMS *Ajax*.'

'*Ajax*? So it was you shelling me the other day.'

'They were shelling northern Piraeus,' says Dimitriou, frowning. 'You couldn't have been up there?'

'Yes, I was. With McCall.'

'But North Piraeus, Tom,' says Dimitriou. 'That's taking your commission a bit too seriously, surely?'

'It wasn't work,' Tom says. He draws in the condensation on the table with a paint-stained finger. 'I was looking for Zoë Valavani. You remember me talking about her, don't you?'

'Of course! Your mysterious singer from Smyrna. Wait a minute. Don't tell me that's why you're here?'

Tom starts to answer, but at that moment, Seferis returns with Egyptian beer.

'George has been with the Winston circus as well,' says Dimitriou.

405

'Ah, yes. Finally, the British Empire has noticed us.' Seferis shakes his head. 'I am as yet undecided if this is a good or a bad thing.'

'Bad,' says Dimitriou.

'Chris would like ELAS to be triumphant,' Seferis tells Tom. 'And I would have agreed with him, even a few months ago. But everything has changed since October. The KKE dominate ELAS in a way that they did not during the occupation. When the choice was between Greek heroes and Nazi barbarians, well, that was no choice at all. Now, though, the choice, as I see it, is between Stalin and Churchill. I truly believe we are seeing the first shots of a new war: Soviet Empire against British Empire. If I am to be forced to choose – and we shall all be forced, alas – I will throw in my lot with Churchill.'

'But why, George?' Dimitriou is shaking his head with friendly exasperation.

'Archbishop Damaskinos is to be the new regent: that's decided. He is a bit of a peasant but he is a republican and a liberal and he is stubborn enough to resist these bloody monarchists. If the king returns, there will be disaster. But Churchill, and Ambassador Leeper, have convinced me that Britain won't allow that. I too am a republican and a liberal. I couldn't live under some sort of Greek politburo.'

'I had the same thought today,' Tom says. 'About new beginnings. Something dreadful waiting to be born.'

'What were you doing?' Dimitriou asks.

'Identifying bodies. A massacre of civilians. Seven dead, all shot in the back of the head. No apparent reason. I was with the unit which was detailed to collect any identification.'

Luckily, Seferis decides to steer the conversation to sunnier places, and when Tom goes up to bed it is with a head full of discussions on art, writing, landscape, home and exile. And an invitation to dinner tomorrow night, at the Seferises' house on Kydathinaion Street. After Seferis said goodnight, though, Dimitriou paused in the lobby.

'You know, I'm in the press office but I'm also military intelligence,' he said. 'If you like, I can put out some feelers. The Germans left their usual terrifyingly efficient paperwork behind, so there are lists of people they didn't like, and people they killed. Ditto the police and the gendarmerie. You don't want to find your Zoë on one of those, but I can look. We have our own lists: casualties; ELAS members and sympathisers; men and women we've rounded up. We've been sending them to camps in North Africa. Did you know that?' Tom shook his head. 'We have. And there are lists for them, obviously. Now I'm not saying she's going to be on any of these, but perhaps it would be a good thing to check?'

'Would you, Chris?' Tom's hand was trembling again, and he pretended to look for his cigarettes.

'Sure. She was from Smyrna, wasn't she? Like me. Children of the Catastrophe. I'd like to help if I can. Valavani isn't a very common name so it won't be difficult.'

'Thank you, Chris. She has a brother called Pavlo but I don't think there's any other family.'

'Leave it with me. Goodnight, Tom.'

'Night, Chris.'

George Seferis and his wife live in a ground-floor flat in one of the narrow streets of Plaka. Tom drives over from Syntagma in a diplomatic car with Dimitriou. Maro welcomes him like a long-lost relative and ushers him into rooms lined with bookshelves and piled with more books and manuscripts. The other guest is George Katsimbalis, a poet and evidently one of the Seferises' oldest friends. He dominates every conversation but only, somehow, to make it more interesting and entertaining. The house, as Seferis explains over a bottle of wine from Cyprus, belongs to his family. His brother Angelos – whose wife has just left him, Maro explains – lives on the middle floor, and his sister and brother-in-law, a government minister, live at the top. One of the ground-floor rooms is being used as an army dressing station. 'There was another body in the street this morning,' Maro says. 'The dreadful things that Athenians have grown used to. And we, of course, safe in Cairo . . .' Maro stares at her plate for a moment, then smiles at Tom and asks him whether he knows Lawrence Durrell. The circle of friends, from all over Europe and beyond, with George and Maro at its centre, seems immense, and Tom can't help feeling that, just for this evening, he is included.

After dinner, George goes to look for another bottle, and Maro disappears into the kitchen with Katsimbalis. Tom hears him start to sing over the clink and plash of wet dishes. Tom and Dimitriou go outside and stand in the dark street, looking up at the star-framed Parthenon high overhead. There is an army guardhouse across the street, and through the open door they can see soldiers gathered around a brazier. Gunfire rattles hollowly but it isn't nearby. As they watch, a flare arcs up from the Acropolis and floats down northwards.

'I found a name,' Dimitriou says. 'Don't worry, it isn't your friend. But I thought I'd better tell you. Pavlo Valavani: that was her brother, wasn't it?'

'Pavlo.' Tom leans hard against the doorjamb. 'He's dead, isn't he?'

'Afraid so. Some chaps I know are going over the records

from the city morgue, collating info with the new government. I thought I'd have a look.'

'How did it happen?'

'An overdose. Heroin. He died around the beginning of October. Sorry, old man.' Dimitriou shakes his head. 'He almost made it to Liberation. Wish I could have brought you some better news.'

'Still, thank you,' says Tom. He pictures Zoë's brother as he first saw him, propped against a tree and covered in blood, and as he was in the Cordelio, long fingers fluttering up and down the neck of his bouzouki. The tall, thin young man, beautifully dressed, who sat with him in the little house, waiting for the soldiers who would help him escape. Zoë said something about her brother: what was it? Too sensitive for this world, too much like a musical instrument. How terrible for a man like that to be trapped in this torture chamber of a city. 'I didn't know him well at all, but I don't think he would have liked being liberated like this.' Tom's bad arm is throbbing and his left hand feels as if it is being chewed by sharp-toothed creatures. 'There are so many bodies out there, Chris,' he says. 'What the hell are we doing to this country?'

'Reinstating their beloved Danish king, old boy,' says Dimitriou bitterly. 'Cheers. Did you know, incidentally, that the new regent, the archbishop, used to be a professional wrestler? I have decided that this whole thing is nothing but an exercise in surrealism, and I have surrendered to it. I strongly advise you to do the same.'

'Trouble is, I never was that keen on the surrealists,' mutters Tom. 'A Romantic, that's me. And a modernist. A modernist Romantic.'

'Can you be both?'

Tom sighs. 'I wish to God I was neither,' he says.

* * *

409

The next day he gets up before dawn, washes in the hotel's rusty water and eats breakfast in the Grand Bretagne's vast, almost deserted dining room. A tall, gaunt general with protuberant ears is drinking coffee at the far end of the room – it is General Hawkesworth, head of military operations – and trying to ignore Earl McCall, who is obviously trying to wheedle a story out of him. For some reason, the hotel has superb bacon and eggs – there is no other decent food on offer, at the Grand Bretagne or anywhere else in the city. He stayed up late, reading *The Waste Land* in Greek, which seems more and more appropriate these days. He slept badly, and dreamt of Pavlo, in an odd way: he was trying to buy him a train ticket at Paddington Station, but there was some confusion over the change at Newton Abbot, so he went back to the window again and again, Pavlo waiting patiently in the noise and smoke of the station, until at last Tom came out with the right tickets, to find him gone. After he has eaten he goes out into the early morning. *Unreal City / Under the brown fog of a winter dawn.* He walks slowly up Ermou, listening for gunfire, making for the sounds of battle as they start up with the rising sun.

CHAPTER FORTY-TWO

'Zozo!' Zoë struggles to the surface. Sleep, for the past days, has been like drifting under a thin skin of ice on a dirty, frozen pond. She spends most of her time on the floor by Andromache's bed, wrapped in an old peach-coloured quilt. She falls asleep when exhaustion wins over desperation, and wakes with her eyes and mouth crusted with the residue of fever dreams.

Apostoli is shaking her. 'Andromache is worse. I'm worried, Zozo. I'm so worried!'

Someone is screaming outside, a high, almost mechanical sound. Andromache is gripped by a spasm and gasps. Suddenly the room feels completely unreal, like a photograph, like Mickey Mouse. *I'm going to die here*, Zoë thinks. *No, Andromache is going to die . . .* In her mind she sees the room, the house, the street flickering, like at the cinema when the projectionist makes a mistake and the film slows down. *Everything's coming to an end*, she thinks. *It's all going to end, and no one else will know. We'll be gone, and it will be as if we were never here.*

Zoë struggles upright and looks at the woman on the couch.

Andromache's colour is livid and sweat is trickling over her sharpened cheekbones. 'She has to have a doctor, Toli.'

'Where is there a doctor? And I can't leave her . . .'

'Listen. Efi says there are some in ELAS. And the British have medics. The British are here in Psiri. I'll find a patrol. I speak English, remember? I'll be back soon.' She picks up the Italian gas mask bag she has been using as a handbag and slings it over her shoulder. It holds her identification papers and ration card, an almost empty powder compact and some cigarettes.

'What if you're killed? I don't know what I'll do.' Apostoli looks up at her, his face twisted with emotion.

'If I die, remember what I told you. About my family. Can you remember?'

'I . . . What was it?' he mutters. 'You'll have to tell me again.'

Zoë bends down and kisses the bald spot on the top of his head, brushes the back of her hand across Andromache's stringy hair. Then she turns and hurries out of the room. Going down to the ground floor is like diving into a sunken ship. The windows are boarded up and everything is shrouded in dust and lumps of plaster shaken loose by explosions. She crouches behind the front door, listening. The screaming has stopped and the gunfire seems to have shifted to the next street or perhaps further away. There is a white flag, a large square of sheet tacked to a broom handle, next to the door. Andromache made it to wave on her dashes to the standpipe, to show that she is neutral, but Zoë has never been quite sure if it makes her more or less safe. She has been shot at a couple of times while carrying it: neither ELAS or the X approve of neutrality, let alone surrender. She takes it anyway as she unlocks the door and peers out, waving the flag in front of her, wincing in expectation of the crack of a bullet.

But the street is empty. Cartridges are scattered over the pavement, and a wide brush stroke of red shows where a body – the screaming one? – has been dragged away. She steels herself, then steps out. She turns left and runs towards the corner. The tank was down there, she reasons. There must be British soldiers nearby. The square of fraying linen flaps above her. When she reaches the corner, she sees a couple of civilians edging from doorway to doorway, but no soldiers. This street leads, in one direction, to Ermou, which in turn leads straight to Syntagma Square. Ermou is a battlefield, though, and its straightness and length make it a place of lethal crossfires. She decides to cut through the narrower streets, still heading east towards Syntagma. Which means, she realises, that she is turning her back on ELAS, on Efi and Sólon, if they are even still alive. *So I'm going to the English*, she thinks. *At last. I suppose that makes me a quisling. But ELAS won't save Andromache. They've gone mad, like the X, like the government.*

Zoë runs across Karaiskaki Street and into the alley opposite. She keeps running until she comes to the next main street. Crouching on the corner, she looks up and down. South, towards Ermou, she sees a line of British tanks and a group of soldiers in red berets. *Perfect*, she thinks, but then a machine gun begins firing and the soldiers take cover. One of the tanks reverses into the middle of the street; its gun turns in her direction. She runs back the way she has come, turns north towards the Central Market and Omonia Square, slows to a walk. The flag hangs limply over her arm. Leaving Psiri, she heads towards the sound of a loudspeaker which is broadcasting something in English. A Blenheim bomber circles overhead. Although there are clusters of civilians here and there, peering out of shopfronts or crouched by standpipes, she has the strange feeling that she is completely alone in the city. She keeps going, sometimes rushing between doorways, sometimes waiting with other people to cross a road where there might be a sniper. As she gets closer to the market, she finds herself alone again. And there, parked beneath a plane tree next to a small church, are two British Bren carriers. She gives a sigh of relief, though in a way she would prefer to keep walking. Towards the sea, or the mountains. But she holds up her flag and yells out the first thing she can think to say in English: 'Excuse me!'

She sees faces turn towards her as, waving the flag resolutely above her head, she steps out into the road. A shot echoes nearby and she crouches and begins to run towards the Bren carriers. She is almost next to them when she sees that the men hunkered down by the caterpillar tracks of the carriers are not wearing British uniforms but a mixture of civilian clothes and Wehrmacht tunics. And on the arm of the nearest man, the man pointing his sub-machine gun straight at her, is a white armband on which a black X and a crown show up all too plainly.

'Come here, my pretty,' he says, and the other men begin to laugh.

'I'm . . . looking for a doctor,' Zoë stammers.

'We're all doctors here, aren't we, lads?' The man grins, yellow teeth beneath black moustache. 'And we've got the cure for communist sluts.'

She could run. How far would she get? Two steps? Three? She puts up her hands. 'I'm no one,' she begins to say. 'My friend is sick . . .' And then she sees two more people step out from behind the church. She knows them both immediately. One is the killer of Christos Vlessas: Captain Ioannis Pandelis. The other, thin peroxide-blonde hair trailing from under an old Metaxas-era gendarme's cap decorated with an X badge, is Feathers.

'Look, Ioannis!' Feathers exclaims, almost squealing in delight. 'It's my sister-in-law!' She begins to laugh, a thin, unhinged sound that reminds Zoë of the screams she heard earlier in front of Apostoli's house. Captain Pandelis is striding towards her, his hand undoing the flap of his holster. *I didn't get away after all*, she thinks as she turns away from him, smells the shockingly familiar scent of Feathers's cheap perfume mixed with his sweat. She feels the barrel of his pistol shoved hard into the dip behind her right ear, and closes her eyes almost gratefully.

The pistol's muzzle digs harder. Her eyes are squeezed shut, waiting for the shot, which she knows she won't hear, but will she feel it? *Christ and the Holy Virgin protect me* . . . A hand clutches her wrist and jerks her arm up between her shoulder blades, almost wrenching it out of its socket. The pistol pivots agonisingly in the dip behind her ear, forcing her to turn her head towards the Bren carriers. Captain Pandelis shoves her, using the pistol to steer her across the pavement and up to the nearest carrier. 'Get in.' The vehicle is a riveted steel box on tank tracks. The pistol digs deeper, the blade of the front sight drawing blood. She can feel it trickling down her neck. She has to put a foot up on the track and lift her leg up and over, the men hooting at her stockinged legs. She can feel the cold wind on her bare thighs. Pandelis pushes her and she falls forward into one of the narrow rear compartments, hitting her head viciously. Panicked, she twists around so that she can look up at a rectangle of grey sky. She can taste blood in her mouth and her vision is swimming. Someone gives a whistle. A man jumps into the driving seat, another two men into the compartment beside her. A pair of legs clad in baggy tweed trousers swings above her and a scuffed but plainly expensive brogued boot lands hard on her stomach. Feathers' face appears, outlined against the clouds. She puts the sole of her boot against Zoë's face and pushes. Zoë feels the skin beneath her left eyebrow split.

'Move over, sister-in-law!' Feathers says jauntily, as if they happen to be sharing a taxi. Zoë scrabbles backwards, drawing her knees up as hard as she can, and Feathers squats down opposite her. She is holding a large revolver with a ring dangling from the butt. Zoë's memory produces an incongruously pleasant memory: Tom Collyer unbuckling his service revolver and laying it on her table in the house on Hozanitas Street. The gun is too big for Feathers' skinny arms to support and she grasps the butt with both hands and rests them on her knees, aiming the barrel straight into Zoë's face. She is wearing a frilly blouse beneath a British Army battledress tunic. The engine starts – it is behind the panel that Zoë is leaning against and she gasps in fright. Feathers burst out laughing. The carrier jerks forward and the pistol jumps against Feathers' knees.

'Nearly shot you!' she squeals.

The carrier lurches into the street and turns, gathering speed.

'Where are we going?' Zoë manages to say.

'You'll see, Sister-in-law!' One of Feathers' sleeves has ridden up and Zoë sees the familiar dirty red lines and scars like pockmarks.

'Stop calling me that.' *Don't antagonise her*, Zoë tells herself. 'You didn't come to Pavlo's funeral,' she goes on, trying to sound relaxed, as if they were back at Hozanitas Street, sitting around the table by candlelight, trying to talk to one another because anything was better than silence.

'You didn't invite me.' Feathers pouts.

'You'd vanished.'

'I never did! I just went to stay with some friends!'

'These bastards?'

'That's right. Good Greeks – but you wouldn't know about that, would you, you dirty Turkish whore?' Feathers giggles. She bursts out laughing: *Like a schoolgirl*, Zoë thinks, *swearing in the playground*. '*Kouliana, poutana*.' Sister-in-law, whore.

416

Zoë's heart is beating painfully hard. She takes a deep breath. 'Pavlo loved you, Feathers,' she says. 'Christ knows why, but he did. More than anyone else. Is that why you call me *kouliana*? It's fine. Do you have a doctor in your unit? I need one. For Apostoli's wife. Remember Apostoli, who played in the band with Pavlo?'

'Don't worry, *kouliana*. We're going to take care of everything.' She closes one eye and sights along the barrel. 'And don't talk about Pavlo.' Her mood has suddenly turned cold. 'How dare you fucking talk about him? He *hated* you! Shut your filthy Turkish mouth!' She reaches out and grabs the strap of Zoë's bag, pulling it over Zoë's head and looping it over her own shoulder. The carrier slows down with a series of jerks and stops. Feathers leans forward and grabs a fistful of Zoë's hair.

'Out!' She pulls Zoë off balance. 'Out, I said!' The barrel of the pistol slams into Zoë's breastbone. Hands above her head, eyes and nose running and mingling with the blood from her cut eye, Zoë stands up and half climbs, half falls out of the carrier. She lands on her knees in dry grass. Looking around, she sees where they are: Koumoundourou Square. The other men are gathering round. 'Remember the song, Zozo?' Feathers says, reaching down and pulling her up again by her hair, the pistol digging into her throat. 'Douru douru, in the square at Koumoundourou? This is a famous singer, boys! Why don't you sing for us, Zozo? Go on!' The pistol digs into Zoë's throat and she coughs. 'Go *on*!'

'Oh, God,' Zoë moans. 'Oh, oh . . .' She coughs and tastes blood. *'You tell me one thing and you do another. You've made up your mind to drive me crazy.'*

She hugs herself, sobbing. The words are barely words at all. *'Ah, if your mother won't give you the Kokkinia house, I'll go and fetch that girl Mario from Podonifti.'*

417

Zoë stops: the words are choking her. 'The Kokkinia house. Is that what you wanted, Feathers? Pavlo's house?'

Feathers grabs Zoë by the hair and pulls. Their faces are almost touching; Zoë can smell cheap face powder and vinegary sweat. 'It was Pavlo's house and it should have been mine,' Feathers hisses. 'You should have given it to me. Just like you should have let Ioannis fuck you. People like you *never do the right thing!*' Feathers is screeching now. 'That's why I despise you.' She pushes Zoë away and jabs the pistol at her breastbone. 'Come on, boys!' she shouts. 'Join in!'

Dourou dourou, dourou dourou,
In the square at Koumoundourou!

'What the fuck is that Turkish grunting supposed to be?' Captain Pandelis appears at Feathers' side.

'It's our famous singer!' Feathers giggles, waving her pistol at Zoë.

'Search her and let's get on,' he snaps.

Feathers steps up to Zoë, who feels herself enveloped in the familiar sweet, cheap perfume. She bites her lip to stop herself whimpering as Feathers sticks the barrel of her gun up under her chin. 'You're wearing my jacket.'

'I . . .'

'Take it off!'

Zoë pulls off the jacket as quickly as she can. Feathers shrugs off her own tunic and kicks it aside. She puts on Zoë's jacket and admires the fit. The sleeves are too short, but she doesn't seem to notice. Then she shoves Zoë, sticks her hands into the pockets of her skirt and runs them up the front of her blouse. Zoë feels a hand turn into a fist as it finds something. Feathers yanks savagely; the silk cord burns against Zoë's skin and snaps.

'What's this?' Feathers holds up Tom Collyer's badge. 'It's British, isn't it? What are you doing with this, *Tourkála*? Holy Christ! This is your boyfriend's! Your poor lost English boy!' She screams with laughter. 'The famous Captain Tom! What would he say if he knew you were an ELAS hooker, eh, Zozo? The British are on *our* side, not yours. You know, he might even be here! Kapetanios!' she shouts, and her voice echoes around the empty square. 'Kapetanios!'

'Shut up, you madwoman!' Captain Pandelis shoves Feathers and she lurches away, cackling, pistol waving in Zoë's face.

'He's not here, though, is he? He's dead. He must have died years ago. You've been fucking a ghost all this time.' Still laughing, Feathers throws herself against Pandelis and kisses him, mouth open. The captain's fingers dig into Feathers' meagre arse. The other men cheer, raggedly.

'That's enough. Let's sort this out and get going,' Pandelis says, pushing Feathers off him, more gently this time. 'We have a rendezvous with that British company in . . .' He glances at his watch. 'In thirty-five minutes. We're going to get the bodies out here and bury them – we're not going to leave them lying around like those communist butchers, are we?'

Zoë turns her head and sees, beyond the leering men, a mound of earth beside a long, shallow trench. Her skin turns cold and she wants to sink to her knees but somehow she forces herself to stay upright.

'What about her?' Feathers asks petulantly. She is still holding the cap badge in her fist.

'She's going to help us, then she's going into the hole. You' – he points at Feathers – 'and Yorgo, Stellios, Evripides, Christo – drag the stiffs out here, and be quick, would you? No fucking around this time.'

419

'Come on.' Yorgo – no older than eighteen, with an outsize British beret slanted across his head, takes Zoë by the arm and begins to lead her towards a corner of the square. Beyond the old buildings, peeling stucco the colour of Hymmetus honey – *I'll never taste honey again*, Zoë thinks – the conical tower of the Armenian church rises. Rifle shots crackle not far away, and one of the guns on the Acropolis opens up, such a familiar sound that Zoë barely notices it. The paving stones are cracked and the lawns are trodden and brown. All the trees have long since been cut down for firewood. A machine gun lets off a burst two or three streets away.

'Oho, we're pushing the bastards back,' one of the men says gleefully. They come to the door of a burnt-out house and Feathers pushes Zoë inside. The others crowd in behind her. The first thing Zoë registers is the choking stench of burnt wood and furniture. Then she sees, huddled against the far wall of the room, a pile of corpses, all lying face-down, limbs tangled.

'Go on, bitch,' says Feathers, prodding Zoë with her pistol. 'These are your friends.'

'Please, Feathers . . .'

'You want to give them a proper send-off, don't you?' says Feathers. 'Take that one.' She points to a corpse lying a little to the side of the others, a young woman, barefoot, in man's trousers and a thick wool sweater. Her close-cut black hair is stiff with dried blood. Zoë gasps; stumbling over, she turns the body onto its back. 'No, no, no,' she whispers, but she already knows. Efi's eyes are half open and there is blood around her nose and mouth. Her body is beginning to stiffen and her arms are twisted unnaturally. Rocking on her heels, moaning, Zoë begins desperately to wipe away the blood with her sleeve. Efi's face is freezing: colder than her own skin. Much colder. She wipes and wipes, but the blood won't shift.

'Get a move on!' Feathers shoves Zoë with her boot so that she sprawls across Efi.

'Shoot me!' Zoë screams. 'I don't care!'

'Shut up. Get her by the ankles and drag her outside,' says one of the men, as if addressing an imbecile. Feathers grins at her and waves her pistol towards the door. Zoë finds herself taking hold of Efi's bare ankles. They are hard to the touch and terribly cold, but she starts to pull. The body doesn't move at first and then it begins to slide across the soot-covered floor. The smell of burning is covering other smells but there is a presence in the air that makes Zoë start to gag. Somehow she manages to get Efi to the door, working with her face turned as far away as possible, and out into the square, across the road and onto the grass where Pandelis and the others are gathered around the grave, smoking. Feathers is walking beside her with her pistol, and another fighter is covering her lazily with his rifle. She tugs, step by step, walking backwards, placing her feet so as not to trip, one step, another, another, towards the grave.

'Hurry up,' Feathers shouts. 'Hurry up, you Turkish—' Zoë's eyes are closed, and she opens them in time to see a fine red mist drifting around Feathers' garish yellow hair. A split second later she hears the bang of a rifle.

The fighters crouch and start firing at a point somewhere behind Zoë, who has let go of Efi's corpse and thrown herself down onto the dirty grass. Another bullet buzzes very close to her and wisps of grass drift through the air. She turns her head to the right and sees Feathers, arms flung wide, eyes glaring in terror, her hair splayed out, its livid yellow turned more garish by the spray of fresh blood. Air is gurgling and whistling through a small hole just below her collarbone and every time she breathes, a jet of blood shoots up out of the wound. One hand is clenched around the butt of her pistol, the other . . .

Zoë crawls over to Feathers and grabs her left hand. The woman's fingers are clenched so tightly around the cap badge that her nails are drawing blood from her own flesh. Zoë starts to pry the fingers loose. Feathers gasps and turns, her terrified gaze fixing itself on Zoë. She drops the pistol and, with a great effort, turns on her side and wraps her free hand around Zoë's.

'I . . .' Feathers mews like a blind kitten. 'I . . .' Her hand tightens, and Zoë realises the dying woman thinks she is being comforted.

'It's all right,' she says. 'It's all right, Feathers. You'll be fine.' All the time, her fingers are trying to work the other woman's free, but she can't move them. Feathers' eyes are fixed on hers; her mouth is a blood-flecked circle.

'It's all right . . .' Zoë feels herself begin to cry. 'You stupid, stupid girl! Go easy. It's all right. Go easy, Feathers.'

Feathers starts to choke. She lets go of Zoë's hand and starts to tear feebly at her blouse, her eyes all the while fixed on Zoë's, and then, in a second, she is gone. Zoë becomes aware of bullets kicking up the earth all around them. Feathers' fist is still clenched fiercely around the badge. A bullet hits her corpse and it jolts. The fighters in front of Zoë are firing from behind the mound of earth and the carriers. She can't see the others. She only sees a gap between two houses, and she scrambles to her feet and runs, like a madwoman, like an animal. Bullets sizzle and buzz through the air around her but she has reached the opening, she is through.

CHAPTER FORTY-THREE

Tom is sitting in a doorway watching two medics working on a corporal who has just taken a heavy machine-gun round full in the chest. The rest of the company, strung out along a half-wrecked street just south of Omonia Square, watch in silence. Tom knows it is useless. So do the medics. The other soldiers watch, dragging on cigarettes, their eyes red in their green-and-black-streaked faces. Only a couple of blocks away from what passes for the front line, this is a relatively safe area, and the locals seemed genuinely pleased to see them today: several times, someone – usually an old lady but once a young boy wearing shorts despite the cold wind – ran out into the street with a tray of sliced sweet bread: vasilopita, baked only on New Year's Day. '*Xronia polla!*' people called from their windows and doorways. '*Kai to xrono!*'

'What's that mean?' one of the soldiers asked.

'"And next year too,"' Tom said.

'Christ, I fucking hope not,' the soldier muttered.

Later, he chews his little corner of vasilopita and stares at the blank sheet of watercolour paper in his lap. The cake is dry, almost tasteless. He imagines its creation: the flour saved for weeks; an egg bought for God knows how much money, or bartered for; a precious tablespoon of sugar. All this, shared with strangers, foreigners, offered with the same angry love he found in the woman who came out to bandage that soldier. *Xronia polla*, he tells himself. *Many years*. The corporal died in the street. An hour or so later, the squad he was following found a couple of young men who tried, too late, to throw away their tin helmets on which ELAS had been crudely painted. They shoved the boys through the shattered window of a dressmaker's shop and shot them both. Tom painted the dying soldier and then he painted the murdered boys, but he knows that he will never send the last picture back to London.

It is almost dark by the time he gets back to the Fortress. He goes straight to his room and is unlacing his boots when the telephone rings. He didn't even know it was working. He picks up the receiver and a polite voice tells him the concierge has an urgent message for him. He sighs and makes his way back downstairs. The only person he can think of who knows he is in Athens is Mr Gregory of the WAAC. Probably a query over expenses, he decides, walking into the lobby, where he finds the concierge standing with Chris Dimitriou.

'Tom,' Dimitriou says. His sombre face looks more hollow than usual.

'Evening, Chris.' He turns to the concierge. 'I think you have a message for me?'

'That was me, Tom.' Dimitriou takes his arm. 'Come to the bar. I need to buy you a drink.'

'Oh, yes? Terrific. I need one. Why?'

'I'll tell you in a minute.'

Tom hears something in his friend's voice. 'You can tell me now, can't you?'

'I'd rather . . .'

'Chris. Please tell me now.'

'OK. I'm so sorry, Tom. A platoon of Royal Welch found an execution site this afternoon. A bad one. They managed to collect identification from some of the bodies, and . . . well.'

Everything has slowed down. 'What are you talking about, Chris?'

'There was a bag with a ration card and some other effects. Which was lucky: most of the bodies were badly damaged, apparently. There'd been an artillery bombardment . . .' Dimitriou takes a carefully folded piece of paper from his pocket. 'Look, for what it's worth, I wish it was something else. I wasn't sure if I should tell you at all.'

Tom looks up, takes the offered paper with the stiff fingers of his bad hand. He opens his mouth, trying to think of something to say. As it often does when he is tired, his left hand has gone almost completely numb. It obeys his commands after a fashion, but as a thing that doesn't properly belong to him any more. So now he can't feel the slip of paper between his thumb and forefinger. *You should paint this*, a voice in his head says, very distinctly. He observes his good hand unfolding the paper, once, twice. Inside, several lines of black type.

Surname: Valavani
Name: Zoë
Father: Valavani
Race: Greek
Born in: Smyrna
Year: 1916
Lives in: Kokkinia
Identification no.: 6214
Profession: Singer

Street: Hozanitas, 317
Picked up by 2nd Platoon, A Company, Royal Welch, Lt.
Burchinshaw, mass grave in unnamed square near Athens
central market Koumoundourou Square, unit established in
Observation Post 'Beans' SW corner of square.

Tom walks towards the door, almost knocking over a small table, blundering into the backs of chairs. 'Tom!' Dimitriou's voice sounds very distant. He ignores it. The armed guards at the door salute him but he ignores them too and goes out into the blackout void of Syntagma.

'Need an escort, sir?' they call after him, but he shakes his head and waves them away. The night is almost completely silent. No traffic, no tanks or armoured cars. No voices or footsteps. Just his own. He begins to walk as fast as he can, turning into Stadiou Street past the sandbagged guard post. A West Country voice asks him for the password and he gives it. The men on guard make no effort to stop him: if a paratrooper major wants to be out at night, then so be it. He hugs the buildings, stepping over rubble and fallen lamp posts, sometimes clambering over an abandoned ELAS barricade. There are tanks parked in the middle of Klafthmonos Square, the glow of cigarettes and the low mumble of voices. He hears a weapon being cocked from behind a half-destroyed kiosk and gives the password. The shadow of a man in a paratrooper's helmet leans out and waves him over.

'Bit late to be out, sir,' says the soldier.

'I'm heading for Koumoundourou Square,' says Tom. 'Classified business.' The lie comes easily and he feels nothing as he says it.

'Can't let you go any further in the dark, Major,' says the captain who Tom finds in command of the tanks. 'But I'm sending out a patrol at 0600 hours and you can tag along. Make yourself comfortable.' He waves to where a tarpaulin has been stretched between two tanks. A brazier glows in the shadows, picking out seated figures in its faint, slightly infernal light.

He spends the night rolled up in a borrowed blanket under one of the tanks. He obviously sleeps, because he remembers nothing, just a cold blackness, because he is woken by someone tapping politely on the toe of one of his boots. A tank is revving its engine and the captain is giving orders to the commander. They set off, Tom holding on behind the turret, and in a few minutes are at the end of Evripidou Street. The commander points into the darkness.

'If you're looking for the Royal Welch OP, it's down there, sir. Round this corner, turn right into the square, it's about ten yards along in a row of shops.'

Tom steps out into the street and immediately an English voice hisses, 'Who goes there?'

'Major Collyer, 4th Battalion,' Tom says. A soldier with the butt of his rifle tucked into his shoulder steps out of a narrow street opposite, followed by another man. 'I'm looking for OP Beans.'

A building has collapsed on the north side of the street, and the soldiers lead him over the fallen wall, through a jagged thicket of beams and tiles and into a tiny courtyard. They knock on a door. Tom steps into a room filled with men, tobacco smoke and the smell of rancid olive oil.

The lieutenant in charge of the rifle section is almost comically puzzled by Tom's presence. 'I'm here for two reasons,' Tom explains. 'Intelligence gathering, and my other job, which is Official War Artist.'

'War artist?' The lieutenant looks suspicious. Tom is used to that.

'I won't get in your way,' he says, as he has said countless times to countless pleasant-faced young officers. 'As to the intelligence, I understand that you found some civilian bodies around here.'

'That's right, sir,' says the lieutenant, obviously relieved to be on familiar ground. 'There's a fresh grave out there in the middle of the square. Whoever was doing the burying didn't get to finish the job.'

'And you sent the identification you found on to Military Intelligence.'

'I did, sir.'

'Good work,' he says. *Just let me see her*, he wants to shout. *Let me see her, and I don't care what happens after that.* 'I'll take a look when it gets light enough,' is what he does say.

There are twelve men in the room besides Tom, a full rifle section, and it is crowded. Tea is brewed. Men talk in low voices, cadge cigarettes. To Tom, it is as though he has spent his whole life in these places, with these people, waiting for the sun to come up. At first Tom can see nothing beyond the tree just in front of their position, but gradually, so gradually it seems like a malfunction of his eyes, the sky turns from slate to royal blue and begins to wash out, seeping light down into the square. The world – this is the whole world now, there doesn't need to be any more of it – begins to take shape. A burnt-out Bren carrier rests in a circle of scorched grass in the middle of a small square. Near the burnt car, a mound of black earth next to a hole, a black slot in the grass, and to the right of the hole, a row of soft shapes. The first thing Tom sees is bare feet, the whiteness of them. Five bodies are lying neatly but the others are jumbled, forced into knots and humps, dismembered. So familiar, the dead. The human body, when emptied of life, when taken apart by high explosives or fire or bullets, becomes predictable, almost mundane. The lack of novelty is part of the horror, Tom has always thought. And now Zoë has been reduced as well, broken down into shapes and ugly, mediocre colours.

Tom grinds out another cigarette on the floor and stands up. 'I'm going out now,' he says. He climbs over the barricade and out into the sharp air. A few stars are still shining. Birds are singing. He walks across the paving stones and out into the grass, kicking silver sprays of dew, towards the blackened carrier, which he can smell now: burnt paint and rubber. Towards the pale row of bare feet.

The first body is a middle-aged man wearing nothing but a pair of pinstriped trousers. He has been shot through the chest. The second . . . He walks along the line. The bodies are all men, shot in the head or chest, up until the first shell crater. The burst has thrown two bodies up into the air and they have landed, all in a muddle, in the shallow pit. Both men. Next to them, a woman in tweed trousers, blouse shredded and soaked with blood. Black hair cut very short. Tom is glad she is lying on her face. Another man next to her, one leg, no arms, squinting at the bullet hole in his forehead. A short, middle-aged woman in a jarringly happy floral print dress, knotted between her legs. And next to her, another woman wearing tweed trousers, on her back, arms flung out. From her breastbone up, there is only blood-blacked grass. Tom swallows, and kneels. The navy blue jacket she wears was once smart. A bag, some sort of canvas army haversack, the strap wrapped around one of her wrists. He looks inside: empty. But as he bends his head he picks up the faintest of smells, a needle of perfume spiking, for a moment, through the reek of burst bellies and high explosive. The headless woman's left hand is closed in a loose fist. On an impulse, he lifts it gently and studies it. *I can't remember*, he thinks. *Why can't I remember her hand?* He sees something dark between the

429

white fingers, the thing she was holding when . . . He finds himself easing the fingers away. *Why are you doing this? You should stop now. You should . . .* Something falls into the grass. He picks it up. A cap badge: cannon and crown. *UBIQUE.*

He doesn't even notice the bullets as they start to whine and sizzle across the square. Only when a mortar round bursts a few yards away and the shrapnel clatters against the shell of the car does he look up. Then he hears shouting. 'Major Collyer! *Major!*' Soldiers are waving urgently through the door of the observation post. The Bren gunner fires a long burst and Tom hears the bullets smack against the wall of the block of flats behind him. He doesn't move, waiting for something to strike him, to rip him open and spill him out. But another mortar round bursts and his training takes possession of him. He begins to lope back towards the shop. A bullet kicks up the grass next to his feet but he ignores it. *Lousy shots*, he thinks. *Nothing works out the way you need it to.*

They pull him back inside the observation post and he senses the soldiers' professional admiration. *Always a special place for madmen and lost causes like me*, he thinks. 'Did you get what you wanted, Major?' the lieutenant asks. Tom nods.

'Yes, thank you.' What else is there to say?

Tom works quickly, as his discipline has taught him. Quick dabs and strokes of the brush, the journey from water bottle to paint to paper almost unconscious. Soft lines for the men lying or squatting in rubble, greens and browns of camouflage, red slashes for their berets. Hard outlines of the windows and sandbagged doorway, the curve of a Bren gun magazine. White daubs, the lettering on the walls, ΚΚΕ. ΒΑΛΑΤΟΣ scrawled across a painted advertisement: fat butter beans spilling from a jar, golden-yellow on green. Observation Post Beans. When he moves his leg, the cleats of his boot rattle across dried olives and spent cartridges. The tiles beneath him are sticky with olive oil and the air around him is heavy with it, cloying and rancid, twisted through with cordite and other things rotting in the chaos of tumbled crates and cases around him.

The Bren starts up again, the gunner squeezing off short bursts, his spotter pointing and shouting in his ear. 'Left. Left! See him?' Tom winces. He licks his thumb and smudges the rectangle of the doorway. The ash from his cigarette is drifting and speckling the damp painting. It isn't a bad effect.

The soldier crouching next to him adjusts his sights and tenses. 'I see you, you little bastard,' he mutters. 'Can you get that fucking sniper, Jim?'

'If I could find him,' says the Bren gunner tersely.

Tom blots the painting carefully, and folds it back to reveal a fresh page. He rolls over and stands up, crouches so he can look over the soldier's shoulder. He doesn't feel anything at all, except for cold emptiness. But he still needs to look. He's still working, though he is almost finished. He stares out at the long, shallow trench in the grass near the burnt car, where the bodies are. He takes a cigarette, lights it and puts it between the stiff fingers of his left hand. He notices that his right hand is shaking slightly. He makes a fist and when he opens it again, his hand is steady. He picks up his brush and paints.

Surrounded by a wash of dirty green, a black hole. He begins to mix grey. Bodies in sunshine. He knows the exact shade. *She isn't there*, he says to himself. *Don't worry: she isn't there any more.*

A runner comes with a message: the corporal is ordered to blow through the side wall into the next shop and consolidate the position. The level of excitement inside the observation post increases but Tom hardly notices. He sees that he has given the bodies next to the painted grave small individualities: quirks of hair, face shape. One woman has heavy blonde hair and he has picked out her eyebrows, two tiny black commas above blank eyes. But that isn't what she looks like. Not now. Not out there. He rubs his numb hand again.

There is a flash and the shop lurches around them. Plaster rains down from the ceiling. Through the dust, Tom sees the men around him pressed against the walls and floor, hands over their heads. 'What the hell was that?' the corporal shouts.

Tom licks his brush, lays it carefully into its slot in the paintbox. *I'm finished now*, he says to himself. The squares of watercolour are all hidden under dust. All the colours he chose to paint the war, that day in the shop on Great Russell Street. Olive green. Terre vert. Burnt umber. Mars black. Manganese blue. The young lieutenant is adjusting his beret with unsteady fingers. Someone is cursing in the dull sing-song of the newly wounded. Cadmium red. Magnesium brown. Tom forces the box into his stiff left hand. The Bren fires three rounds and the cases dance through the swirling dust. Green gold. Chinese white. He knows exactly how long it takes to load a gun like the one ELAS have just fired at them. He can almost feel his own fingers on the hand wheel, sliding the shell into the breech, gripping the firing lever. In the observation post, someone shouts an order. The men around him are clamping their hands over their ears. There is a bang that drives the breath out of his lungs, and part of the side wall of the shop collapses, then everyone who can move is crawling through into the next shop or through the back door. The wounded man is being dragged by the collar of his smock.

'Get a move on, Major!' someone screams at him. Tom looks over at the hole in the wall. If he throws himself across the room, he might just make it, but why should he escape? He is going to see Zoë. She is just a few steps away, out in the burnt grass.

'I wanted to hear her sing again,' he says aloud, just in time, as the air goes solid and the shop dissolves into light.

CHAPTER FORTY-FOUR

She runs, dimly aware that she is heading east, towards the market, legs scissoring on the very edge of balance. She tastes blood in her mouth and her nose is full of its iron stench and she wonders if she is hit but she can't be if she is running.

It isn't far to the house but Zoë can hardly walk and the sunlight is deepening to amber by the time she gets there. Surely the street wasn't this damaged when she left? There is shattered glass everywhere and a stalled tank squats in a tangle of railings and a telephone pole. The door of the house is slightly open. She falls inside. The deserted ground floor echoes as she calls out, 'Toli! Andromache!' Stumbling up the stairs, head spinning, she trips on the top step and sprawls across the bare floorboards. On the floor, breathing in the familiar stench of imprisonment – stale tobacco and the overflowing toilet – she starts to shiver. 'Apostoli!' On her hands and knees, she crawls to the door of the room where they have been living. It is empty. There is the bed, sweat-stained sheets hanging from the mattress. There is the tin full of cigarette ends. But she is alone. 'Apostoli!' she shrieks, staggering from room to room. But there is no sign of them. She goes back downstairs, clinging to the bannister, and out into the street. A woman in a black coat, with a black headscarf around her head, is prodding the tank with her walking stick. Zoë knows her vaguely: before the war she and her husband sold cheese and cream, but now, widowed, the woman spends most of her time in church.

'It's blocking our shop,' she says angrily, when she sees Zoë.

'Have you seen my friends?' Zoë asks. She is shaking badly now; her teeth are chattering. 'Mr and Mrs Vikos, from number 14?'

'What a day! Christ and the Holy Virgin . . .' The woman crosses herself. 'First it was the fighters, ELAS boys and girls, coming down the street, banging on doors. They took people away, dear. Then the British came. There was a lot of shooting – dear God!' She presses her hands to her ears, then holds them up towards heaven. 'But now it is over.'

'My friends. Apostoli and Andromache Vikos. Did you see them?'

'Aren't you well, *kyria*? You're covered in blood. Will you come and sit down?'

'No!' Zoë sees hurt appear in the woman's eyes and she feels her own eyes growing wet. 'I'm sorry. Please, please tell me what happened to my friends.'

The woman shakes her head. 'But I don't know. I saw some people being taken away. Then this tank . . .' She hits it viciously with her stick.

Zoë leaves the old woman and goes back to the empty house. She is so cold that it feels as if flames are licking her. She finds her dirty peach quilt and wraps herself in it. *I'll just sit here for a minute to warm up*, she tells herself, but in a moment she is asleep.

She sleeps for a long time, but when she wakes she feels worse. Her clothes are drenched in sweat. A freezing wind is blowing in through a broken window. She shifts, stretching her legs, and the pain is so sudden that it makes her scream. Still, she manages to stand, pushing herself upwards against the stone. She totters into the street and begins to walk, holding onto the wall like a blind woman.

She must bury Efi before the dogs find her. After that, she will look for Andromache and Apostoli, but when she thinks of where they might be, the city spreads before her in her mind, vast, maze-like and broken. Her friends have disappeared. Everyone has disappeared. Even Tom. Feathers' words keep threading themselves through Zoë's fever, needle-sharp and bitter. 'You've been a ghost all this time,' she whispers. 'Just a ghost. But I have always loved you, and I always will, now.' She reaches into her pocket for Tom's badge and then remembers where it is: locked away in a dead woman's hand. *Charon, you are too greedy*, she thinks. *We've all gone to you now. I'll be going too, in a little while. The horse and cart will take me, or perhaps just the dogs and the crows. When there is no one left to bury the dead, to sing over the dead* . . . She stops, and rests against a lamp post. She is freezing and shivering uncontrollably, but her stomach feels like a bucket of hot coals. But she knows now. At last, she knows what she must do. There is one last thing she can give.

By the time she gets to Koumoundourou Square the sun is beginning to set. She has had to stop and relieve herself twice, almost crying for the shame of it, in a ruin and behind an abandoned car. In the square, a party of British soldiers is busy in the far corner, stacking things, talking loudly. The odd word comes to her but where before she would have gathered up the foreign words like crumbs, she doesn't listen now. She walks straight out between the trees and onto the grass. There is a wrecked Bren carrier there, and she stumbles where the earth has been rutted by explosions. *I left Efi here*, she thinks, *and Feathers* . . . But there are no bodies. She stumbles on.

A person must give some thought to the hour of her death
When she will go down into the black earth
And her name will be erased.

The old song. A boat slipping by in bitter, smoke-filled darkness, the splash of oars, the city on fire. The dead woman's skin in her grasp, her flesh and bones, this nameless one . . . *I was Zoë Haggitiris; I am Zoë Valavani.* She tells herself these things as she struggles backwards towards the grave. *I lived in Bournabat. I had a pony. My mother was Mary, my father was George. My mother was Katina, my brother was Pavlo.* There, next to the carrier, is a neat patch of earth, a large, dark rectangle in the brown grass. She drops to her knees at the edge of it, lets her hands sink in to the damp, stony soil. *Efi,* she thinks. *And all you nameless ones. Feathers, even you.* The grave, she knows, is bottomless. Pavlo is lying there with Mama, Mary and George Haggitiris, Vangeli, Marika. The famine dead, the shot, the hanged, the ones swallowed by fire. The stilled voices. The things the refugees knew, that are no longer to be found in this world. All of them under the earth.

She closes her eyes and sees that Tom Collyer is with them, grey eyes filled with earth. No more colours. No more heart beating against hers in the morning. She sits back on her heels and crosses her arms across her body, holding herself to calm the shivering, and lifts her head. She can only remember one song, but what other song has there ever been?

Chapter Forty-Five

Tom wakes after what seems like a second, travelling from black void to vivid reality with no warning. Instead of the observation post, he finds himself strapped to a stretcher that is cantilevered off the back of a jeep. The jeep is crawling along in a thick cloud of blue smoke behind a convoy of tanks. They seem to be pulling into Syntagma Square. The pink slab of the Grande Bretagne is just ahead, if it isn't a hallucination. He remembers an explosion. He'd been waiting for it. But he is still alive. He opens his mouth and instead of words, a ragged shout spills out. The orderly driving the jeep yelps in surprise and brakes, hard. Tom is unbuckling the straps holding him to the stretcher with his good hand.

'Let me off here,' he croaks at the orderly, who has jumped out of his seat and is trying to restrain Tom.

'Bloody hell, sir! I'm taking you to the hospital.'

'I'm perfectly all right.' He can barely get the words out.

'Excuse me, sir, but you ain't. I thought you'd already pegged out. You gave me one hell of a fright. Just lie down again and we'll get you fixed up in no time.'

'Look, Corporal.' Tom's vision is settling. He spits plaster dust onto the pavement. 'This is my billet. There are doctors here. Lots of doctors. I'm not hurt. I just need a drink and my bed.'

'Honestly, sir . . .'

'It's an order,' Tom says, and the orderly stands back reluctantly as Tom eases himself onto the pavement. 'Thanks for the lift,' Tom says, as the worried-looking man salutes him.

Now that he is standing, watching the orderly drive away, Tom's head is starting to swim again. He finds himself staring into the square. There are people moving about in the shadows beneath the trees, bent shapes, shuffling and bending. He realises they are scavenging for twigs to burn. He limps across the road and down the marble steps leading into the park. After a while his leg feels as if it is about to give way so he sits down on the bottom step. *I should draw this*, he thinks, but his eye is caught by a dog, skeletal, with chewed ears, who is watching the wood-gatherers in its turn.

'I'm going back,' he says aloud, and tries to stand up, but a stabbing pain in his leg forces him back down. He is just gathering himself for another attempt when he sees someone waving to him from across the road: it is Chris Dimitriou, with Earl McCall behind him.

'Tom?'

'Oh. Hello, Chris.' Tom waves a hand. 'You couldn't give me a hand up, could you?'

'What the hell's happened to you, old man?' McCall asks as he puts a hand under one of Tom's arms. Dimitriou takes the other arm, and Tom manages to stand, leaning heavily on his friends. 'We were looking for you last night. Seferis had us round for dinner. I thought you were invited?'

'No,' says Tom. 'I need to go now, chaps.'

'Are you all right, Tom?' Dimitriou is looking him over. 'Christ, you're wounded!'

'I'm fine. Really. I have to go back to Koumoundourou Square.'

'What's over there, Tom?' They are leading him over to one of the iron benches.

'I found her,' Tom says.

McCall lights a cigarette and gives it to him. 'Oh, man,' he says.

'Zoë Valavani?' Dimitriou sits down next to Tom. 'I'm so sorry, old chap.'

'I found her, and now I have to bury her. I can't leave her for the dogs. I can't leave her . . .' He closes his eyes. 'Like that.'

'You need to go to hospital.'

'I will. I will. But first I need to bury her. She's all alone. Do you understand?' He finds the cap badge in his pocket and takes it out. 'She had this. She was holding on to it all this time. We'd both been holding on to each other. And when I found her . . .' He presses his fingers against his eyelids to blot out the image. 'It wasn't enough. I didn't save her. We haven't saved anyone, Chris. Now please let me go.'

'All right, all right,' Dimitriou says gently. 'I've got to meet Archbishop Damaskinos in a few minutes, but after that, we'll find some men and drive over there. Meanwhile, let's get a doctor to look you over . . .'

'I'll take him,' says McCall.

'Mac . . .'

'No, I want to. It'll be OK.'

They half carry him to McCall's jeep, which is parked outside Police Headquarters. Dimitriou waves them off and they drive up Stadiou. Some sort of calm has returned: there are civilians on the street, standing in clusters, staring at the wrecked trams and demolished buildings. A military policeman with white gloves stops them at a crossroads.

'I understand,' McCall says over the rattling engine. 'You know that. You know why. I couldn't do a thing when Emmie died. Not a damn thing. I was in the jungle – New Guinea – and I got a letter. Just a regular letter. It came up with the rest of the mail. And you know what? It was so fucking horrible out there that I read it and it hardly registered. I thought . . . I don't know what I thought. But when I got back to the rear, it hit me. I was sitting on a beach, sort of a shitty beach, covered in dead leaves and these pale crabs, but the sun was shining and my pants weren't rotting off me and I thought, I'll write to Emmie about this, and I'll make it kind of funny. And then . . .' The MP waves them on, but McCall pauses, his hand on the gear lever. 'I haven't been back. I know where she's buried but I haven't been. I could have gone home but I haven't.' He shoves the jeep into gear. 'I guess I won't. So I understand. And I'm sorry.'

They have gone quite far when a couple of paratroopers step into the road, blocking their way.

'I'm with the press,' says McCall, showing his pass. But they shake their heads. 'Booby traps,' they explain. 'Should be taken care of by tomorrow. There's nothing to see, anyway.'

'I'm going,' says Tom. 'It's all right, Mac. I can manage by myself.'

'I'm not sure, sir,' says one of the soldiers, but Tom knows they won't argue with a major.

'Thank you,' he says to McCall. 'I'm sorry as well.' He swings first one leg, then the other out of the jeep and walks away, up the first street he comes to. His left leg is in agony but functioning: he is used to its moods and grits his teeth against the familiar pain. Pain like this is nothing. There is a cold wind blowing, rattling the sagging wires above the street. Catching sight of something in a windowless shopfront, he pauses and finds himself, reflected full-length in a cracked cheval glass. His face, distorted slightly by the broken mirror, seems very white and very thin, like something long-underground. He bats feebly at his jacket, raising clouds of plaster dust and revealing the green and brown smears of its camouflage. *This is what the war has done to me*, he thinks, rubbing his leg, trying to massage some proper life into the badly knitted strands of his flesh. *And I'm one of the lucky ones. Christ, I used to be young. I used to be in love.*

You'll never be young again, the ghost in the mirror seems to say, *but you'll always be in love. You made a promise, and there's no one who can release you from it. You'll always be in love, now.*

He walks faster, his heart almost choking him, rolling on quickly, favouring his bad leg, skirting groups of people who are clearing away rubble. Not far, now. But stepping over a lump of concrete he feels something give way abruptly in his knee and he falls sideways against the iron bars of a shuttered butcher's shop and has to clutch at them to keep from sliding all the way to the pavement. The pain is much worse. He curses, pulling himself upright, and staggers along, leaning against the wall. But the wall ends, and a side street stretches before him, a chasm. Nothing to lean on. He will have to crawl. And then he feels a presence at his side. An old woman is standing there. Short, wide, dressed in the black headscarf and black dress he has seen so often these past weeks. Her deeply lined face holds a pair of bright hazel eyes. He sees that she has put down a bundle of twigs tied with a piece of string.

'Where are you going?' she demands in Greek. Tom can just about understand her. She leans down and touches his leg very gently. Her touch is much more gentle than her harsh voice. 'Where are you walking to, my darling son?'

Tom tries to smile. 'Bad leg,' he says.

'Very bad!' the old woman agrees. 'Where are you going?'

'The square. Koumoundourou.'

'Square . . .' She studies his face intently, then grins, showing almost empty gums. 'Come,' she says, and pulls Tom's left arm over her shoulder. He leans against her, trying not to put too much of his weight on her shoulders, but she is surprisingly strong. Together they hobble across the street, along the next stretch of pavement. They cross another two streets, Tom almost crying with pain.

'Let me rest for a minute,' he gasps, in Greek. He slides down the wall of a half-collapsed building with an ornate balcony, a section of which has fallen. It makes a lopsided bench. The old lady sits down next to him as though it is the most natural thing in the world. Tom rests his head against the wall. It is throbbing sickeningly and the pain in his leg is excruciating. He imagines it laid open, gleaming meat and yellow bone, raw nerves jumping like severed power lines. Madder and caput mortuum.

'What is the matter, dearest one?' The old woman has very gently taken his hand without his noticing, but now he feels her rough, dry palm against his own skin. 'You have been fighting. You have been brave, my son. *Aman*, but you are finished with that now.'

'She's dead,' Tom says, the Greek coming easier with the firm grip of the woman's hand. 'I found her, but I was too late. I could have saved her.'

'You did what you could.' She smiles, revealing almost toothless gums.

'So many dead. I've seen so many corpses.' Tom feels tears begin to trickle down his face. 'I don't know what to do with them all. I thought I could tell the living about them. But in the end, they have no names. They're gone.'

'It is true,' she agrees.

'Her name too. Zoë. It was Zoë. And when I'm dead, no one will remember her at all.'

'When one goes, and one is left behind, that one must stand up. That one who knows suffering, my dearest, who knows loss, must stand up and cry for those who have gone to the strange land.'

'But I don't know what I can do, Mother.'

'We sing for the dead, don't we, dearest one? I know. I have sung my heart out. Right out, dearest boy: nothing left. But you are strong.' She lets go of his hand and spreads her fingers across his chest, over his heart. 'Listen. There is someone singing already. Are you ready to go now?'

'I don't know,' says Tom, but when the old woman takes his arm he finds he can stand. He can bear the pain.

'Good, good,' his companion says, cackling. She helps him across the next street and there is the square just ahead. They step out into the thickening amber light. The bare trees are cutting deep veins of shadow across the dead grass.

'Good luck, my son. *Kalí tychi!* ' she tells him, and points. 'There. Go.'

'Thank you!' he calls after her, but she doesn't even raise her hand as she walks away, much smaller than she seemed, back into the shadows. He turns to see where she has pointed, and sees the humped shape of the Bren carrier. The wind has picked up, shushing through the branches, freezing cold. Dry twigs clattering against each other. Dry words.

And something else. There is a broken branch in front of him and he picks it up and, leaning his full weight on it, limps onto the grass. There is no mound of earth any more, just a patch of freshly turned earth among the litter of war: an oil drum, discarded ammunition boxes. A gust of wind blows a flurry of paper across the grass. His head is pounding and flashes of purple and orange light are flickering at the corner of his vision, but as he gets closer, he sees that there is a person on their knees at the edge of the bare soil. He can hear his own breath, and a voice that he knows is just a memory, but it is beautiful. Someone buried her, after all. He feels a surge of gratitude, but it is so painful that he almost falls. He has to press his eyes again to clear them. When he takes his fingers away, the square forms again, slowly, first in negatives of black and silver, then in slabs of colour, oil paint squeezed and smeared roughly over canvas. The block of flats, the trees, shapes scraped into the paint. Tom stumbles on. He can smell the earth now. *What can I sing?* he thinks. *I can't sing. I've lost all the words.* Someone, though, is singing for him. 'Thank you,' he whispers. The branch sinks into the loose earth and he stumbles, dropping to his good knee. 'Thank you,' he says again, and the singer looks up.

She is a woman, almost young, shivering feverishly in an old black dress many sizes too large for her, her bare arms clasped across her chest. Ribbons of dried blood eclipse one side of her face. Her cheeks are hollow and the shadows under her eyes are like smudged soot. Her hair, honey-coloured, yellow ochre, falls in heavy tangles to her shoulders. Her long neck, in which a blue vein is pushing through almost-translucent skin, is hardly touched by the collar of the dress. Her mouth is open, and her song comes to him like wind over a field of long grass.

She looks up and sees a gaunt man in a filthy camouflage

smock, his black hair thick with dust, his skin scabbed and stretched tightly across his bones, a thick scar across his forehead, one ear clotted with blood. His long fingers are rubbing at his eyes, but when he takes them away, she knows him.

'Zoë?' he whispers.

'But I'm singing for you,' she says, and drags her hands across her own face. *He'll go*, she is thinking. *He'll go back into the earth.* But he is still there. 'Are we dead?' she whispers.

'I came. I promised. I thought . . .' She realises that he can't walk any more, and stumbles across the grave to him, across the black earth. 'I thought I was too late.'

'No, no.' When she puts her arms around him, she feels sunlight on her skin. But the sun has gone down. It is getting dark. She can feel his ribs against hers, his heart beating faintly, and her own little pulse chattering with fever: two birds left too long, left to starve, alone in their cages. She presses her face into his neck and hears the rhythm of his blood. Such a small sound. Still, a sound. A song. She feels his hand in her hair and she raises her face to him. His lips taste of blood, and metal things: of the war. But only for a moment, and then she doesn't have to remember any more.

'My God. There's almost nothing left of us,' she says. 'But there's enough. There's just enough.'

PHILIP KAZAN was born in London and grew up on Dartmoor. He is the author of two previous novels set in fifteenth-century Florence and the Petroc series following a thirteenth-century adventurer. After living in New York and Vermont, Philip is back on the edge of Dartmoor with his wife and three children.

philipkazan.wordpress.com
@pipkazan